O9-ABF-878

Praise for the No Ordinary Hero series

"The latest from the ever-popular Enoch is steamy and bubbling with humor, a scrumptious tale to begin her No Ordinary Hero series."   —*Booklist*

"Stirring historical romance . . . with colorful secondary characters, judicious lashings of Scots dialect, and . . . a heady romantic atmosphere that's sure to captivate the genre's eager audience."   —*Publishers Weekly*

"Thrilling and sexy."   —*Kirkus Reviews*

"Romance not to be missed."   —*BookPage*

"Wonderfully romantic . . . marvelous."
          —*RT Book Reviews*

"Enoch at her finest! No one does it better."
          —*Reader to Reader*

"A delightful mix of sexy bantering . . . a picturesque Scottish setting, and likable characters . . . A WINNER."
          —*Addicted to Romance*

Also by
SUZANNE ENOCH

A Devil in Scotland
My One True Highlander
Hero in the Highlands
Some Like It Scot
Mad, Bad, and Dangerous in Plaid
Rogue with a Brogue
The Devil Wears Kilts
The Handbook for Handling His Lordship
A Beginner's Guide to Rakes
Taming an Impossible Rogue
Rules to Catch a Devilish Duke

It's Getting Scot in Here

SUZANNE ENOCH

St. Martin's Paperbacks

NOTE: If you purchased this book without a cover you should be aware that this book is stolen property. It was reported as "unsold and destroyed" to the publisher, and neither the author nor the publisher has received any payment for this "stripped book."

This is a work of fiction. All of the characters, organizations, and events portrayed in this novel are either products of the author's imagination or are used fictitiously.

IT'S GETTING SCOT IN HERE

Copyright © 2019 by Suzanne Enoch.

All rights reserved.

For information address St. Martin's Press, 175 Fifth Avenue, New York, NY 10010.

ISBN: 978-1-250-29637-5

Our books may be purchased in bulk for promotional, educational, or business use. Please contact your local bookseller or the Macmillan Corporate and Premium Sales Department at 1-800-221-7945, ext. 5442, or by e-mail at MacmillanSpecialMarkets@macmillan.com.

Printed in the United States of America

St. Martin's Paperbacks edition / March 2019

St. Martin's Paperbacks are published by St. Martin's Press, 175 Fifth Avenue, New York, NY 10010.

10 9 8 7 6 5 4 3 2 1

For my mom, who still insists on purchasing
extra copies of all my books to make sure
I remain gainfully employed.
I love you, *màthair*.

Prologue

Once upon a time—in May 1785, to be exact—Angus MacTaggert, Earl Aldriss, traveled from the middle of the Scottish Highlands to London in search of a wealthy bride to save his well-loved but crumbling estate. Aldriss Park had been in the MacTaggert family since the time of Henry VIII, when Domhnall MacTaggert, despite being Catholic and married, declared publicly that Henry should be able to wed as many lasses as he wanted until one of them got him a son. Aldriss Park was the newly minted earl's reward for his support and understanding.

For the next two hundred years Aldriss thrived, until the weight of poor harvests, the ever-intruding, rule-making Sassenach, and the MacTaggerts' own fondness for drinking, gambling, and wild investments (including an early bicycle design wherein the driver sat between two wheels; sadly, it had no braking mechanism and after a series of accidents nearly began a war within the MacTaggerts' clan Ross) began to sink it into disrepair.

When Angus inherited the title in 1783, he realized the old castle needed far more than a fresh coat of paint to keep it from both physical collapse and bankruptcy. And so he determined to go down among the enemy Sassenach and win himself a wealthy bride. The English had made enough trouble for him and his over the centuries, so they could bloody well help him set things right.

On his second day in London, he met the stunning Francesca Oswell, the only offspring of James and Mary Oswell, Viscount and Viscountess of Hornford—who had more money than Midas and a bevy of very fine solicitors—at a masked ball where he dressed as a bull, and she as a swan. Despite the misgivings of nearly everyone in Mayfair, Angus and Francesca immediately fell madly in love, and married with a special license ten days later.

A week after that, Angus took Francesca back to Aldriss Park and the Highlands, where she found very little civilization, a great many sheep, and a husband who preferred brawling to dancing, and he discovered that her father's solicitors had arranged to keep the Oswell family money in Francesca's hands. This made for some very spectacular arguments, because there is nothing more combustible in the world than an impoverished Highlands laird in disagreement with an independently wealthy English lady about his own ancestral lands.

Over the next thirteen turbulent years the estate prospered, and Francesca gave Angus three sons—Coll, Aden, and Niall—and with each one became more concerned that this was not a life for any civilized person. She wanted to bring the boys back to London for proper educations and to live proper lives, but Angus refused, stating that what had been good enough for him would be good enough for his lads.

When a fourth child, a daughter, arrived in 1798, Francesca reached her breaking point. No daughter of hers was going to be raised with an uncivilized accent in a rough country where she would be ridiculed by proper Society and unfit to marry anyone but a shepherd or a peat cutter. Angus refused to let his lads go, but he allowed Francesca to take young Eloise and return to London—on the condition that she continue providing for the maintenance of the estate.

Francesca reluctantly agreed, but given that she controlled the purse strings, she had her own conditions to try to keep some influence with her wild sons: All three boys must marry before their sister, they must wed proper Englishwomen, and at least one of them must marry someone of her choosing.

She knew Angus would raise them as he pleased, but they were her children, too, by God, and she meant to see to it that they had some semblance of propriety in their lives—she was a viscount's daughter, after all, and certain things would be expected of her offspring. She refused to allow them to be viewed as unsophisticated wild men by her London neighbors, and she remained determined to have a presence in their lives.

To enforce her will, she convinced (or rather, coerced) Angus to put his signature to the agreement, which contained this provision: If young Eloise MacTaggert *did* marry before any of the boys, Francesca would cut off all funds to the estate. If they were to insist on defiance, they would have a heavy price to pay for it—one they and their tenants could not afford.

Angus had no choice but to agree, and considering that Coll, the oldest, was only twelve at the time of Francesca's departure and Eloise was but a wee bairn, he was willing to wager that he would have time to renegotiate. Angus and Francesca remained married, but neither would bend enough to visit the other ever again. As far as the lads were concerned, their mother had abandoned them.

In the spring of 1816 Angus received a letter from Francesca announcing their daughter's engagement, and he promptly collapsed. He'd hoped his sons would have found themselves Scottish lasses by now and shown their mother she couldn't control their lives after all, but the lads were defiant and wouldn't be rushed. Now it appeared to be too late.

He summoned his sons to his apparent deathbed and confessed all—Francesca funding the estate, the pernicious agreement, and their mother's grasping claws, which he explained was a symptom of all Englishwomen and their weak, clinging, cloying ways. For the sake of the property and their tenants the young men must go to London. At once. No sense even taking time to put him in the ground, much less mourn him, because Francesca wouldn't excuse the loss of time, and they needed to marry before their sister.

The lads—grown men, now—were not at all happy suddenly to learn about the responsibilities and rules foisted upon them by a woman they barely remembered. Being wily, freehearted, and exceptionally handsome men accustomed to doing things their way and certainly not bowing to the demands of a demented Englishwoman, they determined to go down to London not to comply, but to outwit their mother and upend any plans she had for them. And thus, dear reader, begins our story.

Chapter One

"I can smell the shite from here." Niall MacTaggert pulled up his bay gelding, Kelpie, at the top of the low rise. "Bloody Saint Andrew," he muttered, swinging down to the ground. The sight before him—a vast sprawl of hazy, smoke-shrouded streets, the peaks of bell towers here and there the only bits that had managed to break free of the gray to stab into the overcast sky—had both a scent and a sound he hadn't even the words to describe. "Have ye ever seen the like?"

"Nae." His oldest brother, Coll, Viscount Glendarril, remained aboard his massive black Friesian stallion, Nuckelavee, but he leaned forward to cross his wrists over the saddle's pommel. "I reckon we've found hell."

As they gazed at the loud, fog-bound morass, Niall's second oldest brother, Aden, drew up behind them. "Finding a bride here's nae the first thought that strikes me," he commented, patting his chestnut thoroughbred, Loki, on the withers. "I reckon we should rescue our sister from that blight and make for the Highlands."

"And send her to a nunnery," Niall added. "If we can keep her from marrying, we've nae reason to tote posies about and read poetry to some fainting English hothouse flower."

That had been the plan he suggested, but Coll had over-ruled him, insisting that the three of them could convince Francesca Oswell-MacTaggert to tear up the agreement. Coll had always favored battle, a direct confrontation, over delicacy or subterfuge. And his methods generally succeeded—the main reason Niall and Aden had agreed to give it a go.

Niall turned to see the quartet of outriders and two wagons of luggage accompanying them come into sight. It all looked impressive, which had been the point; they all knew that no Sassenach traveled far without half his worldly goods accompanying him. Now, though, he had to consider that having to repack all of it would considerably slow any getaway they might attempt. Then again, they could always taxidermy another red deer stag if they had to leave behind the one they'd brought along.

Most of the rest of it was nearly as unnecessary. Then again, Francesca claimed to want her sons about. Well, here they were. All three of them. And not a one in the mood to be cooperative. Niall stepped into the stirrup and remounted Kelpie as his brothers returned to the rutted, muddy road and the wagons. *London.* He'd rather take a wade through a peat bog than spend an hour in London. Their da had signed a paper, though, and then seventeen years later had refused to rise from his sickbed—his death-bed, according to himself—to join his sons in disputing it. Angus MacTaggert, Earl Aldriss, a roaring giant of a Highlands warrior and evidently too scared of his es-tranged wife to leave his estate and go set eyes on her. Not that Angus would ever admit to that.

On a sunny day, if such things existed here, the oak and elm trees scattered along the road might have provided a pleasant shade. Today they mostly made Niall miss the pines and the craggy, snow-topped peaks of the Highlands. Christ, had it only been five days since he'd last seen them? It was warmer here, or at least the breeze, even with the rain hanging just behind it, didn't have that chill that dug into a man's bones.

He fell in beside Aden, with Coll and his great black warhorse a few feet ahead of them. The outriders had been more for show than for anything else; he doubted even some damned Sassenach highwayman would care to run up against the MacTaggert brothers. Still, someone had to lag behind with the wagons and protect the stuffed stag and their shaving kits. Their grand arrival wouldn't change the fact that they'd left behind an ailing father and a busy season of new lambs and growing crops, that they'd had to postpone the Highlands games that had been a tradition in June for the past two hundred years, and dozens of other things that all needed tending. And a fair crop of young ladies who'd be lamenting his absence.

"Ye ken if yer face freezes like that a hundred lasses will perish from sorrow."

Niall sent Aden a sideways glance. "If I'm forced to wed some pinch-faced flower of the south, those hundred lasses will all be perishing from loneliness *and* sorrow. Even the lot chasing ye might frown for an entire minute once they read about yer nuptials."

"Dunnae underestimate Coll's lack of enthusiasm at having Francesca choose a bride for him."

"Aye. Thank the devil he's the one lost the card turn. I'm surprised he has any teeth left, the way he's been grinding 'em for five days."

With a swift look at their brother's backside, Aden pulled a deck of cards from his coat pocket and shuffled it one-handed. "I reckon he'll fight harder for us with himself in the hangman's noose."

Aden's swift expression of amusement as he pocketed

the cards again might have been simple appreciation, or it might have been one of his rare admissions of trickery. Either way, Niall was abruptly grateful not to be the present Viscount Glendarril. It was horrifying enough to be ordered to choose a Sassenach bride; to have a woman he'd not seen in seventeen years pick out the lass he was to marry would have been enough to make him consider fleeing to the Colonies, regardless of the consequences to Aldriss Park.

The scattering of farms gave way to densely packed shops, businesses, hotels, inns, brothels, taverns, and stately homes, looming out of the fog like giant, steep-edged ravines to tower halfway into the sky. Along with the buildings came the people, shouting in a hundred accents and several languages, offering oranges, fish, pies, glimpses of the far-off Orient, and themselves. So these were the civilized folk, turning to stare at the trio of riders as they passed—as if the Highlanders were the odd birds. "It's a madhouse," he muttered, reining in Kelpie to avoid a scampering, nearly skeletal young girl scooping horse shite into a bucket.

"What in Saint Margaret's name is that?" Aden commented, flicking the end of his reins toward a street corner.

Niall followed the gesture to spy a tall, thin man dressed in a lime-green jacket so tight he wouldn't have been able to lift his arms above the elbow. The points of his shirt, white and stiff, dug into his earlobes, and his blond hair had been curled tighter than sheep's wool. His trousers were a peacock blue, his waistcoat a patterned yellow and green, and the black boots he wore shone like water and had heels as deep as a horse's hooves. "I saw one of 'em in a fashion catalog Eppie had on her bed stand," Niall replied. "That, Aden, is a dandy."

"I'm stunned enough that I willnae ask what ye were

doing in Eppie Androw's bedchamber. A dandy. Do ye reckon he can walk?"

"If he takes wee-enough steps, aye. And ye know damned well what I was doing in Eppie's bedchamber. I'm four-and-twenty, nae eleven."

Ahead of them Coll consulted a folded paper, then headed right down a narrower, quieter lane. The houses here were larger and didn't share common walls, with more windows and quaint-looking gardens in the back. A street or two beyond them, the homes had short front drives, overhanging roofs for leaving carriages without getting rained on, and stables alongside the gardens in the rear.

Though Coll had initially been against it, they'd sent word that the MacTaggert brothers were traveling down to London. Niall could see the benefits of surprising Francesca Oswell-MacTaggert, putting her back on her heels and maybe even frightening her into tearing up the damned agreement. On the other hand, she'd sent the letter announcing Eloise's betrothal, so she would have a fair idea that her sons would be arriving sooner rather than later. And he personally didn't relish the idea of having to sleep in the stable because no additional rooms had been opened for them.

They trotted past a small park dotted with bairns in frilly dresses or short pants, together with women dressed in caps and dowdy gowns—nannies, he supposed—before Coll led them down another lane. A labyrinth of climbing roses and wrought-iron gates surrounded them now, not as closed in as the bordering streets but just as suffocating. When Coll finally drew Nuckelavee to a halt, Niall felt somewhat relieved; he could imagine a hell where one rode through flower-choked lanes endlessly searching for a tavern that would never appear.

"This one," Laird Glendarril grunted, his gaze on the stately gray house on the right.

"Write out the direction for me before we step outside again," Aden requested. "I'll nae find it again otherwise."

"With any luck we'll be back home before ye have to memorize it," their oldest brother returned, and sent the big black warhorse up the half-circle drive. "Hallo the house!"

The front door opened. Servants started fleeing the house in front of them, maids and kitchen help and footmen all straightening caps and coats willy-nilly as they ran out the door. For a hard half a dozen heartbeats Niall thought they'd caught the house on fire and were running for their lives, until he realized they were lining up on either side of the doorway. He did a swift count—fifteen of them. With that many servants, a man wouldn't even have to hold his own kerchief to blow his nose.

"We've merited a parade," Aden noted. "Do ye reckon they do this every time someone approaches the house?"

Niall stifled a grin. "That wouldnae seem very practical, but the English are all mad anyway."

The narrow man with the most gentlemanly attire bowed as the three of them lined up on horseback. "Welcome to Oswell House, Lord Glendarril, Master Aden, Master Niall." Down the line the other servants bowed and curtsied in fairly impressive unison. "Lady Aldriss awaits you inside."

Behind them the first wagon turned onto the drive and stopped, the other one just behind it. Charles and Wallace, the two men seated beside the drivers and brought down expressly for one purpose, stood and pulled their bagpipes from beneath their wooden seats. At Coll's nod and after a few off-key groans to fill the bags with air, they began playing "The White Cockade" at full volume. Now that felt like a proper greeting.

Niall dismounted, handing Kelpie's reins off to a

stunned-looking lad who wore stable livery. Windows of the neighboring houses began flying open, maids and footmen and anyone else in earshot trying to get a look at whatever was making that noise. Before the first refrain they'd gathered a crowd on the street behind them, clapping to the reel.

"I reckon we're overdressed," Aden commented as he handed Loki off to another stableboy.

Sweet Andrew, Oswell House seemed to have a lad for every horse in the stable. "That was the point, wasnae?" Niall straightened his fox-fur sporran and fell in with his brothers. Scarlet plaid with thick lines of black and green, the colors of clan Ross had to be the grandest and brightest in the Highlands. And with the three men all pushing past six feet tall, they were definitely not about to be missed—or mistaken for anything but what they were.

"Won't you . . ." The butler fellow cleared his throat. "Won't you come inside?" he repeated, more loudly.

"They havenae played 'Killiecrankie' yet," Coll returned. "And ye've nae introduced us to all these folks who've lined up so proper to say hello."

Because he'd been watching the doorway, Niall saw Francesca Oswell-MacTaggert, Countess Aldriss, the moment she left the shadows. He'd been but seven years old the last time he'd set eyes on her, but he would have recognized her among a crowd of hundreds. Aye, her black hair had lightened to a peppered gray, and the angel's face he recalled had widened a bit at the jaw, but it was her. In fact, the one thing he hadn't expected was that she would be so . . . tiny. The top of her head wouldn't even come to his shoulder.

She walked slowly outside to stand in front of the doorway. Her gown of deep blue likely would have sparkled in sunlight, but there was none of that to be found today. "I see I won't need to inform the neighbors that my sons have arrived," she said, her voice that cool, sophisticated accent he'd found very exotic as a bairn. Now it merely sounded English. Unlike his own. "Thank you for that."

"Aye, we're here," Coll returned, his eyes narrowing. "Thanks to yer threats, Francesca. Ye managed to put Da on his deathbed and took me away from mending the irrigation ditches, but ye've brought us out of the Highlands."

Her left hand flew up to her throat and a delicate gold necklace there before she lowered it again. "Your father has passed away?"

"He might've, by now. Made us swear nae to delay heading south and risk ruin for Aldriss, so we've nae idea. Pogan—our butler, if ye've forgotten—is to send us word."

"I haven't forgotten Pogan," she returned. "Nor will I discount Angus's dislike for London. Until I hear otherwise I shall credit his so-called deathbed antics to be just that—antics." Rubbing her hands together, she took a breath and stepped to one side of the doorway. "Now. Given that the future of Aldriss lies in you agreeing to my wishes, I do *wish* you would come inside."

Niall stole a glance at Coll. At nine-and-twenty, the current Viscount Glendarril and future Earl Aldriss had the clearest memory of Francesca; he'd been twelve when she'd left for London, after all. Coll stood four inches above six feet, and men—much less women—generally didn't argue with him. Even fewer attempted to order him about. This might not be an order, but it was close enough. Niall wondered if Francesca realized she'd just invited a bull into her glassware shop. An angry bull.

Coll met Francesca's gaze, then turned his back on the house. "Keep playing, lads," he called, then whistled for the wagons to pull onto the drive. "We've a bloody mountain of luggage to move inside, and I'd rather hear the pipes than the groaning of the footmen."

"Or the neighbors, I reckon," Niall muttered. He

hadn't put much hope into Coll's plan of stomping up to the Oswell House front door, bellowing that Francesca had best rethink her plans because the MacTaggert brothers did not bow to anyone, and marching back to the Highlands. They looked to be trapped here for a few days, at least.

He looked up at the half-a-hundred windows that adorned the front of the grand house. None of the past six days had gone as he expected, though he had enjoyed the ride down from Scotland. Instead of a head-to-head battle, *he* would have chosen to find a London-based solicitor of their own to fight Francesca's agreement. Another Englishman would have had better odds of finding a way out of an English agreement than Coll and his preference for straight-up brawling. That suggestion had been overruled as well, of course, because everyone knew a Highlander couldn't trust a Sassenach. Not even one in his own employ.

Either way, he'd never been averse to making trouble. While Coll and Aden issued orders to their outriders and the Oswell House staff, he strolled up the pair of low steps to the front doorway. "I'm told I knew ye when I was seven years old," he drawled, sticking out his hand as Francesca looked at him. "I'm Niall."

She faced him, taking a quick half-step forward before she stopped again. Being a MacTaggert in the Highlands meant running across plenty of men wanting to make their own reputations on his back, to prove their strength or power or wealth by attempting to set him on his arse or in his grave. He'd become deft at determining who was an actual threat and who was actually angry or terrified or—more than likely—drunk. That was how he knew he'd just struck a blow against Francesca Oswell-MacTaggert, and that he'd hurt her. While he generally didn't hold with battling a woman, she'd started it.

Lifting her chin a little, she moved again, reaching out

to grip his hand. "You don't need to introduce yourself to me, Niall. For goodness' sake." Her fingers trembled just a little, but as he shifted to let go, she tightened her hold on him. "I expected your hair to be red."

Shrugging, he ran his free hand through the overlong mess hanging into his eyes. "It got darker. Brown mostly, with a wee bit of fire here and there in the sunlight."

"You were a handsome young boy, but my heavens. You'll have half the girls in London swooning at your feet. And those eyes of yours—they're very like your sister's, you know. Such a pale celadon, like new leaves in sunlight." She reached a hand toward his face.

Niall stepped sideways into the house, freeing his hand and avoiding her caress in the same motion. One hello did not make them friends, or family. In the strictest sense it made them acquaintances. Aye, that's what they were—barely acquainted, with the caveat that Francesca happened to hold the purse strings that could determine the future of the estate and all their tenants. His future as well.

"It seems to me," Aden drawled, stepping between them and into the long, dark foyer beyond, "that if ye had a curiosity about the color of Niall's hair or his pretty eyes, ye had a simple way to satisfy it. A visit, mayhap. Or a letter." The middle MacTaggert brother hefted a monstrous stuffed boar's head mounted on an oak plank. "Where am I lodging?"

The skinny butler skittered up on Aden's heels. "That . . . Perhaps one of the footmen could carry that for you, sir. John? And—"

Ignoring that, Aden started up the wide, elegant staircase and paused at the landing where the steps separated to climb to the left and right wings. "Give me a direction, or I'll just choose whichever room strikes my fancy."

"Smythe, show Aden to his bedchamber," Francesca said.

"Of course, my lady."

"Och, ye remembered my name, Francesca," the lean twenty-seven-year-old drawled. "Then again, I am rumored to be unforgettable."

"When you've deposited your trophy, join us in the morning room," the countess instructed, turning to head into a room just off the foyer. "Niall, please join me, won't you?"

Time to do a bit of scouting the terrain, then. Niall started after her, then stopped abruptly when a hard hand clamped down on his shoulder. "Ye shook her hand," Coll muttered.

"And I introduced myself, as if we'd nae met before. I'm charming, if ye'll recall. But I'm nae a traitor."

"Dunnae forget that, *bràthair*. Ye heard Da's warning. She may look a flower, but many a man's been drowned in a soft voice and tears. If ye dunnae have the stomach for this, then step back. Aden and I will manage it."

If they went by Angus MacTaggert's last description of his estranged wife, the one he'd presented them from his self-proclaimed deathbed, Francesca Oswell-MacTaggert was a weeping, fainting damsel in distress who used her feminine wiles to manipulate every man within hearing into fulfilling her whims. Niall didn't know if he believed all that or not; contrary to what he'd said, he did have a few memories of her, and she'd been warm and pleasant in most of them. And she'd smelled of lemons. But then he'd been a bairn, and he wasn't one now. Far from it.

"The only good reason to marry an Englishwoman would be because the weeping pansy would do as I said, and I could leave her behind in London," he returned in a low voice. "It worked for Da, after all."

"Aye. As ye say. Nae marrying one at all is my first choice, though. Especially one some stranger's picked out for me," Coll returned, releasing him again to follow him inside the room.

Niall took a seat close by the morning room door, while Coll stomped around for a bit, eyeing the neat shelves of books and vases and delicate, feminine knickknacks. The moment Aden reappeared, the two of them took command of the couch to Niall's left. That left Francesca facing the doorway into the foyer and well able to see the ridiculous chaos of things they'd toted down from Scotland as each was brought into the house. This should be interesting, at least, even if he doubted it would go as well as Coll hoped.

"My boys," she said, her quiet voice just audible over the bagpipes outside.

"Ye'll have to speak up," Coll announced. "The lads are enthusiastic this morning."

"I said I'm more pleased than you could ever know to see my boys again," the countess restated, her voice firmer now.

"We're nae yer boys," Coll returned. "Ye summoned us here with a threat, and so we're here to answer in kind. If ye wanted affection, ye should've asked more kindly, and written more frequently."

She sank down in the available blue chair, her skirts rustling around her as she folded her hands onto her lap. Every move she made seemed studied, as if she had a painter in the next room ready to leap out and sketch her portrait. "So I'm to take the blame for your father not bothering to inform you that we've had an agreement for seventeen years. Very well. I can accept that."

Aden tilted his head. "*He* didnae leave us behind, Francesca."

Looking down, she opened her mouth and shut it again, while Niall waited for the weeping and lamenting and pleas for sympathy to begin. Instead she cleared her throat. "My greatest fear was that Angus would raise you boys as wild, unmannered barbarians, and evidently I had the right of it. That said, as we all know that your futures depend on you doing as I say, let's begin with this: You will not call me Francesca. I am your mother, and you will show me some respect. I'll give you four choices—you may refer to me as Mother, Mama, my lady, or Lady Aldriss."

That didn't sound at all weepy. "Then might ye tell us where we can find our sister, Lady Aldriss?" Niall asked, covering his surprise.

"I might," she conceded, "if you'll give me your word that you won't blame her for the agreement or for her engagement. It's not her fault that you're here."

Niall scowled, putting aside the thought that he'd suggested kidnapping her. That had been one of a dozen ideas thrown at the dartboard. "Do ye reckon we're mad enough to mean harm to Eloise? She's a MacTaggert. And she's our wee sister."

Something about what he'd said seemed to please her, because Francesca smiled. "Good. I'm glad to hear it. She wanted to be here, but she'd made a previous engagement to go shopping with some friends, and I made her keep to it. As I said, I wasn't certain how she might be greeted. She'll be home before dinner."

"I reckon ye might want to tear up that agreement," Coll stated. "Ye dunnae know who we are, or whether we might already have a lass in mind for marriage. If ye force us to wed some milquetoast female or other, ye may nae see grandbabies, my lady."

"I know you've had less than a week to conjure some defense against your father's and my agreement, but that's the best you could come up with?" she countered. "No grandchildren? You are, after all, speaking to a woman who left her own sons behind."

"Ye said ye were glad to see us," Aden put in, scowling.

"I am. I hope that eventually you'll understand how pleased I am. But the agreement stands. You will all three abide by it, or I will withhold the funds your father has been using for the past thirty years to keep Aldriss Park from collapse. *I* certainly don't care about the place. But you do. I can see that."

"Aye, we do, Lady Aldriss," Coll growled. "And all our cotters and servants and villagers."

"Then you know what you need to do. It's very s . . ." She trailed off, her gaze on something in the foyer behind them. "Is that a stag?"

"Aye," Aden returned. "That's Rory. We keep him in the library."

"Not in *my* library, you won't."

"I reckon he'd look just as fine on the staircase landing, then," Coll took up. "Joseph, Gavin. Leave Rory on the stairs, so we can all admire him." Lifting an eyebrow, Coll turned his gaze back to Francesca.

"Well," she said, clearly not realizing she'd just lost that argument, or not caring, since she'd won the larger one. "I suppose we can decide on his placement later." Rising, she walked over to the wall and tugged twice on a gold tassel pull by the doorway. "This does not need to be an adversarial business. For the moment, however, since you are all my prisoners and evidently are disinclined to engage in polite conversation, Smythe will show you to your rooms. Luncheon will be set out in the small dining room between one and three o'clock, and we sit for dinner tonight at seven. If you don't sit for dinner, you will not have dinner."

The butler appeared in the doorway. "Yes, my lady?"

"Aden's seen his, but please show Coll and Niall to their bedchambers." Inclining her head, she started out of the room. At the last moment she turned around again. "As you've read the agreement, I presume you're aware that one of you is to wed a lady of my choosing. And as you're the one with the title and inheritance, Coll, I've decided it should be you."

They'd already decided that among themselves, but Coll hadn't liked losing to begin with. Having it shoved at him all over again wouldn't gain Francesca any affection. Lord Glendarril stood, all six feet four inches of him coiled and ready for a fight. Moving quickly, Niall climbed to his feet, as well. "Coll said it should be him," he lied, "so ye've nae surprised us, Lady Aldriss, though I doubt ye can find an Englishwoman to match him."

His jaw clenching, Coll flexed his fingers. "Aye. Ye find me some swooning, untouched lass, then. I reckon we'll deal as well as ye and Angus MacTaggert did."

Her cheeks paled a shade or two. "The young lady I've selected will make you a fine Viscountess Glendarril, and a better Lady Aldriss when your father does see fit to expire," she returned, ignoring his other comments. "You'll meet her tonight at the theater. You may bring *one* of your brothers; I don't wish her overset by the three of you all glowering at her."

"Ye might give me a bloody day to catch my breath before ye bring the axe down on my neck," Coll snapped.

She sent him a smile that wouldn't have warmed ice. "There's no sense in wasting time. What if Eloise and Mr. Harris were to elope? You might lose everything over poor timing."

Well, this hadn't gone at all the way Coll had described. Niall would have been amused with the way Francesca had stomped all over him if that wouldn't have encouraged his oldest brother to punch him. But still, thank God he had at least a small say in finding his own bride, a milquetoast lass like Coll had described, a woman he could bed and then leave behind while he went back to the Highlands and lived as he pleased. "Ye might as well set eyes on her, Coll," he said aloud.

Coll swiveled his head around. "Niall likes the theater. He'll join us tonight."

Niall took a breath. *Bloody wonderful.* "Och, I'd be delighted," he lied. Just what he wanted, to spend an evening watching Coll trying to make some weak-willed lass faint from his mere presence. At least, he supposed, if any of the nearby females succumbed as well, he'd have his first chance at finding a weepy, dim-witted one for himself.

Francesca wanted them tied to London, it seemed. The countess likely hadn't reckoned on them pursuing a set of lasses none of them wanted anything to do with. One visit to London, and perhaps a second one from Coll to make himself an heir, and Aldriss Park funded permanently. Not ideal, but better than whatever Francesca imagined for them.

Chapter Two

I'm nae wearing that, Oscar." Niall turned away from the dressing mirror to eye the large, emerald cravat pin nestled in an ornate gold setting. He could swear the figures of mini cherubs frolicked along the rim.

"Yer ma brought it to me especially for ye," the valet said. "She said it belonged to her da, the old Laird Hornford."

No doubt Francesca had sent a bauble to Coll and Aiden, as well, and now she waited in the foyer to see which of them would wear her gift. It wasn't going to be him. "Put it down," he ordered. "I'll wear the thistle pin, and naught else. I'm nae some English dandy."

"Aye," Oscar said, setting the fancy thing on the table. With a sigh he retrieved the small silver thistle pin Niall generally wore with his dress kilt. "I'd appreciate if ye'd make certain the lady kens that I did as she asked."

"Dunnae ye fret about what some underhanded Sassenach lass thinks of ye. We'll nae be here long enough for it to matter."

"What about the brides ye and Master Aden are supposed to find here? And the one Laird Glendarril's to wed? Ye have to be here long enough for that."

Niall frowned at his reflection in the dressing mirror. Coll might still claim it hadn't been settled yet, but that conversation in the morning room had sounded fairly definite to him. "Only long enough for a wedding. I reckon Da's been living a fine life in the Highlands without his wife for the past seventeen years. Nae reason we couldnae do the same." The more he thought about it the more sense it made—marry some Englishwoman about whom he didn't give a damn in order to save Aldriss, and not have anything else to do with her. That would show Francesca she couldn't control everything, and especially not her sons.

That was still the worst-case scenario, though, to be used only if he and his brothers couldn't persuade Lady Aldriss that they weren't fit for English consumption. She'd yet to see them in public, after all. Perhaps after an evening of uncooperative Highlands lads, she would return to Oswell House and tear up the agreement of her own accord and send them packing back to Scotland.

A soft rap sounded at his door. "Aye?" he called.

He saw her in the dressing mirror's reflection, a petite, slender sprite with long dark hair piled atop her head, nearly colorless green eyes made even more striking by a deep-emerald evening gown, and a smile that looked hopeful and nervous all at the same time. His heart thumping, Niall climbed to his feet.

"Eloise," he said, meeting her halfway across the room and pulling her into a sound hug. She was as tiny as Francesca, and even more delicate-seeming.

Her smile deepened. "You couldn't possibly recognize me," she said, her cultured English accent surprising him despite the fact that he knew precisely where she'd spent the past seventeen years of her life. She was his sister; she was supposed to be Scottish.

"I have a clear memory of poking ye with a stick so ye'd

cry and I could wrangle another biscuit from Mrs. Ross. She's our cook, and she loved giving ye milk-softened biscuits."

"I don't remember that," she returned, her brow furrowing before it smoothed again. "I do love biscuits quite dearly, though." The eighteen-year-old tilted her head, taking a closer look at him.

"Do I have a bug on my forehead?" he asked after a minute of her scrutiny.

"What? Oh, heavens no. I . . . I just met Aden, and he said I look like you." She took a half-step closer. "I can't figure him out. Coll said I was a wee bairn and shouldn't be thinking of marrying anyone for at least ten more years, but Aden just looked at me, said you and I could be twins, and then asked where he could find a good game of faro."

Niall grinned. "Nae a one of us can figure out Aden. He *is* fond of cards. Ye're coming to the theater with us tonight, aye?"

"No. I'd like to, but I have a dinner with Matthew and his parents." She cleared her throat. "I think Mama wants to give you a few days to become familiar with London before you meet Matthew and everyone."

That, or Francesca might still be trying to figure out if London was ready for the MacTaggerts. When he returned his attention to Eloise she was still gazing at him. "I wasnae happy to come down here to London," he said, "but I am happy to have ye back in my life."

She smiled, tears gathering in her eyes. "I have brothers," she said, her voice breaking. "I always knew I did, and Mama told me stories about you, but they were always the same stories, of things you did when you were all very young. It was like hearing a tale about someone else's family." She stood up on her toes and kissed him on the cheek. "I'm glad you're here, Niall."

With that she left the room again. Behind him, Oscar sniffed loudly. "That was damned touching, Master Niall."

Niall turned back to the dressing table. "Aye, it was. If Da had told us *why* he resented Francesca all this time, I might've written Eloise other than on her birthday. Mayhap I'd have come down to visit her."

No doubt Angus had been embarrassed to have been put in such a vulnerable position by such a wee woman as Francesca Oswell-MacTaggert, but the family patriarch hadn't done his sons any favors by keeping that damned piece of paper and its contents a secret from them until the moment he'd learned of Eloise's betrothal.

If they'd known earlier, they might have had time to hire an English solicitor to find them a way out of this mess. They might have come up with a strategy on their own to get around all of them having to marry Englishwomen, and Coll being forced to wed the one his mother chose for him. They might have married Scottish lasses, and then dared Lady Aldriss to do her worst.

His door swung open again. "Here," Coll said, and tossed him an apple.

Niall caught it. "We're nae sitting for dinner then, I assume?" he asked, biting into the fruit.

"Ye assume correctly. I'll go to the damned theater because I gave my word, but I'm nae sitting and eating beside that woman and pretending we're a family."

An apple might suffice for a few hours, but it was not a long-term solution. "If it comes down to it, we're eating yer horse first, then."

Coll paced to the window and back again. "She has us over a barrel."

"Aye, that she does."

"I suppose, then, that it doesnae matter who this lass is, as long as she's spineless. If I cannae get around a marriage, the duller the better. I'll sit through having eyelashes batted at me and talking about the weather and Parisian fashion, and I'll wed her as soon as possible. Ye and Aden find yer lasses, and then we'll go home alone. Francesca may have won, but she willnae like the prize."

Niall had never thought he would be looking for a simpering lass, but he hadn't anticipated any of this. "I'll follow yer lead. The MacTaggerts stand t—"

"Together," Coll finished, approaching to clap him on the shoulder. "Aye. Aden's already gone out, so what say we throw some darts in that fancy billiards room until Lady Aldriss calls us down for the theater?" He scowled. "I hope it's at least *Macbeth* or someaught bloody."

As they found the billiards room someone banged a gong downstairs. Niall supposed that meant dinner was served, but since Coll had already decided they were to survive on apples tonight, he ignored the reverberating clang. A gong, when someone yelling up the stairs would have sufficed just as well. Then again, their father had once fired a pistol into the floor to get his sons into the dining room.

Generally Niall would be the one smoothing the rocks between Coll and Francesca. Aye, he liked a good fight, especially when the two sides had equal power, and in this instance he hesitated even to name Francesca as family, but he knew both his brothers and his father turned to him looking for common ground. And it wasn't just them. Whenever it had happened, he'd become the valley's peacemaker. Their diplomat, his father called him. If that meant that he had no use for bullies or that he protected the people around him, then he supposed he accepted the moniker. How that all played into being hamstrung into a marriage, he had no idea.

"There you are," came from the doorway, and Niall turned to see the butler straightening his waistcoat. "You've missed dinner, my lord, Master Niall, I'm afraid."

"Aye," Coll replied, and threw another dart.

"I'm to inform you that the gong sounds the commencement of dinner every evening, and that it will only sound once. I'm also to say that the coach is on the drive, and that Lady Aldriss wishes to see you join her there without delay."

Coll coiled his fingers around his last dart. Sighing inwardly, Niall nudged his shoulder against his brother's. "Ye dunnae have an alternative plan," he muttered before the viscount could begin putting holes in people. "And there is the wee chance that the lass ye're to meet favors just the sort of man *ye* are. Ye know, dull, stupid, and pliable."

"Ye're an idiot," his brother grumbled back at him, tossing the last dart into the dead center of the board. "Let's find out, aye?"

"Mother, should I wear Grandmama's pearls, or the onyx necklace from Aunt Louise?" Amelia-Rose Hyacinth Baxter called, leaving her bedchamber with a bauble in either hand and stopping at the top of the stairs.

Her mother appeared downstairs from the direction of the sitting room. "You cannot think to wear pearls with that white lace at the neckline—you'll make them look yellow." Her brow furrowed. "Don't you have blue glass beads with the matching earbobs? They'll bring out your eyes."

"I'm already wearing a blue gown," Amelia-Rose countered, twirling. "That's too much."

Her mother, Victoria Baxter, flipped a hand at her. "Wear the onyx, then. Just hurry. We must have you seated before Lady Aldriss and her son arrive."

Yes, of course. A lady always looked very fine curving her neck to glance behind her, and then rising and turning to greet her admirers. It made her gown swirl about her waist and thighs. Amelia-Rose hurried back to her bed-chamber and handed the onyx necklace to Mary. "We've spent too long on my hair," she told her maid, sitting so Mary could fasten the gold chain behind her. "Mama's worried we'll be late."

"But you have to concede that your hair looks very fine this evening," the maid returned, putting a finger through a delicate blond curl and twisting it. "A golden waterfall, it is."

Amelia-Rose looked at her reflection in the mirror. Her hair did look very nice this evening. Too nice, perhaps. She straightened her left sleeve a little. "Do you suppose my intended has bothered to bathe?"

Mary chuckled. "I would imagine Lady Aldriss has in-sisted that he do so. He is half English, you said."

"Yes, and half Scottish. Highlander Scottish." She sighed. "You've seen them about. They're all brutes with great bristly beards and kegs slung over their shoulders."

"Those are the ones working at the docks, Miss Amy. This one's a viscount. And he's to be an earl, one day."

"I know. And being called 'my lady' and having people bow and curtsy to me would be very nice." Amelia-Rose grimaced as she stood again. She'd begun parroting her mother even when Victoria Baxter wasn't there to notice. "I don't object to his status. Only to his location and the quality of his upbringing. Scotland is very far away from London. If I were to hold a soiree there, who in the world would even know it?"

That had been her concern since her mother and Lady Aldriss had come to their agreement a fortnight ago. London boasted soirees, recitals, theaters, amusements, rides in the park, museums, and everything else imag-inable. Scotland had . . . sheep. One could not dance or have witty chats with sheep. Or Highlanders, in her ex-perience.

The small bell that usually sat on the table in the foyer began ringing wildly, a sure sign that her mother was, at the least, growing impatient. Stifling a sigh, Amelia-Rose headed downstairs, pulling on her deep-blue gloves as she descended the straight staircase.

Her mother met her at the bottom. "You'll do," Victoria said, eyeing her. "Though I wish you'd woven ribbons through your hair."

Blue ribbons, no doubt. "Mama, this is Drury Lane, not a grand ball," she countered, putting on a smile. "And I certainly don't wish to look too eager."

"Why shouldn't you look eager?" her father put in, emerging from his office. "It's all arranged. All that's left is you and Lord Glendarril meeting, and the two of you choosing a date for the wedding. I daresay we've done the difficult part in all this."

"Oh, nonsense, dear Charles," his wife put in, surprising Amelia-Rose. "Our daughter has been the toast of London for two years now. She's already had . . ." She paused, glancing at Amelia-Rose. "How many proposals have you had?"

"Four," she answered, taking her light silver shawl from Hughes the butler and wrapping it around her shoulders.

"There you have it, Charles. Four proposals in two years. Why should she be eager to meet a man who has both a title and wealth and who cannot flee when Amelia-Rose says something untoward?"

Ah, so it wasn't a compliment after all. She should have known better. "I am trying, Mother. And I thank you for taking the trouble to come to an agreement with Lady Al-driss."

Victoria put a hand to her forehead. "Gratitude, at last. I am quite overcome."

"Now, now, dear," Amelia-Rose's father soothed, ushering them past Hughes and out to the waiting coach.

"Three of those proposals are from this year. She is making an effort."

"Thank you for saying so, Father." And she *had* been making an effort. She hadn't said anything truly scathing since late last Season, when Lord Albert Pruitz, the Marquis of Veyton's thirdborn son, had compared her to a pitcher of milk. She'd learned her lesson after that calamity, and she'd minded her tongue. Her thoughts hadn't been all that cooperative, but at least the entirety of her did understand that no one would ever offer for her again if she couldn't refrain from accusing a suitor of having the imagination of a turnip.

In her second Season now, she'd learned to temper her expectations and to accept her own shortcomings. She'd hoped to find a man who admired her for who and what she was, who appreciated that she had a wit, and that hadn't happened. Now her parents had gone and found a man for her—one who apparently met none of her qualifications. The only actual benefit she could see to marrying Lord Glendarril would be that she could move out of Baxter House. But going from there to the Highlands didn't seem much of an improvement at all.

No one arrived early at Drury Lane Theater, because being early meant there was no one there to admire one's gown or cravat as one walked up the wide, curving staircase. On the other hand, they were seated in Lady Aldriss's box and provided with drinks within two minutes of leaving the carriage.

Three open seats remained in the box. Lady Aldriss, of course, and Lord Glendarril, but who else? Not Eloise MacTaggert, because Amelia-Rose knew her friend to be dining with the Harrises this evening. One of the other brothers, then. She stifled a scowl as people below began to wander to their seats. Nothing had been officially declared, but people knew who she would be meeting tonight, and she wasn't about to give anyone fodder for gossip by allowing a careless expression. Not any longer.

Across the theater in a box nearly opposite the one in which she and her parents sat, Lady Caroline Mays and her younger sister Lady Agnes, together with the Duke and Duchess of Hildergreen, took seats in their own box. Caroline lifted her opera glasses, spied Amelia-Rose, and gave her a wave.

Smiling, Amelia-Rose waved back. Inwardly, though, she cringed. She liked Lady Caroline—they were dear friends, really—but the duke's daughter couldn't keep a secret to save her life. She would see everything that went on in Lady Aldriss's box, and by morning every one of their mutual friends would know it, as well. Wonderful.

She sighed. If she couldn't somehow avoid all this, perhaps it would go well. Perhaps Coll MacTaggert was handsome and agreeable and had always wanted to live in London. His accent would fade over time, hopefully his manners weren't horrid and could be corrected, and she could therefore avoid having her entire life upended.

"Ah, good, you're here." Lady Aldriss's voice came from the box entrance behind her.

Amelia-Rose took a deep breath, leveled her shoulders, and turned her head just so to show off the curve of her neck. The action was wasted, though, because only Lady Aldriss, lovely in mauve-and-black silk, stood in the curtained entryway. Perhaps the MacTaggert brothers hadn't arrived, after all—and that would be fine with her. Her calendar for the Season was already full to bursting.

She stood, curtsying as the countess moved into her private box. "Good evening, my lady." Because she and Eloise were friends, she'd become quite familiar with Lady Aldriss, and had come to appreciate her rather straightforward manner, so different from Amelia-Rose's own mother and her half-complimentary, half-insulting "suggestions."

"Victoria, Charles, so good to see you," Lady Aldriss said with a smile, offering a hand to each of Amelia-Rose's parents. "And you, my dear, are a vision."

"Francesca, thank you for inviting us this evening," her mother returned. "Did your sons not arrive?"

One side of the countess's mouth quirked. "They did." Taking a step backward, she reached through the curtain.

A tall man, his shoulders so broad he barely seemed to fit in the doorway, half stumbled into the box as if pushed from behind. With a low word that sounded like a curse he straightened, and all at once she took in green eyes so light they looked nearly colorless, a straight, well-proportioned nose, a mouth that turned down at the corners in a half scowl, wildly overgrown brown hair, those shoulders, a lean waist, and—oh, good heavens—a vibrant red, black, and green kilt. And those Scottish shoes with the long laces wound around his legs nearly up to the knees.

Thank goodness he was wearing that kilt, though, because otherwise her first thought might have been that he was extraordinarily handsome in a wild, uncivilized way—some pagan god of virility. Now, though, she had no choice but to remember that he was a Highlander, and that she really didn't want one of those. His gaze caught hers, something she couldn't decipher but that felt . . . warm, touching his expression and then vanishing again. *Oh.* Abruptly she wanted a breath of air.

"Oh, for heaven's sake," Lady Aldriss muttered. "This is Niall, my youngest son." She vanished briefly, then reappeared through the curtains on the arm of an even larger man. "This is my oldest, Coll MacTaggert, Viscount Glendarril. Coll, Mr. and Mrs. Baxter, and Miss Amelia-Rose Baxter."

Lord Glendarril looked very like his younger brother, though his eyes were a much darker green, his mouth harder, and his brows straight slashes that shadowed his eyes but didn't hide his direct, disconcerting stare at her. *This* was the man her parents wanted her to marry? This huge, hard-edged, staring brute?

Her mother nudged her in the small of her back, and Amelia-Rose belatedly curtsied. "My lord. I'm so pleased to meet you."

"Are ye?" he replied in a thick Scottish brogue. "Will ye be pleased to wear my ring and call yerself Lady Glendarril?"

"I . . ." Heavens, he was terrifying. "I think we should become acquainted first, my lord. Don't you?" she asked, trying very hard to remember she was supposed to be polite. Oh, this was *not* going to happen. This brute would cart her off to the Highlands to milk his cows and give him strapping Highlands babies while he stomped about in his great boots. *No, no, no.*

"Well, that's what we're about tonight, isnae?" He unceremoniously took the empty seat beside her while his mother and silent younger brother sat beside her parents. "Tell me someaught about yerself, then." Lord Glendarril folded his arms over his chest.

He made her feel firstly like she was being questioned at the Old Bailey, and secondly like some sort of harpy who'd sacrificed a goat in order to find herself a husband. Amelia-Rose opened and closed her mouth again. What in the world was she supposed to say to that? Clearly he wouldn't approve or appreciate whatever she uttered.

Behind her, her mother reached forward to straighten one of Amelia-Rose's sleeves. "My daughter has already received four marriage proposals, my lord," Victoria said grandly, her voice pitched just loudly enough that those in the boxes on either side could overhear. "I daresay Amelia-Rose has secured her place as a diamond of the first water over the course of her two Seasons."

"What the devil is a water diamond?" the viscount retorted, snorting.

"It's an expression," Amelia-Rose returned. "My mother exaggerates, of course."

He lifted a straight eyebrow. "So ye're nae a diamond?"

"I'm . . . I have rarely wanted for a dance partner," she stumbled. How did one explain a brag without sounding either too humble or too haughty?

"Ye like to dance, then."

"Oh, yes, I do," she exclaimed. Perhaps he was just nervous, too, and had less practice at polite conversation. Well, she excelled at conversation, and she'd been working on the polite part. "Especially the waltz. This Season has been mad with balls, and Lady Jenkins's soiree had three waltzes. It was scandalous, but now everyone else wants to do the same. Do you dance, then, my lord?"

"Nae if I can avoid it."

She caught her expression before it could fall. For heaven's sake, he wasn't even trying to be pleasant. "What do you enjoy then, my lord?"

"What do I do that hasnae a purpose, ye mean? When I'm nae seeing the sheep sheared or the crops planted, the cotters fed, roofs repaired, and whatever else comes to my attention? I reckon I drink, and I curse, and I brawl. What do ye do that *isnae* for yer own enjoyment?"

Amelia-Rose kept her lips tightly closed. What a rude, insufferable man. If her parents thought for one second that she wanted this . . . Highlander for her husband, in her bed, well, they were very, very mistaken. And they might as well realize that now. "I am n—"

"Amelia-Rose," her mother interrupted, "tell Lord Glendarril about the Sundays you've spent aiding the poor." Victoria leaned forward, evidently unwilling to leave the explanation to her daughter. "On the third Sunday of every month our church donates clothing, shoes, and hats to the poor. Amelia-Rose always attends, helping women find the most charming ensembles. She is much beloved, I assure you."

That sounded horrid. Is that how her mother actually saw it—that she was helping underprivileged women play dress-up? "It's not that frivolous," she said in a low voice, forcing a smile.

The gaslights along the front of the stage sparked into life, and the crowd below them tittered and quieted. It dawned on her that she didn't even know which play they were here to see. Hopefully a comedy, something to lighten the mood and amuse the brute beside her. Because even though she'd resolved not to marry this man, she didn't wish to sit next to a giant, angry Highlander for hours and hours.

The curtains opened, and a single man in hose and doublet took center stage and began to speak.

Two households, both alike in dignity,
In fair Verona, where we lay our scene,
From ancient grudge break to new mutiny,
Where civil blood makes civil hands unclean.

Oh, wonderful. Shakespeare. And not *Much Ado About Nothing* or *A Midsummer Night's Dream.* No, Lady Aldriss had invited them to see *Romeo and Juliet.* Now she was meant to sit there and listen to a tale of misunderstanding, of families at war, of a love that ultimately ended in yet more misunderstandings, tragedy, and death. And during the intermission, she would no doubt be expected to be polite and charming while he would continue to glower and call her frivolous.

"Dunnae faint yet, lass," the mountain rumbled from beside her. "Tell me about the weather or someaught. Or what passes for weather here in the south."

The weather. That was what he thought of her, that she was just some simpering, empty-headed miss. Well. Her pony had just left this race. "I might, my lord, if I thought you would understand what 'cumulous' and 'precipitation' mean. Perhaps I should just say 'rain wet' or 'sun warm.' Or is that more than you expect of me? I could nod silently, of course, but then you wouldn't have dialogue over which to bully me. 'Dialogue.' That means 'words.'"

Lord Glendarril's jaw clenched, and he stood. In Gaelic he muttered something to his brother seated behind them, and then he shoved out through the curtains at the back of the box. "What was that?" Lady Aldriss asked quietly as the play continued below them. "I'm afraid I never learned much more than 'hello' and 'goodbye' in Gaelic."

"Coll went to find someaught to wet his whistle," the other MacTaggert brother, Niall, replied after a beat. "He'll be back shortly."

"He is fond of English beer," Lady Aldriss said in a voice that sounded a bit too flippant, as if she'd realized what a disaster Amelia-Rose had just precipitated.

The play below them continued, the men in the crowd roaring approval when the famous actress Persephone Jones took the stage as Juliet. Not everyone had eyes only for the onstage tragedy, though; Amelia-Rose could see the glint of opera glasses turned in her direction—or more specifically, at the chair beside hers.

Having her almost-betrothed absent now was almost worse than having him glowering there beside her. Everyone knew they were to be a match. At least, all of her friends knew, and that meant everyone else likely knew as well. And what they saw was her, sitting there with an empty chair. *Oh, dear.*

She'd done it again. Perhaps they should all leave, and later they could claim some unforeseen emergency had arisen to call them away. That would be better than her having to explain tomorrow why Lord Glendarril had vanished five minutes into the play and twenty minutes later hadn't returned. Had he left? Was he coming back at all?

She half turned to suggest an exit to her father, but then stopped when something rustled behind her. Abruptly the seat beside her wasn't empty any longer. Stifling a sigh, annoyed with herself for being relieved that he'd returned when she'd already decided she didn't like him, Amelia-Rose sent him a sideways glance and opened her mouth to apologize.

"I couldnae see from back there," the viscount's brother Niall MacTaggert said from beside her. "Coll can boot me out when he gets back. If ye reckon ye dunnae mind me sitting here."

Considering that he lacked only an inch or two of his brother's height, she "reckoned" he could see quite well from any spot in the theater. But he'd bothered to move, and in the dark no doubt one Highlander looked nearly like another to the theatergoers below. "He's not coming back, is he?" she whispered back at him.

She could feel those nearly colorless green eyes gazing at her. "Nae. Ye insulted his knowledge of the weather; that's nae someaught ye do to a Highlander. We ken *all* the words for snow, and for rain. Precipitation, rather."

That, she hadn't expected. At all. Her lips curved before she could catch her expression. "You heard that?"

"Aye. I've been led to believe that all English lasses are soft and gentle and weepy and nae in the least bit contrary. Is that nae so?"

"I . . ." She trailed off, swallowing. "I spoke too sharply," she confessed, not certain why she was doing so.

"Ye're generally softer, then?"

Amelia-Rose hesitated again. "I try to be," she said, even though admitting such a thing couldn't possibly benefit her. "I will apologize to him. This . . . he . . . took me somewhat by surprise." No, she didn't want Glendarril, but neither should she have chosen the least politic method to tell him so. She had put her own reputation in jeopardy—again.

"There's nae need. His leaving had naught to do with ye, truthfully. None of us knew till six days ago that he'd an obligation to marry a lass of Lady Aldriss's choosing."

"It would have been nice if someone had mentioned that to me earlier," she returned. "I didn't have much notice, either, and you don't see me stomping about or trying to encourage people to faint or cry." Oh, she likely shouldn't have said that, either.

"Ye've a slightly better hold of yer temper than Coll does."

"A dragon would seem to have an easier temper than your brother," she blurted, then put a hand over her mouth. *What was wrong with her tonight?*

He snorted. "I cannae argue with that." Niall MacTaggert leaned a breath closer. "Now. The lot of ye English dunnae speak like those Montagues and Capulets on the stage, do ye? Because it sounds like frilly nonsense. I barely ken a word of it."

That made her grin again, and she lowered her hand. Her parents couldn't see, so they couldn't chastise her later for being frivolous after driving away her almost-beau. They had several other things to chastise her about, after all. "No. Saying hello would take far too long, and we're all quite busy discussing the weather, you know."

For a second she worried that she'd gone too far again, but his amused expression only deepened. "Aye," he returned. "We stopped on a hill above London, and all ye Sassenach looked like a colony of ants scurrying about. It was enough to make even a great, stout heart like mine shiver."

The idea of this big, well-muscled man being afraid of London made her chuckle. She'd expected a brute, and had found one in Coll MacTaggert. The brother, though, could at least carry on a conversation. Nor, at least for the moment, did he seem to find her "too free with her opinions" or "trying to pretend she was more than a silly girl," as her mother frequently complained.

Niall MacTaggert's humor made her reassess his brother's bullying. They couldn't be so different after all, could they? Perhaps Lord Glendarril had merely been put back on his heels by this entire morass, and after another day or two to become accustomed to all this, he could be reasoned with. The idea did give her a little hope that they might find themselves on the same side—and thank goodness for a little hope. And for Niall MacTaggert.

Chapter Three

Your brother is aware of the consequences of his actions, is he not?" Francesca snapped, shedding her gloves as Smythe the butler pulled open the front door of Oswell House.

"Aye, he's aware." Niall had nothing to remove for the butler, but he paused in the grand foyer anyway. As much as he wanted to confront Coll, reasoning with his brother would have to wait until the woman who funded their livelihood stopped raging. Damn his brother anyway. The man had never wielded more than an ounce of patience.

"Then just what does he expect I will—"

"I said he's aware," Niall interrupted. "I'm here. Dunnac bellow at me. When I find him, then ye can yell at *him*."

"I . . ." Francesca took in a deep breath through her nose. "Yes. Do that. And inform your brother that he is taking Amelia-Rose to breakfast in the morning. That is decided. If he doesn't, I will have to—"

"He will," Niall broke in again. "We didnae come all this way to lose Aldriss."

She looked at him for a moment, her green eyes assessing. Lasses. Just when he thought he had them all figured out, one of them stood up to Coll in admirable fashion.

"Yes, you came to save Aldriss from my unforgiving claws, didn't you?" Francesca said, handing her shawl to the butler, as well. "Then you'd best keep that in mind. Smythe, please have peppermint tea sent up to my bedchamber. Is Eloise home yet?"

"Yes, my lady. She returned an hour ago."

"Send her up to my room also, if you please."

"Yes, my lady."

Niall watched the countess up the stairs until she vanished down the western-facing hallway. "Has my brother returned?" he asked, facing the butler.

"Neither of your brothers is presently here, Master Niall," Smythe informed him.

Of course they weren't. The devil knew where Aden had gone, and while Coll would generally be found either at the Bonny Lass or in the bed of any one of half a dozen actual bonny lasses, down here in London, Niall had no idea where to even begin looking. Somewhere with food, he hoped; one of them might not starve, that way.

Sidestepping into the morning room, he picked up the whisky decanter and headed for the stairs. "Good night, Smythe."

"Shall I send Oscar up to tend you?"

"What for? I reckon I can put myself to bed. Havenae had a mama to kiss me good night since I was a wee bairn."

"Good night, then, Master Niall."

Pausing on the stairs, Niall looked down at the butler. "Just Niall, for Saint Michael's sake. Ye'll give me a swelled head."

Between "Master" this and "have a cup of tea" that, he'd be wearing a crown by the end of the week. The English seemed to think very highly of themselves and their so-called civilized ways. Or most of them did, anyway. Amelia-Rose's conversation hadn't been remotely what he'd expected. She'd handily sent Coll fleeing, and even after that hadn't been able to rein in her tongue. Not entirely. Not even the Scottish lasses spoke that way to him or his brothers, because however friendly they might be in bed, the MacTaggerts were, after all, their lairds, and Laird Aldriss, their chieftain.

No wonder Coll had fled—his oldest brother had pushed her, expecting compliance and submission, and she'd snapped back at him like a fox in a trap. Unless he was greatly mistaken, Amelia-Rose wasn't any happier at any of this arranged marriage shite than Coll was. His brother should have noticed that, and taken it into account.

Niall had noticed, but then she was striking. Despite the tongue-twisting name the lass was pretty, fresh-faced, and blond. No MacTaggert male had ever complained about that combination. With a night to consider, Coll might well come around. Keeping Aldriss funded was important to all of them, but especially to its heir. He could still leave the lass behind in London, regardless of whether she meekly agreed to it or not. Though firstly Amelia-Rose seemed a lass who just might put up a fight about being abandoned, and secondly, leaving her all alone in a grand marriage bed would very likely be a sin.

On the main landing, Niall patted Rory the deer on the head, noted that someone, likely Aden, had given the buck a cravat around his neck and a blue beaver hat over one nine-pronged antler, and continued up the stairs. He pushed open the door of his borrowed bedchamber and immediately scented, then spied, the thick ham sandwich on the dressing table. *Thank God.* Shrugging out of his proper black jacket, he made for the food and the small note propped beside it. He unfolded the missive. *Idiot. Eloise*, was all it said, and he grinned as he took a huge bite. Evidently having a sister about could be more useful than he'd realized.

His evenings generally didn't end until much closer to

dawn, so as he ate, washing down the meal with a generous portion of the whisky he'd liberated, he wandered over to the bookshelf located perpendicular to the trio of windows. A compilation of Byron poems, some Shelley and Wordsworth, three Shakespeare folios, and a history of Hereford cattle. All very English, and very unappealing tonight.

Laid flat on a lower shelf and topped by a black-and-white porcelain cow, though, he found an unexpected treasure—*The Lord of the Isles* by Sir Walter Scott. So Francesca did have Scottish things other than her three sons in the house; she merely preferred to keep them hidden. Pulling off his boots and tossing them over by the door, he took the book, the sandwich, and the whisky decanter, and hopped onto the over-pillowed, too-soft bed to read. And drink.

He woke confused, half inside a dream where Amelia-Rose Baxter kept asking him to dance and then twirling away before he could answer, and half aware of Oscar flinging open the bloody curtains—until he become fully aware of the sunlight stabbing him in the eyes.

"What the devil do ye think ye're doing?" he growled, putting a pillow over his head.

"I'm waking ye up. It's near eight o'clock," the valet answered.

Eight o'clock? "Fetch me a damned pistol."

"A pistol? Why do ye require a pistol?"

"Because I'm going to shoot ye for waking me up when I didnae ask ye to do any such thing, ye damned lummox. Go away and leave me be."

"I cannae. Yer mother—her ladyship, that is—is asking where yer brother is, and why he's nae on his way to escort the Sassenach lass to the coffeehouse."

Niall shoved the pillow aside and sat up. "Coll's nae returned?"

The valet shook his head. "I checked the bedchamber. Nae a rumpled sheet or muddy boot in sight. And the window's latched, so he didnae come in and slip out again."

That didn't bode well. Aye, Coll had been annoyed, but mere annoyance wouldn't have kept him out all night when Aldriss was at stake. "Does Francesca know that?"

"Nae. She sent her maid to ask me to fetch him down. Hannah —that's her highness's maid—said the lady wasnae at all happy."

With a curse, ignoring the pounding of his skull, Niall lurched to his feet. "Tell Hannah that Coll left to meet the Sassenach lass already. Say he stopped to fetch her some posies to apologize for last night."

Oscar began nodding. "Aye. I can do that. But what will ye be up to? I cannae fool everyone."

"I'll be getting dressed. Tell Gavin to saddle Kelpie, and I'll go meet the damned lass myself. Keep an eye out for Coll; ye'll have to tell him what we've decided he's been up to before the countess catches sight of him and he bellows out the truth."

"I'll see to it. Saint Andrew knows it willnae be the first time I've bent the truth into a knot for one or the other of ye." The valet sniffed. "I put clean clothes out for ye," he went on, pointing a finger toward the chair by the dressing table.

"*Tapadh leat*," Niall returned, thanking him with a grateful nod. "Where's Aden? I'll wager ye didnae try waking him up."

"That Smythe fella said he came home about dawn. Ye can sack me, but I'm nae risking my neck to wake him up unless his bed's on fire."

Niall finished pulling on his dark-brown buckskin trousers. "First of all, *this* isnae home. Scotland is home. Aldriss is home. This is our prison, where we're to stay for a time because that woman ordered us here. Second, aye,

leave Aden be. He sounds like he'll be more trouble than
he's worth. Go tell yer tale before someone else delivers
the countess a different one. If Aden wakes, tell him, too."

"Aye." With a resigned scowl Oscar fled, shutting the
door firmly behind him.

Niall stifled his cursing long enough to shave. Damned
Coll knew how important this match was. Even if the viscount didn't want the lass, he needed to at least make it
look like he'd put some effort into courting her, and make
the failing look like her doing. And he couldn't go about
saying things like he had last night. They weren't the only
Scotsmen in London.

If Francesca spoke any Gaelic, all three of them might
have woken this morning to find themselves destitute, cut
off from their mother's funds. Because Coll hadn't said he
was going off to find an English beer during *Romeo and
Juliet*. No, Viscount Glendarril had declared he would stab
himself in the eye before he'd wed a sharp-tongued harlot
who'd likely try to make him prissy and English. And that
was a very large problem. The only positive thing he'd
done was to say it in a language both the lady and his own
mother didn't understand.

Oscar had laid out a brown waistcoat and a cravat in
addition to the buckskin trousers and a blue long-tailed
coat; evidently they were supposed to dress like Sassenach here. Well, they'd dressed up on occasion, for some
lass or other's come-out party, so he supposed he could
manage it again. He didn't have time to dig through draw-
ers and find where the valet had stashed all his clothes,
anyway.

As he shaved and dragged a comb through his unruly
hair it occurred to him that he did this fairly often. Not go
out to escort English ladies promised to his oldest brother,
but sweep up after Coll's misadventures. A large man with
a larger stubborn streak, a title, and a very short temper

frequently didn't consider how a sharp word from him could be construed as a blast from a twenty-pound cannon by most mortals.

Aden had mastered the technique of stealth, which left him free of most of the consequences of the MacTaggert brothers' follies, including his own, but Niall couldn't manage that. He liked mayhem in general, but when it affected people without their resources or standing, he'd always felt . . . responsible for setting things right again. And here he was, doing it once more. In this instance, with the outcome vital to not only their futures but those of the nearly three hundred cotters and villagers on Aldriss land, it seemed both necessary that he step in, and very nearly unforgivable that Coll continued to make himself scarce.

He put a simple knot into his damned cravat and headed for the bedchamber door, nearly taking a blow to the head as it flung open again. "Oscar, how many times have we asked ye to knock before ye barge in, for the devil's sake?"

"I knew ye didnae have a lass in here," the valet returned, looking over his shoulder as he crowded into the room and shut the door again. "I told her majesty yer brother went out already, and now she's headed up here to, and I quote, 'see if Niall can provide me with some insight into Coll.'"

Niall cocked his head. "Ye do a fine Sassenach accent," he noted. "For a minute I almost thought ye were civilized. Did ye tell Gavin to saddle Kelpie?"

"Aye."

Retreating toward the window, Niall pushed it open. "Then I've left for the morning to go prancing about the park and ogle all the eligible English lasses there," he said, and ducked outside to grip the garden rose trellis. Thorns made a wreck of one shirtsleeve, but he tucked it up into his jacket sleeve as he reached the ground.

As he made his way to the stable he brushed rose petals

from his jacket and trousers. Out in front of the wide double doors Gavin, the groom they'd brought with them from Aldriss, shoved an English fellow away from Kelpie's bridle as the bay stomped restlessly. "Gavin, it's too bloody early for a brawl," Niall warned him.

"This *amadan* says all the horses in the stable are in his charge. I'm about to introduce his backside to the ground."

The older man tugged on his coat. "I am Farthing, Lady Aldriss's head groom," he said stiffly. "This . . . buffoon is permitted in *my* stable only as long as I say so."

"Gavin, ye buffoon, dunnae shove Farthing unless ye reckon Nuckelavee's about to eat him," Niall ordered, naming Coll's notoriously bad-tempered stallion. There was a reason Coll had named him after the black demons of the northern isles.

Gavin snickered. "Aye. I reckon I could be persuaded to save the Sassenach's life."

"Good." Taking the reins, Niall swung up on Kelpie. "Now. How do I get from Upper Brook Street to Wigmore Place, Farthing?"

Farthing furrowed his brow. "Weymur?"

Niall sighed. "Wigmore," he repeated, enunciating it as Mrs. Baxter had last evening when Amelia-Rose's mother had insisted on the outing.

"Oh. Wigmore Place. Head that way"—he pointed east—"on Upper Brook Street, then north up Duke Street. Turn right onto Wigmore Street, and you'll find Wigmore Place on your left. It's just about half a mile from here."

With a nod, repeating the street names to himself, Niall kneed Kelpie into a trot. He'd been to Inverness on half a dozen occasions, so the crowded streets of a town weren't entirely foreign to him. London, though, felt more like a noisy, smelly maze than a place where anyone would choose to live.

Kelpie didn't like it, either; the bay skittered every time

an orange girl scurried into the street or a milk cart rattled out in front of them. Niall patted the gelding's withers. "Easy, lad," he crooned. "We'll nae be here for long."

That didn't reassure either one of them, but since Farthing's directions were good, at least they didn't become lost in this devil's bog. He turned Kelpie up Wigmore Place, hopeful that he remembered the street number he'd heard from Mrs. Baxter. He did not want to spend his morning riding up and down the road to find his brother's Sassenach lass.

The door at 129 opened as he approached, and a stoop-shouldered man in black livery stepped into the doorway. "Lord Glendarril, I presume?"

"Nae. I'm his brother. He sent me to fetch the lass."

The butler opened his gobber and shut it again. "Your calling card, then," he said, holding out a hand, "and I'll inform Miss Baxter of your arrival."

"I've nae card. Tell her Niall's here, and I'll be taking her to the damned coffeehouse to meet Coll."

"Hm. Wait here . . . Niall."

The door shut again. Well, that was fine, then. He was dressed very respectably, if he said so himself. If the residents of Baxter House thought him too shabby, then they could go soak their heads. Coll wouldn't have stayed standing here on the bloody front step.

The door opened once more. Amelia-Rose stepped outside, wearing an extremely proper blue bonnet that hid her sunshine hair and most of her face, and a pretty peach muslin gown that revealed a nice portion of her bosom. A blue shawl that matched the bonnet covered her shoulders. Abruptly Niall was grateful that Oscar had found him some English-style finery to wear, himself. She was a bonny lass, Amelia-Rose Baxter was. Damned bonny.

"Good morning," he said, remembering his manners enough to incline his head.

She dipped a curtsy. "Mr. MacTaggert."

"Niall, if ye please. My other brother's a Mr. MacTaggert, too, and it's confusing."

Her mouth curved a little. "Niall, then. Let's go meet your brother, shall we?"

"Aye. The—"

He stepped sideways as a second woman emerged from the doorway. This one was a giant, nearly six feet tall with coal-black hair scraped back into a bun that looked solid as iron. Her gown of green-and-brown muslin was nice, if plainer than Amelia-Rose's, but the dress didn't do her straight figure any favors.

"And who are ye?" he asked.

"I'm Miss Bansil. Miss Baxter's companion."

"Did we invite ye as well, then?"

"I cannot go anywhere with you unless Miss Bansil is present," Amelia-Rose put in. "It would be scandalous to do otherwise."

"Well, we dunnae want anything scandalous," Niall returned dryly.

Coll's almost-intended took a step toward the street, then stopped. "Where's your carriage?"

Niall frowned. "Carriage? I rode my horse. Kelpie."

She faced him. "So you think to carry the three of us on Kelpie?"

He tilted his head at her. Was she teasing at him, or was she genuinely annoyed? "I didnae think that far in advance at all," he admitted.

"Ah." Amelia-Rose turned around. "Hughes, have John saddle Mirabel and Daisy," she told the butler. "And a mount for himself."

"At once, Miss Baxter," the vulture returned, and sent a footman back into the depths of the house.

"If I'd known we were forming a parade, I'd have

brought drums and a piper," Niall observed, taking Kelpie's reins back from the waiting groom.

"That would . . ." She trailed off, sending Miss Bansil a quick glance. "We'll be down shortly," Amelia-Rose amended, as she and the tower turned back to the house.

Niall was fairly certain she'd been about to say something witty. A shame she'd stopped herself. "What, are ye off to gather more people to ride with us?" He kept his expression cool, but beneath that he continued his long barrage of silent profanity at Coll. Neither of them had any real experience with escorting fashionable ladies to fashionable places, and this morning he'd clearly waded into the loch and found himself in waters well over his head.

"I'm not dressed to ride," the blond lass returned, her tone amused, as if she'd never run across anyone who wouldn't know that a horse gown was different from a carriage gown. "Wait by the stable if you don't care to come inside."

Well, no one had invited him inside, but he preferred the stable anyway. Horses, he understood. "Aye."

The groom from whom he'd reclaimed Kelpie had vanished, so with the bay following close behind him he headed around the side of the house toward the strongest smell of hay, mud, and manure. Kelpie bumped him in the shoulder, and he shifted to let the gelding draw even with him.

"Dunnae ye complain," he said, patting his mount on the neck. "Ye've had breakfast, at least. Coll's likely at some tavern downing half a hog right now. I'd be happy with a bowl of cold porridge and a handful of wild berries."

He had to ask the groom who'd be accompanying them how to find St. Alban's Street, then had to fit that into the nearly blank mental map he was trying to put together in his head. It wouldn't do to lead the lass into a dangerous part of Town, however much the idea of brawling with a Sassenach or two might appeal to him at the moment. Alone he reckoned he could manage just about anywhere, but evidently he was to lead an entire brigade today.

A dozen bruised-looking apples sat in a bucket by the stable door, and he snagged one when no one was looking. It was overripe and mealy, so after one bite he gave the rest of it to Kelpie. The bay wasn't as particular as he was. If not for the sandwich Eloise had provided him last night he would likely have perished from hunger by now. The damned coffeehouse, if they ever reached it, had best be stocked with an entire roasted cow. A large one.

Mirabel turned out to be a spirited gray mare, which surprised him given the delicate lass meant to ride her. Amelia-Rose seemed very . . . breakable, even if her tongue had been a wee bit sharp last night. The companion's horse, Daisy, on the other hand, slept through being saddled. Miss Baxter liked to ride, even if her companion didn't. That boded well; Coll rode nearly every day, as did he. One thing in common was at least a beginning, even if Lord Glendarril meant to have as little as possible to do with his unwanted wife—if he ever reappeared to marry the lass.

The side door of Baxter House opened, and the two lasses emerged once more. The tall stick wore a plain brown riding habit, but as she stepped aside, something deep in Niall's chest—and somewhere a bit lower—jolted. Amelia-Rose had donned a crimson riding habit that boasted little black buttons from her waist to her chin. Rather than being demure, though, the heavy material showed every curve above her waist, while the red skirt flowed around her hips and swirled against her legs as she walked.

And she was walking now. *Good glory.* For a dozen hard beats of his heart he envisioned her with her blond hair tumbled past her shoulders, her expression wide-eyed and breathless, and all those buttons broken open and scattered to the floor. Beneath his proper trousers, his cock jumped again.

He shook himself. Every time he set eyes on her, she pulled at him. Aye, he could admire a bonny lass; he wasn't dead, after all. But he shouldn't be admiring this one. He damned well shouldn't be lusting after her. Amelia-Rose was Coll's lass. Niall was there merely keeping the agreement open until his oldest brother came to his senses. Nothing more.

Of course if Coll got a look at her this morning, he might just propose on the spot. She was a lithe, sensuous goddess. The thing that troubled Niall most was the idea that Coll could marry such a lass and then decide to leave her behind in London. No, that wasn't the thought that troubled him the most. But he refused to acknowledge the other one. It would serve nothing but damned bloody trouble.

"Let's be off, shall we?" she said pertly, apparently unaware she'd nearly made him split his seams. "We shouldn't keep Lord Glendarril waiting."

Lord Glendarril was most likely somewhere sleeping off a large dinner and a woman, but that wasn't for her to know. "Aye."

He let the groom boost her up into the sidesaddle; until his brain caught up with his cock he wouldn't be touching her. If he hadn't been tired, hungry, and boasting a headache so grand that even his hair hurt, he wouldn't have been imagining doing anything naked and sweaty with Amelia-Rose Baxter. And still somewhere in the back of his mind he knew that was a lie, too.

When everyone else was mounted he swung up on Kelpie and led the parade south and east. Lines of connected townhouses, broken up by small parks filled with more nannies and prams and bairns, gave way to fancy-looking shops, hotels, and gentlemen's clubs.

The gray mare drew even with him. "Do you know where we're going?" Amelia-Rose asked.

"More or less. I reckon ye'd inform me if I make a wrong turn."

"Certainly. We're a bit too far south at the moment, but this is the less complicated route."

"I asked yer groom for directions," he said, indicating the man riding at the rear of the parade. "He looked at me like I was an idiot, so it follows he'd give me the simplest route."

She cleared her throat in what might have passed for a chuckle. "This is truly your first time in London?"

"Aye." He felt more than saw her sideways glance at him. Next she'd be asking if he'd ever kissed a lass, because from what he'd always heard about the Sassenach, they thought every man who'd never been to London was no man at all. "Is that White's club?" he asked, indicating the plain building front that looked very much the same as all the others, with the exception of its prominent bow window. He'd seen a drawing or two of that, as he recalled.

"Yes. Is your father a member?"

Niall snorted. More English snobbery. "Nae. My da is a chieftain of clan Ross. That's the only club he'd ever care to join. A gaggle of Sassenach sitting about and arguing over how important they are is a bigger waste of time than milking a cat."

Her smile loosened a little. "That's a bit severe, isn't it?"

Was it? "I've nae seen a thing to change my opinion."

"That's because you haven't seen anything at all but an evening at Drury Lane Theater and a morning riding down the street." She squinted one eye.

"Either ye've a twitch, or ye're wanting to say someaught more, lass. Dunnae be shy with me. I dunnae offend easily."

Aside from that, he'd very much appreciated the way she'd blasted at Coll last night.

With a barely audible sigh, she nodded. "We're to be friends, aren't we? In-laws, if our parents have their way. Tell me, then, if your father so dislikes London and the English, why did he marry your mother?"

"That's a question we've debated for two decades," he answered truthfully. "He claims it was for her da's money. I reckon he got cracked in the head by Cupid, but he willnae admit it now out of pride."

Her mouth, with which he'd been fascinated all morning, quirked again. She'd be terrible at card games, because every emotion she felt mirrored itself on her pretty face. For God's sake he hoped it wasn't the same with him, or they'd all be in trouble.

"'Cracked in the head by Cupid,'" she repeated, chuckling. "Not quite as poetic as being struck by the cherub's arrow, but I imagine falling in love could be somewhat . . . chaotic." She sent him another glance. "Would you agree? Have you ever been in love, Mr. MacTaggert? Niall, I mean?"

"I've been near to it half a dozen times, Miss Baxter," he returned, spotting the next street plaque and turning the group north accordingly. "Nae close enough to fall over the cliff." At this moment he was wishing one of those lasses *had* caught his heart; if he'd been already married, especially without knowing about the bloody agreement his parents had signed, he would likely have been excused from this mess and happily still in the Highlands.

But after last night, that wasn't quite true, either. The play had been better than he'd expected, but so had the conversation. Especially when he'd thought to be seated in the back row watching while Coll attempted to speak to an empty-headed flower about nonsense. It had begun that way, aye, until Coll had pushed too hard. Had his brother suspected he was being bamboozled? More likely he'd just been overly annoyed by the entire thing, but she'd definitely taken her moment to speak her mind.

"What about your brother?" she asked.

Niall blinked. "What about him?"

"Has he . . . been in love?"

Oh, that. "Nae that he's admitted." He sent her another look, catching a glimpse of blue eyes slanted in his direction before she faced forward again. "Ye definitely caught his attention last night."

"If you try to tell me he was intrigued rather than entirely put out, I will call you a liar, sir."

A laugh burst from his chest. He tried to stifle it with a cough, but doubted he'd been at all successful. "He wasnae indifferent about it. I'll admit to that."

"Well, I shall be minding my tongue this morning, just so you know. I misspoke last night, however . . . provoking he might have been. I know better."

That seemed a damned shame, but since Coll wasn't anywhere about and Niall had lied to get her to the coffee shop, he was almost willing to wager that she would be misspeaking again this morning. He looked forward to it.

Just past the corner on the left in front of them, a wooden sign bearing a drawing of a Turkish coffeepot and fancy lettering proclaimed that they'd arrived at The Constantinople. The shop below the sign boasted large windows and a rich, exotic scent that drowned out the coal-and-manure smell around them. His stomach rumbled. While he'd had coffee, he'd never been to a place dedicated to the brew.

This morning might have been worse, he supposed; Mrs. Baxter might have sent them to a recital or a tableware museum. What he knew about finer folk's music and dinner plates wouldn't fill a thimble.

Niall dismounted. Miss Baxter, still up on Mirabel, held out a gloved hand to him and smiled. Blowing out his breath, he stepped forward. His ancestors had fought off the English for decades. Surely he could keep one lass at arm's length for one morning while he told her charming and complimentary tales about his eldest brother. And then with any luck, he could hand her over to Coll and go take a gander at other lasses—ones who weren't practically engaged already. Ones he could imagine leaving behind while he returned to the Highlands.

Chapter Four

If she'd known that the first MacTaggert with whom she would have to interact this morning would be Niall rather than Lord Glendarril, Amelia-Rose might have had a less fitful night's sleep. Or perhaps a more fitful one.

His brother the viscount had an almost aggressive handsomeness to him, rather like a dark-haired lion who hadn't decided whether she was a friend or a meal, but not only did Niall have a face that half her friends would simply swoon over, but his sense of humor almost dared her to misbehave. And that was not a good thing. Whatever she decided to do about this marriage nonsense, she wanted it to be her decision, not something she accidentally destroyed or got trapped into because of her unreliable tongue.

Perhaps the youngest MacTaggert brother had only been attempting to counter his brother's fierceness last night, but he'd made an impression, regardless. Those light, light green eyes, complemented by long, dark lashes, a nose and jaw to which not even Michelangelo could do justice, wild brown hair that practically begged her fingers to brush it from his temple—if he hadn't been Scottish, he would very nearly have been perfect. Or rather, he would be perfect for some other young lady. The name on the agreement her parents had signed was Coll MacTaggert.

While John saw to Jane Bansil, Niall approached her and Mirabel. She held out a hand for assistance in reaching the mounting block, but before she could do more than grip his shoulder he put his hands around her waist and lifted her out of the saddle without any apparent effort. The sensation of being lighter than air, of flying, quite took her breath away.

A gentleman should ask for permission before grabbing hold of her so intimately. Everyone knew that. But then he *was* a barbarian Highlander and barely a gentleman even if he seemed to know how to dress like one. "That was improper," she said a little breathlessly, reaching up a hand to straighten her bonnet as he set her feet on the ground.

He kept his hands around her waist. "Should I put ye back up, then?"

"No, it's done now. Do release me." That wasn't what she wanted to say, but it seemed like the proper response. "We wouldn't want your brother to see you putting your hands on me."

His eyes narrowed a fraction. "Nae. We wouldnae want that. So being helpful is a sin?"

"Of course it isn't. But . . . Oh, never mind." As if she was qualified to give lessons in propriety. "Just ask a female before you lift her into the air."

That brought another devastating grin to his lean face. "Aye. I checked the wind first, though, and I reckoned it wasnae strong enough to carry ye aloft, even with that great hat on ye."

She opened her mouth to retort that by some standards her bonnet was quite modest, but that would trip over her mother's advice never to apologize for being well dressed. Aside from that, Amelia-Rose saw the twinkle in his eye. "Troublemaker," she muttered, taking a step backward.

When Jane took her arm, Amelia-Rose actually jumped.
"You said he was handsome," her companion whispered,
"but goodness' sake. I look forward to comparing him
to the one with the title." She chuckled. "Perhaps you
could send this one toward one of your less discriminating
friends. Rebecca Sharpe doesn't require a titled gentleman,
does she?"

No, Rebecca's father was already a viscount, and a
wealthy one at that. All Rebecca required was a pretty
face. And perhaps someone to balance her rather . . . self-
absorbed character. Somehow, however, Amelia-Rose
couldn't imagine Niall MacTaggert blithely fetching sweets
and glasses of Madeira every time Rebecca snapped her
well-manicured fingers.

"I think he would eat Rebecca for breakfast," she whispered back, ignoring Jane's surprised look as they reached
the coffeehouse door.

That was neither here nor there, anyway. She was here
to give Lord Glendarril another opportunity and, according to her mother, to give *herself* another chance to charm
their best hope for a title since Baron Oglivy, who was
nearly sixty years old. That, of course, had made her wonder if her intentionally acting like a complete shrew
would cause this horridly unfair agreement to fall apart.
It would likely ruin her, but she still wasn't ready to dis-
card the idea entirely.

At the same time, she couldn't help reaching for hope.
The little Niall had mentioned about his father's antipathy
toward the English certainly hadn't encouraged her at all,
but if his brother the viscount simply felt forced into something he didn't want, she could muster a large degree of
sympathy. A Highlander who would remain in London
might do, though his rudeness and lack of propriety certainly wouldn't either curb her own tendencies or encourage her to improve. But she couldn't know anything for

certain until she spoke with him again. Over a cup of coffee, as it were.

John waited outside with the horses, and she followed Niall's broad back around the crowd of tables and morass of conversations to a spot close by the front windows. He held a chair for her, and she took a seat, impressed that he did have some manners.

When he'd seated Jane as well, he vanished back into the crowd. Coffeehouses, she knew, weren't quite as popular as they'd once been, but The Constantinople buzzed with conversation. Mostly male conversation, but her mother had always pointed out that she wouldn't find a husband in a dress shop.

Of course she had a man now, at least on paper, even if she didn't particularly want him—and even if he didn't seem to be present. Niall took the chair opposite her and set a heaping plate of biscuits on the table. Jane reached for one of the treats, and for a second Amelia-Rose thought Niall might pull the plate away. "You appear to be hungry," she noted.

"Aye. I dunnae see the point of a shop that serves a drink but nae any food. A man could starve to death." He wolfed down a biscuit and then a second one.

The cups of coffee arrived at the table, and she took a sip of the hot, rich brew before adding a trio of sugar lumps. As Niall alternated between biscuits and gulps of coffee she watched him. A man with an appetite, clearly. Was it just for food, she wondered, then blushed at the thought.

This had nothing at all to do with the morning she'd imagined for herself, but at the moment she couldn't call it disappointing. Even so, her mother would ask how she'd gotten along with Lord Glendarril, whether they'd dealt better today than they had last night.

"I can't help noticing," she said aloud, "that your brother doesn't seem to be here."

Niall looked up at her. "Aye, he does seem to be a wee bit tardy, doesnae?" he said around a honey biscuit. "Mayhap he found a broken carriage and stopped to hold it up while they change the wheel."

"So he's heroic, is he?"

"Oh, aye. Pulled a trio of sheep out of a bog all on his own just a fortnight ago. He had to go for a swim in Loch an Daimh just to get the top layer of muck off himself. I'm surprised he didnae get mistaken for a *cirein cròin* and get himself shot."

"What's a . . . one of those?" she asked, deciding not even to attempt the pronunciation.

"A *cirein cròin*? A great sea monster. It can eat half a dozen whales at one go."

She snorted, covering her mouth with her hand in a belated effort to hide the sound. "He is very large," she agreed while Jane elbowed her beneath the table.

"That he is. One time we were repairing the thatch of Widow MacDougal's roof, and he fell right through onto her bed and broke that, too. I think the old lass wishes she'd been in the bed when he fell, but she'd have been flat as a plank. She did get a fresh roof and a new bed for her trouble, though. Coll saw to that."

"Is Widow MacDougal one of your tenants?"

"One of our cotters, aye."

So he meant to spend the morning until Lord Glendarril's arrival telling tales of what a fine man his brother was. That was well and good, but she preferred to judge for herself. And carefully chosen tales did not paint an entire portrait, anyway. "Does your brother assume all women are empty-headed watering pots?"

That made him frown. "He doesnae."

"Just me, then?"

"Lass, I—"

"I propose a game of questions and answers," she broke in. "With no lies allowed."

Tilting his head, he ate another biscuit. "Nae. I reckon ye want to try to trick me into saying Coll's nae fit for polite company, and that's nae so. I ken ye've heard tales of Highlands barbarians. Well, we've heard tales of delicate, fainting Sassenach lasses. Ye werenae what he expected, is all."

"Fair enough," she conceded. "And yet I cannot help but notice that he still isn't here." Should it have mollified her that Coll MacTaggert hadn't planned on a marriage, either, and didn't particularly want one? It didn't; at least she'd attempted to play her part. She hadn't blamed him for all her troubles, at least.

"Coll's stubborn. He'll come to the proper conclusion; it may take him a day or two, though. In the meantime, have a biscuit." He scooted the plate in her direction.

He, and the biscuits, were obviously meant as a distraction, but they both looked tasty. And if she hesitated, the biscuits, at least, would all be gone before she had a chance even to sample one. As for him, thinking about that delicious-looking subject wouldn't harm anything, she supposed. A little amused despite herself, she selected a sugared treat.

Whether Coll MacTaggert was being cowardly or heroic, the fact remained that he was not there. Perhaps this could work to her advantage. Telling her parents that Lord Glendarril hadn't bothered to appear could cause them to cancel their agreement with Lady Aldriss. That would set her back into the spinning teacup of being assessed and judged and sent after another man with an impressive-enough title to earn her parents' approval, but it wouldn't be her fault for once.

If she said nothing, though, or better yet allowed them to believe that she and Coll MacTaggert were slowly becoming acquainted, she would have something she'd never had a chance to experience before—a measure of freedom. Even if she and Coll were ostensibly courting, she could see her friends, go on outings, dance through the London Season she so adored.

It would all work better without Coll being present, of course. Heavens, as a nearly engaged woman she could dance with nearly anyone. Perhaps with all the weight lifted from her shoulders she might find a man whose company she actually enjoyed, one who didn't insult her, one who didn't warrant her disdain or indifference, and one of whom her parents might even approve. All she would need was a plausible escort.

"Ye've a sly look about ye, lass," Niall noted, bringing her thoughts back to the ground.

"I am going to find you a decent map of London," she said.

"That's thoughtful of ye."

Amelia-Rose nodded. "Yes. And this afternoon your brother is going to escort me to Lady Margaret Hathaway's alfresco luncheon. I've been wanting to attend, but my mother wouldn't let me accept without knowing what plans Lord Glendarril might have for us."

His brows dipped into a scowl. "I—"

"Your brother isn't here. That makes you his second, does it not?"

"He's only a bit late, as I s—"

"Then one or the other of you will arrive at my home at two o'clock, in a proper carriage. And one or the other of you will drive Jane and myself to the luncheon, for which I will provide directions, and he or you will spend the afternoon being charming so that I don't look like a fool for being involved in this marriage of convenience, which everyone wants to pretend is anything but."

Niall MacTaggert set a half-eaten biscuit on the wooden

table. "So ye reckon I'm yer lapdog now?" he said, a slight cooling in his voice that nearly made her shudder. Easytempered as he seemed to be, she abruptly realized that it may well merely have been the face he chose to show her. Well, she had other faces, too.

"Not at all," she replied, with more confidence than she felt. "If you don't wish to participate, I will simply return home and tell my parents the truth—that Lord Glendarril isn't interested in me. Because how can I assume otherwise?"

He took a breath. She couldn't read his thoughts, of course, but she imagined he was weighing spending a few hours with her against facing his mother and informing her that Coll MacTaggert had been thus far utterly unimpressive and utterly absent as a beau. That was in no way *his* fault, but he'd been the one to step in both last night and this morning. Whether he'd done so to save her or to keep his brother from embarrassment she didn't know, but it would seem to be in his best interest to continue to do so. Or so she hoped, because once she did tell her parents that Lord Glendarril wanted nothing to do with her, this nonsense *would* begin all over again—and she was running out of men she hadn't driven away or insulted or who were otherwise unacceptable.

"Seems ye've got me roasting on a spit," he commented, more mildly than she expected.

"I do. For this afternoon, at least. Perhaps you can tell me about more of your brother's heroics, and I'll fall for him before we even meet again."

A muscle along his jaw jumped. "Aye. That could happen. Very well. Coll or I will escort ye in a proper carriage to yer picnic." He sat a breath closer. "What I'd truly like to know about this party is if they'll be serving food. Or will it be frilly snacks that couldnae fill a bee's stomach?"

She laughed, her absurd degree of relief telling her just

how much all of this had gotten to her already. *Oh, thank goodness.* No arguments with her parents, no sending her to stand beside friends who happened to be speaking to earls and marquises. Not today, at least. "As soon as I return home I will personally send a note to Lady Margaret to clarify that you are not a measly bee and that you wish to be fed. If I'm not satisfied with her response, I will pack you a basket luncheon myself."

"I'll hold ye to that."

"Very well. For your information, a coach or a phaeton would be an acceptable conveyance, but I do prefer a barouche."

He lifted an eyebrow. "A barouche. Aye. Anything else, Miss Baxter?"

"No, that should suffice. But as you are standing in for my nearly betrothed, you may call me Amelia-Rose," she decided, despite the sharp look that earned her from Jane. Her shy second cousin had become exceedingly proper as she aged, and while Jane did serve to remind Amelia-Rose to behave, she also represented what happened when one was too reserved. Amelia-Rose was nineteen, and she had no intention of becoming a thirty-three-year-old spinster.

Niall downed another biscuit. "Nae," he said, his tone amused. "Amelia-Rose is a damned mouthful for a barbarian Highlander. I reckon I'll call ye *adae*."

"Why? What does that mean?" she countered, deeply suspicious even though it sounded quite pretty in his deep brogue. "I won't agree until you promise me you aren't calling me a turnip or something embarrassing."

When he grinned, her heart gave a stutter. No man should be that handsome. Especially not the brother of the man supposedly courting her. "I'd nae call ye a turnip, lass. It means 'rose,' like yer name. Only less twisty on my tongue."

Rose. Well, it was half her name, which people generally tried to shorten anyway, but in Scots Gaelic it felt . . . prettier than the "Amy" her mother disliked so much. *Adae*. It was very nearly poetical. "Very well," she said, with an exaggerated sigh. "But if I find out it does mean something else, I shall wallop you."

He laughed, the sound deep and musical and enticing. The pair of women seated behind him both turned their heads to look. One of them fanned herself, and they leaned together, whispered something, and both blushed. Amelia-Rose took another sip of her sweet coffee and pretended not to notice, but of course she did. She knew both of them. And even if Niall was just her beau's brother, the reaction of other ladies to his presence was mollifying. She'd spent the last two years trying to be just like everyone else and falling short. Let someone envy *her* for once.

Especially considering last night, when the viscount had vanished five minutes into *Romeo and Juliet*, a bit of envy was nice. If she didn't wish to become a laughingstock, though, she would have to encourage the displays of manliness and charm from whichever MacTaggert appeared to escort her, and she would have to discourage the barbarian Highlander behavior.

What a tangle this was becoming, and only after one day. Jane looked like she'd been forced to swallow an insect, Niall sat eating biscuits as if he'd been starved for a month, and she had an absent almost-fiancé. She should have been embarrassed and even more troubled, she supposed, as a proper lady would be when the man she was supposed to pretend was falling for her didn't bother to make an appearance. But at this moment she wasn't troubled. She was having a blasted good time.

At the table directly beneath the side window a trio of men argued over whether a pheasant was a more noble creature than a swan. One of them had even brought drawings to support his claim for the swan, and loudly recounted the law that allowed only the aristocracy to eat them—a sure sign of their high standing.

"Do we request more coffee?" Niall asked, setting his cup aside. "Or do I get ye home so I can fetch Coll and a carriage before two o'clock?"

"We should go," Amelia-Rose replied. She still had to write Lady Margaret and ask to be re-included in the luncheon even though she'd canceled just yesterday. And she had to make certain there would be enough food to satisfy the tall, lean man seated opposite her. She had no doubt that Coll MacTaggert wouldn't be her escort, and that was fine with her. More than fine.

"Aye." He stood and moved around to hold her chair out for her.

"You cannot be serious, Francis," one of the bird men exclaimed. "The entire world acknowledges the nobility of the swan. A pheasant must be hung for three days before it's even edible."

"You, sir!" one of the men said, putting a hand on Niall's shoulder. "Which bird do you prefer?"

Niall looked straight at his newfound friend, all trace of easy amusement gone from his face. The man abruptly lifted his hand away and took a half-step backward without Mr. MacTaggert having to say a word. Everyone seemed to be looking at him, as a matter of fact, and all he'd done was stand and be taller and more muscular than every other man in the shop.

He held out a hand to her, and she placed hers in it. For a hard beat of her heart she felt . . . regal. Protected. Anyone would be a fool to cross such a fine, fit specimen of a man—and yet she'd done just that. Well, not so much cross him as use his own desire to hide trouble in order to gain herself an escort to a luncheon she wanted to attend, but that only seemed to have amused him.

"Since ye asked," he said, glancing over her head at the bird admirers, "I prefer a swan poached in a sauce of peaches and saffron."

With that they strolled out of the shop. "You shouldn't have said that," she commented as they returned to John and the horses. "Coffeehouses are the home of meaningless philosophical arguments, especially from professors— which they looked to be. And only the nobility is permitted to dine on swans."

"So ye reckon they're jealous?"

"What? No. It's . . ." She glanced at him, to find him wiping a soft grin from his face. "You were teasing them."

"I'd nae be able to call myself a Highlander if I ever ate swan poached in saffron. It's nae bad stuffed with mushrooms and oysters, but I prefer duck."

"You do know you could be tossed into gaol for eating a swan."

He tilted his head. "Did ye forget I'm an earl's son and a viscount's brother?"

She *had* forgotten, and that was very stupid of her. She was practically engaged to said viscount, after all. "It's just that you don't . . . act like an aristocrat." Immediately she regretted her words. *Stop talking*, she ordered herself.

"I'll take that as a compliment, *adae*. Ye didnae offend me, if that's why ye willnae look me in the eye now."

Before John could give her a hand into the saddle, Niall stepped up, standing so close she had to lift her chin to meet his gaze. He looked at her while her heart did an odd flip-flop again. "Yes?" she prompted when she began to worry she would wrap her arms around his shoulders and kiss him.

"Permission to put my hands on ye, lass."

"Oh. Certainly. If the wind's not too strong."

Holding her gaze, he slid his hands around her waist

and lifted her into the air. For a split second she forgot what they were doing, until her backside bumped against Mirabel and her sidesaddle.

Pay attention, Amelia-Rose, she ordered herself, fitting her knee around the saddle horn and then refusing to hold her breath when Niall grasped her ankle and slid her foot into the single stirrup. For heaven's sake, since her debut last Season no fewer than five men had helped her onto Mirabel. None of them, though, had given her the delighted shivers. Of course she'd been attempting to impress them with her manners and decorum, while here she didn't have to trouble herself.

"Ye've a delicate ankle," he mused, his hand still on her foot. "It's a wonder ye can stand on it."

Her cheeks warmed. "I assure you that though I'm not constructed of iron and tree trunks like you are, I manage quite well," she retorted. "What did you think I tottered about on?"

Blowing out his breath, he released her ankle and stepped back. "With all those long skirts and immense bonnets, I reckoned *all* ye English lasses floated above the ground on the morning breeze."

Amelia-Rose laughed. The image of half a hundred young ladies being carried aloft by a gust of wind actually didn't seem that far-fetched, now that she considered it. "You are not what I expected, Niall MacTaggert," she said, walking Mirabel in a circle around him.

"Neither are ye."

She stiffened a little. "Is that bad?"

"Nae." He continued looking at her, pivoting to keep her in view as she circled. "Nae."

Niall didn't care to be walloped, even by a petite, delicate English lass, and for that reason he hoped she never discovered that *adae* didn't mean "rose." It meant "trouble."

And she was presently causing him a great deal of that. Truthfully it wasn't all her fault, because if Coll had done as he was supposed to, as he'd sworn to after they'd all drawn cards and he'd lost the game, it would be the viscount taking Amelia-Rose to coffee and the damned picnic.

But his . . . annoyance, he supposed it was, wasn't about an imagined inconvenience, of having to take her to a luncheon when he had something better to do—because riding off to find a dim-witted wife didn't particularly appeal at the moment.

He liked the way Amelia-Rose laughed. Aye, he charmed people all the time, put them at ease, heard them laugh at his jests. She gave out her laughter like it was a prize; as if someone had told her that ladies didn't laugh out loud and so she'd determined not to do so, but she couldn't help herself. She'd promised to be more proper today, as if she hadn't felt justified in handing Coll that well-deserved insult last night. In the tales his father told, females of the English variety were all coy and self-concerned and not a match for any Highlander. This one, Coll's almost-betrothed, didn't fit that mold. At all.

Niall shook himself as he reached Oswell House again, after only one wrong turn. This townhouse was nothing at all like the sprawling castle up in the Highlands. Pogan, the butler at Aldriss, had complained for years that he never had any idea where any of the MacTaggert brothers might be, because they were in and out at all hours of the day and night, and often enough didn't even use the doors to enter and exit. Niall had once literally butted heads with Aden as his brother left the mansion through a library window while he climbed back in through the same window after a night spent in a bonny lass's bed.

The entire front of Oswell House, though, overlooked the street. One rear door led into the tidy brick-walled garden and then a small park behind that, which had more possibilities for secrecy at least in the middle of the night— as long as none of the neighbors happened to be looking out their own windows. The side door opened to a covered drive with the stable directly behind it.

Niall swung down from Kelpie and handed him off to one of the stableboys. Before he reached the plain back door it swung open, and the bony butler eyed him. "The countess is looking for Lord Glendarril," he stated, stepping aside to allow Niall through. "She's been looking for him all morning."

"And a bonny day to ye as well, Smythe," Niall returned, heading for the main part of the house.

"She says that if she doesn't speak to him by sunset, there will be consequences."

Niall kept walking. The fine mood he'd been in shredding with every step, he made for the stairs and the second floor. "Oscar!" he called, stripping off his damned heavy jacket as he went and tossing it over Rory's unoccupied antler.

Without waiting for an answer he counted doors until he reached Aden's temporary bedchamber, where he shoved open that door and stalked in. The heavy curtains were still closed, and his brother lay in a massive pile of blankets and pillows crossways on the large bed. The sprawl wasn't unusual; his brother had always been as restless in his sleep as he was during the day.

"Aden," he said, continuing on to the window and pushing open the first set of curtains.

"Damn ye and the horse ye rode in on," came from the bed in a muffled growl. "Close the bloody curtains or I'll thrash ye."

Niall shoved open the next set of curtains. "I've nae seen Coll since act one last night, and I just had to take his nearly betrothed out for coffee in his stead."

The blankets erupted outward as Aden sat up. "How horrible is the lass? Pig? Coo? Clucking hen?"

"She's bonny enough," Niall returned, her artistic tangle of blond hair and those sky-colored eyes still fresh in his mind. "Less meek than Coll reckoned for, I suppose. Instead of bothering to talk to her, he got up and left. The rest of it didnae matter a whit." She wouldn't like that he'd pointed out her sharp tongue. Beneath her varying levels of propriety she did have an air of daintiness and delicacy about her, something that made a man wish to protect the lass, to step between her and any danger.

His older brother nodded, swiped lanky black hair out of his eyes, and slid to his feet. "Did he take Nuckelavee?"

"He left the theater on foot. He's still that way unless he stole someaught."

Oscar skidded into the doorway. "Och! Waking ye up wasnae my idea, Master Aden. I warned him n—"

"Go fetch me a strong coffee and some food," Aden cut in. "And have Loki saddled."

"Aye. Right away," the valet said, and vanished again.

Niall watched him go. "Ye've got poor Oscar terrified of ye, ye ken."

Aden shrugged out of his nightshirt and dug into the immense wardrobe that dominated the room. "I warned him to leave me be. If I'd truly wanted to do him harm, I would have thrown something heavier than a boot at him."

"And while I'm certain he's thankful ye didnae, it still knocked him out cold."

"Th—"

"There you are, Niall," Eloise said from the doorway behind him. "Mama asked—Oh!"

Niall looked from his sister's startled face to Aden's bare arse as his brother searched for clothes. Aden straightened, grinned at her, and went back to his task. With a sigh Niall stepped between them, heading for the door.

"Ye've just allowed several arses to move into yer house, Eloise. I reckon ye're bound to catch sight of one or more of 'em from time to time." Nudging her backward into the hallway, he shut the door behind him.

Her pink cheeks darkened further. "Here in London we close our doors while we're dressing," she snapped. "What if I'd had a friend with me?"

"I doubt Aden would've minded. What did yer mother want with me?"

She sent another glance at the doorway, then visibly shook herself. "She's your mother, too, you know."

"So I've heard."

"Really, Niall? You're going to put me in the middle of this?"

He'd hurt her. Niall reached down and took her hand. If there was one thing all three of the MacTaggert brothers could agree about, it was that none of this mess was Eloise's fault. She'd grown up, and she'd fallen in love. Not one of them could fault her for that. "Thank ye for the sandwich last night. Ye saved my life."

That earned him a smile, at least. "I left one for Coll, as well, but it was still there this morning—or at least it was until I caught that valet of yours wiping crumbs from his shirt. Coll hasn't been back. So he didn't escort Amy—Amelia-Rose—for coffee. And since Mrs. Baxter hasn't sent over a note complaining about that fact, I am willing to surmise that someone else *did* escort her daughter."

"Clever lass. Coll's still settling in," he said, not knowing whether he was lying or not. "He'll come around."

"Amelia-Rose could be a good match for him. She's very witty, though I think she tries not to be."

"Why is that?" he asked, his interest immediately snared.

"Well, I wasn't out last Season, but I heard that she . . . wasn't scandalous, really, but spoke a bit boldly. For a lady. I haven't asked her about it, of course. I have noticed, though, that she's both frightfully well read and very cautious with her speech. There are a few of us that she chats with more freely, and she is delightful."

Amelia-Rose did sound like a perfect match for Coll—if he'd been looking for a lass who could counter his recklessness and wouldn't tolerate his heavy-handedness. Interesting that his brother would say the woman she'd been attempting to be, and had failed at being last night, would suit him better.

His sister continued to look at him, so he nodded. "They just need to have a chat where half of London isnae staring at them."

"I hope so, for his sake. For Aldriss Park's sake. I've always wanted to go back there. I was nine months old, I'm told, when Mama and I left." She retrieved her hand and placed it over her heart. "I did not know about this agreement between Mama and Father. The first I heard of it was after we had dinner to celebrate the engagement. I found Mama writing a letter, and she looked up at me and smiled, and she had tears in her eyes. She said, 'That stubborn old man has to come here now. And your brothers, too. We finally get our boys back, Eloise.'"

That was interesting, and he put it in the back of his mind where he could contemplate it more closely later. He damned well didn't have time to unravel any of it now. "That letter wasnae quite so joyous for us," he countered. "Da swears it's killed him, and . . ." Niall trailed off at the alarmed look on her face.

"You weren't just jesting about that? I thought you were trying to point out how little you all wanted to be dragged down here."

"I'd nae put too much stock in Da turning up his toes, *piuthar*," he went on. "I've killed him twice all on my own, and between Coll and Aden he's taken his last breath at least a dozen times."

Her expression eased a little. "How did you kill him, then?"

He grinned, relieved that he hadn't made her dislike him. They were family, but barely acquaintances at the same time. "I jumped off the roof of Aldriss into a snow-bank when I was sixteen," he admitted. "And I'm nae telling ye the other one because ye're a lass and have delicate sensibilities." And because Lord Marmont had sworn to cut off his balls if anyone ever breathed a word about Niall's escapade with Delilah MacDougall, the marquis's youngest daughter. Niall remained rather fond of his balls, and he preferred to keep them just where they were.

Eloise sighed. "I wish I'd been there to see that," she said, clearly not reading his mind, thank Saint Andrew. "Father wrote me on occasion, but he never really talked about anything scandalous. Mostly sheep and lambs, and sometimes how proud he was of one or all of you." Eloise leaned forward a little. "Please don't ever tell him I let Mama read his letters. I think the first letter she sent him directly in seventeen years was the one that brought you down here."

"I'd nae tell. Da swore up and down he'd nae ever communicate with her again, in writing, in person, or as a spirit." Coll and Aden would never believe their father had written to Eloise, even, given Lord Aldriss's dislike of "civilized extravagances" like reading and writing. "Ye said Lady Aldriss wanted someaught from me?"

"Oh, yes. I forgot. She wants to know where Coll is, how his rendezvous went, and whether you met any likely young ladies in the park."

And there he was again, standing in the middle, mending the angry edges back together. Whether he liked the position or not, for the moment, at least, he needed to remain there—right in the middle. They had too much to lose for him to step aside.

"I'd appreciate if ye'd tell the countess Coll's nae back yet from seeing Amelia-Rose, Aden and I are going to familiarize ourselves with Mayfair, and I met a large herd of lasses but couldnae tell ye any of their names to save my life."

She nodded. "This time." Eloise held up one finger. "This time only. I don't make a habit of lying."

He leaned down to kiss her cheek. "I dunnae, either. Now. What's a barouche, do ye have one here, and where would a lad go hereabouts if he wanted to punch someone?"

"I . . . Good heavens. A barouche is a large, open-topped vehicle, yes, we have one here, and I have no idea about the other thing. Gentleman Jackson's is the only boxing establishment of which I'm aware. Smythe could give you the address, I'm certain."

"That's a beginning, then. Thank ye." Niall turned around to open Aden's door as Oscar arrived with a heaping tray of food.

"But you cannot have the barouche today, if that's what you're asking," Eloise went on. "Matthew and I are taking it to a picnic this afternoon."

Niall faced her again. "Lady Margaret's alfresco fete?" he asked.

"Yes! How did you—"

"I reckon I need another favor, then." He explained about Amelia-Rose's request for an escort and a barouche, but left out the bit where she'd more or less threatened to bring down his already tottering stack of half-truths if he didn't comply. The lass had outmaneuvered him, and he could appreciate that. Coll likely wouldn't, but Coll wasn't there.

"Of course you may join us," Eloise said, smiling. "This is why I wanted my brothers about."

"To join ye on picnics?"

"To be here. To disturb my plans and frown at the unacceptable men of my acquaintance."

Niall frowned. "Are ye acquainted with any unacceptable men?"

She laughed. "Oh, yes! That frown, right there."

If she expected him to go on picnics every day she was daft, but he didn't say that part aloud. Instead he returned to Aden's bedchamber to catch his brother up in more detail about the theater, coffee, their mother's threats, and the picnic. Again he left out the devious bits, telling himself that there wasn't time for all that now. He also left out the exact color of Amelia-Rose's eyes, and the way her hair turned golden in the sunlight, because he was fairly certain he wasn't supposed to notice those things.

"Amelia-Rose Baxter?" Aden repeated, in between pulling on his boots and devouring what looked like an entire damned chicken. "That's a mouthful."

"Aye. So's that food. I've nae seen much of it since I got to London."

His brother shoved over the plate. "I'll make for this Gentleman Jackson's, then, and see if I can drag Coll to yer wee picnic. Ye'll have to meet Eloise's beau and decide whether we should permit him to wed our sister or crack him over the head and ship him off to India or someaught."

"And if Coll's nae boxing?"

"I reckon if I can track a deer through the mountains in the rain I can find a six-and-a-half-foot Highlander clomping about London."

"Aye." Aden likely could, at that. The middle MacTaggert brother favored slightly more cerebral pursuits like gambling, but he also had an eye for seeing things in people most of them would prefer remain hidden. "Before ye get him to the picnic, make sure he's going to behave. His growling last night was damned unfair. It was her parents who shook hands with Lady Aldriss. Nac Amelia-Rose. I reckon Coll wanted to see if the lass would surrender, but he didnae have to do it with half of London watching."

Coll needed to be more pleasant. Amelia-Rose wouldn't agree to marry him if she didn't like him. And so she needed to like him. Or at least to converse with him long enough to see that he did have a pleasant, humorous side—when he wasn't being dragged to the altar against his will. Even if she wasn't as malleable as Coll had expected, she was the one Francesca had chosen. This needed to happen.

In the meantime Niall would remain Coll's proxy. The fact that he didn't mind that fact, that he actually looked forward to seeing her again, would have to be something else he tried to keep back for later perusal. One thing was certain: If there was another English lass in London who had the same wit and charm, he was going to find her. If he did so, he was *not* leaving her behind when he returned to the Highlands.

One thing he couldn't leave to consider later was that he was already holding Amelia-Rose up to measure every other lass against her. That he wanted to hold her, period. *Adae*. Trouble, indeed.

Chapter Five

"And?" Victoria Baxter prompted.

Amelia-Rose jumped. "My goodness, Mother, I didn't hear you come in," she said, twisting in her dressing chair to see her mother standing in front of the closed bedchamber door.

"Oh, I've lost the braid, Miss Amy," her maid, Mary, said with a grimace. "Please do sit still, or we'll never have you ready in time."

"It's Amelia-Rose, Mary. Please don't make me correct you again," Victoria said, moving into the depths of the room.

The maid curtsied, her blush reflected in the dressing mirror and making Amelia-Rose clench her jaw. "I'm sorry, Mrs. Baxter. I'll remember."

"I'm sorry, Mary," Amelia-Rose cut in, facing forward again. "You're performing miracles as it is."

Her mother joined them in the mirror's reflection as she sat on the end of Amelia-Rose's bed. "Why are you dressed for an outing? Are you avoiding me?"

"No, Mother. Of course not. Coll—Lord Glendarril—is escorting me to Lady Margaret's alfresco luncheon." It wasn't precisely a lie, since Niall had promised that either he or Coll would be there to fetch her. It should be Coll, of course, especially if she was to judge his character honestly. As of this morning she'd somewhat softened toward Highlanders, which left her willing to give him another chance.

"I told you, Lady Margaret is too forward. You don't want to be seen with her and have anyone think the same thing about you." Victoria sniffed. "You have enough to overcome."

This again. "Margaret is not forward. She's friendly. And I'm not going alone, anyway. You said you wanted this to look like a love match. The viscount and I must therefore be seen together."

"True enough." Her mother folded her hands primly into her lap. "I am somewhat confused, though. For the previous fortnight you've done little but complain that you would rather reside in a nunnery than wed some brute of a Highlander no matter if he was the Duke of Scotland."

"That was before I met him."

"It was, indeed. Which, considering that he left the theater last night before Juliet even appeared on stage, makes me wonder why you're suddenly so eager to be seen with him in public. I have to assume that this morning he gave you an assurance that his suit is indeed serious? Because otherwise I might think you simply want to go to a picnic."

Amelia-Rose relaxed a fraction. Of course her mother didn't care about the details of any conversation or how her daughter felt about Coll MacTaggert now. She only wanted to know if everything looked well after the poor showing the viscount had made last night. And that her daughter was still set to become a viscountess, and a future countess. "Yes, I am much reassured," she said aloud.

After all, now she knew that her almost-betrothed repaired cotters' roofs and saved sheep from bogs. It wasn't at all that his brother had bothered to apologize on the viscount's behalf, or that he'd amused her and left her feeling appreciated. It wasn't that for once she hadn't had to apologize for being blunt or impertinent. Nor that having someone else, especially an exceptionally handsome man with indescribable eyes, attempting to make amends to her felt refreshing. Or that she wanted to see him again.

"I'm pleased Lord Glendarril's character is better than my first estimation," her mother said crisply. "The Spenfield ball is on Thursday. He may escort us there and prove his worth in person. I should like to witness it for myself."

Drat. "I don't know that he's been invited," Amelia-Rose countered. "He's only been in Town for a day, after all, and you know that the Spenfield ball is quite exclusive."

Victoria flipped a hand as she stood. "Don't make excuses in advance, darling. It makes me doubt your veracity. Lady Aldriss will have been invited, so of course her unmarried sons will be welcome. I haven't forgotten, even if you have, that Penelope Spenfield has four marriageable daughters."

No, she hadn't forgotten. That was why she'd been looking forward to the ball before her parents had dragged her into an engagement: The young men would greatly outnumber the young ladies, a phenomenon rarely seen elsewhere. No miss ever lacked for a dance partner at a Spenfield ball, everyone said. Some of Amelia-Rose's female friends had made a point of endearing themselves to one of the Spenfield sisters just to increase their chances of garnering an invitation.

Her mother had paused in the doorway, so Amelia-Rose nodded carefully, trying not to dislodge her maid and her braid again. "I'll inform him, of course. The Spenfield ball on Thursday."

"Splendid. Once everyone has seen how well you two

suit, we'll be able officially to announce the engagement and call it a love match. That sounds much more pleasant these days, with everyone so infatuated with Byron and his silly romantic verse."

Amelia-Rose gave a silent sigh. She had only a handful of days, then, to make a true assessment of Coll MacTaggert in place of the rather colorful one given her by his brother and the sullen one she'd seen for herself. Blast Lord Byron and his romantic verse, anyway. It gave one such . . . impossible dreams of love and passion. No one could live up to that—and certainly not a brute of a Highlander.

None of this solved the problem of the man himself, though. If he should prove to be thoughtful and decent and able to compromise, if he could guarantee that she would be able to spend the Season in London every year and that she wouldn't be trapped in the Highlands, then Lord Glendarril still represented her best chance to escape this household. When she thought about more intimate things—the way his hands felt around her waist, long lashes lifting to reveal a sparkling humor in the depths of his light-green eyes—it wasn't even her supposed beau about whom she was thinking. How like Niall was the viscount? That seemed very important to discover.

Once Mary finished braiding her hair and coiled it into a pert, looped bun, Amelia-Rose requested Jane and a light luncheon in the informal dining room. It would never do to appear famished at the picnic. As she dined, Hughes the butler brought her a letter, and she frowned as she lifted it off the silver salver.

"I do hope Mr. MacTaggert was able to locate Lord Glendarril," her companion commented, sipping at her Madeira. "If they beg off attending the picnic now, your mother will not be pleased."

"My mother is well pleased that Lord Glendarril joined me for coffee this morning," Amelia-Rose said firmly, breaking open the wax seal and unfolding the letter. "And that he has insisted on escorting me to the picnic. She will remain so."

"Yes, of course. You know you may always trust me, Amelia-Rose."

Oh, she hoped that was true. "Of course, cousin." As she read through the missive, she relaxed. "It's only a letter from Lord Phillip," she said, relieved.

Lord Phillip West wrote rather pedestrian letters, and in person he had a bit of a lisp and no title. But his soulful brown eyes . . . Oh, a young lady could perish in their depths. In addition, he was excellent at the waltz. On the other hand, he only spoke of the weather and the latest fashions and horses, which made polite conversation absurdly simple. She'd practiced on him quite a bit at the beginning of the Season. If only he'd been his older brother Lionel, the Marquis of Durst, he would have been perfect.

That was all she wanted, truly: a well-spoken, handsome man who enjoyed parties and Society, had an estate not ten miles from London, and—for her mother's sake—could make her a lady. As her mother said, Father being an earl's second cousin allowed them into Society, but it didn't make anyone bow or curtsy to them.

She imagined a lifetime of conversation about horses and the weather would be supremely boring, but she would have ready access to London to make up for that. She'd never really conversed with Phillip's older brother, though, and she was only imagining them to be similar. Oh, what if he read? What if he enjoyed frankly discussing books and politics?

Except she wasn't all but engaged to the Marquis of Durst. Her man was Scottish and bad-tempered and nearly as tall and broad-shouldered as a mountain. Unless she could convince him to remain in London, this simply wouldn't work. How could she tolerate a lifetime of isolation from culture and friends and the social gatherings that she would finally be able to enjoy without having to worry about catching the right man's eye?

After luncheon she and Jane settled into the morning room for her to compose a letter or two to her own friends, and for Jane to finish some embroidery. Any response to Lord Phillip would have to wait at least two days but not more than four; it was important to appear neither too eager nor too disinterested, however unfit the recipient was to become her husband.

Before the clock in the hallway could finish announcing the hour, she heard Hughes pull open the front door. "I do hope it's the viscount," Jane whispered. "This subterfuge is beginning to make me nervous."

"It's only a little subterfuge," Amelia-Rose replied in the same tone. "We must show some compassion for a man new to London."

"You mean new to civilization, I think," her companion returned.

"Hush."

"Miss Amelia-Rose, that Niall MacTaggert fellow is here for you again," the butler said from the morning room doorway. "Do you wish me to send him away?"

"That's not necessary." A small smile touched her mouth before she could smother it. *Niall had come.* That was only because Niall's presence would mean less weight on her shoulders, she told herself, setting aside her correspondence and picking up her waiting straw bonnet. It was her favorite, decorated with small yellow silk flowers that precisely matched the yellow flowers patterned throughout her light-green walking dress.

"There ye are," Niall said as she glided into the foyer.

She dipped a curtsy. "Your brother is waiting for us, I assume?" she asked, sending a pointed glance at the butler.

"Aye. He rode ahead and will meet us there," the

Highlander returned smoothly, his nearly colorless green eyes practically dancing.

"And you've secured a barouche?"

"See for yerself, *adae*," he drawled, offering his arm.

Trying not to notice the hard, taut muscles of his forearm beneath the material of his black coat, she stepped outside beside him. He hadn't changed clothes since this morning, but being a man—and especially a foreign one—that didn't matter as much as it would have if she'd stayed in her riding habit. She would never live that down.

He had indeed secured a barouche—along with his sister and Eloise's betrothed. "Eloise!" she exclaimed, releasing her grip on his arm to hurry forward and hug her friend. "I had no idea you were coming."

"I refused to hand over the barouche," Eloise Oswell-MacTaggert replied with a grin, pulling Amelia-Rose onto the seat opposite her. "But Niall explained that it was vital to the day, so I agreed to share."

Jane still stood on the front step, but her solemn expression didn't fool Amelia-Rose for a second. "Eloise and I will chaperone each other," she said, shifting over so Niall could sit beside her. "So you are free to hunt down that hard candy Father brought home yesterday."

Her companion nodded, sent Niall a last, speculative glance, and retreated inside the house with the butler. *Hm.* Both she and Niall had made it clear that they would be meeting Coll, but then Jane already knew they'd lied about that very same thing this morning. She and her second cousin were going to have to have a chat when she returned.

"Trouble?" Niall asked, following her gaze.

Amelia-Rose straightened. "No. Not yet. Will Lord Glendarril actually be joining us?"

"With any luck, aye. Aden—our other brother—is fetching him."

"I'd begun to think all three of the MacTaggert brothers were a myth," Matthew Harris said from opposite Niall. "I'm relieved at least one of you is real."

Niall grinned, the expression a little cooler than it had been just a moment ago, reminding Amelia-Rose that he could be much more formidable if he chose. "Just ye bear in mind that I'm the nice one."

Matthew smiled back. "Then I remain relieved that I've met you first."

"Don't listen to him, Matthew," Eloise said, hugging her fiancé's arm with an obvious affection that made Amelia-Rose a little jealous. "They're all nice. Just . . . mountain-sized."

"Ye've grown a mite since last I saw ye, yerself," Niall returned, easing into genuine amusement again. Good heavens, he was handsome when he smiled like that.

"Do you truly remember me? You were barely seven years old when Mama and I moved to London."

He tilted his head. "Of course I remember ye. Ye were wee and plump, as bairns should be, but I see yer eyes in ye still. And yer smile."

The affection between them, near strangers though they were, was palpable. "You two make me wish I had a sibling," Amelia-Rose said aloud. Sighing, she shook herself. "Speaking of which, Matthew, where is your sister?"

"My aunt Beatrice wrote to say she and her three young ones had all taken ill, so Miranda and my mother went back to Devon this morning to help tend them. With any luck they'll be home in a week or so."

"Does everyone know everyone else in Mayfair, then?" Niall asked.

"Very nearly," Eloise answered. "Amelia-Rose came out a year before me, but we go to all the same parties. By now we're practically sisters."

That made Amelia-Rose smile. Eloise MacTaggert had

proven to be much less judgmental than others, perhaps because she knew she had three wild brothers just to the north. "We are, and thank you for saying so. There are others who aren't quite as friendly."

"And why is that?" Niall prompted, frowning. "The lot of ye baffle me."

"Once a lady turns eighteen, there are certain expectations," Matthew offered. "She is foremost to do her family honor, which for most young women means she needs to attract the attention of a man who will offer for her hand."

"She must comport herself with dignity and grace, for every word she utters and every move she makes reflects on her schooling, upbringing, and parentage," Eloise recited. "An offer of marriage is therefore a compliment to both her and her family."

"But it can't be just any man," Amelia-Rose took up, warming to the conversation and rather relieved that Eloise had dealt with the proper-behavior portion. "She may have any number of suitors, but she is to choose and marry only the best of them. The one with the loftiest heritage, of course. He must also have the means to support her and quite possibly the rest of her family. If he can lift both her and her family's status in Society, that is the most ideal."

"I'm beginning to feel inadequate," Matthew drawled, chuckling. "I'm a mere seventeenth in line to inherit my family's dukedom, and my father has been known to dabble in trade in an effort to keep our coffers full."

"Yes, but you're very pretty," Eloise countered, patting his shoulder.

"Handsome, darling. I'm very handsome," Matthew corrected with a grin, taking her hand in his to kiss her knuckles.

Amelia-Rose found it all slightly too sweet for her taste, but from Niall's expression he remained baffled by the exchange. As handsome as he was, she could well believe that no woman would have dared reduce his worth to his pleasing countenance. "And here you see," she said aloud, her gaze on him, "the rare and much-envied love match. Sugary, full of cooing sounds, and completely oblivious to how very lucky they are."

Niall looked at Amelia-Rose, catching her gaze. Over a day's acquaintance he'd found her to be amusing, clever, very conscious of propriety, and willing to use his circumstance to her advantage—at least as far as enabling her to attend a picnic. She could be sharp-tongued, but he hadn't expected her to be cynical. And yet her description of a love match couldn't be seen as anything but cynical.

Had she hoped for a love match herself? Did she have a man she cared for, a man who'd asked for her hand, and one she'd had to turn away because of her parents' agreement with Lady Aldriss? It hadn't occurred to him previously, but it should have. And he didn't like the idea. At all. "Lass, do ye—"

"Goodness, Amy," Eloise broke in, her cheeks turning red. "I hope you don't begrudge me a bit of that luck you mentioned."

"No, of course not," Amelia-Rose returned on the tail of that, also flushing. "I apologize. That—it didn't sound the way I intended."

"Apology accepted," Eloise said promptly, smiling again. "Let's speak no more about it."

Niall wanted to speak more about it, but apparently that wasn't a conversation they were to have in front of others. "I reckon the lass doesnae need to apologize for pointing out that ye and Mr. Harris here are sugary enough that ye're making my teeth ache," he said aloud, narrowing one eye at his younger sister.

"Oh, stop it, Niall," his sister returned. "I know you and Coll and Aden would have loved to be able to approve of Matthew before he asked for my hand, and I'm certain that would have entailed the drinking of much whisky and some brawling, but it didn't happen that way. He asked Mama for my hand, and she gave her permission."

Niall eyed his sister's betrothed, and had the satisfaction of seeing Matthew Harris shift a little and suddenly find something interesting to view outside the barouche. "Aye, we're too late to have had a hand in yer choosing a lad, *piuthar*, but I dunnae believe it's ever too late for whisky or brawling. We're some of the finest brawlers in the Highlands, if I say so myself."

"Niall, no punching," Eloise stated again.

He sat back and crossed his arms. "Nae promises."

They might be jesting, but he hadn't made up his mind about Mr. Harris yet. Aye, he could assess a man's character fairly quickly, but this particular lad had in mind to marry the MacTaggerts' only sister. Learning whether he was fit to do that would take more than a minute. It didn't help that Matthew Harris likely knew Eloise better than did her own brothers. They should have visited her, however they felt about Francesca. They should have written, at least; they shared blood and heritage, whether she'd ever been exposed to the latter or not.

"I'm willing to have a glass or two of whisky, if that's satisfactory," Matthew put in.

"Ha. Either ye have a bit of spleen, or ye've nae met a Highlander before. I'll see what I can arrange." He sent Eloise a glance. "Nae interference."

"Amy, I may now have some envy of you for being an only child," his sister stated, but since she continued to seem amused Niall reckoned he hadn't done any damage.

Finally they turned into a large, green expanse of trees and ponds and flowers. Niall took a deep breath. It was too orderly and civilized ever to be mistaken for the Highlands, but it wasn't more buildings and noise. For Saint Andrew's sake, he could actually hear birdsongs. "This is more like it," he muttered, his shoulders lowering a little. The mere fact of being in London weighed on him, whether he'd realized it before now or not.

Half a dozen bouncing, flapping lasses met the carriage as they stopped beside a handful of other vehicles. On the far side of the carriages a canopy stood, a spread of blankets on the ground beneath it, while a trio of footmen and a table laden with plates, baskets, bowls, and glasses stood close by and awaited their dining pleasure directly to one side. *Ah, food.*

"—must be Lord Glendarril," one of the young ladies, a bosomy redhead, said in between giggles, her gaze on him. "Oh, Amelia-Rose, he's heavenly."

Amelia-Rose clambered over him and out of the barouche. "No, no, no. This—this is his brother—one of Eloise's other brothers, I mean— Oh, dear. This is Niall MacTaggert."

Niall stepped down from the carriage. "Lasses," he said, inclining his head.

They all dipped curtsies like a flock of bobbing doves. Bloody hell. Perhaps he needed to be more thankful that Coll had dodged his responsibilities so far today; at least with Amelia-Rose by his side, Niall had a bit of protection from the muslin horde. On the other hand, if he wished for some companionship, that would be easy enough to find.

His sister took his arm and yanked on it. She couldn't have budged him if she wanted to, but he relented and moved a few steps away with her. "If ye're worried, I'll nae brawl with anyone here," he said under his breath. "Unless there's stronger drink than what I spy."

"These ladies are all—or most of them are—my friends. Don't ruin any of them."

Niall lifted an eyebrow. "All I did was say hello," he returned with a half grin.

She tightened her grip on his forearm. "Mama said you're to find an English wife. Even if you don't want to, I know you're at least thinking about it. Don't let what our parents did cause you to misbehave with these nice young ladies."

"*Piuthar*, I'm four-and-twenty. I'm nae some pup getting the scent of my first fox. And if I reckoned these lasses were to blame for my predicament, ye'd nae find me escorting Coll's lady just to keep everyone else happy."

That didn't sound quite right, because the only person being kept happy by all this subterfuge, as far as he could tell, was Francesca Oswell-MacTaggert. And perhaps Amelia-Rose's parents. Which didn't mean that he was *un*-happy, because she looked like warm springtime in that yellow gown, and the smile on her lips made him think about kissing.

"My sweet, everyone wants to meet your brother," Matthew Harris said, stepping in to take Eloise's free arm. "And I'm being peppered with questions for which I have no answers."

Niall shrugged out of his sister's grip. "Dunnae ye fret, lass," he said. "I'm charming as the devil."

"And just as wicked, no doubt. Behave, Niall."

What she'd said, despite his attempts to shrug off her words and remember at least half the names of the lasses present, started something roiling in his gut. He'd been sent down here. Dragged down here. He'd been told to behave. He'd been told to find himself a wife. No room for questions. But now he abruptly did have one or two of those, and it had occurred to him that he hadn't asked himself many questions about anything lately.

Days at Aldriss Park were busy, filled with tending to the property, aiding the cotters, shearing sheep, farming crops, fishing, hunting—all the things he'd done practically since he could walk, with the notable exceptions of drinking and women. Those had come later and been well worth the wait. But they were all things he did. Ways he occupied himself and helped those for whom his family was responsible.

This could not be another of those times, where he simply did whatever was asked of him because firstly it was simpler, and secondly he was that charming man who liked it when the people around him were happy. Now he needed to ask himself a damned question, and he needed to find the damned answer for it. What the devil did *he* want?

"Niall," Amelia-Rose said, walking toward him and arm in arm with another of the pretty young lasses, "this is Lady Margaret, daughter of the Marquis of Hampfer. Peggy, this is Niall MacTaggert, Eloise's brother and youngest son of Earl Aldriss."

"I'm very pleased to meet you, Mr. MacTaggert," the marquis's daughter cooed, curtsying.

"And ye, Lady Margaret. Thank ye for including me in yer festivities."

She giggled. "I had an additional pheasant prepared when Amy told me how hungry you were likely to be."

He sent Amelia-Rose an appreciative grin. "I thank both of ye, then."

"So tell me, Mr. MacTaggert, we had expected to meet Lord Glendarril. Is Amelia-Rose merely teasing us, and such a person doesn't actually exist?"

"Oh, he's real enough, lass. We dunnae come into London often, though, and when we do, he has a thing or two to tend to. He may be here later."

"I hope so." She spied another carriage full of arriving guests and pranced off to greet them.

"I do hope you're able to keep your stories straight," Amelia-Rose said in a low voice.

He looked at her, trying to pay attention to her words

and not how her eyes matched the color of the deep-blue afternoon sky. "What?"

"You told me that your brother is adjusting to London and your mother's demands. Now you've said he's attending to business. Since he's known at least by rumor to be nearly engaged to me, I would appreciate if you kept your tales in order. I do not wish to be embarrassed by his poor behavior or your lack of ability to prevaricate about it."

"Och, 'prevaricate,' is it?" he returned, leaning his head closer to hers as they made for the stream to the right of the canopy and blankets. "Ye English've made an art of using long words for simple things."

"I can say 'lie' if that will convince you to do as I ask."

"I'll keep my tales untangled, *adae*, if ye'll answer a question."

She slowed beside him. "What question might that be?"

"What did ye have in mind for yourself before yer parents made an agreement with Lady Aldriss?"

"That's none . . ." She trailed off. "We all have our fairy-tale dreams, Niall. I haven't quite given up on mine, silly as they may be, and your brother will have some work ahead of him if he means either to live up to them or to convince me to give them up."

He admired her for saying that, even if it didn't bode well. This damsel wasn't going to sit by and wait while Coll stomped about London being angry. They had an estate and a great many cotters relying on his brother doing the correct thing. And now he hoped that Coll *didn't* show up this afternoon. They needed to have a serious conversation first.

"I told ye we were led to believe we'd find naught but delicate, mild, fainting lasses this far to the south. Give a man a day to think, *adae*."

Her eyes narrowed. "I'm not mild, then?"

He opened his mouth and then closed it again. "I honestly havenae a bit of an idea how to answer that question without getting myself smacked in the head," he finally replied.

Amelia-Rose sent him a sharp look, then shook her head. "You make me forget."

"Forget what?" he pressed, far more interested in her answer than he likely should be.

"To mind my tongue." She gave a rueful smile. "Answer me honestly, if you please."

Niall rather liked her tongue, and all her other parts. "Truly?"

"Truly."

"Then nae, I'd nae choose 'mild' to describe ye. Keen-eyed, mayhap. Or clever-tongued."

The grimace on her face didn't look entirely displeased, though he reckoned it was supposed to. "Your brother wants someone mild, then, does he? Someone meek and unassuming, easily cowed and led about?"

"If I said aye to that, would ye be inclined to be the lass he wants, or the lass he doesnae want?"

Her gaze focused somewhere past him, on the lines of trees and the small stream at their feet. "Last year I decided I would be myself. I acquired one proposal, made a baron's son weep, and had to convince my parents I was not trying to ruin my own chance for marriage. Your brother isn't the only man in London who prefers meek and mild, Niall."

"Ye said that was last year," he prompted, abruptly angry. And not at her. Her parents, and most everyone else, apparently, had tried hobbling her. They'd tried to break her. And now she couldn't decide if she was wild or tame. "What of this year?"

"This year I am attempting—and failing, according to

you—to be more . . . ladylike. I have three proposals, not counting the one your mother gave on behalf of your brother, and no one has shed a tear. Not in public, anyway."

He smiled, though what he truly wanted to ask was whether *she* was happier this Season. "I reckon Coll and I are more damaging to yer calm than most men would be. We being barbarians and all."

When she looked at him again, a trace of humor had returned to her expression, thank Saint Andrew. "Lord Glendarril did make an impression."

"Aye, like a great boot in the mud." Niall turned them back in the direction of the canopy and the growing group of picnickers. "Between ye and me, *adae*," he went on, lowering his voice, "I've told ye what Coll says he wants, and ye could be that lass if ye tried, I imagine. I'm nae certain, though, that's what's best for ye. I reckon I'll get clubbed for telling ye this, but at this moment I'm nae convinced ye and Coll are compatible. And ye willnae be compatible unless ye decide to cast aside the keen-eyed lass I spy before me. The . . ." He trailed off, deciding he'd potentially caused enough trouble.

Blue eyes held his attention, drew him to her. "Please go on," she whispered.

He wanted to. Badly. "I like ye as ye are, lass," he settled for saying. "The sweet and the sour. I cannae be the only one."

For a second he thought he'd made her cry, but she whisked a hand across her face and nodded. "You've given me some things to consider, Niall. I very much appreciate your honesty."

Not at all certain whether he'd made things better or worse, he seated himself on the ground between Eloise and Amelia-Rose and locked a smile on his face as he memorized more names—even though half of them were Mary or Elizabeth—and pretended to enjoy the conversation about who'd danced the most divinely at the last soiree.

"I'll wager you have magnificent soirees in Aberdeen," one of the young ladies, Tulip or Petunia, he thought, said enthusiastically. "All those kilts and red-haired ladies."

"Aye," he said, wishing the footmen would get on with handing out the edibles.

"Oh, you must say more than that," the flower demanded, to the encouragement of the other lasses. The men didn't seem to care about Scottish soirees any more than he did.

"Aye, I imagine they do," he drew out. "But I dunnae ken for certain because Aberdeen is in the Lowlands, and I've nae been there. I've attended a grand soiree or two in Inverness, and aye the lads wear the tartans of their clans, and there are a handful of ginger-haired lasses. Most of them have Irish in their blood, which I cannae hold against them as they'd nae say in it."

"I . . . Oh." The flower cleared her throat. "Which clan are you, Mr. MacTaggert?"

"Clan Ross." Finally the trio of servants began setting out small bowls of orange wedges and whortleberries and cherries. Of all the things that had troubled him about this trek to London, starving hadn't been one of them. Until now. He scooped up a pile of whortleberries and began devouring them.

"A clan is like a gentlemen's club, isn't it?" one of the lads, a Turner, he thought, asked. "You belong to clan Ross the same way I belong to White's?"

"Could be. When ye swear an oath, is it to God, White's, and England?"

"What? No. Of course not."

"Then it's nae the same. My oaths are to God, Ross, and Scotland." They also on occasion swore to Robert the

Bruce, Saint Andrew, or the Wallace, but he was apparently making a point about something or other.

Eloise nudged him in the elbow. "Be nice," she whispered.

"I am being nice," he returned in the same tone. "I cannae ignore the questions and still be polite, ye ken."

"You don't have to answer so pointedly," she insisted.

Niall sent her a glance. "Ye dunnae know me very well, do ye, *piuthar*? This is as round as my points get."

"What are the colors of clan Ross?" Amelia-Rose asked, breaking what was becoming a nervous silence.

She knew that, as she'd seen Coll and him in their plaid at the theater . . . Saint Andrew, had it only been last night? But he had reason to be more circumspect with her, both because of her importance to Aldriss Park, and because her sharp edges and softer ones near to mesmerized him. Her sharp edges, in particular. "Deep red, with a plaid of black crossed with green. Our chief for the past two years is Lieutenant General Sir Charles Lockhart-Ross of Balnagown."

"But you're not a Ross, yourself," someone else, another of the men, put in.

"I am, on my grandmother's side. Ross and MacTaggert blood's been mingled for the past three or four centuries, I reckon."

"So you're not a member of White's, then," the Turner fellow put in again.

"Nae." Finishing off the whortleberries, Niall leaned forward a little. This man meant him ill; of that he was certain. He could practically scent it on the wind. No, it wouldn't be a ball to the skull or a blade in the back, but Turner had brought the conversation back to White's membership twice, as something he had and Niall did not.

"I've a clan," he went on. "I've nae need for a gentlemen's club. Out in the Highlands if I fall from my horse while hunting deer, or I slide down a cliffside because I've misjudged my footing, my clan will come to find me. Nae just my brothers. My clan. Hundreds of 'em. Just as I've gone to their aid. I dunnae prize a chair because I'm the only one allowed to sit in it. I prize those who'll watch my back, who'll bleed for me if necessary, as I've bled for them." He selected half an orange and straightened again. "Did ye have a question I missed, then?"

Turner surveyed the line of carriages for a moment. "No. No question. Just a statement of interest."

"So it's your brother Lord Glendarril who's to marry Amelia-Rose?" another of the lasses, a pretty, petite brunette with green eyes, asked.

"If we're compatible," Amelia-Rose put in swiftly, with a smile that to his eyes looked forced, especially since he'd been sporting one of those for the past thirty minutes, himself. "He's been so busy; I'm looking forward to spending more time with him."

He remembered the brunette lass's name. "Aye. As Miss Baxter says, Miss LeMere."

"And you have another brother?" Patricia LeMere went on.

"Aye. Aden."

"Also unmarried?"

Ah, so that was it. "Aye. Nae a one of us is wed, yet." He put on a thoughtful look. "And I do hear ye have some lovely soirees in London."

"That, we do."

By the time he'd heard about every ball, dinner, and dance held so far this Season in London, the pheasant came around. Niall wasted no time in polishing off his plate, despite the raised eyebrows around him. They could be dainty if they wished; he was hungry.

"Would the gentleman like more?" one of the servants asked, and Niall handed up his plate.

"Aye, the gentleman would."

"You weren't jesting about being hungry, were you?" Amelia-Rose asked from beside him.

"Since I arrived in London I've had one sandwich, some biscuits, a handful of fruit, one scrawny chicken leg, and this pheasant."

"And you really do hunt your own deer and go hiking about on cliffs?"

He liberated a slice of roasted potato off her plate and popped it into his mouth while he waited for his second helping. "We all hunt; there's a butcher's shop at the village a mile down the loch, and a bakery, but we try to supply our own table. It's a large household, Aldriss. What's left over goes to the cotter widows and bairns."

"Deer don't generally graze on cliffs, though."

Niall chuckled. "Nae. Birds nest there, though. A man tires of chicken eggs from time to time. And chicken."

"What else do you do?"

"Do ye truly want a list of my chores? Most of them involve mud."

She smiled. "Actually, I'm trying to find a way to inform you that my mother is determined Lord Glendarril will escort me to the Spenfield ball on Thursday. We're to show well there together, after which my parents and your mother will be able to make our engagement known officially."

Thursday. That would give them three more days to find Coll if Aden hadn't already hunted him down. And three days to remind his brother that he'd lost the card cut more or less fairly, and that they all had a duty to see to the future of Aldriss Park. And for him to convince himself that Amelia-Rose was merely trouble where he was concerned, and trouble he didn't need.

She might not be the timid wisp Coll had planned for, but she had a strong streak of logic, did Amelia-Rose. She might not disagree with being left behind in London, if Coll didn't fall head over heels for her and hie with her back to Scotland. But the sooner Coll realized she was a good fit to be his viscountess, the better for all of them. Or so he would continue to tell himself until he believed it.

"I'll see to it," he said aloud, when he realized she likely expected a response of some sort.

"Amy, you already have one of them. Leave us the others," Lady Margaret said loudly. It was evidently amusing, because half the lot of them giggled and snickered.

Amelia-Rose blushed. "Mr. MacTaggert escorted me here on his brother's behalf. I have no wish to monopolize him, though. By all means, steal him away."

Niall didn't much like that, and he scowled. "Ye trying to be rid of me, lass?"

"I'm trying not to encourage gossip," she retorted nearly soundlessly.

"Ah, the meek side. Cannae say I'm impressed with it," he noted, rocking up onto his knees and making his way around her. "I'm all yers, lasses. Have at me."

An afternoon of conversation with the other lasses did serve a purpose: It illustrated very clearly that he preferred escorting Amelia-Rose about to chatting with any one of these flighty things who'd realized he was marriageable. And he'd been telling her the truth: The meek side of her, the one Coll wanted, didn't much interest him at all. The other side, the one she'd been trying so hard to stifle, near drove him mad. Until she decided which lass she wanted to be, he'd be much wiser to keep his damned distance.

Chapter Six

As the barouche turned up the Oswell House drive, a muffled bellow sounded from somewhere deep inside the halls. The sight of Loki being led into the stable confirmed for Niall what the yelling had already told him: Aden had found Coll—and Coll wasn't happy about it.

He vaulted out of the barouche as it rolled to a halt. "Gavin," he stated, spying the groom they'd brought with them down from Aldriss, "ye're Eloise's chaperone now."

"I—Aye, Master Niall," the servant called back as Niall ran for the door.

He yanked it open, then paused to look back at his sister. "Dunnae come upstairs," he ordered, and jabbed a finger at Matthew Harris. "Especially nae with him."

The house had erupted in chaos, with half the servants trying to crowd into the hallway and the other half hauling buckets of water up the stairs. He didn't know if Francesca was home or not, but he hoped she was elsewhere. Aye, they'd meant to disrupt London when they'd arrived, but he didn't want her deciding Coll wasn't fit to be married and yanking Aldriss out from under them before they had a chance to secure the estate's future.

At the top of the stairs he turned up the hallway where

the three of them had been lodged. Servants carried water into Aden's room and emerged again, while the door to Coll's bedchamber across the hallway stood closed—with Aden leaning back against it.

"There ye are," the middle MacTaggert brother grunted. The door shook; he rebounded an inch or two away from it, then settled back against the hard oak again.

"Was he at Gentleman Jackson's?"

"Nae. They pointed me to several dodgier establishments, though, including one called The Pugilist." The door thudded again, and he shoved back against it. "They've a pit in the basement where they put a likely lad, and he takes on all comers until one of 'em knocks him out, then that fella takes the first fella's place."

Niall scowled. "And Coll was in the pit?"

"Aye. With a bucketload of black eyes and bruised and broken ribs scattered about the room."

"They're lucky he didnae kill anyone." *Stupid, bloodthirsty lobsterback English.*

Aden did his best to shrug as he and the flimsy-looking lock kept the door shut. "I reckon they thought they had a thickheaded laird with more money than brains, put someaught in his drink so they could shove him down there, and then didnae reckon on how much he would dislike it. They were happy enough to help me haul him out of there once I got him to swear he wouldnae break any of 'em in half."

"And now?" Niall asked, indicating the abused door.

"He's blaming me for nae allowing him to pummel anybody, and I reckon the potion they slipped him has got his head coming off his shoulders."

"He's been drinking?"

"Oh, aye. He smells like a whisky barrel."

One of the footmen stopped in front of them. "Master Aden, the . . . um, the bath is ready. Should we—"

"Go away," Aden cut in. "We'll see to it."

The last of the servants charged down the stairs before he could even finish speaking. Niall gazed after them. "We might've used the help."

"Aye, and our great bear might've liked discussing his frustration about London with any Sassenach in reach."

Aden made a good point. Luckily his brother's door and Coll's were directly opposite each other, so it would be a straight path to the copper bathtub the servants had hauled into the bedchamber. Niall rolled his shoulders. "Are ye ready?"

"Nae, but let's do it."

"One, t—"

"What in heaven's name is going on here?" Francesca demanded, stalking into the hallway.

With a muttered curse Niall met her halfway, stopping her forward progress and putting a hand over her mouth. "We'll manage," he said, keeping his voice low.

"But—"

"I'll meet ye downstairs in half an hour," he cut in. "We can have a chat then." He lowered his hand.

Meeting his gaze with her fern-green eyes, finally she nodded. "Is my oldest son a bedlamite?" she whispered.

She actually looked . . . concerned. Worried. Not over her reputation, but about Coll. Niall shook his head. "Nae. Thirty minutes."

Without another word she turned on her heel and left for the stairs. *Hm.* That had gone more smoothly than he expected. Shaking his head, he returned to Aden. "Where were we?"

"Three!"

Aden yanked open the door as Coll charged it. The viscount came stumbling into the hallway, and Niall and Aden each grabbed one of his arms and kept him moving forward until they could twist him around and shove him into the bathtub.

They stepped back from the explosion of water. Coll, flinging water and curses, scrambled upright. "It's fucking freezing, ye bastards!"

"We didnae have a loch to throw ye into," Aden said calmly. "Sit back."

"My damned clothes are on!"

Well, his dress kilt and boots were. The shirt, waistcoat, and coat had vanished somewhere in the last eighteen hours, likely never to be seen again. Coll looked a mess, himself, with a black eye, a pair of bloody scratches across his chest, bruised knuckles, and his dark hair madder than a bird's nest.

"Then take 'em off," Niall replied, kicking the door shut. All they needed was for Eloise to see another brother's arse today. Or worse, his front bits. "I thought me saying ye were off to find a beer was just an excuse."

Coll slung off his kilt, threw it at Aden, and sank back into the cold water to wrestle off his boots. Aden deftly dodged the wet thing and went to claim the dressing table chair.

"I went to find someaught to punch," Coll rumbled, tossing away both boots and then dunking his head. "But all I found was civilization, and then I got a wee bit angry."

"Which is the last time ye should be drinking," Niall pointed out, folding his arms over his chest. Coll knew that; hell, they all knew that. But they also knew how frustrated he was by all this. "I should've followed ye."

"I dunnae require a nanny, Niall. Some damned coffee and someaught to eat, aye."

Niall eyed his oldest brother. "And ye'll nae leap out and drown Aden the moment I leave?"

Coll narrowed his eyes, sending a sideways glance at

their middle brother. "Nae. I was stupider than a new lamb, wandering into a Sassenach lair, letting 'em convince me to have a drink, and then downing everything they put in front of me. I knew they wanted a fight, but I wanted one, too. Didnae reckon they'd put laudanum in my whisky and then throw me in that wee hole with nae a ladder in sight." He shuddered a little.

Saint Andrew. Drinking and small spaces, and laudanum to put Coll more out of control than the drink or the small space would have made him each on its own. Those fools were luckier than they deserved. But his brother sounded more than half on the sober side already, so with a nod at Aden he slipped out of the bedchamber and made for the stairs.

Lady Aldriss waited in the middle of the foyer, Eloise lurking in the morning room doorway just off to the left. Niall acknowledged their presence but went past them to the kitchen and requested bread and a chicken soup and some strong coffee. "Knock on Aden's door, leave it on the floor outside, and go away," he ordered, and the footman present gulped and nodded.

That was bonny. Now the MacTaggert brothers were both barbarians and monsters, and he couldn't say or do much to convince anyone otherwise—especially since the barbarian part had been intentional. He shed his damp coat, putting it over one arm as he returned to the main part of the house.

"In there," he said as he reached Francesca, indicating the morning room. "I'll tell ye both."

Once inside he shut the door and went to sit on the front edge of the deep, brushed-velvet couch. Eloise sat beside him, but the countess kept her hands clasped in front of her and paced to the window and back.

"He didn't take Amelia-Rose Baxter to coffee this

morning," she stated after a moment. "That was you, wasn't it?"

"Aye. Is that what ye want to chat about, then?"

"No. Of course not. But evidently everyone"—she shot a look at her daughter—"has been lying to me, and I'm attempting to decipher a bit of truth."

"Is Coll well?" Eloise asked, putting her hand around his arm.

"Aye. He . . . About three years ago we figured Coll needed to stop drinking. Liquor. At all. He mostly doesnae drink any longer, but then in the space of a week we thought Da fell on his deathbed, we discovered we were all ordered to wed English wives, and then Coll lost—won—the card turn so he had to marry the lass Fran—Lady Aldriss chose for him. Then without a night to sleep in London he gets dragged off to the theater to meet the lass, and he . . ."

Niall trailed off. How did he describe this part? Coll had called Amelia-Rose a sharp-tongued harlot, but that was hardly fair. The viscount had barely spent five minutes talking to the lass, and it would take far longer than that to decipher Amelia-Rose Baxter. She wasn't sharp-tongued. She was interesting and had opinions, with steel enough in her spine to convince him to take her to the picnic this afternoon.

"He what?" Francesca prompted.

"She's nineteen. He's nearly thirty. At first glance he didnae think they'd be compatible." There. That didn't insult either one of them. "He went off to go find a brawl, and ended at an establishment called The Pugilist."

The countess's cheeks paled. "He didn't."

"Aye. Aden and I reckon those buffoons at The Pugilist figured they'd waylay and rob him, and they . . . convinced him to have a whisky. A few whiskies. And one of 'em with laudanum in it, as far as we can tell. Then they tossed him in the fighting pit, likely with the idea of wagering on who could beat him down. Coll doesnae like small places."

The countess had moved to place one hand over her heart. "I remember. Before you were even born, Niall, he and Aden were playing and Coll got locked in a wardrobe. It took us four hours to find him. He avoided small places after that."

Niall nodded. "He still does. So nae, he isnae a bedlamite. He is angry and mayhap a bit shaken, with a splitting head and too much drink in him." Narrowing his eyes, he willed them to take the next part seriously, for all of their sakes. "I'd nae recommend coddling him or pitying him, because he's likely to fling it straight back at ye. If he wants ye to know someaught, he'll tell ye. Otherwise, I'd feign ignorance."

"Amelia-Rose said he's to escort her to the Spenfield ball on Thursday," Eloise said, her expression somewhere between relieved and worried. And that over a brother she'd never met until yesterday. Eloise was a better sister than the lot of them deserved, and he needed to see to it that Coll and Aden both knew that.

"Aye. I reckon I can convince him to give her a second look."

When Lady Aldriss opened her mouth, he shrugged out of his sister's grip and stood. "I'm nae yer toady, *màthair*, and I'm nae yer ally. I'm here to help Aldriss Park." With that he went back upstairs to make certain he still had two brothers alive.

Francesca Oswell-MacTaggert sank onto the couch beside her daughter. Her oldest son was nearly six and a half feet tall. A man grown. Well grown. Nearly thirty, as Niall had said. And small spaces still troubled him. She never would have suspected such a thing, and in an odd way she found it encouraging. Not Coll's troubles, but the fact that Niall had told her about them. They might still be a united front against her, but she wasn't entirely an enemy.

It wasn't that, however, that made tears run down her cheeks. "Goodness," she said.

Eloise hugged her. "They'll come around, Mama," she said. "It's only been a day, and they seem to be very stubborn. I'm certain they don't detest you."

"That's not why I'm weeping, my darling," Francesca returned, smiling. "Niall just called me *màthair*. That's Gaelic for 'mother.' He called me mother."

Her youngest son. The one she'd had the least hand in raising, and the one who had least cause to remember her. The one about whom she'd been the most worried, even knowing the well-earned reputations of the other two. How odd, and heartwarming, that Niall Douglas MacTaggert also seemed to be the one who most closely shared her sensibilities. She couldn't tell him that; he wouldn't believe her, and would likely be offended at the suggestion.

But then she'd managed to navigate thirteen years with the volatile Angus MacTaggert, and then another seventeen in London keeping her reputation, her wealth, and the entire Aldriss empire intact despite living the length of Britain away from her legal husband. Whether that made her a protector, or a diplomat, or something closer to a martyr, every day of those seventeen years away from her sons had hurt. She'd put aside her own happiness so they could grow up free and wild and independent, not smothered by the rancor festering between their parents.

Now that she had them back, she wasn't about to let anything happen to drive them away again—even if it meant pushing them to marry women they might not otherwise have considered. If they'd known Eloise better, if she hadn't taken her daughter south at such a young age, the brothers might have had more connection with the females of the family. They might even have visited from time to time. That was only one of several regrets she had. Balancing the life Eloise had in London against what she would have found in a wild corner of the Highlands couldn't be measured, though. That had been her compromise.

Francesca looked toward the stairs. From the ease with which Niall had stepped in to keep Coll's disappearance a secret—to give Amelia-Rose a satisfactory-enough explanation that Miss Baxter had apparently not only accepted his presence but lied to allow it to continue—he'd done it before. Given a choice between calling him charming and crafty or charming and protective, she would of course prefer the latter.

She took a breath, standing and pulling Eloise to her feet beside her. "You must tell me how Niall and Matthew got along. I have no doubt that he'll tell Aden and Coll exactly what he thinks of your betrothed, and if there's to be warfare, I would like to know in advance."

Now all she needed to do was set aside all of her private reservations—which could well be her own nerves and nothing more—and settle Coll with Amelia-Rose Baxter, and she could claim aloud that everything was proceeding much better than she'd expected.

"Ye said ye would do what was necessary to save Aldriss," Aden pointed out, picking up a billiards ball and rolling it across the table.

"That's nae how ye play," Coll countered, still squinting a little in the reflected morning sunlight even after a night to sleep off his misadventure. "And I reckon I'll see her for that damned party."

Niall hefted the cue in his hands, beginning to wonder if cracking it across Coll's skull would do more damage to the viscount or to the stick. "So ye'll wed her, but ye willnae bother to become acquainted with her first?"

"Doesnae seem to be a point to that, since Lady Aldriss has decided it's to be. I'd nae try to choose a man for Eloise without figuring out who she is, first, but who gives a damn, anyway."

Well, one person came to mind, but Niall reflected that he did seem to be the only one interested in becoming acquainted with his brother's bride-to-be. "Here," he said, tossing the cue to Aden.

"Where are ye off to?"

"To find a bride, I reckon. Or get some air, at least."

He saddled Kelpie himself, despite Gavin's hovering, and trotted off toward Wigmore Place. He had no idea what Amelia-Rose's schedule might be, and given that she seemed to have nearly every moment of every day filled with social engagements, the odds of her being home seemed abysmal. Still, Coll was supposed to be courting her. It was supposed to look like a love match. And so for the sake of appearances, which Amelia-Rose valued almost to the point of obsession, he would attempt to make it look like one.

Hughes didn't look particularly happy to see him when he swung the Baxter House knocker against the door. "Mr. MacTaggert. No calling card, I presume?"

"Nae. Is Miss Baxter in?"

"Wait here. I shall inquire."

The door closed. Ah, back to exile again. Before he could decide whether to invite himself into the foyer or not, the door opened again, and he found himself face-to-face with Amelia-Rose. "Good morning," he said, grinning, refusing to examine too closely why the day had just become brighter even if he couldn't ignore the fact that it had.

"Good morning," she returned, leaning against the door. "What brings you here?"

He hadn't really thought that far ahead, damn it all. "I . . . Coll and I, that is, were about to go riding, and I reckoned with a mount like Mirabel ye're a rider, yerself. Care to join us?"

"I . . ." She glanced over her shoulder. "I have a luncheon at one o'clock."

Niall pulled out his pocket watch. "It's nae even ten o'clock. We'll have ye back here in plenty of time."

The door swung back and forth slowly, mimicking her indecision as she clearly weighed coming with him. "Very well," she whispered. "Please go have John saddle Mirabel and a mount for himself. I'll meet you by the stable."

"And yer shadow?"

"My shadow hasn't risen yet. Hush." With a slight grin she softly closed the door on him again.

So the lass was ready to be a bit brave then, was she? Good for her. He and Kelpie made their way around the house, where he helped John saddle Mirabel and a gray gelding. If she meant this as a morning's escape, the sooner they could get away the less likely anyone else would be able to stop them.

She appeared in the stable doorway, her crimson riding outfit just as compelling as it had been the first time he saw her wearing it. Even more compelling, really. *Saint Andrew.* "I assume Lord Glendarril is waiting for us?" she asked.

"Aye," he lied smoothly. "He didnae want to risk a row with yer parents, so he'll meet us in the park."

"Which park?" she asked, folding her arms over her attractive bosom, her blue eyes sparkling.

So she didn't believe him. Just as well. "I reckon he said Saint James," he returned. Eloise had mentioned it yesterday as having a pond stocked with swans. That sounded reasonable, anyway. "Ye'll have to lead the way. I couldnae find it without a map."

"I haven't found an adequate one for you yet," she returned, following Mirabel to the stepping-stone. "Evidently everyone knows where everything is the moment they arrive in London."

"I missed someaught, then." Taking a breath, he moved in and put his hands around her trim waist. He lifted her, her hands warm where she put them on his shoulders for balance. Every time she touched him, on purpose or just in passing, a brush of her dress against his legs, a hand up into the barouche, he felt . . . electricity. Lightning. Did she feel it, as well? Was she trying as hard as he was to ignore it?

"You can let me go now," she murmured.

Niall shook himself. "Are ye certain? Ye seemed a bit wobbly," he improvised.

Her cheeks darkened. "Yes, I'm seated quite securely."

Lowering his hands, he turned around to claim Kelpie and swing into the saddle. If he meant to go mad like that in her presence, he likely shouldn't have worn his kilt again, but he hadn't actually planned on seeing her this morning. "Which way, lass?"

She gestured, and he fell in beside her, with John bringing up the rear. "I'm glad you and Lord Glendarril asked me to join you," she said. "I haven't been riding anywhere except the coffeehouse in days, and Jane is . . . Well, she tries, but she does not enjoy it."

"She does seem happier walking." He looked over at Amelia-Rose. "I'm glad ye had a few free hours this morning."

"So am I." She grinned. "I never thought I'd be grateful that Mrs. Evenson had a kitchen fire, but it did cause her breakfast to be canceled."

"If I'd known it was that easy to spend time with ye, I'd have set fire to it, myself."

Amelia-Rose met his gaze, then looked away again.

"You shouldn't say things like that." She frowned. "And I shouldn't say I'm grateful for a fire. You are a bad influence, Niall."

"Am I? Ye be polite, then, and I'll do as I please, and we'll see who's happier at the end of the day."

"That's not fair. You're not a refined lady."

"Nae. And I've nae been happier to be a man than I am today, lass."

"And why is that?" she asked, and he could practically feel her attention sharpen.

Well, he couldn't very well say the first thing that popped into his brain, which was that he was with her. "Ye're wearing that heavy skirt," he compromised, "and I'm in a kilt. Isnae that enough?"

She chuckled. "I'll concede that I do get a bit warm."

"What kept ye occupied last evening?" he asked, and then got to listen to her describe an evening of charades and whist that she somehow made sound interesting. She had a keen eye for people and their quirks—which likely made it even more difficult to not comment on any of it in polite company. Evidently he wasn't polite company, which suited him just fine.

They reached a park filled with trees and rows of planted posies, and an oval pond in the middle. Half a dozen swans paddled about looking untroubled, which he reckoned meant no one dared eat them. "They are regal, aren't they?" Amelia-Rose noted. "I don't think I would ever devour one on purpose."

He grinned. "That statement would depend on how hungry ye were. Are we allowed to gallop here? I tried it on the street the other morning, and some old woman yelled at me and called me a savage."

"Oh, dear. No, there's no galloping here. Only on Rotten Row in Hyde Park. We can trot, though."

Immediately he put a heel into Kelpie's ribs. "Thank Saint Andrew. For a people that scurry everywhere, ye Sassenach make getting anywhere nearly impossible."

"That's the silliest thing I've ever heard," she retorted. "Simply because we don't——"

A pair of ladies and a man with very high shirt points turned a phaeton beside them, and Amelia-Rose clamped her mouth shut. "Good morning, Amelia-Rose," the elder of the lasses said, nodding.

"Lady Caroline. It was lovely to see you at the theater the other night."

"Ah, yes, *Romeo and Juliet*. I recall."

That's why the lass looked familiar. She'd been the one seated on the far side of the stage, a pair of opera glasses aimed at him for most of the night. He started to comment on that, but changed his mind after he took a glance at Amelia-Rose and the forced, placid smile on her face.

"Do introduce me to your friend, Amelia-Rose," Lady Caroline urged.

"Oh, this is——"

"I reckon ye saw me at the theater," he interrupted. "Niall MacTaggert. The last time a lass stared at me like that, she chased me into a loch and tried to take all my clothes off."

Lady Caroline blushed. "I have no idea what you're talking about, Mr. MacTaggert. And I certainly don't stare."

"Then those glasses must've been stuck to yer fa——"

"I apologize, Lady Caroline," Amelia-Rose cut in, her own cheeks paling. "Mr. MacTaggert is not from here."

"Yes, he's one of those Highlanders, isn't he? Lady Aldriss's sons? This isn't the one you're after, is he?"

"'He,'" Niall said, more amused by the nonsense than anything else, "has a pair of ears and speaks on his own."

"Niall," Amelia-Rose hissed, "stop it."

"I do like his accent," the other lass said. She looked enough like the first one that they had to be sisters.

Niall lifted both eyebrows. Leaning over toward Amelia-Rose, he turned his back on the carriage. "I'll behave if ye wish me to, lass, but I will point out that being talked about like a dog isnae someaught I generally tolerate."

"They are my friends," she whispered back.

"Why?"

A brief grimace crossed her face, then vanished again. "Mr. MacTaggert is from the Highlands," she said. "He is Lady Aldriss's youngest son."

"Well, we know he's from the Highlands," Lady Caroline returned. "No English gentleman would wear that, especially on horseback." She giggled. "How does he manage that anyway, do you think, Lewis?"

The man driving the phaeton snorted. "I've heard Highlanders referred to as 'blue skins.' Perhaps that wasn't in reference to the paint on their faces."

"Lewis Jones, you are too much!" Lady Caroline declared, giggling again.

This was about the time Niall would generally begin punching people, but he'd been insulted before, and for less reason. He was more curious about what Amelia-Rose would say, if anything. It would mean something, whether she ventured a comment or not.

"We'll take our leave," she said, and stopped Mirabel.

He halted beside her, but the phaeton went forward a few feet, then turned around and walked back up to them. "You should join us for luncheon," Lady Caroline said. "I'm certain there's an inn somewhere where his attire wouldn't cause anyone to faint."

Amelia-Rose made a sound deep in her chest. "I should be more concerned with Mr. Jones's reception," she said crisply, "as evidently he is unable to resist anything wearing a skirt, including his mother's maid. Hopefully he recognizes the difference between a kilt and a skirt, or Mr. MacTaggert may have to flatten him."

"Amelia-Rose!"

"As for you, Caroline, you did stare at Niall all night at the theater, to the point that I'm surprised you remember which play we were there to see. The difference between being rude from a distance and rude up close is that up close your target is able to respond." She clucked at Mirabel. "Good day, Caroline, Agnes, Lewis."

She trotted off. Niall took a moment to grin at the stunned trio before he kneed Kelpie and caught up to her. "Lass, you are magnificent," he drawled.

Amelia-Rose wiped a hand across her face. "I am horrid. Why did I do that? Why do I always do that? It's a stupid conversation. I don't need to win it."

Damn it all, she was crying. "I reckon ye said someaught because they were insulting me for no good reason," he returned. "It would've been easier to say naught, or to laugh along with 'em. Ye took the harder course, *adae*."

"I am not comforted. You just say whatever you wish."

"They dunnae matter to me. Most I meet here dunnae matter a whisker to me. I ken who I am and what I do in my life. I'm proud of that."

She took a breath, slowing to a walk again. "If my mother hears about this, which she will because she always does, I'll have to sit through another week of lectures on proper decorum and how to keep my useless opinions to myself."

"Dunnae keep them from me," he protested, reaching over to catch Mirabel's reins and bring horse and rider to a stop. "Ye didnae say a thing that wasnae true, and frankly I'd rather listen to ye read a grocery list than hear anyone else recite Shakespeare."

For a long moment her blue eyes searched his face. "Your brother isn't here, is he?" she finally said.

That hadn't been what he'd thought she would say. She surprised him almost constantly, actually, which she would likely say was a bad thing—but which he looked forward to every time he set eyes on her. "Nae. Do ye want me to take ye home?"

A slight smile touched her mouth. Christ's sake, her lips looked soft. Kissable. "We still have two hours, I believe. Let's not waste them."

Two hours wasn't nearly enough. Aye, he should be far away from Saint James's Park and from her. But sooner rather than later he would have no time with her at all— or at least none that he could justify. Until then, he'd steal every damned moment he could.

"No handsome Scotsman to accompany you today?"

Amelia-Rose looked over her shoulder at the trio who took the seats directly behind her. *Wonderful.* Playing the pianoforte in front of an audience gave her the shivers all in itself. To have friends here—ones who wouldn't be performing—made it so much worse. "There are a plenitude of more interesting things for a first-time visitor to London to do than attend a recital," she whispered, and faced forward again.

"Yes, but you're *here*," Elizabeth Sampson returned, speaking well below the sound of Polymnia Spenfield playing the harp. "And I don't so much want to meet your fiancé as I do his younger brother. I hear he's a true Adonis."

"He's not my fiancé," Amelia-Rose retorted, earning her a stern look from Mrs. Spenfield down the row. *Be civil*, she reminded herself. "Not officially. Please don't ruin my mother's wish to make a grand announcement of our engagement simply because we're friends and I told you what was afoot."

There. That had sounded logical, anyway. The last thing she wanted, other than people gossiping about her, was for the gossip to be negative. It weighed on her enough that she had no idea if Coll MacTaggert would actually appear tomorrow night to escort her to the Spenfield ball. If he didn't . . . She shuddered. No, she didn't wish under any circumstances to wed a stupid man who couldn't even be bothered to speak with her for more than three minutes.

But at the same time she already had a reputation for being too blunt. Anyone who already knew about the near-betrothal—which was far too many people for her peace of mind—would assume that he'd broken it off because *she* wasn't acceptable. Yes, she'd handed him a set-down, but only after he'd insulted her first. And then he'd stomped off like an angry bull. At the least she deserved to be the one to cry foul and walk away now.

"No one will hear it from me," Lord Phillip West said quietly, sitting straighter to applaud politely as Polymnia finished her piece.

"I'm only here because I wanted to see his brother again," Patricia LeMere put in. "Niall. Did you see his eyes? I could just swoon."

Oh, please. They didn't even know Niall, or if he would catch any female foolish enough to swoon. She rather doubted it. Perhaps he might pick a lady up after she fainted, but he might well laugh at her first for being so delicate. Coll, on the other hand, might prefer a fainter.

"Where will they be next?" Elizabeth insisted. "I didn't attend the picnic, so I haven't even seen him yet. Everyone says he's too handsome for words. Will he be at the Spenfield ball?"

"But I wasn't invited this year," Patricia complained, a

pout in her voice. "'Too many females,' they said. That isn't fair, is it?"

"Your parents could hold a soiree for you, and invite only men," Amelia-Rose suggested, trying to pay attention as the Duke of Dunhurst's granddaughter Maria attempted something horrid on the pianoforte, poor thing.

"That would make everyone think me unmarriageable and desperate," Patricia whispered back. "Really, Amy."

"You haven't been helpful at all," Elizabeth seconded.

"Then ask Eloise where they might be," Amelia-Rose suggested. "She's their sister." For heaven's sake, she hadn't seen a MacTaggert for better than a day herself, and she was supposedly to join the family. Not that she'd been looking for any of them, or one in particular.

"Don't mind if I do," one or the other of the girls retorted.

Amelia-Rose's mother sat down beside her. "It's your turn next, my dear. Do pay attention, so the others will do you the same courtesy."

"I am paying attention."

"Hush." Victoria Baxter folded her hands in her lap. "I especially arranged for you to go directly after Maria Vance-Hayden; you will show very well, you know."

Privately she'd hoped that Maria's musical skills had improved since the beginning of the Season; the young lady was myopic and shy as a mouse as it was. Squinting and muttering would never find her a husband, but a fair turn at music could only help. Alas, either her ability or her nerves seemed to be betraying her yet again.

Finally the duke's granddaughter stood and curtsied, her music clutched to her chest. Polite applause followed, and then their hostess Lady Curry stood. "Our next recitalist is Amelia-Rose Baxter. Miss Baxter?"

Taking and holding a deep breath, Amelia-Rose stood, nodded, and ascended the single step to the raised stage.

Four dozen faces gazed at her expectantly, at least a third of them more than likely hoping she would be all thumbs. Another third didn't care and had come to the recital for the punch and biscuits, while the last third claimed to be supportive but knew that a horrid showing made for a much better tale.

The benefit, then, seemed mainly to play well and leave everyone with nothing to say about her. Well, she could manage that. Sitting before the pianoforte, she set her music on the stand, flexed her fingers, and began playing. "Mungo's Delight" was a pretty piece, not particularly difficult, but she was only there not to make a mistake. She needed all the perfection she could get hold of.

Amelia-Rose played the country dance all the way through, careful not to speed up as she neared the end, and then set her hands back in her lap. The applause sounded sincere—and so did the whistle cutting through it. Startled, she turned to look.

Niall sat a seat away from her mother, a grin on his face as he put two fingers to his mouth and whistled again. Hurriedly she stood, curtsied, and headed for her chair, then had to return for her music again. *Dash it all.*

"What are you doing here?" she whispered, taking her place between him and her mother.

He lifted a bouquet of white and pink roses and handed them to her. "Eloise told me where ye'd be. Since it sounded formal, I thought I'd best bring ye some posies. Ye play well, *adae.*"

The flowers were very pretty, and as his hand brushed hers, she felt . . . No. She felt annoyed. He was making a scene, and it included her. "Thank you," she said stiffly, "but you haven't answered my question. What are you doing here?"

"Coll wanted to come," he returned, his voice just loud enough that those directly around them could overhear. "I reckon he ate some Sassenach food, because he's nae too well today. But he wanted me to tell ye that he'd be pleased and proud to escort ye and yer ma and da to the ball tomorrow, and for me to ask what time ye'd care for him to call on ye."

Amelia-Rose wasn't certain she believed a word of that, but it did sound plausible, and it gave him an excuse for being there that didn't include one of them being infatuated with the other—which neither of them was. One couldn't be infatuated after only four meetings. Five including this one, though of course she wasn't keeping count. She looked at her mother. "Shall we say eight o'clock?" she suggested.

Victoria sent a tight-lipped smile past her in Niall's direction. "Yes, that would be acceptable. Most persons would send over a note to inquire."

"Coll said I should deliver the flowers in person," he returned, plucking one of the rose petals from her bouquet and lifting it to his nose. "Roses for a rose."

"Amelia-Rose," Mrs. Baxter countered, her teeth clenched. "If you mean to remain here, Mr. MacTaggert, for heaven's sake do stop whistling and making a scene."

"How else is a man to let a lass know he reckons she's talented?" he drawled, lifting an eyebrow and clearly untroubled by the censure.

Seeing her mother flummoxed was rather remarkable. "Applause is acceptable," Victoria said tightly. "As is standing while applauding if it is something you truly admire. Anything else is gauche and barbaric."

When Amelia-Rose caught sight of Niall's profile, he was still smiling. "Stop it," she breathed.

"I'm gauche *and* barbaric," he returned in the same low tone she'd used. "Even so, by yer own rules, Sassenach, I outrank yer ma. If I didnae, I've nae doubt she would have tossed my posies on the floor and stomped on them. But I have the power the lot of ye gave me, and so she cannae."

Her breath caught. "*Your* posies?" she pushed, ignoring the rest of his anarchy. He had brought her flowers. *He'd* done it. And not on anyone else's behest.

His mouth twitched. "Coll's posies," he amended.

She didn't believe him. The flowers *had* been his idea, and she imagined that bothering to track her down at a recital, of all things, had been his idea as well. It didn't have to mean anything, of course; some flowers were a small-enough price to pay to keep his brother in her and her mother's good graces.

But it did mean something to her. Or rather, she wanted it to mean something. What, she didn't dare decipher. "Are you going to stay?" she asked under her breath.

"Are ye going up there again?"

"Yes. I'll play again just before the end of the recital."

He sank back on the narrow chair and crossed his ankles in front of him, long, lanky, and indescribably compelling. "Then I reckon I'll stay. Coll likes music, ye ken."

"Bagpipe music, yes? Not pianoforte music."

"We've nae listened to much pianoforte music. Pipes have an old, mournful sound to 'em, even in a reel. The pianoforte is gentler, like a conversation and nae a lament. I like it."

That was surprisingly thoughtful. "I'm impressed," she whispered.

"Actually it made me want to dance with ye, but since ye were playing the tune, I reckoned that would be a poor idea."

Amelia-Rose was more than half certain he was bamming her again, but it didn't seem worth taking the risk of assuming he was jesting. "No one dances at a recital, no matter who is playing," she cautioned, forcing herself to move past the image in her mind of her holding hands with Niall as they stepped through the country dance. Her fingers twitched, the image was so vivid. *Stop it*, she ordered herself.

"Good thing ye told me," he returned, shifting a breath closer to her. "Have ye considered what I said at the picnic?" he said almost soundlessly. "That ye may not want to be what Coll wants ye to be?"

"I thought you were here on his behalf."

"I am. Mostly."

Amelia-Rose could hear the other young ladies—and their mamas—around her, discussing in murmured tones how very handsome this Highlander was, even if his manners were atrocious. She could hear them passing on the tale of how while his brother was very nearly promised to Miss Baxter, both of the younger MacTaggerts were unattached.

"Ye've naught to say about that?" he went on, his voice flatter. "I suppose that's an answer, too, then."

"You're only teasing me."

"Am I?"

"My parents and your mother signed an agreement. I would very much like not to be a part of it, but I am. Don't make things more difficult." She took a breath. There she went, being too outspoken again, when mostly she just wanted . . . *No.* That wouldn't help anything. "Tell me something else pleasant about your brother. Be his advocate again."

"Nae. I reckon I'm nae in the mood. I reckon I'll sit here in silence and look solemn and brooding."

He wasn't going to march off and embarrass her. Perhaps that wasn't what she was supposed to take away from his statement, but that was what took hold in her heart and didn't let go. Niall MacTaggert liked her, enjoyed her company, and while she felt precisely the same, she'd told him to stop it. And he still remained beside her, when he could easily hurt her fragile reputation.

Oh, this was confusing. It didn't help that the man seated and attempting to brood beside her—three inches above six feet, lean and hard-muscled, very like the ancient pagan god she'd imagined him to be when she'd first set eyes on him—simply couldn't be ignored. That undertone of wildness to him made her wonder whether he meant to behave, or if he might just stand up and dance after all. Or suddenly decide to kiss her. She took a slow breath. Thank goodness she couldn't be chastised for thinking improper things, or she would be in a great deal of trouble.

"Tell me, Niall," she whispered, not satisfied with gazing at his profile in silence, "once your brother is wed, will you return to Scotland?"

"Are we friendly again, then?"

"Were we not? It was a disagreement, not a battle." That sounded like something she should say, anyway.

"If ye'd been a Highlander, we'd have to make amends over a whisky and then throw some darts or someaught."

"At each other? Good heavens."

He snorted. "I'd return if I could," he said, evidently accepting her explanation. "Lady Aldriss's got it in her mind that Aden and I both have to marry English lasses. I'm nae certain if it's because she reckons that'll see us back in London more often, or if she means for them to civilize us."

"That doesn't seem fair," she commented, realizing she'd spoken too loudly when her mother sent her an annoyed glance.

"Aye. I dunnae want to be civilized."

She'd been thinking more about the idea of him marrying just because his mother said so. She didn't have much choice, herself; at nineteen she couldn't wed without her parents' approval, and she had no means other than that which they provided her. He, however, didn't act as if he was beholden to anyone. "You're a man grown, and not the heir. Couldn't you do as you wished?"

"Aldriss's nae a wealthy property," he murmured, his tone intimate. His fingers brushed the edge of her gown, and a slow shiver went up her spine. "When someone else holds the purse strings, it's nae an easy thing to stomp yer boots and declare ye've nae wish to be part of the foolishness."

Perhaps they weren't so different after all. "Oh, I understand that. But—"

"Amelia-Rose," her mother hissed. "For heaven's sake. You don't need to charm *him*."

All the blood left her face. Obviously he'd heard that; half the audience probably had. When she glanced at him, though, a half smile curved his mouth. Before she could face forward again, he caught her gaze with those impossibly light-green eyes of his. "Too late. I'm already charmed, *adae*. Whether ye dunnae wish me to tell ye so or not."

And she was charmed, as well. If only he'd been the oldest MacTaggert. If only her mother wasn't mad for a title in the family. If only, if only, if only.

Chapter Seven

Ye didnae have to say *I* would escort them," Coll grumbled, pulling on his jacket and glowering while Oscar smoothed out any wrinkles across his shoulders. "Meeting them there would've sufficed, aye?"

"It might have," Niall agreed, tossing an apple in the air and catching it again. "If ye hadnae vanished five minutes into yer first meeting and then become a ghost fer the next five days. I've run through my damned list of manly ailments and acceptable business dealings ye could be up to."

"That's nae on me; I told ye I dunnae want an English lass. Even less one that spits back at me after three minutes of conversation. Where are the lasses Da told us about? The ones who'll do as we say and dunnae care where their husbands might be?"

Niall dug his fingers into the apple before he resuming tossing it again. "She gave ye the answer ye deserved, ye clod. Be polite to her, and ye may find she's polite to ye. This isnae her fault. Her parents signed an agreement the same way ours did. Ye might even consider telling her what ye want. Mayhap she'd want to stay behind in London."

He could believe that, since she seemed to enjoy Town far more than he could ever imagine doing. The part she might object to was being left behind while Coll went back to the Highlands to bed whomever he wished, only to return when he wanted to get himself an heir. That could be a problem, but it wasn't his to worry over, thank God. He had his own bride to find, and that fascinating golden-haired lass wasn't available. Even if he imagined she wished she was. Even if he *knew* he wished she was.

The viscount turned around so Oscar could adjust his cravat. "If that's so, we should get on with marrying. Nae need fer me to dress up like a dandy and prance about."

A couple of days ago, Niall might have agreed with him. Making Amelia-Rose's acquaintance had given him some perspective on the importance of appearances to those who spent their time in Mayfair. "The lass would look on ye more kindly if it at least appeared like ye cared enough to try to win her affection, ye great lummox. Ye'd nae have liked it if she'd stomped off and left ye sitting."

With a perfunctory knock on the half-open door, Aden joined them in Coll's bedchamber. "Niall's got the right of it, Coll. Ye ken ye need to wed the lass. Do it with a smile and ye'll at least be able to sleep at night without worrying that she'll slit yer throat while ye snore in yer marriage bed. And if ye get her with a son on yer first night, ye'll nae have to return except to collect the lad."

In response to that, Niall clenched his jaw. Both his brothers could be ham-fisted when the mood struck them. Amelia-Rose didn't deserve the resentment being piled on her. Nor would she enjoy Coll climbing on top of her when neither of them wanted to be there. The idea of the two of them together in bed, even if they did find some common respect, made his blood boil.

He shook himself. They were to be married, unless Coll

couldn't behave himself for ten minutes. They needed to be married, for the sake of Aldriss Park. In logical terms it all made sense. Whenever he closed his damned eyes, though, he saw her smiling, the surprised quirk of her mouth when he demonstrated that he had wits, and the bright-blue sadness in her eyes when she asked him whether Coll would like her better if she was meek.

That thought brought him back to the idea of his brother kissing her, bedding her—Niall stood up. "Get on with it, will ye?" he snapped.

Lord Glendarril lifted an eyebrow. "With what?"

"Ye'd best arrive to Baxter House on time, or they'll reckon ye've run for it again."

Coll scowled. "Ye're coming with me, Niall."

"Nae. I'll nae fit in the coach with ye and the three Baxters."

"I'm nae—"

"The curtains will be open. Ye've ridden in a coach before."

A hand thudded down on his shoulder as he reached the door. "I'm nae objecting to the carriage. *Ye're* the one who arranged this," the viscount rumbled. "I'm nae certain ye arenae throwing me to the wolves now."

Shrugging free of his brother's grip, Niall turned around. "I did arrange this. I also arranged to sit beside Amelia-Rose for the rest of the play ye missed—which had a bonny Juliet, by the by—and I took her to coffee when it was supposed to be ye, and I escorted her to a frilly picnic luncheon in yer stead, and I brought her flowers from ye at a bloody recital yesterday to make certain she'd bother with ye again." And he'd gone riding with her, but his brothers didn't need to know that. "Go yer damned self, Coll."

"Niall, y—"

Niall yanked open the door. "Aden and I'll meet ye

there," he said over his shoulder, "but I'm nae wooing her for ye. Ye have to manage that on yer own."

"I've nae met a lass I couldnae woo, *bràthair*. I dunnae *want* to woo this one."

"Then ye're a damned fool," Niall muttered under his breath, and stalked down the hallway for the stairs.

"Is he going?"

He jumped about a foot in the air as Lady Aldriss appeared at the top of the stairs. "Bloody Saint Andrew, woman," he growled. "Ye near scared me to death."

"I've been standing here for a quarter of an hour. You weren't paying attention." His mother didn't move. "Is he going?"

"Aye. He's going. I'm going as well. So's Aden, if ye care. And Eloise and her beau."

"Yes, well, once I get Coll settled I'll worry over you and Aden."

Niall moved around her to descend the stairs. "If ye worried over us, ye wouldnae have left for seventeen years. Now ye only want to manage us. That's nae the same thing."

"Perhaps not, but I doubt any of you would ever have come to see me on your own. Your father saw to that. I know very well his opinion of women in general, and me in particular."

For the devil's sake. "Then go fight with him. I'm nae in the mood to carry on with other people's battles tonight."

He didn't want to go to this grand Spenfield ball at all. His cravat felt too tight, and his trousers scratched at him. From what Eloise had said, the place would be bursting with lads, because every lass was expected to have a partner for every dance—with a couple of spares in case of drunkenness or injury. He didn't mind the waltz and the quadrille, but that hopping about for the blasted country dances made the lot of them look like pigeons on a hot rock.

Who the hell could do justice to a dance while he was bound up in tight trousers? Kilts would be gauche, though, Francesca had said. That wouldn't have convinced him, except that his mother and Amelia-Rose seemed to have similar views of propriety and proper behavior. The Mac-Taggerts had made a poor showing at the theater; they wouldn't do so at the ball. Not if he had any say.

"I would love for you to come, Jane, but you know how Mrs. Spenfield is. She only allows enough single females to avoid gossip, and that only suffices because she provides no other entertainments."

Jane made another stitch in her embroidery. "I am perfectly content to remain in tonight," she said calmly. "You're the one who's been spinning in circles all evening."

"Perhaps I'm a bit anxious that Lord Glendarril won't appear," Amelia-Rose returned in a whisper, "but I'm certainly not spinning."

While she'd attempted to make it sound like she wanted the viscount to make an appearance, because everything was so much more peaceful when her mother believed everyone to be seeking the same prize, she was more anxious that he *would* arrive to escort them to the ball.

The alternative of course would be Niall again, and if that happened her mother would very likely decipher that they'd been lying all along, and then she would never have a moment's peace for the rest of her life.

"You look very fine this evening, my dear," her mother said right on cue as she and Amelia-Rose's father arrived in the sitting room. Charles made directly for the liquor tantalus.

She didn't blame him; this was definitely an evening designed for the ladies. Last year, when she'd been a fresh debutante, it had seemed almost perfectly like a dream she'd had as a young girl. Gentlemen everywhere, each one vying for a dance, or to bring refreshments, or to exchange a thankfully brief word or two. That had been before she realized that not everyone appreciated her direct manner or her wit or her tendency to speak without bothering first to find the most diplomatic way of expressing herself.

Of course even then she'd almost immediately realized the gentlemen had mostly been attempting to avoid boredom—Mrs. Spenfield had refused to allow a gaming room or even a smoking room, and liquor had been absolutely forbidden. The men were there to eat well of all the dainty, expensive treats, and to dance with her daughters and any other young ladies fortunate enough to be invited. If one of those young men should offer for one of the Spenfield daughters, well, choirs of angels would sing. And that was according to the ladies' own mama.

The ball was probably not the best setting for her and Lord Glendarril to become reacquainted. As far as her mother knew, though, they'd spent part of the past five days together and this was only for public show. Saying anything to counter Victoria Baxter's opinion wouldn't bode well for any of them.

Still, she had a decision to make. Niall had told her the sort of woman Coll wanted. She could pretend to be that woman if she so chose. It would free her from Baxter House, at the least. It would also put her in meek, mild chains for the rest of her life, until she couldn't stand it any longer and went fleeing into the wilderness—thereby causing yet another scandal. But she *could* do it. Coll MacTaggert would have to say the things she wanted to hear and leave her a little room for . . . hope, she supposed it was, but the more her mother dug into her, the more the idea of being anywhere else appealed to her. And tonight had to be about Coll. She didn't have time or room in her withering heart to wish things were different. To wish it would be a different MacTaggert knocking on her door this evening.

She'd worn her finest gown, a sapphire-blue confection with black and silver beading throughout the bodice and streaking down the skirt like shooting stars. The three-quarter-length sleeves puffed at the shoulders and were edged in fine silver lace, as were the low neck and the bottom hem.

The gown had been her at mother's idea, made with the idea of standing out even at a soiree where every young lady would be the center of attention. Just on this one occasion she approved—the gown wasn't risqué or scandalous, but it was, quite simply, gorgeous.

As her father downed a finger of vodka and poured himself another, the front door opened. Amelia-Rose resisted the urge to run her hands down the front of her skirt. She looked very fine, from her gown to her hair twined with silver and black ribbons to her silver dancing shoes. If it *was* Niall, he'd best have a tale ready as to why his brother would be either meeting them later or unable to attend. If it was Lord Glendarril, she could only hope that his youngest brother had informed him which events they'd attended together so she wouldn't have to carry any conversation all on her own. It abruptly occurred to her just how much trust she'd placed in Niall MacTaggert, and how little that troubled her. As to the why of that, now was not the time.

"Mr. and Mrs. Baxter, Miss Baxter, Lord Glendarril," Hughes intoned, as the mountainous man stepped into the sitting room.

She curtsied, dipping her head to give herself a moment. Yes, he was quite handsome, if in a harder, colder way than his youngest brother. His looks, even his size, weren't the problem. Everything else about him was the problem.

Oddly, she'd expected to be a bundle of nerves, worried over how the viscount would react to her this time. Instead, and despite how important she knew this moment to be, she simply wished this to be over with, whatever ended up happening.

"Baxters," the viscount intoned, inclining his head. He hadn't worn a kilt, thank goodness, though he was sporting a black eye that made him look even less civilized. Objectively she could admit that he wasn't some stooped-over, ancient baron—which she'd begun to fear her mother would send in her direction after none of her three proposals this Season had been from a titled gentleman. Victoria Baxter had made it quite clear that this would be her daughter's last Season as an unmarried lady.

Oh, dear. If and when she did turn Glendarril away, would the old, gamy vultures receive her parents' permission to move in, to circle her until she gave in and pointed her finger at one of them? Would it be either this Highlander or an unmarried acquaintance of her grandparents' era? Lord Oglivy, for example?

In the midst of this alarming realization, it dawned on her that her mother was looking from her to Glendarril and clearly expected one or the other of them to say something. And since the viscount continued to stand there looking handsome and slightly annoyed, it fell to her. "Coll, thank you for the flowers you had Niall deliver to me yesterday. They were lovely."

"Ah. Ye're welcome. I'm sorry I couldnae bring them myself."

So far, so good. "It's more important that you recover yourself. Are you feeling well today? I can't imagine what you ate; I do hope it wasn't something at Lady Margaret's picnic."

His eyes narrowed, and for a bare second she thought she'd said something wrong. This was the only narrative she had to hand, though, and Niall hadn't indicated they would be doing anything more than substituting his brother's presence for his. A handful of hard heartbeats later, though, he nodded. "I purchased a pasty from a cart on the way home. That must've done it. Doubled me right over, it did."

"I've a potion that might cure you," her father said, indicating the liquor tantalus. "What's your poison, Glendarril?"

With a smile that looked more pained than grateful, the viscount shook his shaggy, brown-haired head. "I've some prancing about to do tonight. Best not pour good liquor after a bad dinner."

"Will your mother and the rest of your family be attending this evening?" her mother asked.

"Aye. I'm told it's quite the spectacle."

"That it is." Victoria clapped her hands together. "Shall we depart, then? Once most of the carriages have arrived, it's nearly impossible to navigate the filth in the street."

"Well, we dunnae want horse shite on those pretty shoes ye and yer daughter are wearing," Coll agreed, and motioned them toward the doorway and the foyer beyond.

"Don't say 'horse shite,'" Amelia-Rose whispered, drawing even with him.

"What should I call it, then, digested equine grass lumps?"

"That would do," she agreed, relieved to hear some humor from him. Perhaps he and Niall weren't so different. It seemed she meant to cling to every tiny ounce of hope he put into the air.

"Glad to see ye've caught yer tongue in yer teeth," he returned. "I'm to be yer laird; I'll nae have ye snapping at me."

And there it was. The tiny ounce of hope evaporated as she swallowed back her retort. If and when she made a decision, though, it would be one she'd thought through, one that made the most sense for her. She wouldn't throw it away because he'd decided to be arrogant. "Of course not, my lord."

An eyebrow lifted. "So ye do mean to behave. That's a good beginning, then."

"I suppose we're about to find out. But do be aware that if you embarrass or offend me or my mother, you'll become a pariah here in London, and you won't be able to find any other Sassenach bride for yourself." With that she flounced out the front door ahead of him and climbed into the large, black Oswell-MacTaggert coach.

That might have been risky, but for heaven's sake. He didn't even know her, and he'd already decided—again, and without conferring with her—that his was the only way that mattered. *Barbarian*.

He climbed into the coach after her parents, and sat on the padded seat beside her. One muscular thigh bumped against hers. She could edge away, but her parents would notice. Not for the first time she wished someone would be on *her* side, looking to see if this large man made her happy or if they were the least bit compatible. Thus far she'd seen nothing to encourage her to walk down the street beside him, much less marry him. But it was only Niall who'd suggested, to her great surprise, that this was a match she perhaps didn't want to make. And then he'd said that he found her charming, which had kept her awake all night.

"After the wedding, will you continue to live at Aldriss Park?" her mother asked, and Amelia-Rose hid a flinch.

"I reckon so. It's grand enough to fit two dozen MacTaggerts. The abbey at Glendarril was burned down in the lead-up to Culloden. There's nae on that land but broken stones and skeletons. Nae a fit place for an English bride. I may have her stay in London while I have a house built."

Glendarril didn't sound like much of a place for any

bride, but Amelia-Rose didn't say that aloud. She did like the idea of remaining in London, but that was not in any way how she'd imagined her life as a married woman—separated by hundreds of miles and living as a widow in everything but name. Would that be better or worse than making a life with a bully?

"So this soiree is stuffed to the rafters with men, aye?"

She shook herself. At the least she needed to get to know him—if only because she'd supposedly done so days ago. "Yes. No ladies who wish to dance are supposed to be without a partner."

"How does this Spenfield mama manage to lure all these men beneath her roof?"

"With very good desserts and a drawing for a saddle horse," her father supplied.

The viscount sat forward. "They auction off a horse? Seems they could draw in a lad or two with that same blunt and auction off their daughters, then."

"Penelope Spenfield has four daughters of marriageable age. A horse a year for the past four years is what they can manage," Amelia-Rose explained. "A dowry for each of them is, unfortunately, out of the question."

"I reckon if they've been giving away horses for four years, they need a different strategy. Am I to be scared of these lasses?"

Amelia-Rose ground her teeth together. As much as she wanted to bellow at him that he need only be frightened of the girls if poverty and an unfortunate tendency to simper terrified him, she kept those thoughts to herself. One either had empathy, or one didn't. On the other hand, he did seem determined to make this about himself. "How many women do you think would be pursuing *you* if not for your mother's wealth?"

"Amelia-Rose," her mother snapped. "That is enough of that."

She lowered her head, working on not clenching her fingers into fists. When she looked up again, he was gazing at her. "I've a title and lands, lass," he said in an even tone. "But I do get yer point. I'm a lucky man, I reckon."

He sounded mild enough, but she could practically feel his annoyance. He continued to bring out the worst in her. Being incompatible was one thing; him regarding her as uninteresting and unworthy of a moment's conversation was quite another. Especially if that was what he preferred in a wife. Why in the world would he want such a woman? Though honestly, a great many men did.

Refusing to attempt further conversation with him while they were trapped in the coach, she sat holding her reticule in her lap while he gazed fixedly out the window and her mother nudged her ankles to try to encourage her to speak.

As far as she was concerned, they weren't allies. The only thing they had in common was that neither wanted to marry the other. At least she had friends, enjoyed a social life, knew how to converse politely even if she occasionally forgot to mind her tongue in the face of nonsense, and could play the pianoforte and dance all the popular dances. He had a title and his mother controlled the purse strings. That wasn't very much recommending him at all. Not for her, anyway; her parents had heard the words "viscount, eventually to become an earl," and had signed their names and patted each other on the back.

With the coach's curtains open she could see the glow coming from the windows of Spenfield House from half a street away. Glendarril stepped down from the carriage first and offered a hand to her mother and then her. When she gripped his fingers he tightened his hand around hers. Amelia-Rose knew she was no fainting flower—even as a young girl she'd been called fresh-faced and boyish more than she cared to recall—but this man could be exceptionally intimidating. In his presence she was wee and dainty and delicate, because in comparison with him, everything was wee and delicate. Being meek might be easier than she'd realized. Remaining that way . . . She shook herself.

"We need to have a word," he said, shifting her hand to his forearm.

"I'm listening, my lord," she returned, with admirable calm and poise, she thought.

The big man blew out his breath. "Ye've shown me a pair of faces. I'm inclined to believe the first one was yer own, but I'm willing to be convinced. Pick two of yer dances for me, and we'll chat. Ye show me the lass ye want me to see. But ye ken I'm nae asking for a lie. I expect ye to abide by yer choice. I'll make my decision based on who ye show me. That's as much rope as I'm willing to give either of us."

She took a moment to consider. It was more than she'd expected from him, but she still couldn't decide if that boded well or ill for a marriage. Still, she did understand what he asked. She could be the shrew he no doubt thought her, and he would walk away. Or she could be a simpering miss, put his ring on her finger, and then be expected to remain that empty-headed idiot forever. In exchange for what, though?

"If I may ask," she said slowly, "you made a point earlier of saying I might stay in London while you built us a house. How long might I expect that to take?"

"A bit of time."

"Years, perhaps?"

His gaze sharpened. "Aye. Could be. What do ye say to that?"

That explained a great deal. He wanted a fool he could leave behind so he could pretend he wasn't married, and so he could go back to Scotland to live as he pleased. A widow in all but fact, indeed. Would that work to her advantage, or not, though? No one to frown at her, certainly, but also no one with whom to share a life. "I say we should have our dances and converse. We've only chatted for perhaps a total of five minutes altogether, and I was nervous at the theater. Tonight will be our second chance for a first impression."

Coll MacTaggert nodded. "I can agree to that."

"Let's retrieve my dance card, then. I do warn you that we must be quick about it. The moment the card touches my hands, it will be filled very quickly. And I'm not being arrogant. It's merely a matter of mathematics."

Ahead of them, behind the four girls' nervous mother and deeply resigned father, the Spenfield sisters stood to welcome all their guests. The oldest, Polymnia, now eight-and-twenty and well past her marital prime, followed by Thalia, Calliope, and Melpomeni. If their names weren't enough evidence of their parents's obsession with all things Greek, the faux-Ionic columns erected about the ballroom, the gold cherubs littering every wall and tabletop, and the Elgin statues apparently borrowed from the British Museum and standing in strategic view would have been more than sufficient.

"I thought they didnae have much blunt," Coll said in his version of a whisper as they walked into the main ballroom.

"They don't. They do know absolutely everyone, and they have the sympathy of a great many other parents."

"They'd have more of my sympathy if they hadnae named their lasses after the Greek muses."

So he knew who the muses were. Evidently, then, he could read. Until that moment she hadn't been certain. While her mother assured Mrs. Spenfield that tonight was bound to be the night that one of her girls caught the eye of a young man, she led the mountainous Highlander over to the side table to retrieve a dance card. Two waltzes tonight, and oh, she loved waltzes.

"Here," she said, handing him the card and a pencil as a crowd of young men swarmed from one young lady to the next. "I suggest the first quadrille and the second waltz. It gives a proper distance between the two dances. Does that please you?"

He eyed her before he bent his head to scrawl his name in the spaces she indicated. "Ye're full of polite tonight. We'll see if that lasts."

Yes, they would. He continued to aggravate her a great deal. He'd abandoned her, left his brother to apologize and stand in for him, had showed up for the grand moments, had never apologized for any of it himself, and had then declared the fault to be hers. At the same time, he had seemingly put this in her hands. If he'd known how she fared last Season, though, he might have been a bit less confident that she would do as he preferred.

Lady Aldriss walked into the ballroom, two tall, dark-haired men on her heels, and Eloise and Matthew directly behind them. Her heart sped a little in spite of herself. Niall looked fit and splendid in an onyx coat and trousers, and a deep-blue waistcoat. "Your family is here."

He glanced over his shoulder. "Is that Eloise's beau? I need to make his acquaintance."

The way he said "make his acquaintance" didn't sound very promising. Evidently she wasn't the only one that Coll MacTaggert had been ignoring since his arrival in London. Before she could defer, he set off across the ballroom, half dragging her behind him.

She'd never really envisioned what life as a married lady would be like, but then her parents had put her name in ink beside Viscount Glendarril's. A mad Highlander who disliked the English and who hauled her about like a dog. This was her sample of married life with him. She needed to pay attention.

Rather than make a scene she trotted along beside him, stopping before the impressive MacTaggert family. And seeing them all together, they *were* impressive. Aden, the middle brother, lacked an inch or so on Niall, which still left him at just over six feet tall. He had raven hair darker even than Coll's, hanging down to his shoulders and managing to make him look mysterious rather than unkempt. Niall had the greatest perfection in looks, in her opinion at least, thanks to those light, light eyes and brown hair that showed red and gold glimpses in the candlelight. He and Eloise could almost be twins, though of course his angles were much leaner and more muscular than his sister's soft, rounded ones.

"Ye're Harris, are ye?" Coll boomed from beside her.

"Good evening to ye, Coll," Niall drawled, stepping into the middle of the loose circle they'd formed. "I dunnae believe Aden's met Miss Baxter, and this here is Matthew Harris, Eloise's betrothed. Say hello."

The viscount narrowed his deep-green eyes. "Ye dunnae get to tell me how t—"

"Aden?" Amelia-Rose interrupted, slipping her hand from Coll's taut forearm. "Amelia-Rose Baxter. I'm pleased to make your acquaintance." She held out her right hand.

The middle MacTaggert shook it. "Ye've stoppered Coll's mouth," he said in a low, amused brogue. "He's nae accustomed to being interrupted."

She blushed. Oh, dear. She'd been so annoyed with him, but he did outrank all of them here but his own mother. And Highlanders, she'd always known, were very proud and stubborn. Had she been rude? She hadn't meant to be. It was only only that she disliked bullying, and the three brothers more than outnumbered poor Matthew Harris.

"I'm very sorry if I've offended you, my lord," she said, frowning.

"Och, nonsense," Niall broke in. "It's good for him. A mountain still has to listen to the snow."

"A mountain abides despite the snow," Coll retorted, keeping his attention on Matthew Harris. "Have ye gabbed with this sapling, Aden?"

"Aye. He's got all his fingers 'n' toes, knows how to read and write, and can damned well speak for himself. Shake his bloody hand."

"Language," Eloise said. "For heaven's sake."

"Ye've dragged us to a place with nae a gaming table, nae liquor, and a flock of females that look more like vultures than swans," Aden returned. "I reckon if ever a damned curse was warranted, it's now."

Hiding a smile, Amelia-Rose followed his gaze toward the sweets table. Evidently she'd missed the letter that most of the young ladies present had received, because she wasn't wearing pastel colors. She'd heard a rumor that there was a secret signal to alert men as to which young lady was available and which was spoken for—perhaps pastel meant unattached. Whatever it had been last year she must have dressed appropriately, because she'd garnered her one proposal that night. Inwardly she sighed. Perhaps she should have accepted it.

Fingers brushed against hers. "Did Coll fool yer parents?" Niall murmured, his attention ostensibly on the half dozen additional guests currently entering the ballroom.

"Yes," she returned in the same tone. "I wish you'd told me he had a black eye. I could have invented a chivalrous story for it."

"One of us has a black eye so often it didnae occur to me. Ye look lovely, by the way. Yer eyes are the color of cornflowers tonight."

She'd always liked cornflowers. "Thank you."

"Aye. Ye and Coll make a fine pair."

That stopped her smile. Yes, she and Coll were supposed to be a pair. "I thought you'd suggested otherwise," she breathed.

"I reckon it's nae my affair. If he wants ye, and ye're willing to be what he wants, that's between the two of ye."

Amelia-Rose blinked. She'd expected support or at least commiseration from him, because he'd offered it previously. But of course he would have his own family's needs as his primary concern. For her to expect otherwise was just stupid.

Even if there might have been some . . . affection between them, she wasn't meant for him, or he for her. He was a Highlander and a barbarian just like his brother. The only difference, really, was that he didn't have a title. That title was the only reason her parents tolerated the barbarian Lord Glendarril. They had no reason at all to tolerate Niall.

"I've seen more color in snow than ye have in yer face right now," Niall said, glancing at her. "Did ye see a spirit?"

"That's your first assumption?" she retorted, giving up the ruse that they weren't actually speaking. They'd done nothing wrong, after all. "That I must have seen a ghost?"

He shrugged. "Seemed as reasonable as my second guess, which was that someaught's overset ye. Since I'm the only one talking to ye and I only said ye had blue eyes and that I meant to mind my own business, I reckon that made nae a bit of sense."

Her mouth curved before she could stop it. Even when, if she'd truly cared for him, his words might have very nearly broken her heart. "Neither of your guesses makes the least bit of sense. I'm only a little chilled. In a few minutes I imagine it will be sweltering in here, so I've decided to enjoy the cold."

Eloise broke in between them. "The swarm's beginning," she whispered, laughing.

Two groups were indeed forming in the center of the dance floor—one of unmarried men, and the other of all the ladies who wished to dance and who hadn't yet seen their dance cards filled. The Spenfields had outdone themselves this year; two dozen ladies, compared with twice that number of young men. It did leave a problem of sorts, if one didn't wish to be left to choose among the slower, older, less marriageable men. With a giggle Amelia-Rose seized Eloise's hand and they pranced forward together into the maelstrom. And she refused to wonder for a moment what it would have been like to dance with Niall MacTaggert. That was only one of many regrets she would likely have tonight.

Chapter Eight

"I feel like a worm on a hook," Aden commented, taking yet another dance card from a young lady's hand and putting his name beside one of the dances.

"Stop signing yer name and they'll stop chasing ye down. Ye can only have one lass per dance anyway," Niall advised, shaking his head as a red-cheeked lass approached him. "I'm all spoken for," he explained.

"Drat," she grumbled, and pranced off again.

"Where do I put in my name for the horse drawing?" Coll ignored the ladies milling around him, looking more like a lion ready to swat at midges than a man meant to be impressing the lass he needed to marry.

"The what?" Aden asked.

"There's a drawing at the end of the evening," Matthew Harris put in from somewhere on the far side of Lady Aldriss. Wise fellow, to keep some distance between himself and Coll, at least until they'd had time for a conversation. "This year it's a two-year-old bay gelding named Westminster. They say he's a half brother to Wellington's Copenhagen."

"If I get him, his name's nae going to be Westminster," Coll returned. "Wulver, mayhap."

"Shouldn't you be seeing what Miss Baxter is up to?" Lady Aldriss prompted, looking up at Coll's flat expression.

"Before ye chose a woman for me, ye might have thought to ask what sort I'd like," he grumbled. "Where do I put my damned name?"

"For heaven's . . . There. Write your name down on one of those pieces of paper, and put it in the bowl." She gestured at a small table close by the door. The bowl was already half full of wee papers, and Coll immediately headed in that direction, Aden on his heels. "Only put your name in once," she called after them, then looked over at Niall and Matthew. "Oh, get going, then, you two."

With a grin Matthew loped off to join his almost-brothers-in-law. Niall, though, stayed where he was. Eloise and Amelia-Rose stood in the center of a swirl of gowns and coattails, and he didn't trust that they wouldn't be swept off their feet in the turmoil.

"You don't want a horse?" the countess asked.

"I have a horse." He kept his gaze on his sister and the other lass. "Do the Spenfield lasses know that their partners are here to win an animal?"

"It's been this way for the past four years, since Polymnia turned twenty-four and the youngest, Melpomeni, turned eighteen. So yes, I assume they're aware."

"Hm."

"What does that mean?"

Niall could feel her gaze on him. "I'm just trying to decide how the ladies might feel when a lad leaves with a horse but nae a wife."

"I'm not their mother," Francesca returned, keeping her voice below the level of the conversation around them. "It wouldn't have been my plan, but there it is."

"Nae, we've seen what yer plan is, m'lady." Halfway across the room Eloise and Amelia-Rose hugged a third young lady, the three of them bending over their full dance cards and comparing partners. He'd wanted to write down his name—not for the horse, but just for a dance. One dance with that lass before he had to begin calling her sister and watch his angry, cynical oldest brother put his hands and his mouth on her and then leave her behind. Or worse, decide he liked her and take her with him to the Highlands where Niall would have to see her every day.

"Niall, I'm not trying to be rid of you and your brothers. I want you back in my life. You're here now. Isn't that some sort of evidence in my favor?"

"Aye, that ye have a fine solicitor."

The orchestra up on the balcony that overlooked the ballroom played a trio of notes that were evidently meant to warn any dancers to get their arses onto the dance floor. He assumed that because everyone scattered, pairing up, the lasses forming three circles with their partners on the outside. The extra men and those not there to dance—mostly mamas and a few papas—piled onto the chairs set around the edges of the room or returned to the restocked sweets table.

Eloise had paired with Aden, while Amelia-Rose held fingertips with a stocky, pleasant-faced lad who seemed to be admiring the beading in her gown, the bastard. Niall glanced about for Coll, to find him devouring half a plate of strawberries and sugared orange slices. For Saint Andrew's sake.

As the country dance began, he wound around the edge of the room to his oldest brother's side. "Who's yer lass dancing with?" he asked.

Coll lowered an eyebrow. "Some Sassenach," he returned, glancing about the dance floor and then going back to browsing through the fruits and pastries. "If they mean to hold us captive, they should at least serve some meat to keep us happy."

"How did ye find her?"

"I found her at home, with her mouthy mama and pinch-faced, frowning da. Here, try one of these."

Niall took the sweet from his brother and set it aside again. "Those are to be yer in-laws, ye ken."

"We kept apart from Francesca for seventeen years. I reckon I can do at least that well with the lot of them."

"Ye found her more interesting than ye thought at first, though?" Niall prompted. Coll wasn't a chatterbox by any means, but generally the viscount could carry his side of a conversation without Niall wanting to pound him on the head.

"She kept 'my lairding' me, and apologizing for being sharp at the theater. If the lass wants to marry that badly, I reckon she'll nae object to the rest of it. She figured out that this isnae to be much more than a marriage in name, and didnae even blink. Unless ye told her already."

"I didnae." He should have, though, damn it all. If she'd figured all that out and decided she still wanted to be a countess, then he'd been wrong about several things. That disappointed him. No, not disappointed. Saddened.

"Why do ye care if I found her interesting? What does that have to do with the price of wool?"

"Because I've spent my entire time in London split between her and Lady Aldriss and ye, trying to keep that damned agreement and all of Aldriss Park from falling into the loch, *amadan*." For the devil's sake, she'd been far more patient and understanding than Coll deserved, not to mention witty and good-humored, and his brother didn't even appreciate it. His brother didn't even want that from her.

"Then I wish ye'd been the one to draw that card," the viscount said, leaving the table in favor of a section of wall where he could lean back and glower.

"So do I," Niall muttered beneath his breath, well below his brother's hearing, as he followed.

"She may be our savior," Coll went on, "but all I see is a yellow-haired lass who doesnae like me and cannae decide if she wants to tell me so, or if she'll put up with the shite I'm feeding her because she wants a title."

"Did ye bother to apologize for walking out on her at the theater and then vanishing until tonight, by chance? Maybe if she trusted ye, the two of ye could have an honest talk about what ye each want."

Coll narrowed his eyes. "What hornet's gotten into yer ear? She's nae the woman I would choose for myself, and if I *do* marry her, I see nae reason she couldnae remain here while I go home to Aldriss and attend to my life there." He straightened, taking a half-step closer. "Francesca might be able to force me to wed whomever she pleases, but she cannae turn me into a damned Sassenach. And neither can any damned woman I might marry."

For the first time it occurred to Niall that perhaps the MacTaggert brothers had spent too long out in the wilds. They saw every meeting as a battle, every negotiation as a surrender, and every new thing as a threat to the old ones. Coll saw Amelia-Rose as the enemy. Only time and repeated interaction could sway his opinion, and his oldest brother wasn't interested in either. All that so he could force himself to marry a lass he didn't want, and who didn't want him. Unless she'd changed her mind about Coll—or at least his title.

Niall knew he and Aden would be facing the same dilemma, even if they would have a little more choice where the lass was concerned. Marriage had begun to cross his mind even before they left Aldriss, but as the third son he wasn't needed to produce an heir and ensure the line of inheritance, so he'd figured on waiting until he found a lass with whom he cared to spend the rest of his life.

Ignoring whatever Coll was talking about now, he

looked out over the dance floor. There were a handful of pretty girls here, though Eloise had warned him that most of the single female guests would be either as desperate as the Spenfields, or already spoken for. Even from this distance he could fairly well tell which was which, and he could hear the edge of extreme anxiety in the scattered conversations.

Everyone lost in their own wee landscape, with their own fears and worries and threats and wishes. He'd never had a thought about any of that back in the Highlands. The things that had most worried him were the question of whether he could escape Lord Marmont's hayloft and Lord Marmont's daughter without being shot in the arse, and wondering if spring would come late again and the Lowlanders would snag the best wool prices for the year.

His shoulder jolted, and he whipped back around to face Coll. "What?"

"I said ye seem to be mending fences with Francesca," his oldest brother repeated, glancing toward the group of parents where their mother stood, no doubt trying to sell off Aden and him to the best family.

"I barely remember Francesca," he retorted. "I've nae loyalty to her. I dunnae want us to lose Aldriss. And we've a sister who has friends here and a life she's trying to build. Ye behaving like a wild bear reflects on her, too, ye ken."

Coll grimaced. "Aye. Though if she parted from the pretty Englishman, I'd nae have any cause to wed. Neither would ye or Aden."

Yes, he'd previously jested about putting Matthew Harris on a ship bound for America himself, but he didn't mention that tonight. Coll might consider it a fine idea. And little as Niall liked being forced into anything, it seemed innately unfair that Eloise and Matthew should have to be punished for falling in love. "I'm nae about to cause harm to Eloise, and if ye'd stop thinking like a trapped badger ye might have half a chance of being happy."

"Ye—"

The dance crashed to a close, and amid the applause Amelia-Rose returned to her mother's side. She continued smiling, but Niall reckoned this evening wasn't any more pleasant for her than it was for Coll. Why no one had considered sitting the two of them down across a table and just letting them chat, he'd never understand. She could certainly hold her own in a conversation, and without other voices butting in, without her trying to be the lass she imagined she was supposed to be, perhaps Coll would realize what a delight she was.

"It's a quadrille next," Eloise said, prancing up to them on Aden's arm. "Are you dancing at all, Niall?"

"He's studying the herd," Coll put in. "Try these lemon wafers, Aden."

"Coll, this is your first dance with Amy," their sister reminded him. "Go get her."

With what might have been a growl, the viscount stalked off toward his nearly betrothed. "I'm ready to wager that Coll's going to make a run for it back to Scotland." Aden pulled out a coin, spun it in his fingers, and pocketed it again.

"I don't want any of you to go, now that I finally have you here with me." Eloise took Niall's arm, standing between him and Aden. "Coll is aware that I didn't know about the agreement either, isn't he?"

"Aye, he is," Niall said, kissing her on the cheek. "And Amelia-Rose is a finer lass than he gives her credit for. He's just decided they'll nae get along because he doesnae want to like anything English."

"Coll likes a challenge," Aden put in. "Someaught he can see and fight through and declare victory over. This is all about him surrendering to someone else's will, and that's nae in his character."

No, it wasn't. Aden, though, was the one who'd apparently stacked the deck to make certain Coll lost the card turn. And this agreement between the Baxters and Francesca wouldn't work with either of the younger brothers, anyway; Mrs. Baxter wanted her daughter to be addressed as Lady something or other, and a simple mister would never do. Even if he'd drawn the low card, Amelia-Rose Baxter wouldn't have been meant for him.

Niall shook himself. The doldrums didn't suit him. And he had no idea why he should be feeling them after making the acquaintance of an English lass only five days ago. There was no destiny they'd been denied, no fairy tale written. He liked her, aye. More than he would ever take the time to decipher, now. Because she would marry his brother. He wouldn't spend endless nights wondering how things might have been different. He wouldn't imagine she tasted like strawberries and tea, or that her hair smelled like lemons. Or that her skin would be soft beneath his rough hands, and that she would shiver in delight when he touched her.

Niall shook himself again. *Stop it, ye idiot.* "Do ye nae have a partner, Eloise?" he made himself ask.

As he finished speaking, a tall, whip-thin young man edged forward, his hand outstretched as if he wanted to collect Eloise and at the same time stay as far away from her brothers as possible. "If I may, Lady Eloise?"

"Who's this one?" Aden asked, narrowing one eye.

The tall lad swallowed, his Adam's apple bobbing like a worm in a rook's throat. "I . . . Um . . . I'm Frederick. Frederick Spearman."

Niall took a step closer. "Spearman, eh? Ye come from warrior stock then, Frederick? Did yer ancestors get bloody coming after mine?"

"I . . . Oh, dear. The—"

"Oh, stop it," Eloise cut in with a nearly hidden grin, freeing her hands and rescuing Frederick from whatever the lad thought they meant to do to him. "Aden, go find your partner."

"She's definitely a MacTaggert," Aden commented, and strolled off to take the hand of a very large, pink-cheeked lass.

That was Aden, seeking out the ones who heard everything, who were generally ignored and discounted and for that reason knew everything about everyone. If there had been a lass without a partner he would have stood with her, himself, but as far as he could tell every lass who wanted to dance was doing so.

The circle of dancers Amelia-Rose and Coll had joined turned and dipped and held fingers all the way across the ballroom. Even as he realized he would never be able to hear any of their conversation from where he stood, Niall stopped himself from relocating. Coll might bark at her, but he'd never harm the lass—and she could hold her own. If she chose to do so. Whatever they might say was none of his affair, anyway.

"I continue to appreciate your assistance in keeping Coll from making a disastrous decision."

Taking a breath, he looked away from the quadrille to face Francesca. "I told ye why I'm involved. Ye might consider that putting a bull and a swan together to suit yer own whimsy might have been a piss-poor decision to begin with. But then ye dunnae ken who Coll is, or Aden or me, so I dunnae reckon what we want figures into any of this meddling of yers."

Her brow furrowed. "You strike at me every time we speak. Your brothers just ignore me, which to my surprise I find preferable."

Niall inclined his head. "As ye wish."

Turning on his heel, he stalked over to the open balcony door and made his way through the crowd of parents and unmatched men to the wrought-iron railing. Lady Aldriss could say his brothers ignored her, but he was the one she kept approaching. Did she reckon he was the softest of them? Or that he had the fewest memories of her, and so had less reason to be angered by her departure?

"You're one of that Highlands mob that belongs to Lady Aldriss, aren't you?" a very proper British voice boomed behind him. "You should be wearing a kilt so we recognize you."

Rolling his shoulders, Niall turned around. The man standing there was nearly his height, but broader and . . . squish-faced in a way that put his nose and mouth too close together and his eyes too low on his forehead. A toad, he decided. The fellow looked like a great, sullen toad. "Aye, I'm a Highlander, though I dunnae belong to anyone. Ye have an insult to hand me, I reckon. Get on with it."

The pair of men standing to either side of the toad sidestepped away from him a little. It might have been to make flight easier, or it might have been an attempt at flanking their quarry. Niall didn't much care. All day he'd been angry, and tonight had put a nice, heady foam on his fury. He knew the exact reason for his anger, and the fact that he couldn't do anything about Amelia-Rose's future only made it worse. So there he was, and a fight seemed a damned fine idea.

"There you are, Lord Eddlington," Francesca cooed from the doorway. The toad stiffened his shoulders.

"Lady Aldriss." He inclined his head, no easy task, Niall imagined, for a man without a neck.

"I had heard the silliest rumor, my lord," the countess went on, gliding to stand between Niall and the toad, "about you letting go your chef. You must tell me if it's true, because I would very much like to hire Miss Beasley if she's left your household. She is a wonder."

"It was a disagreement over wages, my lady," the toad grumbled. "All settled. She's not available."

"I thought it must be a mistake," Francesca went on with a warm smile, taking the toad's arm and guiding him toward the ballroom door, his two toadies following along behind like dogs. "Everyone knows how fond you are of Miss Beasley's . . . cooking. Do give her my regards."

With that she gave a small push, and abruptly she and Niall were alone again on the balcony. "That toad's bedding his cook?" Niall commented, looking back inside through the window. "Poor lass."

"I never said any such thing." She moved back in front of him again. "But *that* is how we battle here in London. Not with our fists."

"He started it. I reckon he wanted a brawl."

"Yes, he did. Everyone's whispering about his affair with his cook, and with one punch he could have turned the gossip to those MacTaggert barbarians that Lady Aldriss set loose on London. He thought you an easy and convenient target, Niall."

He snorted. "I may have been willing and convenient, but in two seconds it wouldnae have been just me he had to worry about. Coll would've broken him in half if I didnae drop him first."

Francesca sighed. "That isn't the point, my dear. Yes, the three of you could likely take on the entire male guest list here and triumph. But Lord Eddlington was attempting to use you. If you'd bloodied his nose, all the better. It's not as if he has any good looks to protect, anyway."

That surprised him a bit. "Ye've insulted him now."

She shrugged. "I *am* a MacTaggert. I am the mother of MacTaggerts, and I am very proud of that fact. My weakness was that I need *this* battlefield. I enjoy the intricacies and intrigues of London. The direct, physical battle of living in the Highlands, and with your father, was more than I could bear. It broke me, Niall. It broke me, and I fled."

Inside the dance ended, with footmen wheeling in bowls of punch and trays of biscuits apparently to refresh the dancers for the next round of revelry. "I dunnae ken what ye want me to say. Ye left us. To me that said loud and clear that ye valued Eloise and London more than ye did the three of us."

She stepped closer. "That isn't so. Not at all. I tried to take all of you. Your father wouldn't have it. If I'd stayed you would have grown up between two parents who couldn't stand to be in the same room together, who detested each other's lifestyle and, eventually, each other. It would have been a household full of hate and loathing and resentment. So instead of that, you grew up in a household without a female."

He could see that; he understood it, now, at least. Back then, his clearest memory of that time was him demanding of his father that his mother return at once, and Lord Aldriss responding that MacTaggerts made do, and that they didn't cry like wee bairns. At seven years old, it had very much seemed like the law. "I made do," he said aloud. "We all did."

"But that doesn't have to be the end of the story, my son. You have access to two worlds now. If you would try not to resent being here so much, you might find something— someone—you enjoy. And I am here, if you should ever want to chat about . . . anything. However far apart we've been in distance, you have always been in my heart."

"And I still reckon ye might have better luck with bringing us to yer table if ye'd asked instead of ordered. Now if ye'll stop pecking at me like a mad hen for five minutes, I've some lass to go meet."

Maybe, eventually, they might find some balance, but tonight he wasn't in the mood. He already had enough to mull over, and while he might owe her for stopping a fight before it could happen, he wasn't ready to sit down and embroider a handkerchief with her.

He had a long damned evening ahead of him, and evidently he meant to watch every dance—or rather, watch one woman dance with every man in the room except for him.

"I still cannot believe your parents would sacrifice you to a Highlander in exchange for his title," Lord Phillip West said, taking Amelia-Rose's hand to dip and turn with her, then releasing her to rejoin the line of male dancers. He caught her gaze with his soulful brown eyes, then moved in to circle her again. "Actually, I can imagine your mother doing precisely that," he continued.

Yes, so could she, even before Victoria had done it. Her father would enjoy it, of course, being able to puff out his chest and declare that yes, his daughter had married the heir to an earldom. For him that was as far as it went: a moment to brag to his fellows at some club or other. Her mother's motivations were much deeper. Amelia-Rose couldn't count the number of times Victoria Baxter had told the tale of how she'd very nearly caught the eye of the Duke of Ramsey, and how only a spilled glass of wine had sent His Grace into the arms of another.

If defeating true love was as easy as bending over to retrieve a wineglass and missing an introduction, Amelia-Rose didn't have much faith in such a thing. Missing a dance, however, could very well end an agreement, and it was tempting to slip away into the garden for five minutes. The waltz would be next. Coll wasn't on the floor now, but he'd already given his opinion of dancing in general. His brother Aden was close by, dancing with—oh, goodness, he was dancing with Thalia Spenfield. If he wasn't cautious he would be a married man by the end of the evening.

Niall remained in the ballroom as well, as he had for nearly every dance this evening. He hadn't danced any of them, though. She couldn't help noticing him. She wasn't the only one, either; at least eight of her female friends had managed to find a moment to take her aside and ask whether her beau's brother was attached, if he preferred brunettes, or if he had a favorite hobby someone might use to take up conversation with him.

Evidently none of her advice had been successful, because he remained alone, close by the blissfully cool air drifting in from the open balcony door. And while she didn't feel like he was staring at her, their eyes met with a frequency that told her he was very aware of where she was, and with whom she danced. Just as she was aware that he wasn't dancing, and that no young lady had caught his attention tonight. She shut her eyes for a heartbeat. He was meant for someone else, and she very plainly loathed that idea. Was that how he felt about her and Coll? Part of her hoped so, however wretched it was.

"You're being quiet," Phillip observed, joining her again as they reached the end of the line and pranced back up the center of their fellows.

"Am I?" She forced a smile. "This isn't a dance conducive to deep conversation."

He chuckled. "That is true enough. Are you going to the Thames boat races on Tuesday? My brother may be down from York in time to join us."

She'd been smitten with his brother Lionel, the Marquis of Durst, since her first glimpse of his honey-colored hair and brown eyes even more soulful than his younger brother's. If the marquis hadn't recently been romantically linked to an heiress from Yorkshire, and if she didn't have a great many other things on her mind, her heart would likely be fluttering at the idea of seeing him. "It would be lovely to see Lord Durst again. May I let you know in a day or two?"

"Certainly. I'll always save a place for you, Amy, regardless. You make the rest of us look better by the addition of your presence."

Amelia-Rose smiled. "You, Phillip, are a true gentleman."

London abounded with true gentlemen, true ladies, and excitement. Scarcely a day passed during the Season when someone didn't offer to accompany her shopping, or to a museum, or a luncheon, or hundreds of other amusements. Even the past two years since she'd been out, since she'd discovered that while a girl might speak her mind, a lady did not, she'd had London to distract her. And a few friends who didn't cluck their tongues at her when she expressed an opinion. She didn't think she'd ever tire of this Town.

And that was why she didn't want to leave it. Certainly not for some brute who disliked her simply because she enjoyed a bit of culture and because she didn't like being thought of as meek. If she remained in London as Lady Glendarril, everyone would know she'd made a mercenary marriage and then been abandoned. Would she still be able to do the things she loved? Niall—and Coll—had encouraged her to be the person she wanted to be, rather than the one she wanted to be seen as. And it was becoming more clear that those two ladies were very different. *Oh dear, oh dear.*

The dance ended, and her heart began pounding more quickly as Glendarril reappeared in the ballroom. Lord Phillip offered his arm, ready to escort her over to her mother, or to her next partner. If she went to her mother, she would no doubt hear a litany of everything she should want and everything she should be doing to achieve it.

With a sigh, she nodded toward the viscount. "If you please, Lord Phillip."

"He's not going to eat me, is he?" Phillip muttered.

That question actually struck her silent for a moment. Coll MacTaggert was undeniably formidable, but in order for him to take some sort of action, he would have to care that she'd danced with another man. And she honestly couldn't conjure any expression, any word, that made her think he had any feelings for her at all other than annoyance.

Rebecca Sharpe and Melpomeni Spenfield intercepted them as they left the floor. "Amy, why isn't Niall MacTaggert dancing?" Melpomeni asked, eyeing him over her glass of pink punch.

"There are more men than women here," Amelia-Rose returned. "Perhaps he didn't step forward in time."

"Or perhaps he was wounded doing one of those dangerous Highlands dances, and he cannot take the floor tonight," Rebecca suggested.

"Was he in the war? He might have been wounded there," Elizabeth Sampson surmised, joining them.

"You saw him two days ago. He wasn't limping," Amelia-Rose countered. *For heaven's sake.* Sometimes a man didn't dance simply because he didn't wish to do so.

"Is he shy?" Melpomeni asked, sending Niall a longing look.

"Oh, he didn't seem shy. He was very bold, in fact. It gave me the shivers." Elizabeth Sampson shivered again for effect.

"What gave you the shivers, Elizabeth?"

"That brogue of his. And talking about living in the Highlands. Did you see his eyes? Such a light green. Maria calls them celadon."

At least they didn't need her to participate any longer, Amelia-Rose reflected. She had enough on her plate. But now she could add the . . . concern over whether she would ever see Niall again if she did break with his brother. Would she and Eloise have to cease their friendship, as well? Or if she did marry Coll, would she and Niall chat from time to time? Would he call her *adae* in that way that made her shiver? How silly that her name in Gaelic sounded so . . . sensual.

They reached Lord Glendarril, and with a nod Phillip released her. "Our second dance," she said, shifting her hand to Coll's arm.

"Aye."

Amelia-Rose bit the inside of her cheek, holding back the desire to ask him some very pointed questions. Other people would overhear, and her mother would collapse on the spot if Coll abandoned her at the side of the ballroom. "We should have a little more opportunity to converse, at least," she offered.

"Aye."

Before she could roll her eyes at his apparent stoicism, the music began. She put one hand in his, placed the other very far up on his shoulder, and gasped a little as he put his free hand around her waist and plunged them into the dance.

"What's it to be, then?" he asked without preamble. "Married, or nae?"

"Firstly, my lord, I'd like to be certain I have everything straight. Your plan is that we marry, you go back to Scotland and continue to live as a bachelor, and I remain in London. Yes?"

"Aye. That about sums it up. Ye'll be Lady Glendarril, and later Lady Aldriss, which is what ye want, I reckon."

"What about children?"

"I'll need an heir. Two would be safer. So we'll have our marriage night, and if that doesnae do it, I'll send for ye once in a while."

"Where will these children be raised?"

"In the Highlands."

Without her, then. She would remain utterly alone, and be expected to tolerate all of it without comment. "And what of affection?"

He snorted. "Ye ken this is an arranged marriage, aye?"

Slowly she nodded, the awful, lonely horror of what lay before her clearly laid out in its most matter-of-fact, bleakest terms. She was grateful for that. It left no room for flights of fancy, of wondering whether they might eventually settle into a loving marriage. He didn't intend to become well enough acquainted with her for that to ever happen. "I understand."

"Then we're in agreement. I'm glad this nonsense is over with. We'll wed as soon as I can arrange it, I'll bed ye, and then head back north to where I'm needed."

If she'd been the fainting sort, the type of woman he expected and wanted her to be, she would have collapsed to the floor on hearing that. Instead, a loud buzzing started in her ears, one that got louder and louder until she realized it was the entirety of her, trying to scream.

"Nothing is worth this," she said aloud.

"I beg yer pardon?"

"What you're proposing—and I use that term loosely—is that you go and do as you please, while I sit in a house somewhere, assuming that you've provided me with one, and have no companionship, no affection, no children to occupy me, nothing but the occasional summons from you to go to the Highlands so you can bed me, then send me home again."

"I reckoned ye could live with yer ma and da."

Oh, that settled it. "My main reason for agreeing to this was to be able to leave that wretched house," she snapped. "No, my lord. You are an arrogant, thoughtless, self-concerned . . . buffoon, and I will not throw my life into a dustbin so you can continue shearing sheep and lifting the skirts of tavern wenches. I don't care who signed what. I will not yield."

They stopped. In the middle of the waltz, in the middle of the other dancers, they simply stopped. And then he lowered his hands from her, turned his back, and walked off the highly polished floor.

With a hard breath she turned around. Couples swirled in front of her and behind her, sweeping across the ballroom floor. Farther away, among the nonparticipants, a low murmur began. Amelia-Rose clenched her fists. *Oh no, oh no.* This would ruin her. She'd turned Coll down, and he'd just ensured that she would never, ever make another match. She would be living in Baxter House until she was so old she turned to dust.

"Look at me," a low brogue came from directly in front of her.

A shiver ran up her spine. *Niall.* "I don't want to," she whispered.

A warm, rough hand took hold of hers. "Then just waltz with me, lass," Niall murmured.

His free hand encircled her waist, and she did look up to meet his impossibly light eyes. "You don't have to, you know. I'm ru—"

"I want to," he returned.

He swung her back into the waltz, and she closed her eyes against her sudden tears, dug her fingers into his shoulder, and she danced.

Chapter Nine

"Thank you," Amelia-Rose breathed when she began to feel a bit steadier, looking up to meet Niall's pale-green gaze.

"Ye're white as a sheet, for Christ's sake," he said, his tone low but sharper than she was accustomed to hearing from him. "What the devil did he say to ye?"

"Give me a moment, will you?"

His fingers around hers flexed. "Aye. I can do that."

A moment ago she'd been in a battle, and she'd won. And then she'd very soundly lost. Every nerve felt sharp and raw, and she held on to Niall to keep from stumbling. She had effectively ended the agreement and the engagement; even if Coll for some reason changed his mind, her mother would never allow the marriage now.

Coll's actions did prove how little regard he had for her. Yes, she'd insulted him, but she didn't think that had anything to do with his abandonment. She'd simply ceased to be useful, and so he'd walked away.

"Ye and Coll are like oil and water, lass, but ye knew that already," Niall went on after a moment. "I reckon then that whatever just happened, it went past what either of ye expected."

"I . . . He was very honest. I can't fault him for that," she said finally, wishing her voice would stop shaking. "I lost my temper. I don't want a marriage where I'm ignored and abandoned. If that's selfish, then I suppose I'm selfish."

"I cannae think it's a sin to want a measure of happiness," he replied.

"Exactly." She'd told her parents her opinion at the very beginning of this, but that had been more nebulous, more about being forced into a marriage with a stranger simply because he had "Lord" in front of his name. "I could have been less strident about it. I shouldn't have called him a buffoon." Tears welled in her eyes, and she blinked them away. No crying where anyone else could see.

He made a sound deep in his chest that might have been amusement. "I've called him that, if we're being honest."

Amelia-Rose lifted her chin. "I told you that I like my life. I see no reason I should give it up for a boor who offers me nothing but criticism and sheep and loneliness, wants me to continue living at my parents' home and, if I have children, means to take them from me."

His grip didn't shift, but she had the distinct feeling that he'd just become angry. Quite angry. At her? That, she didn't know. "He said he'd take yer bairns?"

"He said I was to live in London, and they would live in Scotland."

They twirled in silence for a turn. "I reckon he meant to make ye angry. If he can claim this is yer fault, then he still hasnae broken the agreement between my parents."

"What makes you say that?"

"He was raised without a mama. To claim up front that he'd take any bairn from its mother's arms . . . He'd nae do that." Niall frowned. "I cannae imagine him doing that." He muttered something else that sounded like a curse.

"Have you asked him?"

"Nae. I reckon I will, now."

"I did try to keep an open mind, Niall," she told him. "And you . . . Your friendship and consideration lifted my estimation of your brother. You're the better man, though. Don't let him tell you otherwise."

"Nae. I'm different, is all. In some ways. I'm as much a MacTaggert as he is, and I shear as many sheep as any of us."

"You actually do shear sheep?" she asked, snatching at a chance to change the subject. She needed to keep speaking, though; dancing in his arms felt . . . not quite safe, but protected. It was heady after her previous fear that she'd sink right through the floor, and she needed all her wits about her right now.

"I do. We're nae at Aldriss just to be pretty. There's always plenty of work to be done, and I've a strong back. I reckon I can do my part to help."

She nodded, lowering her gaze to his simply tied cravat. Unlike most of her male friends he hadn't arranged the stiff white cloth into a waterfall or a clever bow or a billowing cascade. Just a single pin in the shape of a thistle provided decoration. Likewise his black coat and dark-blue waistcoat were without ornament, the plainness of them broken only by their rows of silver buttons. No gold-threaded stitching, no stiff, high collar or faux medals or paisley patterns or embroidered monograms.

"If you're so busy working, how do you know the waltz?" she asked.

"Is this what ye want to chat about?"

"Very much so," she said feelingly.

Niall drew her a breath closer as the swirled about the room. "A long-legged fellow, a dance master, he said he was, came to the village offering to teach all the lasses for two shillings apiece. Anyway, we convinced this stork to teach us, as well."

She could imagine it, three dark-haired lions and a stork

teaching them to dance the waltz. The poor man must have been terrified, but for heaven's sake, in her opinion it had been well worth the fright. He danced without effort, every ounce of his attention seemingly on her. With Coll it had been a battle; with Niall, she soared.

"Will you lose Aldriss now?" she asked slowly, swallowing away her nerves. If this waltz could last forever, that would be magnificent.

He cocked his head. "That, I couldnae say. Ye're the lass Lady Aldriss chose for him, but he made it look as if ye turned him away . . . Francesca keeps telling me she wants us back in her life. Forcing Coll into a marriage neither of ye want doesnae seem the way to do that. She may agree to choose a different lass for him."

"And then you'll go and charm that lass on your brother's behalf, I imagine?"

"Nae. I dunnae think I have it in me to charm another lass." Niall glanced down at their joined hands for a moment, then lifted his gaze again. "In the theater box that night, Coll meant to send ye into tears. Instead ye sent him running like a scalded cat."

"I didn't intend to do that, though. A lady doesn't show discomfiture or annoyance. It's not proper."

"For a London lass it's nae proper. The lasses in the Highlands can hold their own. When I sat next to ye, ye looked me straight in the eye and dared me to make an excuse for Coll." His mouth curved in a slow smile. "Ye caught my attention."

The corners of her mouth lifted in response. "You saw all that just from me looking at you? I'm somewhat skeptical, Niall. Yes, I was annoyed, but more that your brother had just revealed himself to be exactly the caricature of a Highlander I had imagined."

"I can safely say ye're nae at all what I had in my mind when I rode down to London. I told ye I reckoned I'd find ye'd all bc pale, simpering, dour husks that didnae have a drop of warm blood in ye."

That was what she'd been trying to be, really. When he described a proper young lady, she sounded horrid. Was it so awful, then, that she wasn't quite one of them? Being a husk would certainly be easier, but it left no room for warm-blooded things like laughter and happiness and love. "What did you find?" she asked aloud, though she wasn't certain she wanted to know the answer.

The music stopped before he could answer. It felt . . . odd, as if she'd accidentally stepped onto a cloud, only to realize that a cloud couldn't possibly hold her. The audience applauded, and she belatedly let go of Niall's shoulder and his hand to join them. As she turned away, though, he caught her left hand and tucked it around his forearm. "What did I find?" he repeated, and before she was even aware of it, they were outside on the balcony overlooking the garden.

"What are—"

"I found ye," he interrupted, and leaned in to catch her mouth with his.

A delighted thrill sent shivers up her arms, her previous tragedy forgotten—or at least sct well aside. *Niall MacTaggert.* He slid his arms around her waist, pulling her against him. Amelia-Rose drank in the heat and taste of him, putting her hands over his broad shoulders and lifting up on her toes. In return he deepened his kiss, his breath warm along her check and his mouth teasing at hers in a way that left her both satisfied and yearning all in the same swirl of warmth.

Far too soon he broke the kiss, lifting his face an inch or so from hers. "Ye needed a breath of air, *adae*," he whispered, "because of yer shock over Coll leaving ye cold on the dance floor."

"Wh—"

"Amelia-Rose." Her mother's sharp voice came as Niall ducked out from under her arms and took a long step sideways. "Where are y— Whyever are you out here, unchaperoned?"

She turned around as her mother's footsteps tapped up behind her. "I needed a breath of air," she said, her mind feeling misty and dreamy. *Wake up*, she ordered herself. Now was not the time to lose her wits. She'd just been kissed, not rescued.

"I'm not surprised," Mrs. Baxter retorted, sending at glare at Niall—who now stood a perfectly respectable distance away from her. "You. Where is your brother?"

"I'm nae his keeper, Mrs. Baxter."

"Well, someone needs to be. This is unforgivable. I can't even imagine the gossip now. I'll be the laughing-stock of London. What did you say to him, Amelia-Rose? For heaven's sake."

"He told me what he wanted in a wife. Someone to remain here in London, living with you, and to wait for him to send for me so he could get me with child, take the babe, and then send me back to London again. Like a . . . a brood mare or something! I told him that was unacceptable."

Victoria snapped her mouth shut. "He would have married you, then?"

Of course that was what would matter to her. "Yes, he would have married me. I will *not* marry him."

"You have ruined everything. Again." Mrs. Baxter put a hand to her temple. "We may not have announced it officially, but everyone knew he was to marry you. Everyone." She turned to glare at Niall. "You barbarians!"

"Mother, Niall saved me," Amelia-Rose protested, though "helpful" wasn't the first word that came to mind when she looked at him. "Improper," definitely. And "scorchingly desirable."

"That is more than enough from you, Amelia-Rose.

Where is your mother, Mr. MacTaggert? I will not carry on with this farce for another minute. He insulted my daughter in the middle of the Spenfield ball. In front of everyone. That cannot—will not—be tolerated. Do you hear me?"

"I'm nae deaf," he returned coolly, leaning a hip against the iron railing of the balcony. "And I'm nae about to scamper off and fetch my mama to deal with ye."

"Well, you certainly have no say in matters here. Promises were made."

He sent Amelia-Rose a sideways look. "I didnae promise anything. Did ye promise anything, lass?"

"No, I didn't."

She would never have said that if it had been her alone. But she was tired of being caught up in all these machinations for status and respectability, and Niall's plain, outspoken manner felt refreshing. And she wanted him to kiss her again.

"Amelia-Rose Hyacinth Baxter," Victoria snapped. "You will return to that ballroom at once and dance your next dance." She pivoted to glare again at Niall. "And you will inform your mother that Mr. Baxter and I will be calling on her at ten o'clock in the morning and that we are most displeased."

"I'll alert the pipers, then," he said dryly.

Amelia-Rose didn't know if he was jesting or not, but her mother practically dragged her off the balcony and back into the ballroom, so she couldn't ask him. Part of her hoped he wasn't.

So she and Coll had apparently broken their agreement, but a whole new box of troubles had just opened. At this moment only two things comforted her—that Niall had saved her on the dance floor, and that whatever happened, she wasn't going to have to marry Niall's brother.

As for that kiss . . . *Good heavens.* She didn't want to

think logically yet, but she did have to acknowledge that Niall possessed the very same detriments as his older brother—he was a rough-hewn, mannerless Highlander who disdained London. He'd said he wished he could return home. He was even less acceptable to her parents—and oh, she wanted him. She did. Trying to convince herself otherwise . . .

But nothing had been resolved. No one had pledged anything, and she still had a very large problem.

She could conclude now that what she'd suspected was true, that the past days he'd spent in her company hadn't been solely on his brother's behalf, just for the sake of Aldriss Park. He'd as much as warned her that she and Coll wouldn't suit. But had he done that for her, or for him? Just because he'd been correct didn't excuse the way he'd essentially backstabbed his brother—or did it?

What did Niall want from her, anyway? Her virtue? Her hand in marriage? He'd never courted her on his own behalf, after all. All she knew was that half the women in the ballroom wanted him, and that her lack of propriety didn't seem to trouble him a whit. And that being the focus of his attention and his desire was the most heady thing she'd ever experienced in her life. Goodness. Her legs felt weak, and she didn't think it was still because of Coll's rudeness.

This was not going to end well. She knew that as well as she knew anything. Niall had stopped a nightmare in midstride, but that didn't make him the answer to all her problems. Even if he had been proper and English, he lacked a title. Her parents—her mother—wouldn't allow any man without a title to walk away with her daughter. Amelia-Rose had heard her say it; she'd been close to aristocracy all her life, close enough to touch, but not inside the door. Victoria Baxter wanted inside that door, even if it was as the duchess's or marchioness's or countess's or viscountess's mother.

Aside from all that, Niall wasn't very proper. In fact he seemed to delight in tossing propriety onto its head. Nor was he English. He had no love for her native land, no respect for the traditions of her or her peers—even though they were his peers, as well—and he'd expected to find an empty-headed, weak-willed lady for himself. He'd told her so, if not in those exact words.

Amelia-Rose shook herself. He'd kissed her. That was all. He hadn't proposed, or declared that he'd fallen for her, or anything more than that he found her charming. Yes, the kiss had been magnificent, and yes, she liked him a great deal, but she had no idea what it all meant. Logically she needed to figure that out before she began lamenting all the things that could never be.

Thomas Dennison hesitantly stepped forward to claim her for the country dance, and after a word from her to explain that Lord Glendarril had choked on something and had had to send in his brother as his second, she was out on the dance floor jumping and twirling again. She tried to enjoy herself; after all, she did love dancing, and the social interaction and conversation and glamour of a grand ball.

With every turn, though, her gaze went to the guests who weren't dancing. Her mother's glare lingered for barely a heartbeat. Her father's annoyance for the same length of time, if that. There was Lady Aldriss, her brow furrowed, her attention on her youngest son. And there stood Niall MacTaggert, saying something brief to the countess and then meeting Amelia-Rose's gaze. And most unsettling and electrifying of all, this time he didn't bother to hide his smile.

"You were unforgivably rude, Coll."

Coll sat back in his chair at the breakfast table and folded his arms over his chest. "Aye. I reckon I'm calling yer bluff, Lady Aldriss. And only because Aldriss Park is involved, I'll tell ye the lass turned me away."

Niall, seated across the small table from his oldest brother, looked down, stabbing another pork sausage to cover the move and his roiling anger. He'd known Amelia-Rose had serious reservations about Coll, and vice versa, but Coll had nearly ruined her. For a lass as sensitive about her reputation as she was, that had been devastating. She had plenty of spleen, aye, but last night could have gone very, very differently.

"And I suppose you haven't got any idea why she would do such a thing," Lady Aldriss countered.

"Nae." He pinned her with a glare. "I only described what I intended for our marriage—one that mirrors yers. Her staying in London, me carrying on in the Highlands, and any bairns she might have residing with me."

The countess's cheeks paled beneath her carefully applied blush. "You're a cruel boy. You wanted to hurt me, and instead you hurt an innocent young lady whose parents put far too heavy a burden on her shoulders."

Coll looked away at that, finding something out the window to catch caught his eye. "She called me a buffoon."

Aden, at the far end of the table, snorted. "Good for her."

"Shut yer gobber. At least ye have a say in which Sassenach ye're leg-shackled to."

"For your information," their mother countered, "and aside from the fact that you've violated the terms of my agreement with your father, I have made inquiries about you over the years. I know you to be hotheaded and abrupt, not one to suffer fools in silence. I chose Amelia-Rose Baxter with you in mind, my son. She is clever and quick-witted and very kind as well as being lovely—a perfect counter to you."

"If ye reckoned I'd trust *ye* to choose any woman for me, ye reckoned wrong," Coll retorted. "I'll nae wed that sharp-tongued shrew. And she'll nae have me. So do yer worst."

The countess opened her mouth and shut it again. "You are . . . forcing me to take an action I had hoped—"

Niall launched himself over the table, catching his brother with a hard fist to the jaw before they both crashed to the floor. Coll had hurt her. And the bastard wasn't even sorry about it. Whipping around, using his speed against his brother's size, Niall hit him again, plowing into Coll as the viscount started back to his feet. A chair cracked into splinters beneath them.

"What the—"

Ducking an arm, Niall swung in again. "Ye nae had any intention of marrying her," he growled, shaking off a glancing blow to his shoulder.

"And so ye wasted a few days being kind to her. Why do—"

"Ye have nae idea, do ye, *amadan*? Ye just decided to ruin her life because ye dunnae like yers, ye fu—"

Aden grabbed him from behind, hauling him off Coll. At the same time, no doubt alerted by the noise, Gavin, Oscar, and Wallace the piper skidded into the room to grab the viscount, pulling him in the opposite direction as Charles the second piper took hold of Niall's other arm.

"Stop this at once!" Francesca yelled. "I will not have this in my house!"

"He started it," Coll growled, shrugging Oscar off only to have the valet reattach to him like a remora on a shark.

"Because ye're a damned bastard!" Niall snapped back again. "Ye dunnae deserve the lass."

His brother swiped blood from his nose. "Ye jumped me over that lass? What are ye, mad?"

"Aye. And ye," Niall said, turning his glare on Francesca, "yer agreement didnae say ye could choose a wife for Coll, anyway."

Francesca looked back at him, her expression wary and very worried. "Yes, it did."

"Nae. It said *one* of yer lads would marry a lass of yer choosing, and the other two would marry English lasses."

"Dunnae pull us into this," Aden murmured, still gripping Niall around the chest.

"Yer agreement didnae say which brother," Niall insisted. "So if it's Amelia-Rose ye have in mind, *I'll* take her. And ye can go hang yerself, Coll."

Silence crashed over the room. If there had been a mouse in the attic, Niall was fairly certain they would have been able to hear it. Even the servants seemed to be holding their breaths. Not him, though. Now that he'd demonstrated his annoyance with Coll, and now that he'd said what he wanted—needed—to say, he felt . . . satisfied.

"Well, damn me," Coll muttered. "Let loose, lads. I'll nae stomp ye."

"Are ye safe now, Niall?" Aden asked.

"Aye. I reckon so. As long as the buffoon there doesnae say anything else insulting about Amelia-Rose."

"As a separate point of interest, then," Aden commented, releasing him and returning to the scattered breakfasts on the table, "I danced with the lass last night, and she explained to me that Niall thought her name too long to say, so he called her *adae* for short. *Adae* meaning 'rose.'"

"And?" their mother prompted, every ounce of her alert and angry and likely expecting more trouble from her sons.

"*Adae* doesnae mean 'rose.' It means 'trouble,'" Aden supplied.

"Did ye tell *her* that?" Niall asked. Damn it, that could lead to some complications. He would have told her himself, when the moment seemed right.

Aden snorted. "I'm nae an idiot. I nodded and smiled and stepped on her toe. Gently."

"That's bonny, then." Niall looked over at the countess,

who was already gazing at him. "They'll be here in twenty minutes."

"So I'm to give in, am I? Pretend the lot of you didn't embarrass me and poor Amelia-Rose? Pretend that *you* didn't have an ulterior motive in escorting her about town, and that Coll never had any intention of honoring his word?"

Coll pushed back to his feet. "I didnae give my word. And I dunnae trust ye to choose me a wife who willnae do to me what ye did to Da. Ye're holding us hostage, *màthair*, and we're—most of us are, anyway—trying to escape." He sent a pointed glance at Niall. "If I sign my name to a paper, I'll honor it. I've nae done so. If he wants her, he can have her. Though ye're nae a viscount, Niall, so ye may find she doesnae want *ye*."

The countess turned her back for a moment. She nodded, though at what Niall had no idea, before she faced them again. "You've found a loophole, then. Very well. I will accept Niall as a substitute for Coll."

"Thank the devil and his wee pointy hooves," the oldest MacTaggert grumbled.

"There is no loophole in the other part of the agreement, however," she went on. "You, and you"—she pointed at Coll and Aden—"are to wed English ladies. I will have something binding you down here, even if it isn't me."

"I'm taking Eloise and her beau to luncheon," Aden stated, pushing his plate away once more and standing. "I'll ask her to point me at one."

"I'll go with ye." Coll headed out of the room, Aden on his heels and advising him to change out of his bloody cravat and not to pummel Eloise's betrothed.

"Coll," Niall called after him, and his oldest brother turned around.

"What?"

"Ye and I still have a disagreement."

The viscount arched an eyebrow. "Nae, we dunnae," he countered. "If ye'd told me ye liked the lass, neither of us would be bloody right now." The two MacTaggerts left the room for the stairs and Eloise's bedchamber.

Francesca uprighted one of the remaining chairs and sat in it as the servants scattered again. "You."

Niall went after his last piece of sausage. "Make another agreement with Mrs. Baxter. I ken I'm nae lofty enough to please that dragon. I want Amelia-Rose Hyacinth Baxter. If she'll have me, I mean to take her. There's nae else about it that concerns me."

"Niall, this isn't the Highlands. It's not about physical ability or determination. There are bloodlines, titles, ambition, so many—"

"And who were ye to marry before ye met Da?" he cut in, standing. "I'm accustomed to keeping the peace," he added, moving for the door. "This nonsense with Coll and my lass nearly . . . If nae for the fate of Aldriss Park I'd have been going after my own brother even before they parted company last night. Now that kin's nae involved, though, I find I'm nae feeling particularly peaceful." Niall stopped in the doorway, but didn't turn around. "That's yer warning."

As Niall left the small dining room, Francesca gestured for Smythe to pour her a cup of tea. Oh, she remembered quite well who she had planned to wed before Angus Mac-Taggert rode into London. She hadn't been engaged yet, but she and Lord Peter Fenwill had had an understanding. She'd enjoyed Peter's company, thought they were well suited temperamentally, and that while he would likely never inherit his father's marquisdom, with her money they would have a comfortable, respectable life.

Angus MacTaggert hadn't cared about any of that. And after she'd set eyes on the handsome Highlander and heard how passionately he'd spoken about both her and his be-loved Aldriss Park, she hadn't cared, either. She'd cast aside the man with whom she'd intended to spend her life in exchange for a heated, passionate mountain of a High-lander.

Luckily her parents hadn't objected, but then his title provided a fair compensation for his lack of wealth. It had ultimately been a disaster, but oh, what a glorious one.

"Do you require anything else, my lady?" Smythe asked, setting the teacup in front of her. "Today is silver-ware day."

She waved her hand. "No, go polish. And thank you."

He inclined his head. "My lady."

Francesca lifted her tea and took a sip. She'd badly underestimated Coll's resentment of her, and Amelia-Rose had very nearly paid the price. But Amelia-Rose was good-hearted if a little frank in her speech, knew all about the proper way to do things, and knew all the proper people. She and Eloise were friends, and she'd seemed to need a bit of a . . . boost. It had seemed perfect, and Victoria Baxter had agreed.

Convincing the Baxters to forget Coll and accept Niall would not be easy. They didn't require money, which she could certainly use as a bribe. Nor was she above doing such a thing. No, they wanted a title. "Oh, dear," she mut-tered.

Niall might be a bit more civilized than his father or his oldest brother, but that still left a great deal of room for trouble. Perhaps she could convince him that it would be in his own best interest to be patient and let her do the negotiating. Because this wasn't only about him and Amelia-Rose. If this didn't succeed, he would blame her, when she'd only just managed a civil conversation or two with him.

She did have one small victory to celebrate this morning. Coll had called her his *màthair*. That was two of them, now. Just Aden left to go.

Francesca took a deep breath. She might only be a Mac-Taggert by marriage, but by God she would do everything in her power to see this succeed. The rest would be up to Niall. And to Amelia-Rose, who'd shown more spirit than she'd expected. At least if this was a disaster in the making, she could hope they would all find that out sooner rather than later.

Niall paced the foyer and pretended to ignore Smythe crammed into the corner by the door. The butler could pretend fright if he wished, but they both knew that the servant had nothing to fear. It had passed ten o'clock seven minutes ago, he'd changed his coat for one with both sleeves still attached, and the Baxters were nowhere in sight. If they'd decided not to argue over agreements and signatures and instead fled to the country with Amelia-Rose, his plans needed a twist. The idea that he waited there while his lass vanished made his jaw clench and his fingers flex. He needed to know if she was well. He needed to know if he should be throwing a saddle onto Kelpie and riding after them.

Wheels crunched on the short drive. Niall closed his eyes for a moment. They'd chosen to argue, which suited him just fine. "Go," he said to the butler, gesturing at the door.

"It's bad form if I allow people into this house and you attack them," Smythe returned, emerging from his corner and straightening his jacket.

"It's also bad form if the butler lands out on the drive on his arse."

"Well." Sniffing, Smythe pulled open the door and moved forward.

A day ago he'd told himself that if Amelia-Rose and Coll fell in love and married, he could live with that. The welfare of Aldriss Park and all those who depended on the MacTaggerts had to take priority over his own attachments. That was how he'd been raised.

It had been a lie. Part of him had known that Coll would never fall for her, and even in his nightmares where the viscount had done so, Niall couldn't imagine himself remaining beneath the same roof as the newlyweds. He couldn't imagine watching as they shared a life, shared a bed. The idea that Coll truly would have left her behind in London, though, was almost worse. None of that was going to happen now, thank God, but it didn't mean he had a smooth path ahead of him.

The Baxters mounted the shallow front step. As Mrs. Baxter handed her bonnet to Smythe, Niall stepped forward, his gaze, his attention, on the daughter rather than either of her parents. "A word with ye, Amelia-Rose?"

She didn't look happy. In fact, as she turned to look at him, he was fairly certain she'd been crying. His right fist closed.

"We are here to see Lady Aldriss," Mrs. Baxter stated. "Not you."

Niall waved the fingers of his left hand toward the stairs. With a loud bellow of escaping air the pair of pipes on the landing beside Rory the deer began a tune. It sounded like a Jacobite marching song, but these Sassenach likely didn't know they were being treated to a rebellion. "Say that again?" he said aloud, putting a hand to his ear. "I couldnae hear ye."

"I said we're not here to see you!" Mrs. Baxter repeated, stone-faced as a gargoyle.

Shaking his head, Niall reached out and took Amelia-Rose's hand in his. "Still cannae hear ye. We'll be in the garden."

Her fingers were cold, but he set that aside as he swiftly led the way through the back of the house and out to the garden. He would have preferred somewhere more private, but she was a lass who could recite all the rules of propriety—and he was fairly certain the two of them alone in a room wouldn't be in her rule book.

Once they reached the small, brick-walled garden Amelia-Rose pulled free of his grip and stepped up into the wooden gazebo, seating herself on one of the benches in front of the low railing. "You've been fighting," she stated as he followed her.

"And how do ye reckon that?"

"Your knuckles are bruised."

He flexed his right hand, looking down at it. "I met a man who deserved a walloping. I obliged him."

"Which man?"

"Ex-beau of yers. He treated ye ill."

She reached out to take his hand, then released it again. "Niall, I'm confused."

He lifted an eyebrow. "What are ye confused about? I kissed ye, and I want ye."

She folded her hands in her lap, only the tightness in her fingers giving away that she wasn't entirely calm. "I do recall the kiss. It was very nice."

"That's nae a compliment." It was nearer an insult, in fact. *Nice*. Ha.

"The first night we met, at the theater, you were being pleasant to me so as not to ruin your brother's chances at winning my hand. Is that correct?"

"Aye."

"And coffee the next morning. And the picnic. And going riding. And the recital. You were there on your brother's behalf, whether he knew about it or not."

By now he'd figured out where her questions were

leading. While he didn't particularly want to visit, mainly because he hadn't sorted it all out himself, he did understand why she'd sent their conversation careening in that direction. "Aye," he answered again. "And nae. But I reckon ye knew that already."

"Last night at the Spenfield ball. You didn't request a single dance from me."

"I wanted to. The idea that I could hold ye in my arms and then have to let ye go again . . . It didnae seem a wise thing to do."

Her gaze touched his, and then she looked away. "I would imagine, knowing what I do now, that you forced your brother to escort my parents and me to the ball."

That made him shake his head. "There's nae a man can force Coll to do someaught against his will. He did have a thing or two other than what I expected on his mind, though."

"I can accept that. But you did *convince* him to escort me."

"Ye play well with words, lass. Get to yer point, then."

She took a visible breath, her shoulders rising and falling. "My point is that I can't decide whether you were lying at the beginning and using your brother as an excuse to spend time with me, or if you're lying now that you must have me for yourself when you're really just trying to save Aldriss Park."

"Neither of those is a lie, Amelia-Rose," he said, beginning to wish he'd opted for somewhere more private after all. Shouting seemed to be in the offing. "I stepped in on Coll's behalf. After our very first conversation I knew ye . . . I liked ye. I liked chatting with ye. Coll being stubborn gave me an excuse to spend time with ye."

"And if your brother had been nicer last night? If he'd offered to spend part of the year in London with me and not steal our hypothetical children away? My mother had planned to send an announcement of our engagement to the newspaper this morning."

"I'm nae certain what I would have done," Niall answered, fixing his gaze on the row of red roses surrounding the wooden structure. "It was like I was reading a story in a book, and I didnae like where the plot was headed, but I couldnae stop it. It had already been written, ye ken. I was too late."

She stood. "I see."

"What does that mean? 'I see'?"

"It means in *my* view the story wasn't already written, and instead of being the hero, you waited until the villain left the room and *then* swooped in, and *then* declared yourself. You kiss very well, sir. As if you've had a great deal of practice. If you truly want me, and I'm not just that convenient 'some Englishwoman' your mother said you must wed, then you're going to have to woo me. And not by pretending it's on someone else's behalf."

He started to snap a reply, but by God she was correct. That was exactly what he'd done, whether he'd intended it or not. He's slipped in sideways without ever having to make a declaration until it was perfectly safe to do so. And his mother was inside the house right now, trying to make his claim official, to bind her to him when he'd done nothing to earn her respect, much less her affection.

"Wait here a moment," he stated, and started for the house.

"What? I will n—"

"Just for a minute, lass. Dunnae leave."

Cursing under his breath, he strode back inside, up the hallway, and to the closed door of his mother's office. Without bothering to knock, he shoved it open.

"Stop what ye're about," he ordered.

Mrs. Baxter had her forefinger jammed at a piece of paper on the desk, with his mother making a conciliatory gesture and Mr. Baxter red-faced. "Niall, I'm in the middle of something," Francesca said tightly.

"No," Mrs. Baxter countered, turning in her seat to face him. "You are a disgrace. I will not sign my daughter over to you simply because you saved her from embarrassment last night. That is not—"

"I dunnae want ye to sign anything. There's nae agreement."

Lady Aldriss blinked. "You've changed your mind?"

"Nae. I havenae. But Amelia-Rose has already been forced once into a match she didnae want. I'll nae see her forced into this one just because it saves me the trouble of winning her." He pinned her mother with a glare. "I will *win* her, Mrs. Baxter. Nae agreement, nae piece of paper but a marriage certificate, signed by her and by me and by whichever priest marries us."

"I highly doubt that, Mr. MacTaggert," her mother returned. "Amelia-Rose is a troublesome girl, but she will not be swayed by your good looks or absurdly quaint accent. She knows her duty to this family."

"I reckon we'll find that out." He wanted to add that her parents had been the ones signing her over in exchange for the loftiest title they could find, but they would eventually become his in-laws. A healthy dislike would be better than outright hatred.

With a last glance and nod at his mother, Niall left the room. Time to begin again. And this time, he'd be wooing the lass for himself.

Chapter Ten

Amelia-Rose watched Niall stomp off back inside Oswell House. *Fine.* The MacTaggerts stomped off a great deal.

No, that wasn't fair. Niall had rescued her last night. His swift appearance had been the only thing that saved her from complete scandal and ruin. And however underhanded his so-called courtship had been, that kiss last night had been more than a moment of mutual attraction. She thought she'd behaved her worst, unable to make a calm reasoned reply when she was clearly being baited, and yet he'd once again been impressed by her spleen, as he called it.

Aside from that, his kiss had absolutely made her toes curl. Better he leave before she accidentally blurted out that she'd half—more than half—wished he'd been pursuing her for himself.

She looked around the garden at Oswell House. It was pretty and well kept, the gazebo freshly painted, with no half-wilted roses and their dropping petals in sight. Lady Aldriss, Francesca Oswell-MacTaggert, had had a father and a grandfather who despite being viscounts had eagerly invested in trade, in this case the tobacco coming in from the Caribbean and the new United States. In addition Lady Aldriss owned part of at least one shipping company, with her father deciding to be sure his untraditional investments went to his only child rather than to whomever she might marry. Now *that* had been foresight.

"Ye stayed," Niall said, returning from the house.

"My parents are still here; I would have had to walk," she replied, belatedly realizing she'd somewhere days ago stopped watching her words when she chatted with him. It made her feel . . . lighter.

He flashed a grin at her. "I've improved to being less offensive than a stroll in the wrong shoes, then. That's someaught."

Amelia-Rose tilted her head at him. She'd met good-natured people before, but they always seemed somewhat dim. Unwilling to see beyond the pretty little garden with which they'd surrounded themselves. Niall was not by any stretch of her imagination dim. Just the opposite. And yet . . . "How do you make me smile in the face of disaster?"

Stopping in front of her, he looked at her for a good handful of seconds. "I reckon I like to see ye smile."

"That's very nice, then."

"Hold on to that compliment, as I've a favor to ask ye."

"A favor? When everything's been going so splendidly? Oh, by all means, ask away."

Niall narrowed one eye, light green still glinting from behind his long lashes. "I'm nae oblivious to sarcasm, ye ken."

"It's no fun to utilize sarcasm on someone who doesn't understand it. What is your favor?"

A muscle in his jaw twitched. "This is my first time in London. I wonder if ye'd show me about."

That, she hadn't expected. Was he attempting to save her again? To keep her well away from any potential social quagmires? He couldn't save her forever. "I'm in the middle of the social Season, Mr. MacTaggert, and I've just parted from an almost-fiancé. Perhaps you should hire a guide."

"Och," he muttered. "Ye're nae even trying to be pleasant now."

"Well, people have been yelling at me since dawn, and you said you liked my spleen."

"I dunnae dislike yer sharp tongue. I'm only pointing out that I noticed it stinging me." Moving closer, he reached out to take her hand and pull her to her feet. "Ye're a stubborn woman."

No one had ever called her stubborn before, except for her mother, and Victoria had meant it as an insult. Stubborn meant she had a backbone, and a lady wasn't supposed to have one of those. "As I said, in light of last night, I find that your motives have somewhat confused me."

"Ye're nae the only one who's been confused, lass." His gaze lowered to her mouth, and her heart did an odd flipflop. *Kiss me*, she thought to herself, since nothing in the world would induce her to say it aloud. *Just kiss me.*

Niall took a half-step forward, lifting his free hand to brush her cheek with his forefinger. Then, lowering his head, he very lightly touched his mouth to hers. Amelia-Rose shut her eyes, warmth, heat, awareness flooding through her.

The press of his lips didn't deepen, and a short moment later he withdrew again. Annoyed, she opened her eyes to find him gazing down at her, a half smile on that impossible mouth of his. "What?" she demanded.

"Ye're leaning," he murmured, stroking her cheek again. "I knew ye liked me, lass. And my 'nice' kisses."

"I already admitted that you kiss well. Do you wish a fanfare now?"

He laughed. "Take me to a museum tomorrow. Ten o'clock. I'll fetch ye in that barouche ye like so much."

Oh, for heaven's sake, she *was* leaning toward him. Belatedly she straightened. "Niall."

"Say aye, Amelia-Rose."

If she didn't, there was no telling where he might next make an appearance—or worse, that he would simply decide she wasn't worth the trouble. "Yes," she breathed.

"Amelia-Rose," her mother's voice came from the direction of the house, "come away at once. We are leaving!"

"I'll see ye in the morning, lass." Niall stayed where he was in the gazebo, no doubt deciding he'd aggravated her mother enough with the bagpipers earlier.

"Don't be late."

"I dunnae mean to miss my moment again," he returned.

She contemplated that last exchange as she joined her parents and they stalked through the Oswell House main hallway while the butler hurried behind them. Was he admitting that he knew he'd very nearly ruined his own chances? It would be nice if he actually had learned a lesson from this disaster.

On the other hand, why, precisely, had she agreed to go with him tomorrow? He was still that Highlander who didn't like London and had no title, and she was still herself. They remained incompatible. Evidently she forgot all her objections to him when he kissed her, and for those moments it was worth it.

But yesterday she'd nearly fallen into a mire well over her head; she had no wish to do it again. Even as she acknowledged that she should stay well clear of his mouth, though, she had to admit that it would be easier to stop breathing. What had she wound herself into? Already she'd begun making compromises in her head, when firstly he'd never asked her for any, and when secondly the two largest walls between them were the ones neither of them could change. He would never be a viscount, and he would always be a Highlander.

"What did that . . . man say to you?" Victoria demanded as the butler handed her and then Amelia-Rose into their coach.

"That he wants to win me," Amelia-Rose returned, sliding sideways on the seat to make room for her father.

"Ha. He should have kept his mouth shut, then. Lady Aldriss was in the middle of trying to convince us to sign a new agreement to give you to Niall MacTaggert in exchange for a share in her shipping company, until he stormed into the room and declared that we were trying to buy and sell you and he wouldn't permit that to happen again. As if he has a say in anything the Baxters do. Ha!"

"He . . . did?" That was where he'd stomped off to, then. To save her again. Even if an agreement would have rescued her from having to decide for herself what she truly wanted.

"Oh, yes. And then he shouted at me that he meant to win you regardless of what your father and I might want for you. The nerve of that heathen. I can hardly believe he's Lady Aldriss's son."

Goodness. Now she wanted to demand yet another explanation from him. His mother wouldn't have written up an agreement without him knowing about it, so he *had* thought to simply . . . purchase her. But then he'd stopped it. He'd listened to her in the garden, and had taken steps to alter what might have happened.

"You are to have nothing further to do with him, Amelia-Rose. Do you understand?"

"We're certain to meet during the course of the Season, Mother. But you needn't worry; I may attempt to reason with him, but I am still as set against marrying a

Highlander as I was when you bound me to his brother."
There. Not much of a lie at all.

"Don't be impudent."

"I'm just saying it may take a bit of effort for me to convince him that we won't suit, but I will be polite about it because I have no wish to make a second scandal out of this. He did save my reputation last night."

"Y—"

"Now, now, dear," Charles Baxter said. "You know that makes sense. Lady Aldriss is a powerful figure, and if we can dissuade her youngest son from pursuing Amy without making a scene, that benefits all of us."

"Amelia-Rose," her mother stated, glaring at her husband.

He inclined his head. "Amelia-Rose."

Yes, that was her, Amelia-Rose Hyacinth Baxter. Mother hated the nicknames, especially "plain" ones like Amy. Victoria would no doubt detest a Scottish nickname like *adae* even more, but she didn't know about that one. At the end, that name might be all she had by which to remember Niall.

She supposed she was willing to be wooed to a point, because he was extremely good-looking and clever and irreverent, and she wanted more kisses and more of the way she felt lighter inside when he was about. Truth be told, just last night she'd had a rather heated dream about him that had involved a bed and nudity and more kissing, though the parts she wasn't certain about had unfortunately been rather nebulous. But unless he could miraculously convince her that the Scottish Highlands was superior to London, and convince her parents that being a mister was superior to being a lord something, it couldn't go any farther than that.

"There was Lord Oglivy," her mother mused. "Of course he's only a baron."

"And he's fifty-seven years old," Amelia-Rose added. "For goodness' sake."

"Hush. You could be engaged to a viscount with a future as an earl right now. But you didn't like the details."

"The details? I don't want to live as a brood mare in a stable while he . . . fornicates with whomever he pleases! And takes any children I might have away from me!" she protested.

"Language, Amelia-Rose! For heaven's sake." Her mother fanned herself. "You would have been a countess, though. There's a difference between a brood mare and a countess."

"Mother!"

"I think we've burned that bridge," her father put in. "She won't be our Lady Glendarril, sadly enough."

"The Marquis of Hanstag's wife is very sickly," Victoria went on, half to herself. "That would entail waiting a year for him to put on and cast off his black, though."

Oh, this was getting worse and worse. "Now we're hoping people die?"

"Not hoping, dear. But if she does, we should be ready. Just think. A marchioness."

"I don't wish to discuss this right now." She didn't want to discuss it ever, but that simply wasn't realistic. It did make her wish she'd gone off walking with Niall, though; his conversation kept her on her toes, but it didn't make her feel oily and ill.

"No, I need some time to consider our options anyway. You will continue attending all your events, and I will find you someone appropriate. And this time you will cooperate."

No one said *or else*, but Amelia-Rose heard it. She'd heard it before. She would end up in a nunnery, or out on the streets, or reduced to being some elderly woman's companion so her mother could pretend she didn't have a daughter at all. If only Niall MacTaggert had been an English baron with a small house in Devon or Sussex and just a short drive from London.

The idea of escaping, no matter the consequences, had once been an occasionally visited daydream. With no money of her own, and no references on which she could depend to help her find employment, it had never progressed beyond that. But she kept hold of it anyway.

As they arrived at Baxter House, Hughes the butler met her at the door with a pile of calling cards on his salver. "For you, Miss Amelia-Rose," he intoned.

She took them. "Good heavens. There must be a dozen here. Who are they?"

"Men, miss," the butler returned. "Most of them asking if you were free for luncheon, or if they could call later to take you walking or riding."

Niall had truly saved her. Not only was she not ruined, but as a newly unattached lady with at least one handsome man shadowing her, she'd become . . . desirable, of all things. She reached out her hand for the stack. "Thank you, H—"

"I see word has already gotten out that you and that barbarian aren't to be wed after all," Victoria said, taking the cards from the salver and sifting through them. "Your usual followers, unfortunately. So common. Ah well, answer two or three of them; a woman in a man's company is always more desirable to other men than a woman alone." She handed them back, except for one. "I shall keep this one. I need to inquire after Lord Phillip's mother."

More likely she needed to inquire of Lord Phillip's mother whether Lord Phillip's older brother the Marquis of Durst was still pursuing that heiress in Yorkshire. If Victoria Baxter deserved credit for anything, it was the way she knew who was seeing whom. It was uncanny, really.

Taking the remainder of the cards, she went upstairs to dress for the luncheon she'd already agreed to attend with Helen Turner and her brother Harry. And then she meant to spend her evening reading one of her father's almanacs about Scottish planting cycles and sheep shearing and weather, and otherwise reminding herself that she had other requirements in a marriage than not being left behind, and that she didn't want Scotland. She would not be thinking about kisses and Niall MacTaggert. Not at all— except perhaps in her dreams.

"Ye're truly after Amelia-Rose Baxter, then," Aden said as he strolled into the breakfast room.

"Aye. If ye're here to tell me we willnae suit, or she willnae take me if she wouldnae take a viscount, then shut yer gobber now. I already had that chat with the countess."

"I've nae a word to say about it. Ye punched Coll hard enough to convince me." His middle brother selected a stack of ham and some eggs, then seated himself at the foot of the table. "I'm here for food, and to tell ye I saw Lady Aldriss leaving her room just as I passed Rory on the stairs. Our stag's wearing earbobs now, did ye notice? I reckon that was Eloise."

"Shite." Niall shoveled in the last few mouthfuls of breakfast, pushing away from the table as he chewed. "Ye bastard," he managed around his ham and gravy, "ye might have warned me about the countess earlier."

"Aye, I might have."

He nearly crashed headlong into his mother as he fled the breakfast room. "Niall," she exclaimed, putting a hand against his chest to steady herself.

"My lady. If ye'll excuse m—"

"I need a word with you, son."

"I'll give ye one later. I've a lass to meet this morning."

She kept her hand over his heart. "Niall, if you want to talk, I'm here."

"I reckon I'm accustomed to keeping my own counsel, my lady. And I've my brothers."

"I'm nae helpful," Aden called from inside the breakfast room. "And ye and Coll arenae speaking, as I recall."

Her mouth curved up at the edges. "I know you may not wish to acknowledge it, but I *am* a female. You've had a scarcity of females in your life, I imagine."

Somewhere behind him he heard Aden snort. "I've had plenty of females in my damned life, woman. I'm nae a bloody monk."

"I mean womanly advice, Niall. Not womanly company."

Niall retreated a step. "I dunnae want to be talking about this with ye, for Christ's sake!"

"Why not? I have years of wisdom, both as a married woman and as a single young lady."

"I am nae having this conversation with my mother."

Her grin broadened. "There it is," she murmured, and went up on her toes to kiss him on the cheek. "I *am* your mother. And you may tell me anything, anytime."

"Bonny. Now go away! Aden's in there, and I reckon he could use some womanly advice." He gestured behind him.

"Bastard! I'm going out the window."

She patted him on the shoulder, then moved sideways so he could get around her. That had been . . . odd, and oddly comforting. Like a family, almost. Like a dim memory of something he'd thought long forgotten.

Shaking himself, he went outside to meet the barouche. The last time he'd had Eloise and her Matthew beside him, but sitting in there all alone while some other fellow drove him through Mayfair would likely look as ridiculous as it felt. "Shift over," he told the driver, and climbed up on the narrow seat beside him.

The driver scooted to the far side of the seat. "Do you wish to drive, sir?" he asked.

"What's yer name, lad?"

"I . . . Robert, sir."

"Robert. I dunnae know my way yet, but I reckon I'll figure London out faster from up here. So ye drive, and I'll watch. To Baxter House."

"Um. Yes, sir."

They set off, and while he did know the way to Baxter House by now, this gave him a few minutes to think. Or rather, to contemplate what he meant to do if the Baxters had actually fled London now that they knew his intentions. He wanted Amelia-Rose—he'd wanted her practically since he'd first set eyes on her. The only difference now was that he didn't have to try convincing himself that she was meant for someone else, or that he would find someone whose company he enjoyed more than hers.

The idea of what he might have missed if he'd been as stubborn as Coll shook him. No, he hadn't set out to find a lass who would twist him up inside and have him near to writing poetry, but then he'd thought to allow this trip to London to upend his life as little as possible. A hollow-headed flower he could show his mother and then leave again, scarcely giving either of them another thought. Now this was between himself and Amelia-Rose. It was a battle he looked forward to, and one he knew he would win. He couldn't imagine not having her in his life.

"I had a look at the mounts you and Mr. Aden and Lord Glendarril brought down from Scotland," the driver said conversationally. "They're fine animals."

"Aye, they are. Nae accustomed to busy streets, though; my Kelpie nearly tossed me over his head when a rag-and-bone man charged out into the street with his wares. A' course I nearly lopped the man's head off, myself, so I suppose Kelpie and I both have someaught more accustomizing to do."

The driver swallowed, eyeing him sideways. "You nearly lopped his head off?" he squeaked.

"Well, he surprised me. For all I knew, the lobsterbacks were attacking."

"I . . . The lobsterbacks?"

"Redcoats, man. Do ye nae speak English?"

"I . . . I thought I did."

Facing forward again, Niall grinned. "Dunnae trouble yerself. I've been told I have an accent."

"Oh. I, uh, hadn't noticed, sir."

Apparently it wasn't polite to acknowledge that a man had a brogue, but so many English rules made no sense to him that he just tossed this one in with the rest. Aye, he'd been raised thinking the English, and Englishwomen in particular, were all inferior to Highlanders, and with one exception he'd seen little reason to alter that opinion. Well, two exceptions, perhaps—Eloise had a level head on her shoulders.

The first exception had warned him not to be late, and he pulled out his battered old pocket watch to check the time. Unless someone had overturned a cart ahead they would be early; he'd have to have Robert stop the carriage around the corner. He meant to be exactly on time, because she'd been worn out yesterday, looking for an excuse to surrender to her parents' demands, and he wasn't about to give her one.

No overturned carts lay in wait, but a pair of coach drivers were blocking the road to argue over which of them had the right-of-way. Niall watched the nonsense, but as it dragged on he put away his pocket watch. Just as he stood to go see to ending the argument himself, one of the coaches trundled off, and the heavy horse traffic began moving again. Such a crush of people; it was something of a miracle that they weren't all at one another's throats all the time.

Robert pulled the bay team to a halt outside Baxter House, and Niall hopped to the ground. "Keep 'em standing," he ordered, and made his way to the front door.

It pulled open as he reached it. "Mr. MacTaggert," the Baxters' butler intoned, moving sideways so Niall could step forward.

"Hughes. I'm here for Amelia-Rose."

"I shall inquire if she is available."

The butler vanished toward the back of the house. They'd allowed him inside, at least, and they hadn't set a guard to watch him, Niall reflected, gazing about the foyer. Some cards on the hall table caught his attention, and with a quick glance around him, he picked them up.

Six of them, all from men, prettily embossed, most with little notes handwritten on the back. One was planning on calling again in the afternoon and hoped to find Amelia-Rose amenable to a conversation. Another inquired as to whether she cared to go riding in Hyde Park in the morning. A third one presented himself as available to help mend a tender heart broken by a heartless rogue.

The rogue would be Coll, he supposed, and these were the vultures swooping in to claim their prize while it was still fresh. Suitors, the bloody mongrels. With another glance over his shoulder, he pocketed the lot of them. If the lads should think her uninterested because she didn't respond, well, he had no problem in the world with that.

"You're prompt," Amelia-Rose said from a doorway halfway down the hall.

"I said I'd be."

She'd worn a pretty green-and-violet sprigged muslin walking dress, partly covered by a pelisse of darker green.

With her hair swept up into a plump, overflowing clip at the back of her head and her blue eyes sparkling, she looked both fresh and supremely desirable.

"Well?" she asked, stopping a few feet from him.

He finished his perusal and met her eyes again. "Ye're made for fresh air and a warm breeze," he said, smiling. "Or should I sweep a bow and just tell ye that ye look lovely?"

Her fair cheeks colored a little. "I still half thought you'd arrive with an excuse for your brother's behavior on your lips."

Niall cocked his head. "I'm nae here on anyone else's behalf. Do ye want to play that game?"

"I just want to be certain of your motives."

"I told ye my motives, *adae*. I didnae lie to ye. Nae intentionally, anyway. I reckoned I was doing my duty. I'm glad being a friend to ye on Coll's behalf isnae my duty any longer, and I can simply declare that I like and admire ye."

She sighed. "You look rather magnificent," she commented, coming forward and setting a green straw bonnet over her honey-colored hair.

He glanced down at himself. Scuffed Hessian boots, his work kilt, a plain white shirt, plainer cravat, and a gray waistcoat and jacket. "I'm being myself. In honor of propriety I'm wearing the jacket and waistcoat, but otherwise this is how ye'd find me on any given day."

"Boots and not ghillie brogues?" she asked, gesturing at his boots.

"Ghillie brogues arenae very practical in the mud. I prefer walking in these." Stepping backward, he made room for her and the butler to move past him to the door. "Have ye decided where we're going?"

"Yes."

He pursed his lips. "I reckon ye can keep it to yerself for a time, but eventually ye'll have to tell Robert, our driver."

Hughes handed over an off-white shawl to her, then pulled open the front door. "Will you be home for luncheon, Miss Baxter? I believe you have several . . ." He trailed off, looking toward the empty hall table, then bending to look beneath the furniture.

"I don't know," she returned, and sent a glance over her shoulder at Niall. "Will I be home for luncheon?"

"I'd like to dine with ye," he said, starting forward and then coming to a stop again as a tall, dark-haired figure pushed past him into the hallway. The companion. Jane something. *Bloody hell.*

Amelia-Rose caught his annoyed expression before he smoothed it out again, and she stifled a grin. He may have decided to toss propriety out the nearest window, but she hadn't. Even if for a bare moment the idea of going somewhere alone with him had been frighteningly tantalizing. "Is something amiss?" she asked, lifting an eyebrow.

"Nae. I forgot we're back to being a trio again, is all."

"We were never not a trio. Your sister simply served as an adequate chaperone previously. Unless you've brought Eloise with you?"

"My brothers stole her today." After a second he lifted his chin again and followed them out the door. "Go whisper where we're going to Robert, if ye're nae of a mind to tell me."

Instead she stepped up into the barouche and settled herself on the rear, forward-facing seat. Jane would have sat beside her, but Amelia-Rose gestured her second cousin to the opposite seat. With an ill-concealed sigh, Jane sat facing the rear of the carriage. "You might as well know," she said aloud as Niall climbed in and sat beside her without even asking her permission. "I thought we should tour the Tower of London. They have a very interesting display of armor and artillery."

"Yer aim's nae to get me thrown into a cell there, is it?" he asked, giving the direction to his driver.

"Oh, only very notorious villains are detained in the Tower," she returned, giving in to the urge to grin. He made it very difficult to remain annoyed, blast it all. However little time they might have together, she might as well enjoy it. "I'm not at all certain you're of their caliber."

Niall snorted. "I once tied a thimble to a rat's tail and set him loose in the wall of Coll's bedchamber. The clicking and knocking kept him awake for a week. He had to chop a hole in his wall to get it out."

"Did he know who did it?"

"Nae. He still doesnae. So now ye know someaught about me that could get me walloped."

"I shall use the information judiciously," she returned, her smile deepening. Good heavens, he was charming, but she already knew that. He knew it as well, no doubt. If not for all the things wrong between them, all of them attached to him like a thimble to a rat's tail, having this man pay her attention, having him declare that he wanted her, would have already turned her head. That might well be the case, anyway.

"I reckon ye will." Niall grinned, shifting a little so that the edge of his slightly faded red, black, and green plaid brushed against her green muslin.

That was who they were: one of them rough about the edges and definitely, undeniably, and proudly not English, and the other carefully and expensively proper—and very English. He wasn't even trying to fit in.

"Have you heard from your father?" she asked. "You said he was in poor health."

"I havenae. Between ye and me, I think he didnae want to face my mother again."

This could be interesting. "They've been estranged for a long while, I understand."

"Seventeen years. She didnae like the Highlands, and he wouldnae leave them."

It abruptly occurred to Amelia-Rose that she needed to have a conversation with Lady Aldriss. If anyone could understand why she felt drawn to Niall but not to his life, it would be the countess. Of course the one obvious solution would be to wish Niall MacTaggert a good day and refuse to see him again, but that idea . . . The idea of not seeing him, of not conversing with him or wondering if he might brush his fingers against hers or kiss her again, tore at her inside.

"That's sad, don't you think?" she said aloud when he continued looking at her.

"Aye." He narrowed one eye. "Are we finished with ye nae trusting what I say to ye, then?"

"I'm still curious what might have happened if I had accepted Coll's horrible proposal. Up until two days ago I genuinely thought you were serving as his surrogate."

"I dunnae ken when I stopped, exactly. He was a convenient excuse for me going to see ye. If ye'd agreed to marry him . . ." He took a breath, looking away from her. "I adore my brother. I'd lay down my life for him. But if I'd seen ye in his arms . . . I've a cousin who lives north of us, up in Skelpick. I reckon I'd have moved up there."

Her heart stuttered a little. "We've known each other for a very short time, Niall."

He sat sideways, compelling her to meet his gaze. "Is it just me, then? I dunnae think it is, but ye tell me, Amelia-Rose. When I first set eyes on ye I couldnae breathe for a good five minutes. And when I sat beside ye, when I jested with ye, ye gave right back to me. I reckon ye're smarter than the lot of us lads put together, and that sometimes ye get tired of hearing all the nonsense we spew. Ye bite yer tongue, but then ye cannae any longer, and ye let fly. Tell me I'm wrong."

Goodness. He'd seen all that? Mostly she just felt like she was staving off chaos, but she did try, for heaven's sake. All the time. "I don't know if I'm smarter than you are, but you're not wrong about the rest of it. Thank you for pointing out my shortcomings."

"They arenae . . . Bloody Saint Andrew," he muttered. "What am I to ye, then?" Niall pursued. "Just a loud Scotsman keeping ye in the good graces of a louder Scotsman and now ye dunnae require my services any longer? I'll nae deny that I had an idea like Coll's, to find some lass just to satisfy that damned agreement between my parents and go home to nae think of her again. But I didnae expect to meet *ye*."

"Of course you're not some Scotsman. I do like you." "Like" didn't seem a strong-enough word, but it was the only one she was willing to give him at the moment. "I'm simply certain we're incompatible."

"Ye like me," he repeated. "The way ye like a dog?"

Amelia-Rose flipped a hand, hitting him in the chest. *Goodness.* That might well have bruised her. "Stop it. I'm being cautious. My parents would be livid. I told them I'm simply being polite to you to avoid further antagonizing Lady Aldriss."

From his expression he didn't like that, but at least he nodded. "That makes sense. I'm feeling lucky that ye and Coll dunnae suit, and ye're wondering why one brother is after ye when the other one isnae." He sank back against the seat again, the fingers of his left hand brushing across hers. "I'll convince ye."

A slow thrill went up her spine. "I shan't make it easy on you. I have some serious concerns about your . . . heritage."

"My kilt-wearing, bagpipe-loving heritage?" he queried, lifting an eyebrow.

"Yes. Precisely that."

"Well, Amelia-Rose," he said, deepening his brogue as he caressed her name, "I dunnae mind convincing ye."

"You shouldn't be sitting so close together," Jane pointed out from the opposite seat.

They were sitting rather close, his shoulder touching hers as they bumped over the road. Amelia-Rose glanced up at his profile as he eyed her companion. Part of her wanted to be convinced, very badly. Part of her wanted him in her life for the rest of her life. It was the logical half that kept crying foul, but even that half wanted kisses—and more.

"We've arrived, Mr. MacTaggert," the driver said, sending them beneath the old portcullis and onto the grounds of the Tower.

Half a dozen other carriages were there already, but hopefully those guests would be viewing the jewels or the menagerie. She wanted this to be just them—and Jane, of course. Yes, Jane must always be present to keep her from scandal.

"Do you have three shillings?" she asked belatedly as he stood and stepped down from the barouche. She'd brought several coins just in case, but it would be much more proper if he paid their way.

Niall held out his hand, and she took it, feeling the calluses on his palm and his fingertips as she descended to the cobblestones. He hadn't been joking when he said he helped shear sheep and all those other things.

"Aye." He curled his fingers around hers. "Ye've brought me to the center of Sassenach power, lass. What do ye wish to show me?"

"Just some history. I'm not trying to convince you that we English never harmed you Scots. I thought you'd enjoy seeing armor and weapons, you being a warrior of clan Ross and all."

To her relief, he grinned as he released her fingers, instead offering his forearm. "That I am. Ye should see my massive claymore."

"Oh, good heavens," Jane muttered from behind them.

"What now?" he asked. "A claymore's a fine weapon, long and heavy, and a wonder when ye ken how to use it correctly."

Abruptly Amelia-Rose didn't think they were talking about swords. "And you know how to use yours correctly?"

"Aye. I'm something of an artist, ye might say. I'd like to show it to ye, lass."

She felt her cheeks heat, and behind them Jane sounded like she might be suffering a seizure. "Stop it," she murmured.

"Aye. I dunnae wish to embarrass ye. But I am thinking about ye in a rather carnal way."

No one—*no one*—had ever said that to her before. In a way, it made her feel . . . powerful. And rather decadent. Because she wanted him, as well. Wanted to feel his rough hands on her skin, his breath warm against her, his—

"Three of you?" the yeoman in the doorway stated. "That'll be three shillings. No touching the armor or the carvings or especially the weapons, as we've just gotten them polished up again. No pretending to battle to scare the ladies, and do not attempt to mount the horses. They are wood, you will get splinters, and I will not help you remove them."

Wordlessly Niall retrieved three shillings from his coat pocket and handed them into the yeoman's palm. The man stood aside, and they entered the stone tower. Immediately the temperature lowered, and with her free hand Amelia-Rose pulled her shawl more closely around her shoulders.

Their footsteps echoed against the stone floor, hers and Jane's a soft tap, and Niall's a harder and heavier drumbeat. In the center of the room, large stands held spears and pikes and halberds, jutting up toward the ceiling, a sea of deadly sharp points. On the right wall, more halberds, together with maces and one- and two-handed swords, axes, and glinting knives, were arranged in circles with the pointy ends facing the center.

"Which one most resembles your claymore?" she asked, daring him to begin speaking in double entendres again.

He stepped closer, moving from the huge, double-bladed weapons of the era of William the Conqueror, toward the narrower, longer swords of Henry VIII. "This one, I reckon," he said, indicating a long, two-edged blade with a cross-shaped hilt, the arms angled slightly forward and a single red gem in the pommel. "Though the gem is an emerald."

"You use that?" Jane asked, sounding both skeptical and slightly impressed.

"In the Highland games, aye. I've nae slain a man with it, if that's yer meaning. Mine came from my great-great-granddad, and last tasted English blood during the Battle of Killiecrankie. Though Aden did nick my arm with it back when we were bairns." Shoving up a sleeve of his coat and the shirt beneath, he revealed a long, straight scar going from his wrist up halfway to his elbow.

Amelia-Rose put her finger on it, feeling the slight rise of white scar tissue. "That must have been a deep cut," she mused, running down the length of it, feeling the play of long, sinewy muscles beneath.

"It did bleed a bit," he admitted, his voice low and rumbling. "The village seamstress sewed it up for me, after Aden and Coll gave me two fingers of whisky."

"How old were you?"

"Eight or nine, I reckon. I cast the whisky up again all over Aden, so we reckoned we were even. Didnae tell Da for a fortnight, and when he did find out he took a look at it, declared that we'd done as we should, then cuffed Aden and told us nae to go about stabbing each other again."

"It sounds like you had a very dangerous childhood, Niall." She looked up, to find him gazing down at her while she still stupidly stroked his bare arm.

"We were wild, aye. Nae a lass about to tell us to mind our manners or nae pummel each other. I reckon our da wanted us to be like the MacTaggerts of old, the ones who defied a king and helped rebel against him, who stood bloody and proud on the battlefield and bellowed their defiance to the sky." He put his hand over hers. "I'm nae quite that uncivilized, but I'm nae some dandy with high shirt points and a snuff box, either."

Would he compromise? Is that what he was trying to tell her? That he might be amenable to spending part of the year in London? Of course she could merely be trying to interpret everything he said as a way they could manage this. Generally she recognized her flights of fancy for exactly what they were—wishes too lofty to be called daydreams. She required a bit of proof before she tossed her heart completely into this battle. But just hearing him say that, vague or not, gave her something she hadn't felt in a while: hope.

Chapter Eleven

I thought Henry the Eighth was rounder than this," Niall commented as they strolled down the line of wooden horses mounted by figures who sat adorned in the armor of the various the kings of England. Most of them were wee lads barely the height of Amelia-Rose. The armor was pretty, improving from the chain mail of William the Conqueror to the steel plate mail of Henry to the obviously ceremonial armor of George III. Henry's was the most lavish, the edges done in gold and with a hell of a generous codpiece jutting out over the saddle of his faux horse.

"Henry was a fine king, and very well respected," she said, her tone absent.

Niall sent her a sideways look. "Ask half his wives about that, lass. Do ye reckon everyone deserves a compliment?"

Her gaze sharpened, as if she'd returned from wherever her mind had been. "No. He got fatter as he got older, I believe," Amelia-Rose returned.

"I can see why he needed all those women, at least," he noted.

Her gaze flicked from the codpiece to the front of Niall's kilt and back to the horse again. "Fanciful thinking, I imagine."

He stifled a grin. She followed the rules of propriety as best as she could, but his lass did have a wicked streak. He looked forward to exploring that. Very thoroughly.

Jane Bansil had seated herself on a bench by the door, and from the tilt of her head and the soft snoring sound emanating from her, she was fast asleep. "We seem to be the only people here," he said, keeping his voice pitched low to minimize the echo.

"I think most people come to see the animals in the Menagerie, or the jewels," Amelia-Rose returned. "We could go see those as well, if you'd like. It will cost you another three shillings, though."

"Nae. I reckon I like it right here." With another glance toward the door he put his hands around her waist and lifted her to sit on the fourth step of a wooden stepladder some worker had left beside the row of kings. "Are ye going to warn me about scandal now?" he murmured, gripping the ladder on either side of her head and leaning toward her. "It's just ye and me, *adae*, and the snoring lass in the corner."

She looked past his shoulder at where Jane sat. "She's a light sleeper," Amelia-Rose whispered, reaching out to run her palm along his cheek. "And someone could come along at any moment."

"Aye. I reckon so." He studied her face, the brief wrinkle between her brows as she frowned at him. "What now?"

"Do ye like to read?"

That made him blink. "Aye, I like to read. Are we discussing literature now?"

"Literature's not scandalous, at least."

"That depends on the literature, I reckon." Niall grinned. "I cannae pretend to know what it's been like to live yer life, lass, but I imagine it's been frustrating."

Her fingers soft on his cheek sent a shiver up his spine. "Why do you think that?"

"I see ye as a lass who's generally smarter than anyone else, man or woman, in the room. It's nae polite to correct a gentleman when he says someaught foolish, so ye just have to listen to the nonsense and smile. When ye cannae stand it any longer and ye speak yer mind, they call ye forward, or mannerless. Am I wrong?"

"No, you're not wrong."

God, he could drown in those blue eyes of hers. "I have to tell ye someaught."

Those eyes narrowed a little. "What do you have to tell me?"

"I've been calling ye *adae*. But it doesnae mean 'rose.'"

"It doesn't? I warned you that if you were calling me a turnip or something, I would not be happy, Niall."

Putting his fingers over her mouth before she could wake damned Jane, he shook his head. "It doesnae mean 'turnip.' It means 'trouble.'"

"Trouble?" she repeated in a muffled tone, not looking very flattered.

"Aye. From the first time I set eyes on ye I knew ye'd be my downfall." He waited a heartbeat. Since she didn't seem inclined to make another outburst, he removed his hand.

"Oh." She sighed. "That's rather nice. And I suppose 'trouble' is better than 'prickly,'" she added with a slight smile. Abruptly she scowled again. "I told your brother Aden that you called me *adae*, and what you said it meant. He didn't bother to correct me. He *did* step on my toe. So does everyone in your family thi—"

He closed the last few inches between them to kiss her.

Her mouth was so soft it made him ache. How she could conjure such sharp wits and still have a mouth like this seemed a marvel. Niall teased her lips open, sending his tongue dancing with hers.

Sliding her hands up his chest and around his shoulders,

she leaned into him. Amelia-Rose moaned softly, and his cock reacted. When they kissed it didn't matter that she was a Sassenach and he was a Scot. It didn't matter that she loved dancing and soirees and picnics in London and he preferred hunting and fishing in the Highlands.

Niall moved in between her legs, deepening the kiss. A woman he'd known for just days, one he'd resented on principle before he'd ever set eyes on her, one who was nothing like the bride he'd thought to find and abandon, and now she was his first thought in the morning, his last thought at night, and the subject of all his dreams.

With another moan she twisted her fingers into his hair and pulled backward. He lifted his head a little, still nibbling at the corners of her mouth. "Ye've a sweet mouth on ye, lass," he murmured.

"And you've a very naughty one," she whispered back breathlessly. "We must stop."

"Why must we?"

"Because I will not be ravished beside King George the Second's armor, for one, and because someone will come in and see us, for two."

"So ye've nae objection to me ravishing ye in a more private setting?" he returned, shifting a hand to cup her warm cheek and kissing her again.

"I have very many objections," she breathed, leaning her forehead against his. "And I am not some wilting flower who swoons into your embrace."

He chuckled. "Och, lass, that ye arenae. Ye're sharp and prickly."

She lifted her head away from his to frown. "That is not a compliment. You're not so smooth and gentlemanly, anyway."

"Seems to me we make a good pair, *adae*."

Her scowl flipped into a grin. "'Trouble' again, eh? How do you say 'scoundrel' in Gaelic?"

"Ye'll use it against me, willnae?"

Her smile deepened. "Aye. Very likely."

"*Skellum.*"

She repeated it. "*Skellum.* It doesn't actually mean 'handsome' or 'virile,' does it?"

He snorted, remembering just in time to stay quiet. "Nae. Though I wish I'd thought of that, now."

That made her laugh, and then Niall had to kiss her once more. Stopping his breath would have been easier than resisting that mouth of hers. He wondered if she knew just how charming she was when she wasn't trying to be that other lass—the one she'd decided made her more acceptable and more marriageable. Here with him, now, she shone like the sun. Warm, affectionate, and witty, Amelia-Rose made all of London less inhospitable to a *skellum* like himself.

Across the room Jane Bansil let out a snort that would've made a boar jealous, and sat upright. In the same second Niall took Amelia-Rose around the waist and lowered her to the ground again. "When are ye free next, lass?" he asked, gripping her fingers in his.

"This is the Season. It's very busy, you know."

"Aye. When can I next see ye?"

"You are serious, aren't you?" she asked, studying his face. "You're not planning on stealing my virtue and then dancing away with another woman?"

"I'm serious as a Highlands winter, Amelia-Rose." He brushed a lock of blond hair from her forehead. "I'm nae asking ye to run off to Gretna Green with me in the moonlight, lass, if the idea of something permanent still troubles ye. I'm suggesting that ye and I spend more time together. I reckon it's worth it. Do ye?"

"Step away from her at once!" Jane demanded, launching herself forward and swatting at Niall with her reticule.

"What are ye, woman, a damned banshee?" he protested, protecting his head with one elbow and moving out of her path.

"You are a disreputable Highlander, sir. I will not have you ruining Amelia-Rose!" She hit at him again.

"Jane, stop pummeling him," Amelia-Rose ordered, though she sounded more amused than worried. "We were just chatting."

"You cannot chat with your mouths fastened together. I am not a fool, cousin."

The companion had seen that, then. "So ye're a witness," he said, catching her rather formidable arm and drawing her closer. "What do ye mean to say about it, then?"

"Mrs. Baxter will want to know what—"

"I reckon ye fell asleep, and I took advantage to sweep in and kiss a lass. I'm a bit of a scoundrel. Dunnae make it Amelia-Rose's fault," he interrupted.

"But—"

"Which will cause the worse uproar?" he continued, noting that his lass no longer looked as amused. "Me surprising a lass with a kiss, or ye telling her mama that ye allowed it to happen?"

He'd never really known his own mother, but he was abruptly grateful that Francesca hadn't yet proved to be as intrusive as Mrs. Baxter. Aye, she'd meddled, dragged them down to London and ordered them to find brides. She hadn't made them feel worthless or attempted to change who they'd become in her absence. Not yet, anyway.

"Jane, please," Amelia-Rose seconded, taking charge of the tall tree's arm. "You know she'll have an apoplexy, and we'll all have to listen to it. And then she'll likely lock me in my room for a week and marry me off to that horrid Lord Oglivy. And he smells like cats."

Whoever this Lord Oglivy was, Niall meant to find him

and suggest he go on holiday to the country for the next few weeks. He looked at Jane Bansil expectantly. He could threaten her, but that didn't sit well with him. She was simply doing her job, even if it was one he didn't much appreciate.

"Oh, very well." Amelia-Rose's companion sagged a little, pulling her reticule back up against her flat chest. "Don't let me catch you again, for goodness' sake."

"That is a promise," Amelia-Rose said, leaning up on her toes to kiss the woman on the cheek.

Jane eyed him as she straightened her gown. "And you, Mr. MacTaggert?"

"I'm nae going to kiss ye," he informed her.

"I should hope not."

"Now," his lass went on, moving around her companion to secure his forearm beneath her hand, "let's go see the jewels, shall we?"

"Aye. Jewels."

Actually he didn't give a damn where they went next, as long as they did it together. If he'd caught some fever, if his new obsession with Amelia-Rose was a signal that he'd been hit on the head one too many times, he needed to know. If by some chance he'd found the one lass in all of Britain that matched him, he by God needed to know that, too.

She leaned against his side. "Yes," she breathed.

"Yes to what?" he whispered back, very aware of the menace stalking directly behind them.

"I reckon it's worth the risk to spend more time with you, Niall. *Skellum*."

Considering that he was presently escorting a lass and her chaperone to a jewel exhibit and then meant to take them driving in an open carriage through Hyde Park before carefully depositing them back at her parents' house, it was entirely possibly that this was the farthest from a scoundrel he'd ever been. Perhaps the London smoke and soot had muddled his brain after all. The only other explanation was one he wasn't quite willing to visit yet. Not when she'd barely begun to spread her wings. This lass could too easily fly from his grasp.

Clearly he needed to find a pair of wings for himself. Something that would make him acceptable to both her and her parents. And at the moment he hadn't the faintest clue what that thing might be. All he knew was that he meant to try.

"We just ride about in circles, then?" Niall asked, twisting his head to watch Lord Alvin and a dozen of his very small dogs drive by in a modified phaeton. The marquis had decided that the dogs needed their own perches, so he'd attached what looked like a wooden, cushion-bottomed open casket at the front and another at the rear of the driver's seat, with all the dogs popping up and down and yammering from within.

"Yes. And we stop and chat with acquaintances," Amelia-Rose supplied. "It's more crowded today because Parliament isn't in session."

He sat back beside her again. "I did just see that, aye? A portly man and coffin dogs?"

Pursing her lips to keep from laughing, she nodded. "Lord Alvin. He's somewhat . . . eccentric."

"We have one of those eccentrics up near Aldriss," he returned, the Mercer twins and their large bonnets now catching his attention. No doubt he felt like he'd stepped—or ridden, rather—into some mad realm of oddities. London was magnificent, that way.

"Do you?" she prompted. "A man with too many dogs?"

"Old Sean Ross. He keeps a wee cottage overlooking

Loch an Daimh. It was a Jacobite meetinghouse in the old days, with a tunnel leading from the cellar out to the nearest hillside and another down to the water's edge for a quick getaway if need be. Old Sean, though, keeps the tunnels full of—"

"Let me guess," Jane interrupted from the opposite seat. "Whisky?"

The fact that she knew a secret seemed to have emboldened Jane. This was actually the first time Amelia-Rose could recall that her second cousin had ever spoken directly to—or walloped—a man. *Hm.*

"Nae whisky," Niall countered, without heat. "Cats."

"Cats?" Amelia-Rose blurted.

"Aye. Every day he goes out trapping for mice and rats and voles, spends the rest of the day fishing and going by the neighbors asking for their vermin, and in the evening he opens the trapdoor to the cellar and tosses his catch down below. Then there's an awful yowling for the next ten minutes or so, enough to make even a stout man's hair stand on end."

"Surely you're jesting," Jane protested.

"I amnae. I've seen 'em. Dozens and dozens of cats, Mollies and Toms down to wee kittens."

"What does he do with them, though? Surely he doesn't . . ." Amelia-Rose swallowed. "He doesn't eat them, does he?"

"He says nae. Old Sean claims, though I've nae seen it so I cannae say if it's true, but he claims he milks 'em. And he has some odd wee cheeses, so I reckon maybe he does."

"No!"

"Aye. I swear it."

Amelia-Rose burst out laughing. She couldn't help it. "That is the most absurd thing I've ever heard. 'Wee cheeses'? Oh, good heavens."

"He brings his cheeses to the fair every year to sell,

along with a selection of Toms and kittens if his tunnels are overflowing. He owns but one sheep, and she's without a lamb, so she isnae giving him that quantity of milk."

"How does one milk a cat?" Amelia-Rose managed, tears of laughter gathering in her eyes.

"I've nae idea, lass. Carefully, I imagine. They're wee, but they do have claws. And teeth."

"I don't believe you," Jane said flatly.

"After Amelia-Rose and I are wed, we'll send ye some cat cheese from the Highlands and ye can see for yerself."

Wed. He's said the word. He hadn't asked her yet, of course, but heaven help her, she'd begun to imagine it, in a faerie dream sort of way. Just the two of them, without her parents to frown and tell her to mind her tongue. Without smelly, old stupid men with whom she was supposed to smile and agree and flirt simply because they were men. They wouldn't even dare approach her with Niall as her husband. Oh, she *could* imagine it.

"I don't see how that could happen," Jane was saying, "since Amelia-Rose detests the Highlands and means never to leave London."

"Jane!" she snapped, her daydream popping like a delicate soap bubble.

"It's true," her companion muttered, hunching her shoulders and turning to look out over Hyde Park.

Oh, now she didn't want to look at Niall, but she could practically feel him gazing at her. She couldn't even accuse Jane of ruining everything, because the subject would have arisen sooner or later. She'd just begun to hope it was later. If they ended up parting ways because of the dozen other things that lay between them, it might not even have come up at all. Except now it had.

Amelia-Rose took a breath and shut her eyes for a moment. "I suppose it's just as well you know," she said, watching the sunlight sparkle across the surface of the Serpentine.

"So if ye'd agreed to marry Coll, ye wouldnae have objected to being left here?" His voice sounded a little flat, but that might also have been her imagination.

"That's the problem. I don't want to leave, and I don't want to be left behind."

"And ye detest the Highlands."

"They aren't London."

Silence. Tears rose in her eyes again, but she blinked them away. He and she would never have made a match anyway. It was only that she'd hoped to . . . enjoy him for a bit longer than one morning.

"Well, that's it, then."

She felt him stand, and looked over quickly as he moved to the barouche's low door and swung it open. "Niall! What are you doing?"

"I'm leaving. Ye've set an impossible tangle, and I cannae see a way through it." With one foot out the door, he paused. "Unless . . ."

"Unless what? Blast it all, you're making a scene. At least drive me home first."

"Unless," he repeated, still hanging halfway out of the barouche with a ridiculous gracefulness, "ye're willing to make a bargain. Say, for example, we spend the Season in London, and the rest of the year in the Highlands?"

Amelia-Rose stared at him for at least a dozen hard beats of her heart. She hadn't just heard what she'd heard. It was far too simple. "P . . . Please sit down," she repeated.

Niall swung the door shut and latched it, then dropped down beside her again. "My point is, *adae*, that I grew up with one parent who'd nae leave the Highlands, and without one who'd nae stay there. I reckon there must be some space in the middle."

She wanted to hug him. She wanted to kiss him. Just

the idea that he would take her reservations into consideration without her first having to plead her side, or that he wouldn't have conjured something he wanted that she could withhold so they could bargain for it, stumped her for a moment. Amelia-Rose cleared her throat. "Where might we stay in London?"

He smiled. "I've nae thought much about it, but Oswell House is grand. Or I reckon my ma would be happy enough to have us about that she'd find us a bonny house somewhere close by." Beneath the level of the sides of the carriage, and more important, beneath the pile of her discarded shawl, he took her hand in his. "I've nae desire to stay at Baxter House, but that's because I've a fair idea yer ma would like to kill me."

"Niall, if I discover that you're bamming me, I will punch you in the head," she stated.

"I'm nae teasing, Amelia-Rose. I am accustomed to making peace in the family, but this is much easier than that. I'm nae about to let a stretch of countryside come between me and a lass with sunshine in her hair and the noonday sky in her eyes."

This couldn't all be true. It couldn't be so . . . ridiculously straightforward. As a child she'd imagined falling in love with and marrying a handsome prince and living in his castle, but well before her debut she'd come to understand that while she might wed a prince, or a duke, or some other title, the rest of it didn't matter to anyone but her. She continued to demand a partnership, affection, but she knew no one was listening to her. She might as well have been howling at the moon.

"Dunnae tell me ye've forgotten how to speak, lass," Niall teased. "I am manly and rather splendid, but ye—"

"I am available tomorrow afternoon after half two," she interrupted. "I will be attending a dinner party with family friends at eight, so I must be home by six."

"Half two till six o'clock tomorrow. Aye." His fingers twined with hers beneath the shawl, out of Jane's sight. "I've an idea for an outing. Wear walking shoes, and I'll fetch ye then."

"I'll meet you around the corner from the house," she decided. "On Wigmore Street." Her mother might accept that she'd taken today to let Niall down politely, but another rendezvous tomorrow would put the lie to whatever excuse she tried to make. Doom still loomed over her shoulder, but blast it all, today she felt like her feet weren't even touching the ground. And *that* was a very difficult thing to walk away from. *He* was going to be very difficult to walk away from. So much so that she didn't want to think about it.

"Your mother will not approve," Jane pointed out.

"Just for once I would like you to be on my side, cousin," Amelia-Rose returned. "Do you truly wish to be the villain of this piece?"

Her companion frowned. "And what happens if I say nothing, your mother discovers that you've been seeing this man against her wishes, and she sends me away?"

"If ye stand up for Amelia-Rose and get sent away because of it, ye call on Lady Aldriss at Oswell House," Niall said. "She'll find ye someaught. I swear it."

"It must be very nice," Jane countered, "to be so secure in yourselves that you can encourage others to ignore the tenets of their employment, to ignore what you know to be the wishes of your employer, on a whim. Mrs. Baxter is my aunt. She has fed and clothed me for six years, and paid me for the past two. It is not villainy to do the job one has been employed to do."

Niall looked like he wanted to argue that, but Amelia-Rose squeezed his hand, and with a glance at her, he subsided. "I do understand, Jane," she said. "My mother expects to be obeyed. I can only ask for your cooperation in this. The decision is yours."

"Yes, it is. And I think we've given you enough time to gracefully end whatever may exist between you and the Honorable Mr. Niall MacTaggert."

She'd given Niall's precise title, the one by which he would be formally addressed. And she'd done it on purpose. Amelia-Rose wanted to clench her fists and scream. If not for that lack of peerage, Niall would be perfect. He *was* perfect, as far as she was concerned.

Could it be enough? She could speak to her father first; Charles did have a firmer grasp on practicality than did his wife. Perhaps she could convince him. She'd been on display for two years now, after all, and though Niall very little resembled Mr. and Mrs. Baxter's ideal, he was technically a gentleman. His brother was a viscount, he was an aristocrat, and he very much seemed to like her. Perhaps more, though she refused to use the word. Not yet. Not when so many things could go wrong.

"Shall I return ye to Baxter House?" Niall asked.

No. "Yes, I suppose we should go." And to think, a fortnight ago she'd claimed to detest Highlanders. But back then, she'd never actually conversed with one.

As they arrived in front of Baxter House, Niall put his arm over the back of the seat behind her. When he half turned to face her, the warmth of him seemed to surround her. It was heady. He made her nearly giddy, and she was not a giddy person.

"Which window is yers, then?" he murmured, looking up at the house. "I'll nae be kept from ye if yer parents decide we're nae a match."

"I think you mean *when* they decide," she returned, wondering if a woman could combust just from wicked thoughts.

He glanced about, then briefly leaned his temple against hers. "I did promise to ravage ye, lass," he murmured. "Dunnae make me into a liar."

Goodness. That began an entirely different kind of heat running through her. With his easy grace and athletic build, she'd been imagining for days what it would be like to be in his arms. To have him inside her. This tall, rugged, independent man who didn't care what anyone thought, wanted her. No doubt he could have half the women of Mayfair if he chose. But for some reason, he continued to look at her. Only at her.

No one thanked him for it. Even she scoffed at him. And yet there he sat, his thigh touching hers, his light-green eyes no doubt trying to decipher what in the world she must be thinking. But today, she was tired of thinking. She wanted to feel, and she wished it could be that simple. "Niall, you know my mother will never agree to a match between us. Ever."

Niall lifted her hand in his to brush his lips against her knuckles. "I will charm her, *adae.* Or at the least, wear her down to my way of thinking. I didnae come down all the way from the Highlands to meet ye and then bid ye goodbye."

"That sounds very romantic."

"It's supposed to." He released her hand. "Point me to yer window."

Jane sat bolt-upright. "She will do no such thing!"

He lifted both eyebrows. "What's this, now?"

"You heard me."

"Well, I reckon the lass can decide for herself what she will or willnae do."

Oh, she shouldn't. But doing what she should hadn't proved very satisfying. "The second one from the left," she said, pointing at the upper floor.

"The yellow curtains?"

"Yes."

"Well, now I'll have to sit up in your bedchamber all night tonight," Jane complained.

"He was only curious, Jane." She looked over her shoulder at him, to see him wiping away a grin. "Isn't that correct, Niall?"

"Aye. Curious."

"Well, dunnae ye look grand."

Starting, Niall looked up as the barouche neared Oswell House. Aden, mounted on Loki, came even with the carriage, gave a half salute, and continued on in the opposite direction. "Where are ye headed?" Niall asked, turning in the soft seat to keep his brother in sight.

"Just out. It's too civilized in the house. And I keep seeing Francesca lurking behind me."

That could be handy. "Wait for me; I'll join ye."

The vehicle turned up the short drive, and Aden circled around to trail them. Generally the MacTaggerts worked alone when pursuing a lass, but this was no ordinary lass, and no ordinary pursuit. Niall could use someone with whom to speak—someone who wasn't Coll. Aden's observations could be useful, if taken with a bit of skepticism.

Clearly he did need some assistance; he'd been distracted enough that he'd ridden back to Oswell House with his backside gloriously cushioned by the overstuffed seat of the barouche, for Saint Andrew's sake. Half of Mayfair likely thought him a softheaded dandy, now.

Once Gavin had saddled Kelpie for him, he and Aden trotted off heading southeasterly. "Did you find a lass while ye were out with Eloise?" Niall asked.

"Nae. A cartload of 'em came at us to say hello to our *piuthar* while we were eating, like a bunch of blushing roses. Nearly had to resort to swatting 'em away like flies. Some pretty ones, but by tomorrow I'll nae recall most of their names." Aden turned Loki directly south along a narrow, crowded street.

Niall caught up with him again. "That's what ye want, isnae? A forgettable lass? That was our grand plan."

"I recall." Aden glanced at him sideways. "I may have decided to look about for someone a bit more . . . interesting. Seeing how well ye've done for yerself, that is."

"Dunnae start that with me, *bràthair*." Niall faced forward again. "It seems like ye do have a particular destination in mind."

"I want to see the grand Thames all the poets write about."

"We're getting close; I can smell it."

"Aye," Aden agreed. "Must be low tide. Either that or a whale's washed ashore." He sent another glance that Niall pretended not to notice. "Isnae Amelia-Rose Baxter the first Sassenach lass ye set eyes on?"

"What of it? I'm nae some moonstruck bairn. She's nae the first lass I've ever met."

"But she is the first one ye've run across who needed this much of a rescue."

The muscles across Niall's shoulders tightened. This was not the advice and assistance he'd come seeking. "What does that have to do with the price of wool?"

"I know ye, Niall. Ye look after the ones who need help. Nae just the lasses; anyone who stands alone."

"I—"

"It's nae a bad thing; Saint Michael knows there's got to be one of us whose first thought isnae battle. My . . ." He trailed off as the docks opened before them, the river just beyond. "That is one grand fucking stink," he stated.

It was that. Crates and nets, sailors and dockworkers and soldiers crowded into every open space. Beyond them wide strips of mud marked the low-tide shore of the Thames, while water continued to flow down the middle of the riverbed. Down in the mud people scampered, baskets and buckets in their hands or on their backs as they dug through the muck. Scavengers, looking for whatever the river might vomit up that they could sell for a penny or a shilling or two.

"Dunnae change the subject," he said belatedly. "I'm nae trying to rescue Amelia-Rose. It's nae pity I'm feeling."

"I didnae say ye were rescuing her. *Ye* said it, just now."

"Because that's what ye were implying. I watched her trying to be polite, and I watched Coll keep pushing at her, and then she handed him the tongue-lashing he deserved. That prim, proper lass, in her pretty, expensive gown, shut his gobber and sent him running with his tail between his legs."

"Ye realize he left because she wasnae a lass he could bend to his way of doing things."

"That was what I thought, until yesterday when he said he didnae care who she was and he'd nae have her as long as our mother chose her for him. But instead of trying to tell me we'll nae suit, why dunnae ye tell me what I can do to convince her damned parents that she belongs with me even if I'm nae a bloody laird?"

Aden dismounted, so Niall followed suit. If they were going mudlarking he wasn't going to be happy about it, but at least he'd dressed more appropriately for it than Aden in his buckskin trousers and very shiny boots.

Instead his brother dug a handful of hazelnuts from his pocket and offered half of them to Niall. Cracking one of them against his palm, Aden popped the plump seed into his mouth. "That's nae an easy question, Niall," he said, after he'd chewed and swallowed.

"Hence me asking for some help. Ma said she tried offering the Baxters a share of her shipping company, but they werenae impressed. They have blunt. They want a title."

"Short of ye murdering Coll and me, that's nae a thing you'll ever have. If there's naught else they want in the wide world, I reckon it's a lost cause." He ate another nut. "Especially when what ye want is for them to like ye."

"I dunnae give a damn if they like me. They just have to accept me."

Aden narrowed his eyes. "That's it, though. They dunnae *have* to do anything. So I reckon ye can either convince them to *want* to accept ye, or decide a way around them entirely. And I dunnae know yer lass well, but she seems to listen fairly close to what her mama tells her."

That, she did—to a point. And every time she did try for some independence, she paid for it. Those had been tears he'd seen in her eyes yesterday. They did make him angry, and aye, he did want to rescue her. More than that, he didn't want to see her troubled. Since he was a large part of the reason for that particular malady, his options seemed severely limited.

"I wasnae helpful at all, was I?" Aden asked.

"Nae. Ye werenae," Niall returned, blowing out his breath. "Ye did make my head ache, if that appeases ye."

"Give me back my nuts if ye're nae going to eat 'em."

Niall handed them over. "Be about Oswell House tomorrow, will ye? Between two o'clock and six. I'm bringing her over for a visit."

"I can do that. What about Coll?"

"He's to be there, as well. He owes a kind word or two to Amelia-Rose."

Aden nodded, pocketing the nuts and swinging back up on Loki. "Dunnae lose yer heart, Niall. I ken what ye want, but I dunnae see a way for ye to get it without someone getting bloody. And ye're likely to be that someone. That's the best advice I can give ye."

Niall watched his brother trot off into the dockside

crowd. His odds were slim. But he did have charm. And a determination to win the lass. Even a MacTaggert, he supposed, could swallow his pride for the right cause. And Amelia-Rose was all that, and more.

Chapter Twelve

Jane, please just go to bed," Amelia-Rose said, pulling her blankets up over her head.

Her cousin jerked upright from her seat by the dimming fireplace. "I am doing my duty," she returned. "I should have told your mother. Since I didn't, I am now solely responsible for your virtue."

"No, *I'm* solely responsible for my virtue," Amelia-Rose countered, sitting up again. "And the stupid window is locked, anyway, so even if he did decide to climb up the outside of the house, managing to not be seen by any passersby in the process, he wouldn't be able to get in."

"You might unlatch the window."

"If you hadn't been in here snoring, I would be asleep already."

That was a lie, but it made her sound less like some wanton minx than she was presently feeling. Her greatest concern at the moment wasn't Jane, but that Niall had indeed been jesting and meant to respect propriety. She didn't want propriety. Not tonight. She wanted to know if he would be able to convince her mind as thoroughly as her body already seemed to be that he was the one for her.

With a sniff Jane stood, picked up her book and her embroidery, and made for the door. "This is madness, Amelia-Rose. And if your mother ever finds out about any of it, you will tell her that I was not involved."

"Good night, Jane."

As soon as the door shut, Amelia-Rose slipped out of bed and tiptoed to the entrance. She listened to Jane's fading footfalls for a moment, then turned the key in the latch. Just in case.

Then she padded to the window, pushed aside the curtains—and yelped when a face looked directly back at her. "For heaven's sake," she gasped, taking a step backward and nearly tripping over her night rail.

A half grin on his face, Niall pointed through the window at the latch. One hand over her heart, she reached up and unlocked it. Accompanied by a breath of chill air the window lifted, and with a swift duck he stepped into the room. "Thank ye, lass," he whispered, turning to close the window and the curtains again. "That was a wee ledge."

"How long have you been crouched out there?" she asked, noting that he'd managed to climb the house in a kilt and boots. She almost wished she'd been outside to see that.

"Long enough to curse Jane Bansil to the devil about a dozen times," he returned. Releasing the curtains, he faced her. "I wasnae certain ye'd open the window at all."

Swallowing, she took him in, six feet three inches of lean, handsome Highlander. He made her generous bedchamber look small and delicate, as if he might take a wrong step and crush a chair. But he wasn't that graceless, or that careless. And what she wanted from him . . . How did one even go about saying it? "Hello," she ventured.

"Hello," he returned. "Ye dunnae have any food in here, do ye?"

Amelia-Rose snorted. This was Niall, after all. "Food again? No, I do not. Are you here for me, or to raid my cupboard?"

"Och, I'm here for ye, lass. I'm nae a fool, though. I ken how important propriety is for ye. Ye're breaking the rules here." Moving deeper into the room, he bent his head to examine the painting on her mantel, dim in the dying firelight.

"Did ye do this?" he asked, glancing back at her.

She flushed. "I did. I was only sixteen, and very unskilled, I'm afraid." It had been meant as a present to her mother, who'd immediately decided it would best be displayed in her daughter's bedchamber.

"Why did ye choose a mountainside?"

"Everyone who paints pastorals chooses mountainsides."

Straightening again, he shook his shaggy head. "Nae. It's usually streams and coos—cows—and meadows. Have ye ever seen a mountain?"

"I've seen other paintings, and sketches. Don't make it mean more than it does, Niall."

"I want to show ye my mountains. The way after a snow the rising sun turns the whole face golden. The smell of pine trees in the wet. The steam rising off the pastured sheep on a cold morning. The scent of fresh bread from the village bakery. The sound of the bagpipes in the evening."

He took two steps forward, closing the distance between them. "The lasses in the village will hound ye, asking ye to show them the fancy way ye put up yer hair. All the lairds and ladies, all the clan Ross chieftains and their families, will accidentally find themselves on the Aldriss doorstep to be introduced to ye. I reckon Lady Marmont will insist on a grand party to welcome ye, and she'll only be the first."

"You don't have to try to convince me that I'll find the same Society in the Highlands that I have here. I know it's vast and empty. I'm—"

Niall took both her hands in his. "The Highlands *is* vast. My mother found it empty, but then my da nae met a soiree he cared to attend."

She narrowed one eye. "So you, being more sociable, would magically arrange for more people to appear?" This conversation wasn't remotely what she'd expected for tonight, but she appreciated that he took her concerns seriously enough to want to address them. What she didn't want to hear, though, was a basketful of wishful thinking. "I don't want pretty lies, Niall."

He blew out his breath. For a bare, dreadful second she thought he'd given up. "I've nae had a day where there wasnae someaught to do," he said finally, "someone who needed a hand with a leaking roof or cutting peat for a fire, or a mama trying to find a way to send her lad to school to train as a solicitor, or a da who received a letter from his daughter in America and needed someone to read it for him."

"That's nice."

"I'm nae finished. If ye want to spend yer days at coffee-houses and shopping, then nae, ye'll nae find that outside of Inverness. If ye want to call on old Mungo Wilkie and help him feed his chickens in exchange for a gander at the finest library in Scotland, he'll thank ye for it. If ye want to teach some wee bairns to read or to dance, ye'll find people willing to give ye their last bit of bread. Do ye want to be entertained, or do ye want to see what it's like to be a Highlander?"

The bluntness of his last statement surprised her. Up until now he'd been encouraging, supportive, and good-humored. But this was important to him. After all, if they married, people would judge him based on her, and vice versa. She wasn't the only one proceeding on faith and hope.

He released her hands. "I've nae wish to force ye into someaught, lass. And I know yer ma doesnae like me and willnae approve. That willnae stop me. Only ye can do that."

"Are you . . . leaving?" she blurted as he turned around.

"I'm going to sit in this chair until ye realize that I already ken the answer ye want to give. I'd nae fall for a lass who only cared for what the world could give her. I'd nae fall for a lass who valued herself so little that she needed to fill her empty soul with pretty things."

A tear, unbidden, ran down her cheek. Was that her? A woman who needed a palace, who needed constant affirmation, before she could claim to be happy? Was she turning into her mother? The thought, just the idea of it, made her feel ill. She'd been told for her entire life that her value lay in making her family proud; in being the perfect, sophisticated, cultured young lady; in marrying a title to improve the family's standing. But was that all she was? "That's not me," she said aloud.

"I know that," he returned. "I know it because I'm a rough-edged man. I've nae made a secret of who and what I am, or of how I want to spend my life. It's nae very fancy, though I dunnae mind a party now and then. And I'm here in yer bedchamber, because ye wanted me in here." Green eyes, darker in the gloom, studied her face. "I've fallen for ye, Amelia-Rose. Hard. I want ye to have nae a bigger life than the one ye imagined for yerself, but a more satisfying one. I love ye, *adae*."

Amelia-Rose put a hand over her heart, feeling it tremble beneath her fingers. He truly believed in her. He loved her, not despite her missteps and hesitations, but because they were part of who she was. It was utterly remarkable. Niall

MacTaggert, the literal opposite of the polished, staid, dull gentleman she'd set out to catch, loved her.

"Ye neednae say anything," he commented into the silence. "I know ye dunnae see a future for us. Ye'd be foolish to risk yer h—"

She threw herself on him, kissing him everywhere she could reach. The chair rocked, nearly going over backward. She grabbed onto his shoulders, gasping against his mouth as the overstuffed thing settled back onto all fours, then resumed with her kisses. Perhaps she didn't own enough hope and faith to say the words, but she could show him how she felt.

"I like the way ye declare yerself, Amelia-Rose," he murmured, settling her across his lap.

Her hair was up in its long night braid, but he tugged the ribbon at the end loose and began stroking his fingers through the mass to free it. Her sunshine hair, he'd called it. Somehow from him that sounded far more sincere and poetical than "spun gold" or "flaxen locks," as she'd heard from other men who thought they might be able to tolerate her in exchange for her parents' money.

"Ye're certain ye wouldnae prefer one of those fancy lads with the high collars?" he asked, brushing his fingers from her wrist and up to her shoulder. "Someone who knows which spoon is for soup and which one's for gruel?"

She chuckled, pushing against him with one elbow so she could reach the trio of buttons closing his gray waistcoat. "They may be the same spoon."

He caught her mouth again. "I want ye, *adae*. If ye mean to send me away, for God's sake do it now."

"I'm not sending you away. I want you, *skellum*. I'm just . . . not quite . . . I don't want to do something wrong." Especially with someone who obviously knew what he was doing.

Niall put a hand beneath her knees and the other behind her shoulders, and stood. "I've nae been with an English lass before," he commented, carrying her with ridiculous ease over to the bed, "so I'm a bit scared. I reckon if ye dunnae pull off any of my important bits, we'll manage."

"You are not scared," she countered, scooting backward on the bed to make room for him after he set her down.

Light-green eyes caught hers. "I may be yer first man, lass, but I mean for ye to be the last woman I ever have. I want to wake beside ye every morning and fall asleep with ye in my arms every night. *That* doesnae scare me. Nae pleasing ye does."

"I'm already fairly pleased," she said as he sat on the bed and took off his boots, carefully setting one and then the other on the floor. Sitting up behind him, she slid her fingers beneath the lapels of his coat to tug it off his arms.

"We've nae gotten to the best bits yet," he returned, grinning as he twisted to kiss her again.

Going onto all fours, he grasped her ankles and pulled her toward him, setting her on her back. Once he'd shed his waistcoat and cravat he knelt with her legs between his and reached down to open the trio of buttons beneath her chin. She'd never thought of a plain white night rail as exotic, but as he opened each button he ran his forefinger along her exposed skin with such delicacy it made her shiver.

When he had them all open he bent down and kissed the base of her throat, moving down along her breastbone with his caresses. Inside her every nerve jangled, every inch of her aware of him. The front of his kilt tented in a rather grand fashion. It fascinated her, made her feel powerful that she could affect this man as much as he affected her. If she'd needed evidence that she aroused him, she certainly had it.

Lifting his gaze to meet hers again, he drew the sleeveless shoulders of her night rail down her arms. When he looked down at her exposed breasts, she had to stifle the abrupt urge to cover them. Modesty, purity, propriety—all the things she supposedly lacked and had been trying so hard to master, she clearly possessed because she now needed and wanted to cast them aside.

"Ye're glorious, lass," Niall whispered, his voice rough at the edges.

As his fingers lightly circled her breasts, brushing her nipples in a way that made her gasp, he seemed almost worshipful, as though he was memorizing her lines and curves. *Intoxicating.* But she wasn't the only one who should be nearly naked. "Take off your shirt, Niall."

His mouth lifting at the corners, he untucked his plain linen shirt from his kilt and pulled it off over his head. Amelia-Rose's breath stilled. He looked like some of the statues in the museum, taut and muscular and lean-waisted. Unlike the marble Greek gods and heroes, though, his skin showed the marks of a life lived. The sword graze down one forearm, what looked like an old, well-healed gash across his left ribs, and a small circular scar in the meat of his left upper arm. She imagined every one of those scars had a story to go along with it, and she wanted to hear all of them.

"Touch me, lass," he urged. "I'll nae break. I want to feel yer hands on me."

Oh, goodness. Except that goodness didn't seem to have anything to do with it, because she felt very, very naughty. His skin beneath her fingers was warm and smooth, covering iron beneath. A muscle jumped at her touch, and she pulled him down over her for more kissing.

His kisses traveled their leisurely way down her again, until he took one of her breasts in his very capable mouth. Gasping, then putting a hand over her mouth to stifle the sound, Amelia-Rose arched her back, a shiver of delight thudding through her.

When he continued nibbling and sucking, her eyes rolled back in her head. This—she could never have done this with some man she'd married for his title. But she trusted Niall MacTaggert, trusted him with her body and her reputation and her heart.

Moving sideways, he continued teasing at her as he pulled her night rail down past her waist, her hips, her knees, and then over her feet. Then his hands trailed down her body, curious, caressing, and unhurried. Breathless, warm, and yearning, she parted her legs as he slid a palm down her stomach, over her mound, and up along the inside of her thigh. As his fingers opened her *there*, she bucked again, nearly sending a knee into his ear.

"I'm sorry," she panted.

"Do ye like this?" he responded.

She wasn't certain she could even get the words out. "Yes," she rasped, her hips wriggling beneath his ministrations. "Very much."

"Then dunnae apologize. I'm mad for ye, lass. Cannae ye see how I want ye?"

She lowered her gaze to the jutting front of his kilt. "I want to see you."

Niall lifted his hands over his head, wrapping his fingers around the canopy beams at the top of the bed. "It's but a tartan, Amelia-Rose. Take it off me."

She sat up a little, figuring out the belt and clasp and the small wolf's-head kilt pin that kept the material from flying open in a breeze. He wasn't a flawed statue, she decided, as she finally got everything unfastened and pulled it from around his hips. He was a strong, wild Highlands warrior, descended from men who'd beaten back the greatest army in the world on numerous occasions. And he was magnificent.

Glancing up at his face to find him watching her, she reached out to grasp his manhood. In response he made a low sound deep in his chest that sent heat and damp between her thighs again.

Gathering up her courage, she stroked the length of him. With another half-articulate moan he settled his knees between hers and lowered himself along her body for a deep, openmouthed kiss. Skin to skin, warmth to warmth, with an unmistakable hardness pressed against her thigh. Good heavens, she wanted him. Even without knowing exactly what to do, she wanted to be part of him.

He moved again, dragging his discarded shirt beneath her hips. Then, parting her knees further, he slipped a hand between them to fit his cock between her folds. Blood, she realized, even as her brain refused to think. She was, for another few seconds, a virgin. There would be blood. And he was sacrificing his shirt to keep it off her sheets. To protect her.

"Now," she breathed.

"Ye ken—"

"I know," she interrupted. "Some of my friends have talked. I won't scream."

Raising up on his hands, he lowered his head to kiss her again. "Hold on, my lass."

Her heart beating so hard she thought it might burst from her chest, Amelia-Rose slid her arms over his shoulders. He pushed forward, the sensation of him sliding deeper and deeper inside her utterly indescribable. Pressure grew, then a sharp, biting pain, and then he buried himself in her fully.

For a long moment he didn't move, and she dug the pads of her fingers into his shoulders while pain faded and other tighter, deeper sensations made her want to press herself against him, wrap her legs around his thighs, keep him there with her.

"Better?" he grunted.

She nodded.

With that he began to move, slowly and carefully at first, in and out, as if he worried he might break her. The slide, the weight of him across her hips drove her half mad. *More, more, more.* When she lowered her hands to his clenching backside, arching toward him, he sped his pace, stroking harder and faster inside her.

Moaning in time with his thrusts, her body tightened, stretched, and, with an exquisite shudder, released. Everything vanished but him and their joined bodies, the deep, jolting rhythm of him claiming her. She shattered harder, a mewling sound she'd never heard before coming from her own chest.

Her mind slowly settled into sight and sound again, just as he pushed in to the hilt, shuddering against her and inside her. Breathing as hard as she was, he settled himself along her body and lowered his head between her neck and shoulder. Amelia-Rose tangled her fingers into the damp, lanky hair at the nape of his neck. *Hers.* He belonged to her now, as much as she belonged to him.

He lifted his head against to kiss her, then went up on his elbows. She tightened her arms around him. If he left, everything might go back to the way it had been. She would be alone, unwanted except for her ability to wear a marriage band.

"I dunnae want to crush ye," he said, looking down at her.

He was getting quite heavy. But he was still inside her, and she didn't want that to stop yet, either. "Stay."

"I mean to, until the dawn." Niall studied her face for another moment, then wrapped his arms around her back and rolled them over.

Abruptly he lay beneath her, and she tucked her head against his chest. "I can feel your heartbeat," she said, the hard, fast tattoo just beneath her cheek.

"Aye. And I can feel yers." He drew his fingers through her wavy, disheveled yellow hair, the gentle tug and pull lifting goose bumps along her scalp. "Ye trusted me, lass. I'll see that ye dunnae ever regret it. I'll figure a way to make this work, as long as ye still want me."

She lifted her head, resting her chin on his sternum to look at his face. This could be them, every night. The thought was nearly enough to make her giddy. But even now, with her body deciding on the next course of action in complete disregard for logical thought, she wasn't a complete fool. "I still want you. I want everything you spoke of. I also know my mother."

"I made it in here despite yer mother. But ye make a good point. It isnae just the two of us in this."

"Exactly. And you don't have a title. And you're Coll's brother, and she hates him almost as much as she hates you." She wasn't entirely certain how she felt about Coll, either, but she didn't want to waste what little time they likely had thinking about Lord Glendarril.

"I want to see ye tomorrow. I can call at the front door and ask for—"

"No, do not call at the door," she broke in. "I'm still free for the afternoon. Will you still meet me on the corner at Wigmore Street at half two?"

"I will be there, lass. And we will find a way for ye and me to be together that doesnae involve climbing through windows, though I'm nae adverse to that."

The climbing-through-windows bit *had* worked out rather splendidly. It couldn't last, though. They needed a solution. She couldn't contemplate the alternative.

Francesca started awake as the front door clicked and opened. Immediately she sank lower onto the morning room couch where she'd settled at just past midnight, and slowly turned her head toward the foyer.

Niall padded past, barefoot with his boots in one hand, wearing only a waistcoat and his kilt with his coat and what looked like a wadded shirt in the other hand. Nearly silently he ascended the staircase, and a moment later another door clicked shut.

Blowing out her breath, she shifted to see the mantel clock. Nearly five o'clock in the morning, bootless, shirtless, and unobservant enough to miss her sitting there in the predawn gloom, blanket up to her chin. Niall Douglas MacTaggert had been up to something. And given the past few days, she had a very good idea what—who—it was.

He should have let her make that agreement with the Baxters. They would eventually have bowed to her terms, because she would have thrown money and even threats of censure at them until they did so. As it was now, while she admired Niall's determination to win Amelia-Rose on his own merits, the young lady was not the one he needed to convince. He'd already convinced her, evidently.

When Eloise had fallen in love it had felt warm and orderly, and Francesca remained fairly certain that young Matthew had not shared a bed with her. Her wild sons, though—while she'd wanted them about, wanted love and marriages for them, she hadn't quite reckoned on how very like their father they were. Angus had seen what he wanted, and taken it, in a spectacularly breathtaking manner. If her own father had been more conventional, things might have gotten bloody.

The Baxters were exceedingly conventional. Amelia-Rose had her moments of rebellion, but then she just as frequently apologized for them. None of it boded well. And if Niall failed—or if she failed him—she might well lose her chance with the other two.

Standing to drape the blanket over the back of the

couch, she headed upstairs to dress. Attempting a few more hours of sleep would be useless now, when she needed solutions. Even if those solutions seemed only to exist in daydreams.

Chapter Thirteen

"This is not wise, Amelia-Rose," Jane whispered, standing close and holding her waxed silk parasol over both their heads. "Your mother *will* notice you're not home."

"I went to her luncheon, and I'll be home in time to join my parents for dinner," Amelia-Rose returned. "I'm only taking the three hours in the middle for myself."

"And when she goes looking for you to see what you plan to wear tonight?"

"She might not," Amelia-Rose hedged. "If she does, then we'll say I was restless and you joined me for a walk. And we've walked here, so it's not even a lie."

A coach rounded the corner up the street, the largest vehicle by far she'd glimpsed in the ten minutes since they'd sneaked away from Baxter House. The blue-and-yellow Oswell crest was emblazoned on the door, and as she recognized it a smile found her mouth and refused to step aside despite the poor weather and Jane's glowering.

As the coach neared them the door swung open. Niall leaned out, grinned, and then hopped gracefully to the street before the vehicle had even stopped. He'd worn his kilt again, and with the rain dripping through his dark, wavy hair he looked like some ancient Celtic warrior come to claim her. To claim her again, rather.

He flipped down the coach steps and took her hand, bringing it to his lips. "Ye look very bonny today, Amelia-Rose," he drawled, the quiet intimacy in his voice making her heart race. "Did ye sleep well?"

"After Jane finally left my room I did," she lied. It was better for Jane, and better for her, even if she did feel a bit guilty about it. "I had very sweet dreams."

That earned her a grin. "I nearly brought the barouche," he said, visibly shaking himself to take the parasol from Jane and hand them into the vehicle one after the other. "But I looked outside and noticed everyone bundled up to their ears and scurrying about like wee scared mice, so I borrowed this beast instead."

"This weather doesn't trouble you?" Jane asked, blowing into her cupped gloved hands.

"It's nae weather if ye can still make out the horizon," he returned, sitting next to Amelia-Rose and then reaching up to pound his fist against the ceiling. "Did ye have a pleasant luncheon, *adae*?" he asked, sitting back in the well-sprung coach.

"Yes, I did. Thank you for asking, *skellum*," she responded, using every ounce of willpower she possessed not to kiss him. "Where are you taking us?"

"Oswell House."

Of all the places she'd imagined he might take her, his family home hadn't been one of them. "Not some secret garden filled with Scottish herbs or a sheep farm or something?"

His brows lifted. "That's what ye reckon I yearn for? Herbs and sheep?"

"I thought you'd want to take me somewhere Scottish,

but I couldn't think of anywhere nearby you might choose."
At least she'd tried to come up with something. "Nothing
nearby enough for a three-hour visit, anyway."

"Fair enough," he conceded. "If ye've nae objection,
though, I want my brothers—my family—to know ye."

She hid a shudder as she recalled the largest member
of his family. "I'm well acquainted with Eloise and Lady
Aldriss, you know. And I have . . . met both your brothers."

"Aye. This time ye be yerself, and *they'll* behave."
He cupped her cheek, his green eyes shadowed and serious in the gloom of the coach, and only lowered his hand
when Jane slapped at him. "Ye're safe with me. I swear on
my own blood. But if ye dunnae wish to go, ye tell me. I'll
find a sheep farm we can tour straightaway. Because ye
know a Highlander can spot a sheep from five miles
away."

There he went, putting her at ease again. Was he even
conscious of how . . . not comfortable, but safe, he made
her feel? And how that made her realize it had been a very
long time since she'd felt precious to anyone? Being in his
company was heady, and could easily be addictive. Was
already addictive. "Oswell House is fine," she said aloud,
ignoring Jane's sniff. "I have been wanting a chance to
have a word with Lady Aldriss."

"That doesnae sound promising, but do as ye will," he
said in a dubious voice. "Keep in mind that she barely
knows me. Ye cannae take what she says too seriously."

That hadn't been her goal, but seeing his discomfiture did make her grin. "Do you think she'll warn me to
flee?"

"I did start a bit of a brawl in her breakfast room just
the other day. For a good reason, of course."

That must have been when he fought Coll. "I'm going
to assume you were defending my honor in some way, and
I can hardly fault you for that."

"That's what it was, then. Aye."

If Jane had been elsewhere, Amelia-Rose would have been willing to call this short coach ride very nearly perfect. She would have been content to chat with Niall and just look at him, trying to figure out what he was thinking and feeling. She'd liked him almost immediately. When had that, though, deepened into this warm, comforting, arousing desire to be with him? As she considered it, she had to wonder if it had begun with that first morning of coffee. If she'd begun to fall for him days and days ago, had that been part of why she'd spoken so harshly to Coll? Not just because she didn't want that life, but because she had a slightly different one in mind?

It would never happen, of course, and she wanted it anyway. She'd wanted it so much that she'd allowed him into her bed. And if the opportunity arose she meant to do it again. Repeatedly. "You're a good man, Niall MacTaggert."

"I dunnae know about that." His pale gaze took her in from head to foot in a way that heated her up from the inside. "Some of the things I'm thinking right now arenae nice. I'd describe them to ye in great detail, but I'm scared yer companion might be armed." He sent Jane a sideways glance.

"Then you just keep worrying that I am, Mr. MacTaggert."

The coach stopped. A second later the door opened, and the Oswell House butler unfolded the steps and reached in to offer her a hand. "Good afternoon, Miss Baxter."

"Smythe. Thank you."

The butler ushered them inside the house to shed their wraps. Niall stopped in the kitchen to towel off his damp mane, then offered her an arm. "I told 'em nae to be formal," he said, heading for the front of the large house, "but that leaves a wide space for nonsense."

"I'm nervous," she blurted, then put her free hand over her mouth. "I shouldn't be; I do know them. Oh, I'm just being silly."

He stopped, faced her, and bent to give her a deep, slow kiss. *Oh, he could kiss.* And do several other things exceptionally well. That thought made heat swirl up from between her legs, up her spine, and settled into a delicious shiver.

"Stop tha—"

Jane leaped forward, but out of the corner of her eye Amelia-Rose saw the stiff arm and upright palm of Niall catch the companion by the shoulder and hold her quite easily at bay. "It's rude to interrupt," he muttered, and kissed Amelia-Rose once more.

"I will scream," Jane hissed, flailing at his hand.

With a sigh and a last nibble at her lower lip, Niall straightened away from Amelia-Rose. "Nervous now?"

She blinked. More than anything else she felt dazed and warm and quite ridiculously optimistic. "No. But you should let Jane go. She has a surprisingly high-pitched yowl."

Instead, still holding Jane Bansil away from him with that one muscular arm, he faced the companion. "Nae harm done, lass," he said. "My brother is the one who did wrong, and I'll nae have my *adae* worried over how *they* see *her*. And aside from that, I reckon I mean to kiss her every time I can manage it."

Jane stopped swatting at his hand, the only part of him she could reach. "You 'reckon' as you will, Mr. MacTaggert. I 'reckon' I will try to stop you every time *I* can manage *that*."

He grinned, releasing her. "Fair enough. Ye're a tiger, ye are. Fierce as fire."

For the first time that Amelia-Rose could ever recall,

Jane blushed at a comment from a man. "I . . . Let's get on with it, shall we?" she mumbled, straightening her plain blue gown.

"Aye, let's." Taking Amelia-Rose's hand in his, he rapped on the closed morning room door and then pushed it open.

They all sat in the large, open room. All the MacTaggerts, save their absent patriarch. Eloise and Lady Aldriss were seated together on the long couch and examining a half-finished embroidery. The middle brother, Aden, lounged in one of the overstuffed chairs and seemed to be reading Francis Grose's *Classical Dictionary of the Vulgar Tongue*, of all things, while Lord Glendarril perched in one of the deep windowsills and peeled an orange.

"Ye're reading a dictionary?" Niall said, lifting an eyebrow as his brothers both came to their feet.

"A bonny, buxom lass told me last night that she wanted a smack," Aden replied with a slow grin. "I reckoned I'd best see what she meant, as I'd nae hit a woman." He hefted the dictionary. "Turns out she meant she wanted a kiss, which means I guessed right."

"Aden," Eloise chastised, setting aside the embroidery and walking forward to give Amelia-Rose a sound hug. "I couldn't say, because you and Coll were supposedly courting, but this isn't the first time I've thought you and Niall look very fetching together."

Lady Aldriss took Amelia-Rose's right hand in hers. "You are most welcome here, my dear. Always."

That word seemed to have additional meaning, but Amelia-Rose attempted to put it aside for now. If the countess had doubts that this pursuit by Niall would be successful, she wasn't the only one. She'd already gone through one MacTaggert brother, after all.

Then Aden strolled up to her. He opened his mouth to

speak, but she lifted an eyebrow at him as both her hands were occupied. "Did you step on my toe so you wouldn't have to tell me what *adae* actually means?"

"Aye, I did," he returned, his gray-green eyes amused. "And I apologize for panicking. Ye're a . . ." He looked down to consult his dictionary of vulgarities. ". . . a prime lass."

As far as she knew that was still a compliment. "Thank you, then."

The window at the front of the room lightened as the viscount left it. *Steady*, she told herself. She'd stood up to him twice already, and that had been without anyone else to assist her. Amelia-Rose curtsied as he rounded the couch. "My lord."

"Ye're English," Coll stated, stopping at Aden's shoulder. "And Lady Aldriss ordered me to wed ye. I wouldnae have done it if ye'd been a princess. Even so, that was my doing. Ye had naught to answer for. I was . . ."

"You were mean," Eloise said under her breath as he paused.

"I was mean," he recited.

"And thoughtless," Aden added.

"And thoughtless," Coll repeated.

"And a buffoon, just as she described," Niall put in.

Lord Glendarril narrowed his eyes. "And a buffoon," he said anyway, "just as ye described." He took a breath, meeting her gaze. "I figured to push ye into breaking off with me, so I'd nae have to pay the price. Ye pushed back. Ye were inconvenient, but ye've spleen, lass."

"And so?" Eloise prompted again.

"Fer God's sake," Coll muttered, then squared his shoulders. "And so, I apologize to ye, Amelia-Rose Baxter. Will ye forgive me?"

He had a fresh bruise on his cheek, while the black eye had begun to fade. Niall had described his oldest brother as a fighter, a brawler, someone who sought out trouble. She wondered how many times he'd previously had to apologize, or if he'd just accepted the consequences. In her opinion, it would have been the latter.

"I will," she said, holding his gaze. "I didn't want this, either. You might have even found me an ally, if you'd asked."

"Aye. I reckon that's so." He furrowed his brow. "Ye've a sharp tongue. If I *had* been looking for a woman, and if ye'd been Scottish, mayhap—"

"No," she interrupted, at the same time as Niall beside her.

To her surprise, Coll grinned. "Nae. I reckon not." With that he went back to his windowsill and his orange.

For the next two hours Amelia-Rose discovered what it would have been like to have a large family. Even Coll joined them eventually, and while she could from time to time sense that all was not entirely well between Lady Aldriss and her sons, they were there. They were together, and they all seemed determined to welcome her as a part of the family.

It was remarkable, really. Warm, and supportive, and genuine, and very humorous. When Jane, seated by the fire, surreptitiously reached over to claim Aden's abandoned book of vulgarities, she nearly burst out laughing. If they could sway Jane toward anything bawdy, miracles could indeed happen.

"I have a question," she said, taking a sip of tea. "Have any of you ever heard of milking cats?"

Aden snorted. "Aye. Sean Ross, one of our cotters. He makes cheeses out of the milk, or so he claims."

"I've seen him do it," Coll added. "It's a tad disturbing, even for me."

Niall twined his fingers with hers. "Ye didnae believe me."

"You were talking about *milking cats*," she retorted, chuckling. "I wanted some verification."

"Well, now I want to hear about them," Eloise piped in. "Because it sounds completely mad."

Lady Aldriss patted her daughter on the knee. "Have your brothers tell you, then. I would like a word with Amelia-Rose." She stood, gesturing toward the door.

For a second Amelia-Rose wondered if Niall would object, but with a gentle squeeze he released her hand. "Ye said ye wanted a chat," he murmured, below everyone else's hearing.

"I do. Please keep an eye on Jane."

He grinned. "I reckon she's fairly absorbed right now."

So he'd seen what her companion was reading, then. Of course he had; he seemed to notice everything. Standing, she followed the countess into the hallway and then down another two doors to a small, neat office. "Yes, my lady?"

"I recall when I first met with your parents about a marriage agreement," Lady Aldriss said, taking one of the two seats before the desk and urging Amelia-Rose to the other one, "that while you didn't say much, you did seem to have a very low regard for Scotland. And Highlanders."

"I apologize, my lady. I meant in general terms, and wasn't trying to disparage your sons in particular." She'd been too blunt again. Would Lady Aldriss rescind her welcome now that they were in private?

"When I met Angus MacTaggert," the countess said instead, "he was magnificent. So handsome and strong, and so very single-minded in what he wanted. Which happened to be me. And I fell for him, very deeply." She glanced down at her hands for a moment, a rare showing of uncertainty. "Scotland is cold in the winter. Rainy in the summer. Filled with sheep and not very many people.

It can be exceedingly lonely and isolated—especially when your husband considers himself too busy to socialize with his peers."

"Are you warning me away from Niall?" Amelia-Rose asked. "Because he suggested that we spend the Season here in London."

The countess blinked. "He did?"

"Yes. Either here, or in a small house nearby." It felt odd to speak about such a future, but here, in this home, she could almost touch it.

"Well." Lady Aldriss brushed at her eyes. "That is unexpected."

"I mean, he hasn't offered for me or anything. We were just chatting. And I know my parents—my mother, especially—won't be easily convinced."

"No, I daresay she won't be." The countess favored her with a rather unsettling look. "Will you be honest about something, my dear?"

That didn't bode well. Perhaps she was as unacceptable to Niall's family as he presently was to hers. Or Lady Aldriss had guessed that her virtue was no longer intact. "Of course I will."

"You are not entirely . . . content beneath your parents' roof. I won't ask you to confirm that, but I do have eyes and ears. My point, I suppose, is that if Coll had been more pleasant, you might have agreed to marry him, however imperfectly you viewed him." She smoothed the front of her burgundy skirt with one hand. "To that, you may respond."

Amelia-Rose grimaced. "I wish I had a braver answer, but yes, I might have."

"And now in place of Coll you have Niall, who *is* more pleasant, and more concerned with the happiness of others."

"I have had four other proposals, my lady."

"Yes, which your mother rejected because of their status." The countess sat forward. "My son seems to adore you. I have no objection to a match—as long as you are not encouraging him because you fear being pushed into marrying some old stick with a title. So tell me it is not his convenience and affability and availability you prize, rather than the man himself."

Amelia-Rose considered all that for a moment. After all the emotion of last night and then today, it felt like a great wave, getting ready to drag her to the bottom of the sea and drown her. "Niall is not convenient," she stated. "Not in the least. He is good-humored, and witty, and warm-hearted, and makes me feel . . . safe. He is a dream—*my* dream, Lady Aldriss—and I'm afraid if I fall for him he will simply vanish. And then if I consider it too closely I realize that I have fallen—quite hard—and I know something will go wrong now, and—"

"Hush," Lady Aldriss said, and hugged her.

Amelia-Rose gulped a sob, and then another one. "I'm sorry," she managed, hiccuping. "I'm not a watering pot. I'm just so worried. I think he is, too, even though he won't say it."

The countess produced a handkerchief from somewhere and gave it to her. "Dry your eyes, my dear. I was raised by indulgent parents, as was my daughter and, I daresay, my sons. A parent . . . Well, you don't need to hear my lecture, but I do believe it to be a parent's duty to help their offspring find the best path and then step aside. Within reason, of course."

Amelia-Rose blotted at her face. "I have no argument with reason, my lady."

Lady Aldriss smiled. "Then know that I will help, however I may."

Someone rapped at the door. "I need to return the lass home," Niall's voice came.

"Enter."

He turned and knob and stepped inside. "I hope ye did-nae . . . Why are ye crying?" Immediately he strode forward and knelt beside her, his kilt settling carelessly around his knees. Niall sent his mother a glare.

"Yes, I made her cry," Lady Aldriss said, walking over to ring for a servant, "but it was an accident."

Far from looking appeased, Niall pulled a handkerchief from one of his coat pockets and wiped at Amelia-Rose's cheek. "Give me someone to fight, lass. Anyone."

She mustered a smile. Affable, yes, he was. And he was also fierce. And for the moment, hers. "Oh, yes, let's wallop my parents and lock them in a wardrobe so they can't frown at me any longer."

He climbed to his feet. "Aye. Ye wait here, th—"

Alarmed, Amelia-Rose grabbed his arm. "Niall! You know I was only jesting."

Niall pulled her upright. "That's better."

"You're not supposed to aggravate me just to stop me from crying," she pointed out.

With a slow grin that quite stopped her heart he brushed a lock of her hair behind her ear. "Ye're assuming *I* was jesting."

"Do not lock my parents in a wardrobe."

He tucked her hand around his arm, heading them back to the loud morning room. "Tomorrow I mean to fetch some posies and a box of cigars and try to convince yer ma and da that I'm a reasonable lad. Then we'll see who's more stubborn, because I reckon it's me."

"It sounds promising," she hedged, "but they may throw you out."

His grin deepened. "I'm persistent as the devil." If he

was as worried as she was, he did a better job of hiding it. If he wasn't worried, then he would be after tomorrow.

By the time they returned to the carriage she felt so full of hugs and handshakes and laughter, she worried she might burst. Even Jane had color in her cheeks, but Amelia-Rose figured that had more to do with her reading selection than the MacTaggerts, themselves.

The rain had stopped, so she was surprised when the coach continued past Wigmore Street and up to Baxter House. "You can't stop here," she said, ducking behind the curtain. "*I'll* end up locked in a wardrobe."

"I told Robert to walk us by, and I'll let ye out just past here. But while ye are in here . . ." He leaned in with a soft, yearning kiss that quite heated her insides.

Jane sat bolt-upright. "Stop that at once, you . . . you chaw bacon!"

He lifted both eyebrows. "I'm a what, now?"

"You heard me."

"I'll have to go look that one up in Aden's book."

The coach stopped, and he pushed open the door as the driver flipped down the steps. "Where can I see ye tomorrow, Amelia-Rose?" he asked, lowering his gaze to her mouth again.

"No, you don't," Jane countered, putting her shoulder between them and pushing Amelia-Rose toward the door. "Out you go, cousin."

"I'll be shopping on Bond Street at two o'clock," she returned, stepping down to the ground. "In case the morning doesn't go as you hope."

"I could use a new hat, I reckon," he returned. "And it's nae hope. It's destiny."

That word lingered with her as the coach trundled off again, and she and Jane turned back up the street. This connection between them felt too delicate, too fragile and too new, for such a strong word. If he was that certain, though, perhaps she needed to see it the same way. *Destiny.* That meant they *would* find a way to persuade her parents. She *would* be able to marry him, to share a life with him. "Destiny" was a very good word.

It wasn't Hughes who pulled open the Baxter House front door as they arrived back home. "There you are," her mother exclaimed, a bright smile on her face. "Where in the world have you been?"

"We went for a wal—"

"Oh, it doesn't matter," Victoria interrupted. "You're here now, and darling, I have the most wonderful news."

Something in Amelia-Rose's chest clenched, and she put a hand against the foyer wall to steady herself. Wonderful news to her mother could only be a very limited number of things. She shut her eyes for a moment and straightened. *Destiny*, she told herself. Perhaps her mother had finally relented and allowed her father to acquire a dog. He'd wanted one for years.

"Take off that bonnet and come along," her mother was still chattering, unknotting the ribbons herself and casting the hat into the corner. "At least your cheeks are pink. This way."

She half shoved Amelia-Rose into the downstairs sitting room. Twenty minutes ago she'd been in a similar room, one filled with smiles and warmth. This one was also filled with smiles, but it felt . . . cold. As she recognized faces, the chill climbed up her spine, rendering her insides frozen and numb.

"Curtsy," her mother hissed from directly behind her.

Amelia-Rose curtsied. "Lord Durst, my lady, Lord Phillip," she creaked out, hearing Jane's very faint gasp behind her. She wondered if her companion had learned any appropriate words for this in that vulgar dictionary.

Lionel West, the beautiful, soulful Marquis of Durst, stepped forward to take both her hands in his. "Miss Baxter.

It seems my mother and your mother have been plotting." He smiled, his deep-brown eyes shifting to the dowager marchioness on the couch and then back to her again. "And they have come to an agreement I feel compelled to accept both for my honor and for my heart. It seems we are to be married."

Chapter Fourteen

Niall didn't know much about flower language, which according to Eloise wasn't a jest, but he figured that white and yellow roses would suffice for Mrs. Baxter, while the expensive box of American cigars he'd purchased for Charles Baxter had nearly cost him an arm in getting them away from Coll.

They knew what he was up to this morning, and despite the words of encouragement and the comments on his eagerness to let go of bachelorhood, he heard the concern in their voices. He had his own worries. The lass—his lass—wanted to please her parents, if only because she didn't think she'd ever managed it before. Pleasing them, though, meant marrying a title. And he didn't have one.

What he did have was a wealthy and influential family on the Oswell side, and a powerful one on the MacTaggert side. He'd never relied much on the Sassenach blood he carried, but it mattered here. His grandfather and the fathers before him had been viscounts for more than two centuries until the last one died with only a daughter—his mother—for an heir. On his father's side, the earldom went back three hundred years, made aristocracy by the decree of fat Henry VIII, himself. That had to matter for something, because it was all he had.

He swung down from Kelpie as one of the Baxter House grooms appeared. Fluffing up the roses a bit with his fingers, Niall approached the door. The butler opened it as he topped the single step. "Good morning, Hughes," he said, nodding. "I'd like a word with Mr. and Mrs. Baxter this morning, if ye please."

The butler lifted an eyebrow. "You would?"

"Aye. I've someaught to discuss with 'em. Now do I wait on the step, or in the house?"

"May I ask what this is regarding? Unless you have a card now and can describe it there."

"I dunnae have a card, and I'd prefer to discuss it with the Baxters."

As he spoke, a lad trotted up to the house, a large bouquet of red roses in his hands. "These are for Miss Baxter," he said, handing them up to the butler before he bounded away again.

Niall looked from the roses to his own posies. "Who's sending Amelia-Rose flowers this morning?" he asked, keeping his tone level.

"I would imagine they are from Lord Hurst," Hughes returned. "Her fiancé."

Some unseen force punched Niall in the chest. He abruptly couldn't breathe. The words the butler spoke seemed to fly right past him, gibberish, but at the same time he knew exactly—*exactly*—what it all meant. Moments flitted through his mind, reminding him that she'd never told him that she loved him. That he'd wondered initially if he might simply have been the most convenient escape from a household she detested.

His first instinct was to charge into the house, find Amelia-Rose, and drag her away from there. His second was to find her parents and make certain they stopped whatever this new hell was and let their daughter be. First, though, first he needed information. Words. Facts. They would be important, so he could fix this. And he would fix it. He had to.

"When did this happen?" he asked aloud.

He thought he'd managed an admirable degree of restraint, but even so the butler took a half-step backward, into the shadow of the foyer. "I'm certain it will all appear in the announcement tomorrow, Mr. MacTaggert. In the meantime, I'll—"

"When did it happen?" Niall repeated in the same tone, centering his gaze on Hughes.

The servant cleared his throat. "Last evening."

After he'd returned her home. He knew he should have kept hold of her, should never have trusted that her parents wouldn't immediately track down another title and sell her off for respectability. "Who's Lord Hurst?"

"I shouldn't be—"

"Hughes."

"Lionel West, the Marquis of Hurst. Brother to Lord Phillip West, and son to Mary, Lady Hurst."

Niall knew Phillip. They'd met at least twice. Doe-eyed lad who seemed to like horses. Whoever this Lionel was, he'd swooped in like a damned vulture. And a marquis, damn it all. "Did she say aye?"

The butler frowned. "What do you mean?"

"Did Amelia-Rose say aye to Lord Hurst? Did he ask her the question, or did they just have her sign her name on a paper? Or shake hands? Did she smile?"

Something that might have been sympathy briefly touched the older man's face. "I wasn't in the room, Mr. MacTaggert."

Nodding, Niall held out the flowers and the cigars.

"With my compliments to the Baxters," he said. He bloody well didn't want the things. Abruptly they felt like poison, like something he'd been tricked into toting about.

The butler took them. "I will pass them along, sir."

Looking down, Niall moved off the step and back toward where Kelpie still stood. He needed to think. He needed to drink. And he needed to figure out what the devil he meant to do about this—when he hadn't the slightest idea where to begin. In the Highlands if one man took another man's woman, there would be a damned fight at best, and a shooting at worst. Here he was fairly certain he wasn't supposed to shoot a marquis.

"Mr. MacTaggert?"

He faced the butler and the half-closed door again. "Aye?"

"Miss Baxter has gone out, but she did make a point of telling me that she would be observing her usual schedule today." He grimaced briefly. "Whatever that might be. She's never had one that I—"

"Thank ye, Hughes." She would be shopping on Bond Street at two o'clock. And she'd left that message for him. Hope blazed through him again, heating the dead chill growing around his heart. This hadn't been her doing. "Thank ye."

"Mr. MacTaggert." The door shut.

Heading out immediately to chase Amelia-Rose across Mayfair appealed to him, but it would be useless. She knew far more people there than he did, and could damned well be anywhere. Four hours. He had four hours until he knew where she'd be. Four hours to come up with more information and a plan. And he did know someone who could help him with at least part of that.

He kicked out of the saddle in front of Oswell House, handed Kelpie over to Gavin, and stalked into the house. "That was fast," Aden observed from up on the stair landing, where he stood draping a gown around Rory's midsection. "Did ye get tossed out on yer arse?"

"Where's Eloise?" Niall asked.

Aden's eyes narrowed a little. "In the music room. Should we be worried over someaught?"

Ignoring the question, Niall headed up to the first floor past his brother and followed the sound of a pianoforte until he found his sister seated alone in the plain-walled music room. "I need a moment," he said, shutting the door behind him.

She looked up, her light-green eyes startled. "You shouldn't be back already," she said, rising and hurrying toward him. "Was it horrid?"

He didn't want to talk about it, and she wouldn't want to hear the stream of profanity that would come with the tale if he did tell her. In fact, the fewer words he spoke, the less likely he was to start bellowing and breaking things like a mad, wounded bear. And he felt wounded. Mortally. "Ye're acquainted with Laird Phillip West, aye?"

"Phillip? Yes. Why? Has some—"

"Tell me about his brother."

His sister scowled, reaching a hand out toward him and then evidently thinking better of touching him. Smart lass. "The Marquis of Hurst?"

"Aye."

Her light-green eyes abruptly filled with tears and overflowed down her fair cheeks. Gulping air, Eloise put her hands over her chest, her fists clenched.

That hurt more than anything she might possibly have said. Those tears told him that he'd very likely lost. That whoever this damned Hurst was, his sister reckoned the marquis was a better fit for Amelia-Rose than Niall was.

But his *adae* had sent him a message. She'd made certain he knew where she'd be. And she had a good idea of what sort of man he was. Not the quiet, subdued type, for certain. Not the type who'd let another man take his woman without a word or a fight.

He nodded. If Eloise had doubts, then he wouldn't include her. "That answers that, then."

As he turned, she grabbed onto his sleeve. "Is it settled? Did she—"

"Naught's settled," Niall snapped, pulling free of her grip.

Whatever the devil had happened between last afternoon and this morning, Hughes the butler had still referred to Amelia-Rose as Miss Baxter. That, as far as he was concerned, was all he truly needed to know. She might have been pushed or fallen into an engagement, but she wasn't married. That meant he could still fix this—if she still wanted him. If the Marquis of Hurst wasn't everything she'd been waiting for when she'd decided to settle for him.

Victoria Baxter let the curtain slip from her fingers. "He's gone, thank goodness. For a moment I feared he might charge the house yelling 'For the Bruce!' or something."

Seated at her dressing table, Amelia-Rose tightened her grip on the handle of her hairbrush. Niall had come calling just as he said he would, prepared to accept her parents' ridicule and insults in order to eventually convince them to see reason. Why *hadn't* he charged the house? If he'd attempted to make off with her, she was fairly certain she would have gone. "Does it mean nothing to you that I care for him?"

"Of course it doesn't. If the MacTaggerts hadn't been attempting to sneak out from beneath their agreement with us all along, you would never have done more than exchange pleasantries with him. Aside from the fact that the Honorable Niall MacTaggert had no business pursuing you for himself, he's Scottish, untitled, unmannered, and would no doubt whisk you away to live in a house filled with sheep."

That had been precisely what she'd originally thought about Coll—except for the title, of course. Now she was glad she hadn't seen Niall from the window. A glimpse of his face would have broken her. As it was, she had no idea what Hughes might have said, or if the butler had delivered the message she'd requested. Did Niall hate her? Did he think she'd betrayed him? That she'd cast him aside without a second thought?

"What now?" her mother prompted into the silence. "Do you mean to stomp your feet? Shout that you won't go along with this? Run away and join a nunnery? A brothel? Because I have no idea how else you might support yourself when your father and I cut you off for your belligerence."

"I haven't decided yet," Amelia-Rose snapped, tears streaking down her cheeks again. "All of them, perhaps."

"And yet I would recommend that you consider thanking me."

Finally Amelia-Rose turned to face her mother. "I am *not* thanking you for anything."

"Ungrateful child. Not a year ago you were mooning over Lord Hurst. 'Oh, he's so handsome,' you said. 'His golden hair and his soulful eyes, I could just swoon.' Well, now you have him. Golden hair, soulful eyes, and a title. You have nothing about which to complain. I've answered all your prayers. Hurst Abbey is only twelve miles from London. You will never be more than a day away from Town."

A year ago she would have been hopeful and excited. As scattered and harried and upset as her thoughts were, she knew that. She'd wanted to please her mother, to be the young lady she'd been raised to be. Winning Hurst would have allowed her to prove to herself that she wasn't a failure.

Her mother came away from the window. "Be grateful, Amelia-Rose. I understand it can be thrilling to have a handsome, virile man's attention. But ask Lady Aldriss if that is enough to make a good marriage. I've saved you. And this is the last time."

"I never asked you to save me." She wanted to say more, wanted to yell that for a day and a night, for an afternoon, she'd been happy. She'd been able to see a future with love and warmth and humor, with a man who encouraged her to speak her mind and surrounded by family who'd welcomed her even with all the trouble she'd caused them.

"I'm your mother. I've done it regardless. Lord Hurst will come by to escort you on your shopping expedition this afternoon, and you will chat with him, you will be pleasant, and you will comport yourself as a woman engaged to be married, because that is what you are."

With that Victoria left the room, shutting the door quietly behind her. Amelia-Rose set down her brush. Everything had happened so fast last evening. She could put things in terms of one emotion or another, surprise, horror, disbelief—but it was so much more tangled and roiled together than that.

She'd tried always to be honest with herself, and for that reason she had to admit that yes, at one time she would have welcomed a suit from Lionel West. Even at the beginning of her first Season, when she'd realized that she would be marrying a title, whoever happened to own it, she'd decided that he would be the least objectionable. Over the course of her two Seasons they'd barely spoken a dozen words together before last night. It seemed more important that he was pretty and seemed kind, and lived close by London.

She would never have called Niall pretty. His looks weren't feminine in the least, despite his long lashes. Those eyes with their impossible color and the laughter in their depths, his strong jaw, the arched brows and brown-red, untamable hair, the lean, hard strength and grace of him— he was entirely, unmistakably, masculine perfection. Her warrior. Her lover.

Did it matter that she'd known him only a handful of days? She'd known Lionel West, if she combined all the minutes together, for perhaps an hour. Of the two, she knew Niall much better, and preferred him indescribably more.

Yes, she'd danced around her feelings for Niall. She'd said that she cared for him, that she valued his friendship, that she wanted to be close by him and kiss him and share his bed. But she hadn't said the last, most important thing—and she hadn't done so because she'd somehow known they wouldn't end up together. Because she'd wanted it too much, and admitting to it would break that future into pieces.

Well, she hadn't said the words, and everything was broken, anyway. She'd waited for the perfect moment, for some promise of ever after, and now it was gone. She'd had it all pulled out from under her, and she'd allowed it to happen. He would know that she'd allowed it to happen, because she hadn't fled or thrown herself out a window or whatever it was that damsels in need of rescue did.

Even that, though, couldn't change one thing. The thing she'd known since probably the afternoon of Lady Margaret's picnic, when she'd been meant for someone else and he'd supposedly been attempting to endear his brother to her. She loved Niall MacTaggert. She loved the way he didn't give a damn what other people thought—except for her, apparently—and the way he looked at her as if nothing mattered to him as much as what she might have to say. She loved his mouth, his body, his brogue, the way she felt stronger just knowing he found her important.

In all this mess she'd done one brave thing. She'd asked Hughes to inform Niall, if he should call, that she would be standing by her schedule for the day. If the butler had passed on that information, Niall would know precisely where she would be this afternoon. Would it make a difference? Would he consider her a lost cause, now? She had no idea what she would say to him if he did appear. Or worse, what she would do if he didn't.

Her door cracked open. "Miss Amy?" Mary said, peering in. "Your mother says I'm to help you dress to go out shopping."

"Come in, Mary. Yes, please fetch my light-blue muslin with the puff sleeves."

"Your mother wished you to dress more grandly, you being newly engaged and all."

"It's a small rebellion, Mary. The blue gown, if you please."

"Yes, Miss Amy."

Whatever happened this afternoon, she had two wishes. First that Niall wouldn't give up on her, and second that someone owed him a miracle. Because on her own, she couldn't think of how this could possibly end well for either of them.

Niall headed south and east toward Pall Mall. When Coll and Aden, a street or so behind him and attempting to remain unseen, fell behind a trio of coaches and an ice wagon, he sent Kelpie into a swift trot north until he'd managed to put enough space between himself and his brothers that they wouldn't be able to track him, then edged west toward Bond Street.

They wanted to help. He understood that, and he also

knew that there were occasions when three large, opinionated Highlands men together caused more mayhem than was warranted. So while he badly wanted to beat Lionel West, Marquis of Durst, into the ground and shovel dirt over him, he would fare better without his two shadows digging the hole for him.

He needed to speak to Amelia-Rose Hyacinth Baxter. Until he heard from her, the doubts kept swirling. Admittedly he wasn't a man accustomed to being turned down by a lass, but this wasn't about his bruised pride. They'd had a plan. Aye, a nebulous plan filled in mainly with phrases like "we'll see to it" or "I'll convince them," but she'd wanted to remain in his life. He still damned well wanted her there.

None of it would matter, though, if he'd merely seen what he'd hoped to see. If she'd allowed him to court her because no one more acceptable to herself or her parents happened to be waiting behind the curtains. If she'd merely been grateful that he'd saved her from embarrassment that night at the ball.

Cursing under his breath, he handed Kelpie and a shilling off to a lad who promised to keep the bay standing in an alley. Beneath his anger and frustration and . . . pain, he knew he could help her. He could fix this. He excelled at fixing things. When a cotter or anyone else had a problem they couldn't settle on their own, they came to Niall. If that made him a peacemaker, or a charmer, then so be it. Today he meant to use all those talents to get Amelia-Rose back in his arms, or to determine once and for all that she'd never wanted to be there in the first place.

He took a position beside a lamppost where he could see most of Bond Street. If he'd wanted to go completely unnoticed he likely shouldn't have worn his kilt, but who he was had become as much a part of this as where she wanted to live. Even with his six-foot-three-inch height and his kilt, he managed to stay out of most everyone's way, though lasses seemed determined to flutter their lashes at him or drop handkerchiefs practically down his front. After the first half a dozen he ignored them, and they lay like wilted, fluttering butterflies at his feet.

After nearly an hour it occurred to him that Hughes might have been lying about Amelia-Rose's schedule, or she might have lied about it to Hughes. It would be an effective way to see Niall well away from Baxter House in the case they meant to acquire a special license, find the nearest church, and wed.

"Bloody hell," he muttered. He should have sent Aden to shadow the house.

Niall straightened. In all this, even with the doubts he made himself conjure about her sincerity, he knew—he *knew*—that Amelia-Rose cared for him. This had been done *to* her, not *by* her. And so he meant to stop it. She wouldn't have lied, because she didn't lie.

As he wrestled with that thought, she stepped out of a hat shop halfway down the street.

She'd worn a pale-blue gown that he knew would deepen her eyes to the color of cornflowers. The plain lines and lack of decoration made her look pure and fresh, a golden-haired English Aphrodite. His feet started toward her before his brain could register that she wasn't alone.

Jane joined her, a hat box in one hand, and behind the companion strolled a slender man with wavy golden hair, a well-fitted brown coat, yellow waistcoat, and black trousers in glinting Hessian boots. Hurst, no doubt. Niall could see why Eloise had described the marquis as soulful; Lionel looked like a poet's fever dream of a young man about to be struck down because he was too beautiful, or some such nonsense.

Squaring his shoulders, Niall continued forward. He knew the exact second Amelia-Rose caught sight of him, because she dropped her reticule and froze. Whether it was good or bad, it was something. She wasn't indifferent.

"Good afternoon," he drawled, crouching to retrieve her bag. "Ye've dropped someaught, lass."

She stared at him, her blue eyes bottomless and . . . stunned? Hopeful? Pleading? Niall refused to put a word to her expression, because it would only be the one he wanted to believe. Her soft mouth opened and closed, and then she visibly shook herself. "Niall. I'm . . . You're here."

"Aye, that I am, *adae*. Did ye wish me elsewhere?"

The soulful dead man stepped between them, reaching for Amelia-Rose's reticule. "I'll take that, my good man. Thank you for your attention."

Niall shifted it backward. "I wasnae speaking to ye, ye soft piece of lambskin."

"I beg your pardon?" Hurst glanced behind him at Amelia-Rose. "Do you know this man, Amelia-Rose?"

"I . . . do." She blinked again. "My lord, this is Niall MacTaggert. Niall, the Marquis of Hurst."

The marquis's expression became a touch less soulful. "You're that Scotsman. I must inform you that Amelia-Rose and I are engaged, sir, and your presence here is unwanted. Please begone."

"That docsnae sound reasonable," Niall returned, wondering if the man had any idea just how narrow the safe path before him lay. "I came upon ye while out shopping for a hat, and greeted this fair lass. Surely ye can spare me a word or two, Miss Baxter, in exchange for yer wee bag?"

"Certainly I c—"

"We're quite busy at the moment, sir. Perhaps you could leave your card at Baxter House." The marquis started forward. "Now, if you'll excuse us, Mr. MacTagg—"

Niall didn't move, didn't step aside, and as Hurst bumped his shoulder the soft man came to an abrupt halt and took a half-step backward. "That wasnae very effective, was it?" Niall observed, looking down at him. The lad was nearly six feet, but most of his exercise looked to be from getting out of bed in the morning. Niall doubted Hurst could hoist a pitcher, much less a sheep.

Hurst lifted his cane, putting his free hand on the ivory dog's head. No doubt he carried a rapier sheathed in there, just in case large Scotsmen refused to move from his path. They were wasting time here, when he needed to speak to Amelia-Rose. And yet, if she did bear this goose-down pillow some degree of affection, perhaps this was what she needed to see. He forced a grin.

"Dunnae make me break ye in half, ye pasty rag doll. I'm just after a word or two. We'll stand right there, so ye can watch over us and keep her from harm." He pointed at a spot directly in front of a shop window.

The marquis began to look rather like he'd swallowed something sour. "I warn you, I am surrounded by friends here. You may think to challenge me to fisticuffs, but you may find yourself taking on the entire aristocracy."

Niall shrugged. He'd tried. No one could say he hadn't. But he wanted to speak with Amelia-Rose now, at once, and hear from her what the devil had happened, and the need to hear her voice, to be close to her, drove everything else out of his mind. "I asked nicely."

Coiling his fist, he took a half turn sideways so he could get his weight behind the punch—and Amelia-Rose put her own fist over his. "Please, Lionel," she said, with a half smile that didn't fool him for a minute, "I don't wish a scene, for goodness' sake. One minute, and we can continue with our afternoon."

"I . . . One minute, then," Hurst agreed. "But not alone. I insist on making certain this rogue doesn't threaten or injure you."

Niall was ready to stomp all over the pretty scarecrow's

demands, but she continued holding on to his hand. "Please," she whispered.

He nodded. "Aye." Not letting her out of his sight, he moved to one side of the walkway. When she and the marquis joined him, he faced her. "Were ye surprised?"

Her jaw clenched. "Yes, I was."

"What surprised you?" Hurst asked, frowning.

"Ye keep yer shite to yerself," Niall snapped. "Ye're to listen; nae speak."

"I didn't agree to any s—"

"That's it. I'm killing him." Niall grabbed the pretty lad by the cravat and hoisted him off his feet.

Hurst yelped, punching at Niall's arms and kicking out at him. "Unhand me, you—"

"Put him down, Niall," Amelia-Rose ordered.

Unless he was mistaken, she found part of this amusing. Niall hoped it was the bits where Hurst nearly wet himself. Clenching his jaw, he set the man down on the ground again, but kept a hand wound into his cravat. "Have ye changed yer mind about anything?" he asked Amelia-Rose, otherwise ignoring the wriggling trout at the end of his arm.

"No, I haven't. I didn't . . ." She trailed off. "I don't know what to say."

Tears rose in her eyes, and he wanted to kiss them away. "He'll give ye what ye wanted," he made himself say anyway. Their words had to be careful, but he needed to know, for certain, what—who—she wanted. What sort of future she wanted, and whether he would be in it. He couldn't rescue a damsel who'd pledged her troth to the dragon.

A single tear trailed down her cheek. Blinking, she swiftly wiped it away. She wouldn't want any other passersby to notice. "How can . . ." Amelia-Rose looked down for a moment, then abruptly met his gaze. "Do you recall that Scottish dish you told me to try? *Skellum?* I did try it. I love it. Very much. I'd like to try it again."

Niall's heart stopped. Simply stopped. Sound, sight, everything seemed clear as a crystal, all around him. He could hear the gulls over the docks, he thought, as far away as they were. Abruptly everything centered again, with the concussion of cannon fire, and his heart started beating. Hard. Fast, and hopeful. Saint Andrew, she was brilliant. And she loved him. *She loved him.* "I'm partial to *adae*, myself," he returned, keeping his voice calm. "It's best with an open window, though. The smell, ye ken."

"I'll try it that way," she said, then stuck out her hand. "That's that then, I suppose. I'm afraid I am occupied tomorrow as well, as Lord Hurst will be taking me to luncheon at noon."

He released the marquis to free a hand. When he took her fingers, they shook. He held on for a bit longer than he should have, then gave her back the reticule. "Aye. That's that."

"That is not that," Hurst stated, trying to straighten his cravat. "I will see you banned from every club in London, you savage."

"Aye. Ye do that, ye wilted lily."

"You might at least wish us well," the lily insisted.

"Now why the devil would I do that?" Niall returned. With a last glance at Amelia-Rose that he hoped said everything he'd been unable to tell her aloud, he turned his back and walked away. He had a thing or two to see to today. And a favor or two to ask.

Amelia-Rose watched Niall walk away. He'd come. And he'd listened. She hadn't been able to say much, but she had the feeling that if she'd been less concerned with scandal, less aware of the fragility of a reputation, she might

well have left with him. The idea of that made her shiver—
her, completely ruined, leaving her betrothed in the street
while she rode off across a Highlander's saddle to a life of
isolation from her friends and family. But she would have
him. She would have Niall. And while he hadn't outright
said so—how could he?—she knew that he meant to help
her. How, she had no idea, but it would involve him visit-
ing her tonight. A low, delighted shiver started up her
spine.

"I cannot believe this," Hurst muttered, still wrenching
at his cravat. "That animal tries to kill me, and you speak
to him about food?"

"I was attempting to calm him down," she countered.
She hadn't been rescued yet. And none of this was Lord
Hurst's fault. "He did let you go, and he did leave, and you
weren't required to resort to violence to defend us."

He looked at her, the scowl on his face dropping to a
reluctant grimace. "You make a point. Even so, I cannot
believe you were eyeing *him* with an idea toward what—
marriage? The man probably lives in a stable."

"I don't think so, but let's put it out of our minds, shall
we?" she urged, placing a hand on his arm.

"Well, I'm quite out of the mood for shopping," Lionel
said, finally giving up on his wrinkled neckwear. "Perhaps
a stroll in Hyde Park will lift my mood."

The more people who saw them together, the more difficult ending an arrangement would be. "I'm somewhat
overset, actually," she decided. "Would you be a dear and
mind taking me home?"

"Yes, of course. I should have considered your delicate
nature." Lifting his free arm, he signaled for his coach.
"You know, now that we've become acquainted, I'm quite
pleased I returned to London when I did. I'm generally
more partial to dark-haired women, due to their naturally
sober nature, but you seem solemn enough."

Amelia-Rose sent him a sideways glance, but he didn't seem to notice. "I do try to be serious," she offered. "I have meant to ask you, do you enjoy walking? Reading? Riding?"

"I sketch," he returned. "Lately I have done a study of the lugubrious saints."

Mournful saints? "Ah," she said. "That must be rewarding."

"Yes, yes, it is." He opened the coach door and handed her up. "You don't read, do you?"

"Why?" she asked, suspicious at the way he'd couched the question.

"It's a horrid habit, you know." He sat beside her, leaving Jane to climb up on her own and claim the opposite seat. "Reading. Spending the day with your chin lowered is very unflattering to the neck. I've heard that it invites sagging skin. And you have a fine neck."

"Thank you."

She'd once fancied herself marrying this man. Knowing him, though, gave her an entirely different opinion of the Marquis of Hurst. A month ago she might have been weighing what she was willing to give up in order to earn herself an escape from Baxter House, as she'd done with Coll's supposed suit. Reading? Smiling, apparently? And she'd had no idea that she had a frivolous hair color.

What she did have was someone with whom to compare the marquis. Someone who asked her questions rather than making pronouncements, assumed she would be interesting and well read, and who enjoyed both laughter and making her smile in return.

Lionel delivered them to Baxter House, promising once more to call on her to take her to luncheon tomorrow, and to bring one of his sketches for her to admire. As he drove away, Jane gripped her arm. "I know what all that *skel-*

lum talk meant," she murmured, walking through the foyer and toward the library. "Have you considered what you're doing?"

Drat. "Jane, you heard Lord Hurst. Am I supposed to marry that?"

"And if you don't?"

Amelia-Rose leaned into the library. Finding it empty, she pulled Jane inside and closed them in. "Explain yourself. And if you mean to tell my mother what happened today, I will—"

"Yes, you won't be happy. I know."

"Jane."

"Amelia-Rose, at this moment you have two men. One who offers you excitement, and one who offers you acceptance. Yes, Lord Hurst is a bit less . . . cerebral than I expected, given his appearance, but he is well respected. It is a good match. You'll have those things you've been lamenting about since before your parents spoke with Lady Aldriss. You will also have a mother who is pleased and proud of you."

"But Niall—"

"Yes, Mr. MacTaggert is a force of nature. Heaven knows if he looked at me the way he looks at you, I might well have fallen for him, myself. He is also a youngest son, dependent on his mother for his income and standing, because he has no reputation here at all except for being a barbarian Highlander. He may have promised you a Season in London, but that still leaves another nine months of the year in Scotland. Living in a house, I assume, with his bachelor brothers and his English-hating father."

After what he'd spoken about the night before last, that prospect seemed much less dire. London was a delicate spiderweb of social engagements, where one misstep could cause one to fall forever out of favor. The idea of a community, of being able to help guide a young man or lady toward a better future than they might find on their own, or of teaching someone to read—that had a mighty appeal.

"What do you suggest, then, for heaven's sake?" she asked aloud anyway, because Jane would expect it.

"I suggest, cousin, that you stop weighing what you're willing to give up, and see who most closely gives you what you want. And then keep your window locked."

With that Jane left the room. Amelia-Rose went to sit in one of the deep windowsills that overlooked the tiny Baxter House garden. Her cousin's rather wise advice surprised her; for too long she'd thought of Jane as a necessary evil, a dour presence meant to help keep her from misbehaving.

Was that what it came down to? Giving up her status or giving up her happiness? It didn't seem that she could have both. So would being with Niall continue to make her happy? When she faced those nine months a year in the Highlands without the friends and parties with which she was familiar, when it rained for days and days on end, would she still be happy?

Oh, this was so complicated. The problem with dreams, she was beginning to realize, was that they only made sense when one's eyes were closed. In the light of day they were as fragile and fleeting as clouds. And she couldn't wager the rest of her life on a cloud.

Chapter Fifteen

Niall crouched beneath a stand of ferns, his gaze on Baxter House above him. The bastard Hurst had appeared about seven o'clock and had stayed until nearly midnight. Aden had ridden by once, but Niall wasn't about to pop out of the shrubbery and announce his location to anyone.

His legs were stiff, even though he'd spent longer hours waiting for a buck to cross his trail. More significantly, the apple and trio of biscuits he'd stolen from the Oswell House kitchen were long gone and he was damned hungry.

The downstairs lamps began going out in succession, and he shifted a little. The windows of Amelia-Rose's bedchamber remained lit, as did the one beside it. She might have left the light on for him, but he doubted it. Either she wasn't in there yet, or someone was in there with her.

Finally her light went out, and then the one in the neighboring room. Niall waited for a late coach to rumble by, then straightened and made his way to the front door. He put a foot on the large pot holding some sort of flowers, then jumped up, catching the eave of the portico with his fingers.

Hauling himself up, he moved from there to the narrow

windowsill beside it, then the decorative fleur-de-lis and the next window. If his reach had been any shorter he would have had to try shimmying up the drainpipe instead, but without much effort he traversed the next pair of windows until he reached Amelia-Rose's. Bracing himself in the tiny corner of the window, he found the bottom of the catch and pushed up.

It didn't budge.

Niall frowned. He pulled on the bottom of the window. Nothing. The curtains on the other side were shut, and he couldn't make out any movement, any light, beyond them. She didn't even have the fireplace lit tonight. Taking a breath, he rapped a knuckle softly against the glass.

Silence answered him. "Damn it, lass," he muttered, and knocked again, a little louder.

The window to the next room down squeaked open. He tried to flatten himself against the wall, but there wasn't anywhere he could go. Just as he contemplated dropping into the flower bed below, a dark-haired head and tight bun emerged into the night.

"She isn't in there," Jane Bansil whispered. "Lord Hurst told my aunt about your meeting on Bond Street, I was sent upstairs without dinner for *not* telling her, and she moved Amelia-Rose to the interior of the house in the bedchamber directly beside hers."

"I need to talk with ye, then," Niall decided, shifting his weight and starting back along the wall.

"No, you don't," she hissed. "I will not have my reputation compromised."

"At least tell me if a wedding date's been set, lass," he countered, slowing his approach so she wouldn't begin throwing things at him.

"Yes. Three weeks from tomorrow. Lord Hurst sent for a special license this afternoon."

Cold stabbed into him. "She doesnae want this, ye ken."

Jane opened and closed her mouth. "I know that. She adores you. You make her smile. But you won't make her a marchioness."

"Nae, I willnae." He reached her window, gripping the top of the sill. "If I cannae see her, will ye give her this?" Niall dug into his coat pocket and produced a dried thistle flower on a short stem. He'd brought it south with him on a whim, pressed between the pages of an old book. At the time he'd had no idea why, except that a thistle was the Highlands, and he was leaving them for a time. Now it represented him, and he wanted Amelia-Rose to know that she wasn't alone.

The companion backed inside a little, as if she feared he would try to yank her outside. "You need to stop making trouble, Mr. MacTaggert."

"The only trouble is the lot of ye trying to stop Amelia-Rose and me." He took a breath. "I cannae see my life without her in it. Do ye reckon Lord Hurst could say the same?"

Scowling, glancing over her shoulder as if she expected to be discovered at any moment, she reached out and snatched the thistle from his fingers. "I am not promising you anything. The decision is hers."

"Aye. It's always been hers."

With that she closed the window, nearly flattening his fingers before he moved them. This wasn't the damned evening he'd wanted. There was supposed to have been more sex, the two of them deciding on the plan he'd concocted this evening, and him holding her for as many hours as they could fit in before the sun rose.

Slowly he made his way back to the portico roof and dropped to the ground. He might have told Jane what he meant to do, but while he didn't doubt the companion cared for her charge, he had no idea if Jane's idea of protecting her would mean tattling about everything to Mrs. Baxter and stopping them before they'd even begun.

Staying in the shadows, he made his way up the street to the inn where'd he'd left Kelpie. Loki stood beside the bay, and he turned around just in time to block his brother from grabbing him. "Enough, Aden."

Aden lowered his arms. "We told ye nae to go off alone. But if ye're back here already, ye're doing someaught wrong."

"They moved her to a different room," he grunted, freeing the reins and swinging up into the gelding's saddle.

"So she doesnae know what ye're about?"

"Nae."

"That makes this all a bit more dangerous, ye ken," his brother returned, mounting beside him.

"If ye're scared, I'll take care of it myself," Niall retorted.

"Nae dangerous for me, ye clod. Dangerous for ye."

Niall shrugged. "She's worth it."

Aden fell in beside him as they made their way back to Oswell House. "I'd make fun of ye for how moon-eyed ye are all of a sudden, but I dunnae want to risk a black eye while I'm after a wife."

"I'd risk it." On Niall's far side Coll trotted into the dim lamplight. "Ye kept us out here for four hours looking for ye, ye lummox."

"If there was a way to reason with the Baxters, I'd do it. If ye can think of something I've missed, for God's sake tell me."

The three of them rode in silence up the nearly deserted street. "I ken that ye're about to make enemies of yer in-laws," Coll finally said, his breath frosting in the night air. "And I ken that that doesnae sit well with ye. The way I see it, someone's going to get hurt here. They've pushed it that way. It can be ye, or it can be them."

"Aye," Aden agreed. "Ye've tried negotiating. Ye've tried making friends. Stick yer hand in the bear's mouth often enough, eventually he'll bite ye."

Niall had to agree with that. "What ye dunnae see in yer metaphor, Aden," he returned, "is that I'm the bear."

This was one bloody bear who was tired of being polite and affable. He wanted Amelia-Rose. And tomorrow she would be the only one who could stop him from taking her.

He went up to bed when they arrived back at Oswell House, but he might as well have saved himself the trouble. Twice he nearly left the house again to make another attempt to see Amelia-Rose, but he talked himself out of it. He'd done what he could. If Jane wagged her tongue about his appearance, the Baxters would consider themselves wise to have moved their daughter out of his grasp, but they would have no idea of anything else in the offing.

Even if Miss Bansil spoke only to Amelia-Rose, neither of them knew what he'd planned—only that he had something in mind. But if he went out again and they caught him, he had a good chance of spending the next three weeks in Old Bailey, and that would be too late to fix anything.

Rising before dawn, he belted on his kilt and headed downstairs to find some breakfast. The footmen were just setting out the first toast and boiled eggs, but then the rest of the family likely wouldn't be rising until midmorning. He hoped they wouldn't be, anyway. He didn't need anyone trying to talk him out of anything or trying to convince him to think of his reputation.

His own reputation didn't concern him. Amelia-Rose, though, was going to have to make a decision. And since he hadn't seen her last night, she was going to have to make it without the benefit of hours of consideration, of weighing the benefits against the storm that would likely follow.

"I thought I might find you here." Francesca strolled

into the morning room, selected a slice of toast and some butter, then sat beside him to pour herself a cup of tea.

Niall closed his eyes for a moment. "I dunnae want to hear that I'm being rash or nae thinking things through."

Carefully she dropped two lumps of sugar into her teacup and stirred it. "Did you tell Amelia-Rose that if you two married, you would spend the Seasons in London?"

"Aye."

"And you meant it?"

With a frown he cracked another egg in its ridiculous wee cup and downed half of it. "Of course I meant it. She likes London."

"I have . . . overheard a few things, aside from what you deigned to tell me regarding Lord Hurst, and I do wonder if you've asked yourself how Miss Baxter might feel about your plans. Unless you've told her, of course."

Niall hadn't told his mother about them, either. Not all of them. "I tried. Couldnae get to her without setting Baxter House on fire."

"Ah. Thank you for not doing that, then."

Smythe walked in, deposited a fresh, wrinkle-free newspaper at Lady Aldriss's elbow, and then exited again. None of the servants were lingering this morning, Niall noted belatedly. His mother's doing, no doubt. No witnesses.

"I've nae a thing to say to ye," he commented into the silence. "Ye'd be better off claiming ye'd no idea what was afoot, anyway."

"When your brothers or your father tell or ask something of you that perhaps you would be better off not doing," she returned, still stirring her tea, "do you hesitate?"

With a grimace, he finished off the egg. "Nae. I do more often than nae end up with a black eye or someaught, though. And I'm nae asking ye for a thing."

She reached over, putting her hand over his. "You are my son. I was apart from you for a very long time, but I am here now. As I told you before, I will do whatever I am able to help you."

"I honestly dunnae know what that might be, *màthair*. Ye're looking the other way for some of it, already, and I reckon that'll be hard enough for ye to maneuver around in yer clever drawing room conversations. The deed, and the consequences, are mine. And Amelia-Rose's." That last bit was what worried him the most; not that she didn't love him, but that he meant to challenge the one thing that could well mean more to her than he did.

"Don't you fret over me and my clever drawing room conversations," she retorted. "I am a very experienced duelist."

"Good." Niall pushed away from the table. "I'll wander back by when they've put out actual food."

"You're not going anywhere yet, are you?"

Whatever he might have thought about Francesca Oswell-MacTaggert, he couldn't mistake the genuine concern in her voice. "Nae. I reckon I'll be about until midmorning."

Francesca watched him out of the breakfast room. He looked tired, worried, and very, very serious. While she hadn't yet been able to discover every detail of his plan—which she meant to do, posthaste—she knew enough to wish again that he hadn't stopped her from negotiating a new agreement with the Baxters. Amelia-Rose would have been angry, but when he won her heart he would have been able to claim the rest of her, as well.

The consequences he'd mentioned would be serious, indeed. She didn't wish them on anyone, much less her own son. The nastiness would interfere with her entire reason for deciding to enforce her agreement with Angus in the first place—to have her sons back in her life.

Sipping at her too-sweet tea, she opened the paper to the social announcements—and set her cup on the table so hard the tea sloshed out. Damn Smythe for not saying something about this, though he frequently had John the footman iron the newspaper in the mornings, and she had a suspicion that the young man couldn't read.

Glancing toward the empty doorway, she lifted the paper so anyone walking by wouldn't know what might have caught her attention. The announcement was small, but not unusually so, with an elaborate spray of flowers across the top and the bottom. It seemed Mr. and Mrs. Charles Baxter were delighted to announce the engagement of their only daughter, Miss Amelia-Rose Hyacinth Baxter, to Lionel Albert West, the Marquis of Hurst. The little script at the bottom, which read *Hearts Entwined*, made her scowl.

They hadn't wasted any time. And with the announcement, anyone who hadn't already heard now knew that Amelia-Rose had found her title. In her eyes, at least, the inclusion of the quotation only pointed out the fact that love had had nothing to do with the match whatsoever.

Francesca debated whether to tell Niall that the official announcement had been made. He knew about the engagement; seeing it in bold black print wouldn't change what he meant to do. It would, though, alert him about just how many other people had hold of the same information.

First she rang for Smythe, wiped up her spilled tea with a napkin, and went to find some writing paper. She hadn't been jesting about her skill in maneuvering through London Society. Now seemed to be the perfect time to make use of those abilities.

"Nae. Make it fluffier."

Oscar narrowed his eyes, giving the cravat a close stare. "If I make it fluffier, ye'll nae be able to see over it."

Turning to face the dressing mirror, Niall looked at his reflection again. His shirt points weren't quite high enough to make him a dandy, but he looked far fancier than he could ever recall. A green coat so tight he could barely lift his arms, a gray-and-yellow-striped waistcoat that could likely be seen even in pitch-black darkness, a damned white waterfall beneath his neck, gray trousers without space for a single damned pocket, and Hessian boots poor Oscar had spent half the night polishing almost to mirror perfection. "I look like a nightmare."

"Be glad Matthew Harris didnae ask too many questions," Coll said from the window, "and that he's near yer size."

"Nae near enough," Niall protested, trying to extend his arms and then giving up the effort out of fear he might pull his own sleeves off.

"Yer hair willnae do," his oldest brother observed, straightening.

"I'm nae cutting it. I'll stuff it under the hat." Picking up the green beaver hat, he set it on his head, grabbing stray strands of hair and pushing them up beneath the dome of the chapeau. He couldn't change his hair color, but at least this way it looked a proper, gentlemanly style. "How's this?"

He turned around, and Coll spent a long moment perusing his attire. "Aye. As long as ye're nae face-to-face with anyone. Ye dunnae look like a poet with consumption."

"Thank ye for that, anyway."

His oldest brother continued gazing at him. "Ye certain about this? I reckon ye could find a lass who's a lot less trouble."

"Aye. Mayhap I could. But she's my *adae*, and I'll nae be without her."

Heavy bootsteps pounded up the stairs outside the

bedchamber, and Aden shoved open the door. "We're ready," he said, out of breath. "Saint Andrew, Niall, ye almost look like a proper Sassenach."

"Nae need to insult me." His heart began a hard, steady rhythm. A great many things could go wrong from this point forward. "And thank ye for this."

Coll clapped him on the shoulder. "Thank us when ye've finished."

Neither of his brothers had hesitated when he'd outlined his plan. Half of it was likely because of the mayhem it could cause, but the other half—and perhaps a bit more—was simply because they were brothers. The MacTaggerts. They always stood together.

Outside Gavin waited on horseback, the reins for the other three mounts in his hands. Not quite certain he could manage to climb into the saddle without splitting his trousers, Niall took his time swinging a leg over Kelpie's back and settling in. Only then did he take a closer look at the groom. "That's nae what ye're to be wearing, Gavin," he said, frowning.

"I asked Farthing, and he said ye gave me the wrong colors. I reckon I'll get some fresh ones in a wee bit."

"Ye brought a Sassenach into this?" Coll queried, his brow lowering.

"Well, they dunnae say '*deas*' or '*clì*' when they turn a team, and I knew it wasnae 'starboard' or 'port.' I deemed I should be authentic, aye?"

"So, what is it?" Aden asked.

The groom reddened. "'Gee' and 'haw.'"

Niall snorted. "That sounds familiar."

"How was I to know that, Master Niall? I'm telling ye, this London is nae a place for sane men."

They set off south at a trot. "I appreciate ye making certain, Gavin," Niall said over his shoulder.

As they reached Curzon Street, they headed right, then

after a block or so turned down a short side street behind a wagon piled with what looked like old furniture. Gavin hopped to the ground, tossing his reins to Aden. "I'll take a look, shall I? It's bonny I'm nae dressed like a harlequin, I reckon."

"Dunnae miss him, Gavin, or ye're walking back to Scotland," Niall warned him.

The groom looked offended. "I wouldnae do such a thing to ye, or stab my eyes with a needle."

Patience, Niall reminded himself. The others had consequences to worry over as well, and none of the benefits he was looking to reap. "I apologize, Gavin. Off with ye."

"There are easier ways to do this, ye ken," Coll commented, edging forward with Nuckelavee just enough so he could see around the corner.

"A straight-up brawl, aye. That willnae gain me what I want, unless ye mean we should murder a man." Niall flexed his hand around the reins. "And me killing a Sassenach lord isnae likely to aid me in finding domestic bliss."

Aden snorted. "'Domestic bliss.' I reckon I'll be after one of those empty-headed lasses, after all. I've a dozen lasses in the Highlands who dunnae expect me to sit in the parlor while they embroider."

"And I hope ye find one who makes ye *want* to give up yer gambling just so ye can sit at home and watch her embroider," Niall returned.

"The hell ye say."

"Gavin's waving at me," Coll announced.

Niall blew out his breath. Once they left this alleyway, there was no turning back. Amelia-Rose was worth this. But he still didn't know the other side of the equation—if she would think *he* was worth this. "Let's go," he ordered, kicking Kelpie in the ribs.

Gavin stood in the middle of the street, gesturing like

a madman. Aden tossed the reins of the gray gelding back to him, and the groom swung into the saddle like a man who'd been born to it. "They turned north," he said. "Came out of the carriage drive like he was late for his own wedding." He sent a glance at Niall. "Apologies, Master Niall."

"Nae need."

Three blocks up they caught sight of the coach, a big black monstrosity with the red-and-blue coat of arms of the Marquis of Hurst. "Aye?" Aden asked, gazing at Niall.

"Aye. Dunnae get yerself killed."

With a swift grin Aden sent Loki into a gallop, Coll and Nuckelavee on their heels. Niall wanted to be the one taking the most obvious risk, but in the outfit he presently wore, he'd end up rolling about on the street with all his seams split. At least his brothers were dressed for battle.

Aden reached the rear of the coach, stood in the saddle, and grabbed onto the luggage straps at the rear to swing over onto the vehicle. Coll caught Loki, keeping just behind the vehicle as Aden scrambled onto the roof and then took a seat beside the coachman.

Having a wild-haired man in a kilt plopping down beside him must have scared the shite out of the driver, and the coach rocked sideways before it straightened again. At the next corner they turned, headed out of Mayfair and its crowds. As far as Niall knew, Aden wasn't armed with more than the single-bladed *sgian-dubh* in his boot, but the middle MacTaggert brother could be very persuasive even barehanded.

They continued on for another twenty minutes, and while Niall didn't see any movement from inside the coach, he knew Hurst was in there. He had to be, because otherwise none of this would work. Perhaps the fool hadn't realized they'd left Mayfair for Whitechapel.

Aden had told him where they would be going, but as they left the opulent West End, Niall frowned. Wherever his brother had been going at night, it hadn't been clubs or any high-end gaming establishments. Aye, Aden could do better than hold his own under most circumstances, but a man alone could always be bested.

Finally they turned up a dirty, trash-strewn street with boarded-up shops on either side and what looked like a pie shop on the corner. The coach stopped. Coll swung down from the black and yanked open the door. "Ah, yer lordship," he said, reaching inside.

The Marquis of Hurst half fell out of the coach, stopped from falling only by Coll's hand knotted into his cravat. "What is the—" He spotted Niall, and his jaw clamped shut.

"Good morning, m'laird," Niall said, carefully dismounting. "Lovely day for a drive, aye?"

The marquis sent a quick look at their surroundings, his pale complexion taking on a gray hue. "There will be witnesses to anything underhanded, you scoundrel. Release me at once."

Instead Coll dragged him over against the front of one of the closed shops. "Send yer lad down, Aden."

The driver climbed down hurriedly but didn't make any attempt to run. "Don't murder me, if you please," he said, raising his hands.

Gavin approached him. "We dunnae need ye, lad," he said. "Just yer clothes. Strip. Now."

The coachman looked toward his employer, and Coll thumped the marquis against the wall. "Tell him."

Hurst squeaked. "Do as they say, Edward."

Gavin and Edward stepped inside the coach and shut the door. Five minutes later they emerged again, Edward in nothing but a long-tailed shirt, and Gavin dressed in a crimson coat, black trousers, and a black top hat. "I feel mighty conspicuous," the groom muttered.

"Ye look bonny," Aden said. "Come up here and take the reins."

Doing as he was bid, he settled into the driver's seat. Aden hopped to the ground and took the horses from Niall. "It's up to ye now, little brother," he said.

"Dunnae hurt him. Just . . . delay him for a bit."

"We know yer plan." He poked a free finger into Niall's shoulder. "All the luck in the world to ye, Niall. We'll see ye soon."

All the luck in the world sounded like just the amount he would need. With a nod to Coll, Niall stepped into the coach and pulled the door shut. "Let's go, Gavin."

Amelia-Rose wasn't certain if she could actually still catch Niall's scent on her pillow, or if it was just her imagination. Either way, her pillow was in her bedchamber, and she was in another room altogether. Perhaps she could ask for it, tell her mother that she could only sleep with her regular bedding or something.

A pillow hardly made up for being separated from him, but until she could figure out what to do next, it was all she had. She'd already tried going out the window, but the height was dizzying and she couldn't make out a single foot- or handhold despite the fact that she knew Niall had made it up to the second floor somehow. But then he probably climbed all sorts of things, and had been wearing boots rather than very impractical slippers.

"You're being very quiet today," Mary observed as she put a last hairpin in place.

"Should I be singing a tune?"

"I . . . I apologize, Miss Amy. Amelia-Rose. I didn't mean to offend."

Amelia-Rose took a breath. "Of course it's not your fault, Mary. Perhaps I *should* be singing. But I've been deemed untrustworthy and I'm being pushed into something I don't want, so I'm irritated. Annoyed." Angry. Furious. Desperate to speak to a man her mother was making every effort to keep from her.

"Lord Hurst is quite handsome, you have to admit. And such soulful eyes. I would imagine he writes poetry."

"Yes. Lugubrious poetry, no doubt."

"I beg your pardon?"

"Never mind."

Her door rattled to the sound of a key turning, and a footman allowed Jane inside the bedchamber before he closed them all in again. If this continued, the entire household would be locked in here before long.

"Good morning," Jane said, sitting on the edge of the bed. "I half expected to see you refusing to get out of bed."

"I considered it," Amelia-Rose admitted. "Going to luncheon with Lionel seems to be the only way I'll find the sun on my face today, however."

Jane cleared her throat. "Speaking of sunlight," she said, pulling a folded handkerchief from her pocket, "I happened across this very recently. Isn't it lovely?" She opened the kerchief to reveal a thistle flower, pressed flat and dried, but still a vibrant purple.

A thistle. Amelia-Rose stared at its reflection in her dressing mirror, before her gaze flashed up to meet Jane's eyes. If she understood her cousin's cryptic description, she'd seen Niall "very recently." How recently? Last night? Had he tried to see her and found her window locked, only to be met by Jane? How could she ask without putting anyone at risk, and also taking into account that the footman guarding the door was very likely listening through the keyhole? "It is lovely," she agreed aloud. "It has a meaning in the language of flowers, does it not? I can't quite remember what it is."

"I looked it up," Jane returned promptly. "It means unity, endurance, and victory." As she spoke, she emphasized each word in turn. "A rather warlike flower, really, don't you think?"

"Definitely a flower to wear into battle," Amelia-Rose replied. "Might I wear it today?"

Jane's jaw jumped. "If you wish. The decision is yours."

"The purple will show well with your yellow gown," Mary agreed, fetching the flower from Jane and pinning it without ceremony to the front of the yellow-and-brown muslin, beneath the edge of the green pelisse she wore over the walking dress. "Even pressed it may prick you, though. Wouldn't you rather wear a gem or a cameo?"

Whether by coincidence or the destiny of which Niall had last spoken, the flower settled just above her heart. "I'll be careful. This should be fine."

She wanted to hug Jane, and most definitely have a moment to speak with her in private, but firstly she wasn't certain how private any conversation of hers would be for the next three weeks, and secondly she had no idea if Jane had reached the limit of her helpfulness or not. If delivering a thistle was as far as her cousin was willing to step away from Victoria Baxter's good graces, then the less said, the better.

The very small chance existed that this thistle might have been Niall's farewell, that he'd realized nothing he did could stop the inevitable. The announcement had appeared in the newspaper this morning, she knew, because her mother had shown it to her. Her future, writ in black and white, impossible to erase, and impossible to change.

Had Niall seen it this morning? Had it hurt him as much as it had hurt her? More? At least she'd known it would be coming. She doubted very much that anyone had warned him about it.

Her door opened again, and Amelia-Rose swiftly drew her pelisse over the flower, hiding it from view as her mother strolled into the room. "Lord Hurst's coach is here," Victoria said. "You will be polite at luncheon, you will profess your eagerness for the wedding, and you will not mention that . . . Highlander in any manner. Is that clear?"

As much as Amelia-Rose wanted to argue, that would only see her locked into this bedchamber for every day of the three weeks remaining before the wedding. Better to cooperate and wait for a moment to send a letter or find a chance for . . . something. Anything. "Yes, Mother."

"Good." Victoria turned to look at Jane. "And you will make certain of that. If my daughter strays from my wishes, you will inform me, Jane. Heaven knows I don't ask much of you, but you will do this."

Jane stood and curtsied. "Of course, Aunt."

"Then let's not keep your husband-to-be waiting." Standing aside from the door, she motioned for Amelia-Rose to precede her.

She descended the stairs, just resisting the urge to break and run for the open front door. Hughes the butler had aided her previously, but not anywhere in his employer's sight. Today he might just as easily slam the door in her face as allow her into the street.

Lionel wasn't in the foyer. Generally he appeared with a bouquet for her and one for her mother, which made Amelia-Rose wonder just how badly he needed the money—by way of a dowry—that would be transferred along with her to Hurst's possession. She could see the rear wheels of his coach outside, then noticed the light drizzle. Ah, that would be it. Lord Hurst did not like raindrops ruining the shine of his boots or flattening his golden curls.

As her mother continued her entreaties and threats from the Baxter House doorway, Amelia-Rose hurried to the coach's open door. A gloved hand in an olive-green sleeve reached out to help her inside, and she took the seat beside him. He offered a hand to Jane, as well, which surprised her a little. Previously he'd barely deigned to notice her chaperone. If she'd cared enough about him to have an opinion, that might have lifted it slightly.

"My lord," she said, scooting as far away from him on the seat as she could, noting only that he was dressed as primly as usual and that he hadn't bothered to remove his beaver hat even inside the coach. Poor fellow, his hair must have been a wreck already.

"Miss Baxter, how very delightful to see you again," a voice in exceedingly proper English accents and sounding half an octave lower than Hurst's replied.

"W—"

"A moment, please." He leaned out and waved toward the front of Baxter House, then shut the door. Sitting back, he hammered his fist against the ceiling of the coach. "Edward, let's be off, my good man."

Amelia-Rose stared at him. Even shadowed behind the coach's closed curtains, the face looking back at her had more color to it than Lionel could manage in midsummer. The mouth was harder, the nose more elegant, and the brows had a slight, sardonic arch that even the hat low over his eyes couldn't hide.

She lunged at him, dragging the hat off to reveal a tumble of disheveled brown hair and eyes of an impossibly light green. "Niall," she sobbed, flinging her arms around him, kissing him over and over again. How he'd managed to appear in Hurst's coach she had no idea, but at the mere sight of him all the ice in her chest melted into warm, hopeful heat.

He kissed her back, then held her away from himself.

"I've come for ye, lass," he said, his voice rough. "But ye need to decide if ye want to go with me. I've a faraway destination in mind, and ye may nae be able to come back here. Ever."

Chapter Sixteen

Amelia-Rose sat back again, but kept her fingers twined with his. Niall didn't want to release her at all; after what he meant to tell her, this could well be the last time he ever set eyes on her.

"Yer parents willnae consent for ye to marry me, ever. They've made that clear, and I cannae steal ye off to a London church firstly because ye're nae yet twenty-one years of age, and secondly because we'd have to have the banns called for the next three weeks."

"I considered that, too," she replied, almost matter-of-factly. "My mother had the engagement announcement posted in the newspaper today. No pastor would read the banns for you and me, knowing that."

"Aye. I saw the damned thing." And had likely taught his mother a few choice words in Scots Gaelic in the process.

"I'm sorry," she said, tears shining in her eyes.

"Lass, dunnae cry. Nae until I've said what I mean to say." He knew what he wanted, what he needed. Whether she would want the same thing once she understood just what would be involved, he didn't know. He hoped, but he didn't know.

She nodded tightly.

"I want to take ye to Gretna Green, in Scotland. I want to marry ye there. There would be nae a thing yer parents could do about it, especially if we stay in Scotland. But that leaves a problem outside of Scotland. The engagement announcement's been seen. I . . . liberated a coach that isnae mine. And an elopement with the brother of the man ye were nearly betrothed to . . ."

"I would be ruined in the eyes of London Society," she finished for him, her fingers tightening around his.

"Aye. It's nae that it *might* happen, either. If ye come with me, it *will* happen. Ye're nae ruined yet, as ye've got Jane with ye and we can call this a kidnapping, or convince Hurst nae to mention it at all." That would be more difficult than she could possibly know, but he was the one who'd had the man forcibly removed from his coach. He would be the one to make it right, if it came to that. If it came to him losing Amelia-Rose.

"Yer parents willnae welcome ye back, either. They'll more than likely disown ye, so if ye change yer mind about me, and about living in the Highlands, ye'll nae have a home to return to."

Surprisingly, she smiled briefly. "That, of all things, doesn't particularly trouble me."

"It's only one of many, lass."

"Are you trying to convince me to refuse to go with you?"

"For God's sake, nae. But I want yer eyes open. Nae regrets. Nae regrets ye cannae live with, anyway."

She gazed at him. "That's your real point, isn't it? That I should be horribly disappointed to lose access to fine parties and refined company and be forced to spend my days with a rough-hewn Highlander on some lonesome loch in the middle of the mountains?"

Niall winced. "Aye, that's it, I suppose. I wish I had more to offer ye, but I've nae been a—"

"You asked me," she interrupted.

"Aye, of course I did."

"I mean, you asked me. You want what's best for me, but you've left it to me to decide what that is."

He frowned. "What else would I do, drag ye off against yer will and make ye miserable? I want ye, Amelia-Rose, but if yer heart doesnae come with the rest of ye, I have naught."

A tear ran down her cheek, and it took every ounce of will for him not to wipe it away. "You just described exactly what everyone else has already done to me," she whispered. With her free hand she lifted one side of her pretty green pelisse away from her gown. His thistle lay pinned over her left breast. Over her heart. "You have my heart, Niall. You are my heart. Wherever you go, I will go."

Niall closed his eyes for half a dozen hard beats of his heart. Of everything he'd planned, of all the trouble he'd caused for himself and for his family and for her, this was what he'd worried over. Opening his eyes, he pulled her forward and lowered his mouth over hers. *His.* She wanted to be his.

"I love ye, *adae*," he murmured, cupping the sides of her face in his rough hands.

"And I love you, *skellum*. I didn't know what I could do to stop this nonsense with Hurst, but I kept . . . I hoped . . ."

"It doesnae matter now. Ye're here, and I'm nae letting ye go." He kissed her again, the touch of her soft mouth against his making him feel protective, grateful, and very, very lucky all at the same time. "All I can give ye is a bit more time to consider. As long as Jane is with us, ye have an escape. A chance at some respectability."

"Yes, about that," Jane said, sitting forward. "Please stop the coach."

Amelia-Rose faced her companion. "Jane?"

"I've watched you two from your second meeting," Miss Bansil said crisply. "I saw you falling in love. According to your mother, my aunt, that is a horror not to be tolerated. As if it's wrong for the brother of a viscount to wed the daughter of the second cousin of the Marquis of Lanford. Does he make you happy?"

"Yes, he does," Amelia-Rose answered with a swiftness that made his heart pound all over again.

"Will the life he's described to you make you happy?"

"Yes, I believe it will."

Jane looked at Niall. "Have you lied to her about anything?"

"Nae. Only about when I fell for her."

"Do you mean to be faithful to her and not abandon her?"

"I do, and I willnae."

"Then you don't need my respectability. You need to head north without impediment. I don't wish to move to Scotland, and so now I mean to worry about my own reputation. I believe I may take a walk, and then go see your mother at Oswell House as you suggested, Niall."

He leaned across the coach and planted a kiss on Jane's mouth. "Thank ye, Jane Bansil," he said, worrying for a second at the lass's stunned expression and hoping she didn't mean to have an apoplexy on the spot. Knocking on the roof, he called for Gavin to stop the coach.

"Jane, do you have money if you need to hire a hack?" Amelia-Rose asked, digging into her reticule.

Niall pulled a five-pound note from his pocket and folded it into the companion's hand as the coach rocked to a stop. "If ye'd take a bit of time for a meal first, mayhap, and then let my mother know where I've gone, I'd appreciate it, Miss Bansil."

She nodded, one hand rising to her lips. "I can do that."

Francesca had likely figured it all out by now, if she hadn't realized it already this morning, but the countess had a reputation here in London, as well. She deserved more than an after-the-fact statement, but that would have to wait.

Jane stepped out of the coach and shut the door, then opened it again and leaned in to take Amelia-Rose's hand. "My best to you, cousin," she said, a tear running down one cheek. "You see, I'm not a villain."

Amelia-Rose gripped her fingers. "No, you're the very opposite of a villain. I'm ashamed I ever suggested otherwise."

She closed the door again and stepped back. "Are we off, then, or do I stop for some tea?" Gavin asked from the driver's perch.

Niall pounded the ceiling. "Go, ye idiot."

As they rolled back into the afternoon traffic, Amelia-Rose pushed the curtains aside to look out at London. Did she have in mind that this could well be the last time she ever set eyes on it? "I wish there was a way to give ye everything ye want," he said, checking his pocket watch. His brothers had had Hurst for an hour, now. If they kept to the plan and didn't throw the marquis into the Thames, soulful Lionel would be receiving some choice warnings about making a scandal and then set loose soon.

She sat back, leaning against his shoulder in a way that spoke of trust and even contentment. "I was actually thinking that I haven't a stitch of clothing with me other than what I'm wearing. I didn't see your trunk tied to the back of the coach, either."

"We cannae take this coach north," he returned, sliding an arm around her waist. "Hurst would have the law after us, and he'd be right to do so. I've another coach waiting just north of Town, and I raided Eloise's wardrobe for a few things for ye. Ye're of a size, I reckon."

"Very close, yes." She twisted her head to look up at him. "Does she know what we're doing?"

"Nae."

Amelia-Rose straightened. "She should know. Your scandal could affect her."

"She's engaged already. And she's a god-awful liar. This way she can claim she'd nae idea what her improper brother was up to, and I reckon her friends will believe her." He'd actually considered telling her this morning, but while he trusted she would do her best to be discreet, she'd more than likely tell Matthew Harris—and Niall didn't know her betrothed well enough to trust him with Amelia-Rose's reputation.

"You thought of everything, then, did you?"

"I tried to. I would've told ye last night, but they moved ye to a different room. The thistle was the best I could do." He drew her pelisse aside, brushing a finger along the flower. "I'm glad Jane decided to give it to ye."

"I'm glad you decided not to give up on me," she returned, cupping his face in her palms.

"Are ye certain ye dunnae wish we'd nae met? I reckon ye and Hurst might have been happier if I'd nae left the Highlands."

"I might have set my cap at Lionel," she confessed, her lips thinning. "He's very pretty, after all. And yes, I probably would have agreed to marry him, just to please my mother—and to get me out of Baxter House. I would have spent my time being precisely the lady he expected me to be, sober, somber, with no opinion but his, no reading because it will make the skin of my neck sag, no—"

"What?" he interrupted.

A smile flickered across her face. "He told me so, himself."

"Now I wish I'd punched him when I had the chance."

"How did you end up with his coach, anyway?"

"My brothers and I dragged him out of it, stripped his driver, and they're . . . seeing to him while we leave London."

"'Seeing to him'? What does that mean, Niall? You haven't hurt him, have you? They'll arrest you, even in Scotland."

"Nae. His sense of self-importance may be damaged, and he whimpered a bit, but we didnae injure him. They'll let him loose at half one, and hopefully he'll go home and sulk and do a bit of thinking before he tells yer parents what's happened."

He felt a shiver run through her. "What if they come after us?"

"They may," he returned, with less concern than he actually felt. "That'll take some time, since I doubt they'll go off on a long trip without preparing first."

"How long?"

"Four days at the most. A little under that if we can hire someone to relieve Gavin and let him snore in here with us. Or he and I can trade off driving." He took her hand again. "My lass, I have ye now, and they'll nae take ye from me. I'll nae allow it."

She nodded, her expression easing. "I won't allow it, either."

Twenty minutes later they turned up a quiet road just south of Hampstead Heath. Beneath a copse of trees the large Oswell-MacTaggert coach stood, four bay horses hitched to it and stomping restlessly while one of the Oswell House grooms watered them. Niall had put the clothes and incidentals he'd selected into a single trunk;

the last thing he wanted was for everyone who saw the coach to realize it was set for a lengthy journey.

"Ye ken what ye're to do, aye?" Gavin asked the groom as he hopped down from the Hurst coach. "Take it somewhere in Knightsbridge and leave it on the street. Dunnae put it anywhere too obvious, but ye need to make certain it gets noticed."

The lad nodded. "Master Niall explained it to me."

"Off with ye, then," Niall took up. "If ye get stopped, dunnae lie. This isnae yer responsibility."

The Hurst coach rolled back out to the road and disappeared behind the bend. One step finished. Two, actually, since Amelia-Rose still stood beside him. Would always stand beside him.

As that thought struck him, though, it also occurred to him that he'd neglected something. But that he couldn't do it while he wore these tight dandy's clothes. Going to the trunk, he unlatched it and forced it open, stripping off the jacket and waistcoat and tossing them inside, followed by the hat and his trousers.

Out of the corner of his eye he saw Amelia-Rose watching him, and he concentrated on thoughts of Old Sean and his mad cats. They would have time to become reacquainted later, but not in Hampstead Heath, and not with Gavin already making grumbling noises about how far they needed to get before nightfall.

Once he had on his kilt and a simple blue coat and waistcoat that actually allowed him to flex his arms, he faced her. Now he was himself again. His heart lurching, he walked up and took both her hands in his. "I need to ask ye someaught," he said, hearing the catch in his voice, and knowing she'd noticed it, as well.

Her eyes widened a little, but she only nodded.

Niall sank down on one knee. "I've stolen ye away with the idea of marrying ye, but I've nae asked ye formally if ye'll have me. I promised ye summers in London, and I promised ye a life ye'll both enjoy and find fulfilling in the Highlands. Ye'll have the second one. I dunnae ken what will happen to yer time in London, but if ye want to come, no matter who looks at us sideways, I'll stand beside ye. I'll stand in front of ye, so I can set every man who looks like he has someaught to say on his arse."

"Niall," she said quietly, teary-eyed and smiling.

"Nae. I'm serious." He took a breath. Rambling was easier, but they were pressed for time. "I love ye, Amelia-Rose. Ye stand on yer own two feet, even with yer own parents set on knocking ye down. Ye've stayed kind, and ye've a wicked humor, and ye've stayed true to yerself. I didnae expect to find ye. I didnae think to look for anyone like ye. But I saw ye, and I was lost. Will ye marry me, *adae*? My *leannan*?"

She sent Gavin, rapt on the driver's seat of the coach, a swift glance. "*Leannan*, Gavin?"

"Och. Lover. Sweetheart," the driver replied, flushing.

Returning her gaze to Niall, she sank down on her knees in front of him. "You are a good man, Niall Mac-Taggert. Without even being aware of it, you look after everyone around you. You've bent over backward to try and give me what I said I wanted. I love . . . I love that it bothers you that I may not see London again. And that you look baffled now, as if you couldn't conceive of why you should think anything different."

She cleared her throat. "I love you, Niall. I tried not to, until I realized that it wasn't you who was wrong for me. It was the things I thought I had in place to make me happy that were wrong. Going to a ball made me forget for an evening how miserable I've been. But that's not happiness. That's just pretending, closing my eyes to the truth. *You* make me happy. And my eyes are open. Yes, I will marry you. Happily. Very happily."

Niall pulled her into his arms and captured her mouth with his own. A fortnight. He'd known her for less than a fortnight, and now he couldn't imagine a life without her. Her practicality, her compassion—she matched him well. And the Highlands wouldn't collapse if they held a dance or two at Aldriss Park, for Saint Andrew's sake. Clan Ross might be better off if a few of its chieftains knew the waltz.

All of that, though, paled compared with the fact that she trusted him, that she wanted him as much as he wanted her. Standing, he took her hand and helped her to her feet, then swung her into the air and kissed her again.

With a yelp she chuckled, folding into his arms. "Don't drop me. We still don't know if your sister's clothes will fit me."

"I'll nae drop ye."

Gavin cleared his throat. "Begging yer pardon, but we've a few miles to go before we sleep. *If* we sleep."

"Aye." Lowering her to the ground again, he took her hand and helped her into the coach. "Let's get to Scotland, shall we?"

One hand on her chin and the other on her hip, Francesca Oswell-MacTaggert stood on the landing of Oswell House's grand staircase and eyed the best-dressed red deer in the kingdom. Her sons had meant Rory the stag as an insult, as a touch of their rough Highlands lives brought into her sophisticated London life. Yet now Rory boasted a beaver hat over one antler, a green bonnet over the other, a single earbob, a wilted, badly knotted cravat around his regal neck, and a lady's skirt around his rump.

She quite adored him, actually, though she would never say so. Whatever he'd been meant to represent, Rory brought . . . fun to the household. A sense of devil-may-care that she'd known in the Highlands, but had since all but forgotten.

How odd, that when she'd lived in Scotland she'd noticed only the loneliness and isolation, the lack of polish and sophisticated entertainments to which she'd been bred. Once she left, she'd done her best to put all but the thought of her boys out of her mind. Now that they were here, she remembered the laughter, the stubborn, proud sense of freedom every Highlander seemed to possess as a birthright. She remembered warm, passionate nights in a chilly room, and the bagpipes that had played to announce the birth of each of her children.

"Do you know if Sally was able to get Hannah to help her sew the hem of my green silk gown?" Eloise asked from the top of the stairs above her.

"Dear?"

"Oh, don't touch the deer. I quite like Rory."

Francesca forced a smile. "Not that deer. You, dear."

Her daughter descended to the landing. "Oh. I was going to wear the green silk tonight, but I can't find it anywhere."

"I wouldn't know, my sweet."

Eloise nodded. "Why is it so quiet? Generally one of my brothers is here stomping about."

It *was* quiet. They'd been at Oswell House for just under a fortnight, and she'd already become accustomed to the different energy that accompanied them. The air of barely restrained chaos. "First, I need to ask if you something."

"Of course."

"Is anything missing aside from your green silk?"

Eloise's brows furrowed. "Have we been robbed? Oh, I hope they didn't get the pearl earbobs that Papa sent me for my birthday." She turned, starting up the stairs again.

Francesca caught hold of her wrist. "No, we weren't robbed. You were . . . borrowed from."

"They didn't put my dress on Rory, did they?" She

looked over her mother's shoulder, then blew out her breath. "Thank goodness. Who borrowed what from me, then?"

"I believe Niall borrowed some of your clothes and necessaries for Amelia-Rose."

She watched her daughter's frown deepen, then clear with wide-eyed understanding. "He—they—Oh, they didn't, did they?" she gasped, putting both hands over her mouth, but not quickly enough to cover her delighted grin.

"No one will confirm anything for me, but yes, I believe they are on their way to Gretna Green right now. They certainly couldn't get anyone to marry them here, not without her parents' permission."

Eloise bounced up and down on her toes. "Oh, I want to tell everyone! I knew Niall would figure something out. And she agreed? But she loves London so!" Her expression sagged a little. "She'll be ruined, won't she? No one will ask her to parties."

"*We* will ask her," Francesca assured her. "And it may not be as bad as all that, if I have any say in matters. Which I believe I do. Or I will, anyway."

"Well, now I want to see what he borrowed. I hope he didn't take the yellow one. That would not be flattering with Amelia-Rose's coloring." Halfway up the stairs, Eloise turned around again, descended, and gave her mother a sound hug. "Please do have a say in matters. I don't want to lose my brothers again. Not any of them."

"Neither do I, my dear."

Below, someone knocked at the front door. Smythe was in the pantry with half the kitchen staff trying to re-estimate yet again how much food the household needed to stock with eight additional people—very large men, rather—beneath the roof, so she returned to the foyer and pulled open the door herself.

A ramrod-straight young woman with black hair pulled into a painfully tight bun looked back at her and blinked. "My lady. I didn't expect y—"

"You're Amelia-Rose's companion, aren't you?" Francesca interrupted, alarm quaking through her bones. "Come in at once." Half pulling the woman into the foyer, she glanced outside and then shut the door. "What's happened? Has something gone wrong?"

"I'm Jane Bansil, my lady," the companion said, dipping a curtsy. "And 'gone wrong' depends, I suppose, on your idea of what 'wrong' is."

"Smythe!" Francesca called, guiding her visitor into the morning room. A footman appeared, and she requested tea, Eloise, and to be otherwise left alone.

"Thank you, my lady," Jane said, taking a seat primly on the front edge of the couch. "I . . . Your son suggested that if I were to come here, you would aid me in perhaps finding another position. I do not think I'll be welcomed back into my aunt's household after today."

"Of course I will. But you must tell me what happened."

"Your son, Niall, asked me to do just that." She folded her hands onto her lap. "Lord Hurst's coach arrived this afternoon to take Amelia-Rose to luncheon, except it wasn't Lord Hurst inside it. It was Niall."

Niall had stolen Hurst's coach? No one had mentioned that bit of skulduggery to her—and she could see why. *Good heavens.* "And then?" Francesca prompted.

"He asked Amelia-Rose if she would accompany him to Gretna Green, where they would marry. She agreed." Jane sat back a little. "Your son was very concerned that my cousin have the option to change her mind if she thought the scandal would be too much to bear. I was therefore to accompany them to bring some propriety to the journey, to give her a way to back out if she changed her mind. In my opinion, however, Amelia-Rose needed to make the decision on its own merits. I therefore declined to flee with them."

Eloise entered the room, the tea tray in her arms. "Jane?" she said, kicking the door closed and setting the tray on the table between them. "What in the world's happened now?"

"An elopement to Gretna Green, as I suspected," Francesca returned. "And a new houseguest. Jane will be staying with us for a time."

"Oh, was it romantic? Did he propose? Did she cry?" Eloise asked, pouring tea despite a distinctive shake to her fingers. "I just want to jump up and down and cheer, and at the same time hit Niall for not telling me what he was up to."

"He didn't precisely propose, but it was definitely understood that a wedding waited at the end of the journey," Jane answered, accepting the cup of tea with ridiculous care. "Thank you."

The poor girl looked as if no one had bothered to offer to pour her tea in a very long time, if ever. Knowing Victoria Baxter as she'd come to, Francesca wasn't surprised. The woman attempted to rule over anyone who as much as dared exist in her presence. She would have to be dealt with. If Amelia-Rose couldn't return to London, than Niall wouldn't do so. And that was unacceptable.

"My dear," Francesca said aloud, "I would very much like if you would tell me everything you observed between my son and Miss Baxter, and between Miss Baxter and her parents. I would find it quite . . . helpful, I think."

Jane looked into her teacup for a moment. "I could manage that, I think, my lady."

Before they could begin, the front door thudded open, swiftly followed by a low-toned exchange, and then the morning room door opening. "There ye are," Aden said, out of breath, disheveled, and grinning.

Francesca stood. "Are they on their way?"

Her middle son lifted an eyebrow. "Ye're supposed to be up in arms, I reckon, lamenting yer youngest boy's lack of good character."

"Don't be ridiculous. What did you come in here to tell me?"

He stepped farther into the room, shutting the door behind him. "Coll and I are going to be away for a few days." Aden glanced at Jane, paused, then gave her a sharper look. "Werenae ye to be somewhere else?"

"She declined to join your brother and Miss Baxter. Which I believe to be a good thing."

"As ye say. I'll bring ye back a signed copy of the marriage certificate, so ye'll have proof that one of us has done as ye commanded, my lady." With a bow he put his hand on the door handle.

"Aden."

"Aye?"

"What of Hurst?"

"We came back to deliver Kelpie and the other mount, *màthair*. Last I saw Hurst, he was hailing a hack and yelling at his mostly naked driver to make his own way home, the bastard. He wasnae happy, and I've nae idea what he means to do next. Another reason for Coll and me to be elsewhere, I reckon."

For the moment putting aside the fact that her third son had just called her "mother," Francesca turned to Jane. "Do you have any idea what Hurst might do?"

The companion pursed her lips. "My aunt offered him a generous dowry to wed Amelia-Rose. A very generous one. He may go after it—and her—or he may send the authorities after them. I doubt he will do nothing."

"I had that feeling," Aden commented. "Coll could

make a lion piss itself, but that sack of oil had something keeping his spine straight."

"How much of a head start does Niall have?" Eloise asked, her hands over her heart.

If nothing else, Francesca reflected, this should discourage her daughter from attempting an elopement, however little Eloise had liked the idea of a long engagement. That had been her brothers' only chance, though, to make good on their father's agreement.

"About two hours, I reckon," Aden replied, "depending on how much it took to convince the lass."

"It didn't take much," Jane said, between gulps of tea.

Francesca stood, joining Aden at the door. "Does Niall know you mean to join him?"

"Nae. He said we're to be our usual ignorant selves and carry on here. Niall's nae content unless he's taken all the burden on himself. I dunnae necessarily agree with that. MacTaggerts stand together."

She nodded. "Follow them, then," she said, keeping her voice pitched low. "Make certain they're able to marry. But then get them back here, as soon as possible. Everything rests on it."

He tilted his head. "What everything? Niall knows she's ruined, and she'll know better than he does."

"My darling, your mother is not entirely without resources. They cannot stay away, and they cannot appear to be anything but a young couple in love who couldn't bear to wait for the reading of the banns. I'm sorry, but you must trust me on this."

"This is London, my lady. I reckon ye ken this madhouse better than any of us ever will. I'll see to it. Coll and I will."

She put a hand on his shoulder, wishing she could be certain he wouldn't pull away if she attempted a hug. "Then go."

Niall being happy meant everything. But she wanted him—them—to be able to be happy here. And while hell might have no fury like a woman scorned, London was about to meet a mother protecting her children.

Chapter Seventeen

Niall opened his eyes to find Amelia-Rose on her side, one elbow beneath her head, gazing at him. "Good morning, lass."

"Good morning."

"I reckon we'll be in Scotland by midmorning, and we'll be married by noon, over a blacksmith's anvil. Nae what ye dreamed about, I imagine."

She frowned. "Stop doing that."

"Doing what?"

"Talking like you think that I think you're a second choice. That I'm disappointed. I'm not. I spent a very long time trying to deceive myself about what would make me happy, because I thought to be stuck into the sort of life where distraction was essential. And then I met you, and I realized the answer to my happiness was me being able to be myself. Not to have to pretend to be horribly proper, not to hold my tongue because the ridiculous person speaking happens to be a man. Because of you, I am me."

That response called for more than a good morning, a getting dressed, and a running out to the coach. Niall glanced at his open pocket watch. It was barely past six o'clock. They had time. A wee bit of it, but enough to enable him to get to the blacksmith's without showing just how much he wanted her even after three nights of deep, deliriously arousing sex.

Pulling on her bent elbow, he turned her flat on her back, kissing her openmouthed. "Ye say such sweet things, *adae*," he murmured against her lips, shifting to splay both hands over her bare breasts. "And what a shame I forgot to pack ye any night clothes."

As he flexed his fingers she moaned, shoving the covers away from herself, trying to pull him closer. "You remembered hair clips," she reminded him huskily, reaching down to wrap her fingers around his cock and stroke him in a way that made his eyes roll back in his head. She was a quick learner, Amelia-Rose was. "I don't think you forgot anything."

"Sweet Saint Andrew, ye undo me, my lass."

Moving over her, he lowered one hand to hook her knee and open her. Sliding his palms up the inside of her thighs, he dipped a finger inside her, her groan of pleasure mingling with his own. She was wet for him, ready. This lovely, perfect lass, who'd just last night taught him which fork to use for a roast rabbit, who delighted in soft sheets and Mozart, had chosen him. He had no other explanation for it but love.

Entering her, he thrust hard and fast, taking her over the edge as she gasped and clung to his shoulders. The sensation of her body pulsing around him pulled at him, tried to draw him with her, but he wasn't ready yet. Instead he slowed his pace until she began to relax again, lifting her head to kiss him.

Then he withdrew, sitting up and folding his legs. "Come here, Amelia-Rose," he beckoned, taking her hand and helping her upright. When she was seated, he took her ankles and pulled her forward, wrapping her legs around his hips and supporting her bottom with his legs.

"Good glory," she whispered, looking down between them as his cock slid inside her again.

With his hands on her arse he pulled her forward in time with his thrusts, the bed beneath them squeaking rhythmically with their movements. Flinging her arms around his neck she came again, and this time he let himself follow, pushing in as deeply as he could and holding himself there as he spilled his seed inside her.

She kept her arms looped around him, her cheek resting against his shoulder. "I had no idea," she panted, "that being ruined could be so invigorating."

Niall laughed, holding her. "I'll ruin ye like that anytime ye please."

"I think I shall please a great deal, Niall."

He kissed her hair. "I love ye, Amelia-Rose."

Amelia-Rose lifted her head to look at him. "That name *is* a mouthful, isn't it? I've always been fond of Amy. It's more me, I think. Would you mind?"

"Mind nae twisting my tongue up every time I say yer name? Nae. Ye're Amy now. It does fit ye, lass. Fresh and warm."

A pebble struck the window of their second-floor room, and with a frown Niall slid out from under Amelia-Rose—Amy—and padded over to look outside. Gavin stood there, another rock in his hand.

Niall shoved open the window. "What is it?"

"I've been feeling a shiver creeping up my spine since dawn," the groom said. "Let's be off, Master Niall."

He'd felt it, too, the sensation that everything had gone too smoothly. Not a sign of a suspicious redcoat, not a stranger coming up from the south by the same road and giving them odd looks, no hard-faced lads from Bow Street appearing to drag them back to London. "Aye," he returned. "Give us thirty minutes to dress and eat."

The groom nodded, trotting back toward the stable

yard. When Niall turned around, Amy already had her shift on, and she was digging into the trunk they shared for Eloise's teal-colored walking dress. He liked it on her; it gave her eyes a bit of green together with the deep blue, like a loch on a clear day.

"That's the dress ye'll be married in," he stated, handing her the borrowed hairbrush as he slung the kilt around his hips and buckled it.

She held the gown up to look at it. "Well, Eloise isn't getting it back, then."

Niall sat on the bed to pull on his boots. "I'd like to take ye up to Aldriss Park after this—another two days of travel. Are ye ready for that?"

"Yes. I want to meet your father, and I'll be happy to settle somewhere after a week in the coach."

He still felt the need to apologize; this wasn't the life she would have chosen for herself. Yes, she said she was happy, and yes, he believed her. But he loved her, and he wanted her to have . . . more. "Ye'll be happy every day from now on, Amy. I swear to that. There's a bonny spot overlooking Loch an Daimh that'll give us a view of the valley and the mountains. I'll show it to ye, and if ye're agreeable, I think we should put a house there."

"It's not too close to old Sean and his cats, is it?"

He chuckled. "Nae. We'd be a good mile or more from old Sean."

"Good. I like cats, but I keep imagining them all escaping from the tunnels and roving the Highlands with little cheeses strapped to their backs."

He laughed. That set him more at ease; perhaps he was taking this change to her plans more seriously than she was. She kept insisting that was so, and it reminded him that she was nothing he'd planned for, either. Meeting her had upended everything, and he embraced all of it, the good and the bad, that had come with loving her.

"Now I'll have nightmares," he muttered with a grin, walking over to help button the gown up her back.

Once they'd dressed he finished repacking the trunk and hauled it downstairs himself. They had a simple breakfast of eggs and ham, and well within the half hour he'd requested they were back in the coach headed north.

"What do ye reckon yer parents are doing right now?" he asked as she leaned against his shoulder to look out the window.

"I imagine I've been disowned," she said, her voice much less concerned than he would have expected from her a week or so ago. "No doubt I'm now a candidate for Bedlam, and my mother will have surrounded herself with her dearest friends, who will all spread the tale that I was always a wretched child and the Baxters are happy finally to be rid of me."

"I cannae believe they wouldn't have any ill words to say about me," he protested. "I stole ye away, after all."

"Yes, yes, I'm sure you're being demonized, as well."

"That's more like it, then."

Amelia-Rose smiled. She'd been smiling a great deal over the past few days, which she supposed under normal circumstances would indicate she'd gone mad. A dash to Gretna Green was the last thing she would ever have expected to find herself doing, but then since meeting Niall she'd done a great many things for the first time. It was an empowering feeling, really.

Through all of this, even when she'd been separated from him, Niall had been beside her. He believed in her. He loved her. His tall, lean form felt like a shield, a man who could protect her, keep her safe, and, most of all, set her free from her own damned, limiting fears.

She looked at his profile as he checked his pocket watch, no doubt estimating just how much longer they had to go before they reached Scotland. The English laws of marriage didn't apply there—at least not the Hardwicke Marriage Act, which said a lady under the age of twenty-one couldn't marry without her parents' consent. Not without the couple risking three weeks of having the banns read in church, anyway. In three weeks she would have been married to the Marquis of Hurst.

"Ye just shivered, *leannan*."

Amelia-Rose tightened her grip on his hand. "I was just thinking about how my life might have gone if you hadn't stolen Lionel's coach."

"Ye'd have bitten him and run for it, I'd wager."

She snorted. "I hope so. I'd like to think I would have."

By ten o'clock her bottom was tiring from another day of riding in the coach, and she was about to suggest that she and Niall switch places with Gavin again so the groom could nap while Niall drove the coach. Then Gavin thumped on the roof with his fist. "Gretna Green," he announced.

Her heart jumped, not with nervousness, but rather excitement. In a few minutes she would be married. She would belong to Niall MacTaggert. He would belong to her. And she would be Amelia-Rose MacTaggert. Amy MacTaggert. That sounded like a fair Highlands name, if she said so herself.

They turned, and then the coach stopped. Niall faced her. "Are ye ready, Amy, my *adae*, my *leannan*?"

"Aye," she said, putting a hand over his heart. She could feel its fast, hard beat beneath her fingers.

He kissed her, slowly, leisurely, in a way that warmed her to her toes. A possessive kiss, an intimate one, a moment she would always remember as the only proof she needed that she'd made the right decision.

"Let's get married, then."

Niall pushed open the coach door and kicked down the

step, then descended to the ground and held out a hand to her. Belatedly she realized she hadn't bothered to wear a bonnet, but she wasn't certain whether one should remove a hat in a blacksmith's or not, anyway.

"Gavin, tie off the team. We need two witnesses, and ye'll be one of 'em."

"I'd be honored, Master Niall. Most honored," the groom gushed, hopping down from the driver's seat.

They walked into the blacksmith's shop, where a large man in Puritan black, a flat-brimmed hat on his head, sat in a chair beside the forge, a mug of something resting on one knee. He set the cup aside and stood. "David Lang. Bishop Lang, they call me. Ye here to marry?"

"Aye," Niall returned.

"Do ye have another witness?"

"Just me," Gavin answered, his hat in his hands.

The blacksmith walked to the rear of the shop. "Mary! I need a witness!"

"I'll be right there, David!"

"That's my wife," he said. "Ye'll need to sign yer names here," he went on, pulling a book from beneath his chair, then paused to look them up and down. "It'll cost ye . . . five pounds for my services."

Five pounds seemed like a fortune, but Niall produced the money wordlessly and handed it over. "Is there a marriage certificate, so we can prove we wed?"

"Aye, for another pound."

"Is there anything else ye'd care to offer us for a fee?" Niall commented with a swift grin.

"I can recommend an inn for yer wedding night. I'll do that for free, because they pay me for every newlywed couple spending the night there."

"Nae. We've a distance to go after this."

A plump woman opened the rear door, a towel in her

hands and the smell of fresh bread accompanying her. "I've ten minutes before the bread burns," she informed her husband.

"Aye. The two of ye, stand before the anvil," Prior Lang ordered. "Hold hands if ye like; it's nae matter to me."

Wordlessly Amelia-Rose took Niall's proffered hand. No, she would never have expected a wedding like this. But what a story it would make for their children. Youngsters with light-green eyes and brogues and hopefully a liking for fine clothes and dancing. She grinned.

Lang looked at Niall. "Are ye of marriageable age?"

"Aye. I'm four-and-twenty."

The blacksmith turned to Amelia-Rose. "And ye? Are ye of marriageable age?"

"Yes. I'm nineteen."

"Are ye related to each other?"

"Nae," Niall said, frowning.

"I have to ask, lad. Now. Are ye both free to marry? Neither of ye is already wed to someone else?"

"We are free to marry," Amelia-Rose answered.

The door behind them burst open. "Just a damned minute!" Lionel West, the Marquis of Hurst, slammed into the smithy.

Her heart clenching, Amelia-Rose backed up, feeling Niall beside her coil like a panther ready to strike. "Ye get the hell out of here," he growled.

"I will not! You belong to m—"

A muscular arm grabbed the marquis around the neck and hauled him backward, out of the building. Muffled yelling followed, and then Aden MacTaggert stuck his head into the doorway. "Sorry about that. He squirmed away from us. Get on with it; he and his friends are promising nae to bring more trouble." With that he closed the door again.

"Did you know your brothers were here?" Amelia-Rose whispered.

"Nae. I should've figured it, though. Prior Lang, if ye dunnae mind? I've nae wish to see that fine-smelling bread burned."

"Ye're certain ye're free to marry?" the smith asked again, pinning Amelia-Rose with a more interested gaze.

"Yes. What that man wants is not what I want."

Lang continued to eye her, then nodded. "By yer kilt ye're clan Ross," the blacksmith stated to Niall. "Do ye have a tartan to use?"

Niall pulled a strip of plaid from his pocket. It bore the same red, black, and green pattern as his kilt, and he handed it to the smith. The big man indicated they should lift their joined hands, and he wrapped the tartan over them. Then he picked up his hammer and struck it against the anvil, the clang sharp and echoing. "Ye're now married. I'll get yer wee paper."

The two of them along with Gavin and Mary Lang signed the wedding register, as did Prior Lang, and then they signed everything again on a small, printed paper. After she put her name down, Niall took the pen from Amelia-Rose and set it back in its stand. "I reckon I'll kiss my bride now," he murmured.

She lifted on her toes, putting her arms around his shoulders, and kissed him. Hope, relief, elation—it all mingled together in a heady joy that made her feel as if her feet weren't even touching the floor. It had been so simple, and somehow that made it more real. She didn't have to dream about a fairy tale any longer. She had better than a fairy tale.

Niall lifted his head. "I love ye, Amy Hyacinth Mac-Taggert. So much it scares me a bit. Ye name anything, any dragon, any quest, and I'll slay it for ye."

"The only request I have is that you don't leave me behind," she whispered back. "I love you, too, Niall Douglas MacTaggert."

"Och, my bread," Mary exclaimed, and left the room. And that seemed to be the end of the ceremony. Carefully folding their certificate, Niall stuck it into an inner coat pocket and motioned Gavin to precede them out the door.

Not until Niall paused just short of the doorway, waiting for Gavin to leave first, did she realize he'd sent out the groom to make certain they wouldn't be attacked by anyone. The fact that Lionel had ventured this far from London during the Season surprised her no end. The idea that he'd done so in such a hurry and had very nearly provoked a fight with Niall made her wonder just how badly he'd needed the ten thousand pounds her parents had promised him in exchange for her.

"All's well," Gavin reported, leaning into the doorway again.

In fact, nothing on the narrow street looked unusual at all, other than the large coach stopped outside the blacksmith's. None of the residents passing by seemed to notice the vehicle, either, which made sense if eloping couples arrived here as often as had been rumored. "Where are they?" Amelia-Rose asked.

Niall let her hand go, hopped up onto the wheel of the coach, then clambered onto its roof. Standing, he did a quick circle, one hand shading his eyes from the sun. Up there like that, in his kilt and boots, he looked once more like a warrior—but then he *was* a warrior. Her warrior.

He jumped down again. "This way," he said, retrieving her hand and heading up the street toward a stand of trees and a quaint-looking stream.

As they topped a short rise, she spied five horses at the edge of the water, one of them unmistakably Lord Glendarril's huge black Friesian, Nuckelavee. Men came into sight, two of them in kilts matching Niall's, and then three more men who appeared to be tied to trees. Amelia-Rose stopped short. "Niall, this will cause trouble."

"An English marquis trying to stop a Highlands wedding? Aye, I'd call that trouble," he returned, tugging her forward again. Abruptly he stopped, as well. "If ye dunnae want to see him, I'll send Gavin back to the village with ye."

Did she want to see Lord Hurst again? Not really, but at the same time the marquis needed to understand that she was no longer available, and had never been interested. Not since she'd met Niall, anyway. "I wouldn't mind a word with him," she returned.

He sent her a sideways glance, then started forward again. "Lads," he said, stopping between the two big men.

"Niall," Coll rumbled. "Are ye wed?"

"Aye."

"Can ye prove it?"

Niall patted his pocket. "Aye."

Moving with surprising speed for such a large man, Coll lunged forward, grabbed Niall, and hugged him. "I'm happy for ye, *bràthair.*"

Niall grunted. "Put me down, ye ogre."

The viscount did so, then turned to her. His gaze on her face, he reached down for her hand, lifted it, and kissed her knuckle. "Welcome to the family, Amelia-Rose Mac-Taggert."

"It's Amy, now," Niall countered.

Glendarril cocked his head. "That suits ye better. 'Amelia-Rose' is a bit pretentious."

Aden elbowed his older brother out of the way. He did hug her, but with a care that said he worried she might break. "I apologize again for letting that toad in the smithy. He looks boneless, but he's got a quick trot."

Niall stepped between her and his brother, accepting another hug. "Did ye know he was following us?"

"Nae till this morning. We passed ye last night, decided to get here first and take a look about." He angled a thumb at Hurst, and Amelia-Rose noticed they'd put a gag over the marquis's mouth. "Good thing we did."

"Did ye have someaught ye wanted to say to Lord Hurst, Mrs. MacTaggert?" Niall asked her.

Previously she might have hesitated. The price she would likely pay for speaking her mind would be too dear. But these three men, these brothers, were part of a clan. Niall had spoken about how when trouble befell one clansman, the others stepped forward to help. And she was a MacTaggert now, as well. She wasn't alone any longer. "Yes, I would," she said.

"Ye wanted him silent, or yapping?" Coll asked.

"Remove the gag, if you please."

The viscount complied, and Lionel spat onto the ground. "You are dead men," he hissed. "I am looking at dead men. You cannot put your hands on me twice. I will see you all transported or hanged."

"Lionel," she said, interrupting the tail end of his rant, "I'm sorry you fell into the middle of this. I know my mother promised you a fortune for my hand, and I understand that this blinded you to any questions over whether I wanted to marry you or not. I did not. I—"

"There is a signed agreement, Miss Baxter."

"You sketch lugubrious saints, you consider women with dark hair to be more solemn than those with blond hair, and you dislike the idea of reading. While I don't have a great deal of knowledge about saints, except to know that Saint Andrew is the patron saint of Scotland, I don't have dark hair, and I very much enjoy reading. In addition, I find you to be dull to the point of ridiculousness, and while you do have a pretty face, I would consider that to be your only virtue."

His mouth gaped open, his face turning purple. He

didn't look so very soulful anymore. Now he more closely resembled a toddler whose toy had been taken away. "You stu—"

"I've two things to add," Niall said, moving up beside her. "She's a married woman, and ye're nae in England. So ye think hard before ye finish that sentence, Hurst. Yer future may rest on it."

As good-humored as Niall generally was, she heard the steel in those words, the utter calm in his level gaze. Hurst heard it, too, because the marquis snapped his mouth shut, the remainder of his sentence unspoken.

"A word, Niall?" Aden asked, moving away from their three prisoners.

She wasn't certain if she was to be included, but Niall took her hand in his callused one again to follow his brother. "Aye?"

"We've a bit of a dilemma," Aden said, lowering his voice.

"Keep 'em here till sunset," Niall returned flatly. "They'll nae be able to follow us north, even if there was a reason for 'em to do so."

"Francesca wants ye back in London. The sooner the better."

Niall frowned. "We're nae going back to London. Even you two ken what's changed for us there. And I'll nae have Amy facing her parents unless or until she wants to."

Coll joined them, shaking his head. "Nae. Francesca's done someaught. Wouldnae tell us what, but she said the longer ye're gone, the harder repairing the damage will be. She said ye need to trust her."

"And what do the two of ye think of that?"

Aden grimaced. "When it comes to London, I reckon she's the expert," he said slowly.

"Amy?" Niall asked, facing her. "This affects ye far more than it does me."

He meant to leave the decision to her. Some of this new independence she'd found was rather intimidating. But she'd always liked Lady Aldriss, and had never heard anything but kindness and understanding from the countess. "I've seen your mother walk through a room and with a glance stop an argument or quiet a rumor," she said. "She is formidable. If she says she can help, I think we should believe her." She shrugged. "At the worst, we travel for another week back to London and then up here again."

"I dunnae ken if my backside can take that," Niall said with a faint grin. "I didnae expect this, though, and I reckon I like the idea of it."

Amelia-Rose nodded. "As do I." The idea that she might gain London again, be able to visit every so often, didn't mean as much as it once would have, but having the freedom to go if she chose to do so—that appealed to her.

"And that's our next dilemma," Aden put in. "Hurst. Back in England. Heading for London, I imagine, on the same road we'll be taking."

Niall rubbed his chin. "Wait here, lass."

She grabbed his arm as he turned away. "You are not going to murder him. That will follow you wherever you go."

"I'm nae that cold-blooded," he returned. "I'd at least make it a fair fight."

"N—"

"Come and listen, then," he interrupted. "I'll nae have ye worried that ye've married a lunatic."

Without waiting for her, he walked back to Hurst's tree and stopped in front of it. Amelia-Rose hurried after him, lifting her skirts over the long grass. Lionel didn't look any happier, but his face had returned to its usual shade of pale.

"Hurst," Niall said, his hands on his hips, "I'm feeling generous today. Mrs. Baxter offered ye ten thousand to take her daughter. I'll give ye five thousand to keep yer mouth shut about ye getting yer coach borrowed, this chase up to Scotland, ye getting tied to a tree, and my brothers wanting to cut yer balls off for insulting my lass."

"I—"

"If ye see any way this story would make ye look the better, I'd like to hear it, because all I see for ye is being laughed at and nae having any blunt to make up for it."

The marquis frowned, his eyes narrowed. He glanced at the two men who'd accompanied him, neither of whom would meet his gaze. Whatever the MacTaggerts had said to them, they wouldn't be talking about anything.

"I don't seem to have much choice, do I?" he finally snapped.

"I'd agree with that. Ye stay here for another day, then head back to London. Say ye had business somewhere. We'll see it all sorted, and ye'll nae have to do a thing but nae have any idea why that engagement announcement appeared in the newspaper."

"And the money?"

"Will be at yer door within a day of ye returning to London. Do we have an agreement?"

"How do I know you'll abide by it, you heathen?"

"Because if I wanted to do someaught permanent to ye, I reckon people go missing up here all the time. Like Amy said, ye got pulled into this. So at the end ye'll be a bachelor with an extra five thousand pounds ye wouldnae have had a fortnight ago. I ask ye again, do we have an agreement?"

Hurst took a breath, wincing as the ropes tightened around his chest. "Yes. We have an agreement."

Niall pulled the knife from his boot. With a swift cut he sliced the ropes, then walked over to do the same for the other two men. "The blue inn there, The Copper, has a fine kitchen. They'll put ye up for the night, as well."

"Don't expect me to thank you, MacTaggert."

"I dunnae. Just go."

When he turned his back, Amelia-Rose joined him, wrapping her hands around his arm. "You are a very good man," she whispered.

"I'm a man who doesnae want blood spilled on my wedding day," he returned, lowering his cheek to her hair. "Ye heard me, aye?" he asked his brothers.

Aden nodded. "Ye're assuming Francesca will hand that rat over five thousand quid, though. And that he'll nae ask for more later."

"Once our mother does whatever she's promising, I'll deal with him again if I have to. He'll nae like it as much, though."

"I wanted to eat at The Copper," Coll stated, scowling.

"Come along, lads," Niall said, heading them back toward the village well behind Hurst and his men. "I reckon I know a place where we can get some fresh bread. It may cost us a fortune, though."

So this was her married life. Amelia-Rose sighed as she walked beside her tall, handsome husband. Her Highlander. She'd expected to find marriage to be a dull duty. Judging by her first hour of being married to Niall MacTaggert, she was in for a grand adventure. She looked forward to every moment of it—even if they returned to London only to have to leave again. Because she would be with Niall. She would be a MacTaggert.

Chapter Eighteen

Francesca rose early. Her son—all her sons—should arrive in Gretna Green sometime today, and at any time now Niall would be married. She did see the irony of it; he'd done as she'd ordered all those years ago when he'd been a very independent seven-year-old and she'd wanted a way to keep her boys in her life; he had, or he would shortly, marry an Englishwoman. His choice and his methods, though, had effectively removed them both from England. From her.

Hannah arrived at her bedchamber, and while she always dressed carefully, this morning Francesca chose a silver-and-blue ensemble, something a bit too fancy for a day she meant to spend in Oswell House. She and Eloise had spent the past three days at home, in fact, not receiving visitors and declining the invitation she'd already accepted to a small soiree honoring a friend's birthday.

"The pearls, or the onyx?" Hannah asked, the maid holding up the two necklaces.

"The pearls. The onyx is more formidable, but I couldn't wear it before sunset without looking overdressed."

When they'd finished, Francesca stood to eye herself in the dressing mirror. The last time she'd dressed this carefully had been the day Coll, Aden, and Niall had arrived in London. That had been a battle that for a short time she hadn't been certain she would win. She still wasn't certain she could call it a victory, though all three had now referred to her as their mother. From Aden and Niall, at least, she'd begun to sense a grudging respect and even a smattering of affection. That meant everything, and gave her enough hope to keep pressing the far more jaded and caustic Coll.

As Hannah left the room, Eloise slipped inside. "Do you think they're married yet?"

"According to Aden, they should be at Gretna Green sometime today. So not yet, but soon."

"I know it's scandalous, but it's so romantic."

Francesca eyed her daughter. "You are not going to elope. If you wed before any of your brothers, I will have to abide by the agreement."

"I want a grand church wedding," Eloise said. "With Papa to walk me down the aisle."

That wasn't likely to happen, but Francesca didn't say anything about it now. Several miracles had happened already, after all. "Mm-hm."

"Mama, may Matthew at least call on me today?" she asked, lifting the folded letter she held in one hand. "He thinks I'm angry with him over something."

"Perhaps later," Francesca returned. "I believe I will have some callers shortly. If everything goes as I hope, then Matthew may join us for dinner."

"Everyone else has seen the engagement announcement by now," her daughter returned. "What does it matter if we've seen it or not? Or if we go out and chat about it?"

"Deniability. We haven't been asked if we've seen it, and we haven't been asked to comment about it. Therefore, we can claim we knew nothing about the silly thing. That will be important, Eloise. Don't forget. We know nothing about it."

"I still don't see why that matters. We're not mentioned in it. Amelia-Rose and Lord Hurst are. Whatever you've planned, we can't stop Lord Hurst from speaking out, certainly."

That was the one part that troubled her the most. Hurst was a marquis. He outranked her in Society, and he had a very wide streak of self-importance running through his skinny frame. In addition he was attractive, which made him well liked. But as far as she'd been able to determine he had been absent from London for the past few days, as well. She frowned. Her sons had said they hadn't hurt him, but she wouldn't put it past them to have locked him in a cellar somewhere.

"Just be patient for a while longer," she said aloud, taking her daughter's arm as they left the bedchamber. "I know there's nothing worse than being housebound in the middle of the Season. I believe the cause is worth the trouble, however."

Eloise hugged her arm. "It is, of course. I'm only worried. And since no one told me anything, I'm also going to have a few choice words for them when they return." She lowered her head. "If they return."

"Coll and Aden still have English wives to find," Francesca reminded her. "Nor am I ready to let Niall go when I've just gotten him to speak to me without clenching his jaw."

"I am very glad they're here," her daughter responded. "I always imagined the household with a big family."

"I'm sorry you had to wait so long."

"I think I appreciate them more now; I didn't grow up with them pulling on my braids and putting spiders in my bed."

That seemed a very likely scenario. Francesca smiled. "You know they would do anything for you. You're a Mac-Taggert. And now I think you have a better idea of what that means."

Her daughter nodded. "It makes me more proud, in a way, which I suppose is wrong, but I can't help it. I do wish they would be more welcoming to Matthew, though. He's better acquainted with me than they are, after all. I think he's a little afraid of them."

"Good."

"Mama."

Matthew Harris was set to marry their only sister. The young man should be a little wary. "If anyone throws a punch, then I'll worry."

The newspaper lay on the table, set in her usual spot, as they entered the breakfast room. Francesca shut her eyes for just a moment. It was done, then. In the next hour or so she would either find a way for Niall and Amelia-Rose to return to London, or she would sink the combined Oswell and MacTaggert names into mire and scandal.

While Eloise selected a breakfast, Francesca requested tea and then sat. Trying to conceal her deep breath, she opened the paper to the sixth page. *Oh, it was magnificent.* Even if she did say so herself.

Behind her, Eloise gasped. "Mother!"

Francesca smoothed the paper flatter. "What do you think, my dear?"

A scroll of thistles outlined the entire page, together with an English Tudor rose and the lion rampant of Scotland. Between those, in bold, black letters, the announcement stated that the Earl and Countess of Aldriss were delighted to announce the marriage of their son, Niall Douglas MacTaggert, to Amelia-Rose Hyacinth Baxter, the daughter of Charles and Victoria Baxter. The blessed day was June the twenty-fifth, which happened to be that very day.

Beneath that she'd intentionally chosen a passage from a Robert Burns poem—an English writer would never do.

O my Luve's like a red, red rose,
That's newly sprung in June:
O my Luve's like the melodie,
That's sweetly play'd in tune.

As fair art thou, my bonnie lass,
So deep in luve am I;
And I will luve thee still, my dear,
Till a' the seas gang dry.

"Oh, it's lovely," Eloise whispered, wiping at her cheeks. She hugged Francesca's shoulders. "You're such a romantic."

"Now we have to pray they actually are marrying today, or we'll look like utter fools." She tried to blink away the tears in her own eyes, but that was no use. She'd wanted to be there when they married. She wanted to see their joy and hope and love with her own eyes, to know that however she'd mishandled her own miseries, she hadn't ruined things for her sons. And now, if everything went well, she would miss the first wedding.

"I think they will," Eloise stated. "I know they will."

"We will have visitors at any moment now, I imagine," Francesca noted, accepting her tea and adding sugar. "When they arrive, please be elsewhere. If there's to be any embarrassment on either side, I don't want witnesses to taint the proceedings."

Her daughter sat beside her. "You're talking about the Baxters."

"Yes, I am."

"Oh. *Oh*. They're going to be furious."

"I imagine so. Make certain Miss Bansil remains up-stairs, as well."

She'd wanted to post the announcement the morning after Niall and Amelia-Rose had fled, to overwhelm the Baxters' engagement announcement immediately with a far grander marriage one. But she'd waited. This might be an elopement, but it was one that she'd known about, and one that had her unreserved approval and was proceeding on schedule.

A slice of toast with marmalade later, and the knocker on the front door began hammering with an almost un-nerving frenzy. "Upstairs with you," she said to Eloise, who snatched up her plate and bolted. Once her daughter had vanished, she nodded at Smythe. "I will be in the morning room."

Rising, she passed through the foyer and into the cozy front room, sitting just out of sight of anyone who might have been trying to see through the window. Then she picked up a random book and opened it. She heard the front door open, and then the high-pitched, clenched sound of Victoria Baxter's voice. Some things remained predictable.

Smythe appeared in the doorway. "My lady, Mr. and Mrs. Baxter insist on speaking with you this morning," he intoned, loudly enough for her guests to overhear. "Are you receiving visitors?"

She did adore her butler. "Yes, I'm much recovered this morning. Show them in, if you please."

It struck her that while she enjoyed the theater, she'd never spared much thought for the actors and how flu-idly they spun tales that were not their own. She had one of those to tell this morning, and her underlying nerves knew that while she did consider herself formidable, she'd never been fond of, or easy with, lying. This was for her son, though, for the precocious boy he'd been at seven and the admirable, honorable man he'd become at four-and-twenty.

"What is the meaning of this?" Victoria hissed, stalking into the room, the half-crushed page of the *London Times* in one hand.

Francesca scowled. "Some tea, Victoria?"

"I do not want tea. I want an explanation for this . . . nonsense! I demand one."

"My dear," Francesca returned, keeping her seat, "I'm afraid I've been under the weather for the past few days, and I do apologize for not consulting you on the wording, but referring to your daughter's marriage to my son—the son of Lord Aldriss—as 'nonsense' begins to annoy me a little."

Victoria snapped her mouth shut. "My daughter is engaged to Lord Hurst, as you well know. We announced it days ago."

"Did you? That's . . . peculiar. Are you certain someone wasn't jesting with you?"

"What? I will not be . . . bamboozled into disbelieving my own decisions, Lady Aldriss. This is outrageous!"

"But if, as you say, Amelia-Rose is engaged to Lord Hurst, where is she?"

Charles Baxter put a hand on his wife's arm. "We should sit, darling. There is a foul fog in the air, here."

"My daughter . . . is unwell. She is at home, resting," Victoria stated, but took a seat on the couch opposite Francesca.

"Your daughter," Francesca returned, setting aside her book, "is in Gretna Green with my son. I asked them to wait for a church wedding, but they are young and impulsive, and couldn't bear the idea of waiting for a special license or for the banns to be read. They took my coach, accompanied by Niall's brothers and Jane Bansil. Surely you know this. Whoever is resting in your daughter's bed-chamber is not Amelia-Rose. If you don't recognize your own child, I wonder if you—"

"No! This is not— I believe nothing you say!"

Stubborn, self-obsessed woman. "Very well," Francesca said, dropping all pretense of bewilderment. "These are the facts before you. Your daughter has been missing for four days. As far as I know, you've told no one, which is fortunate. Amelia-Rose and Niall *are* in Gretna Green. I expect they will be wed by noon. His brothers are witnesses. Your daughter's companion is not. She is nowhere near Scotland."

"She—"

"Hush. Amelia-Rose is ruined. It's happened; it's done. Hurst wouldn't have her now, whatever agreement you made with him. You, therefore, have a select few choices. You can cry to the heavens at what a horrible girl your daughter is, and let her ruin tear you down, as well. You can decry my son as a poacher and a heathen—which everyone knows he is, anyway, because he's a Highlander. The scandal, the ruin, will be yours, and they will not be here to share it. I, on the other hand, will face almost no consequences. Everyone's seen my wild sons. No one could hope to control them. And yet I am quite pleased to see him in love and married."

Victoria opened her mouth again, but her husband squeezed her hand. "And the other choices?"

"There's but one, actually. The notice you placed in the newspaper wasn't actually done by you. It was some sort of jest, but until you discovered the villain you didn't wish to say anything. We've known for better than a week that Niall and Amelia-Rose were going to marry. Being the young couple they are, they couldn't tolerate the idea of waiting, and so with our mutual blessing they, hied themselves off to Niall's native Scotland to wed."

"No!" Victoria burst out, the newspaper shredding in her fingers. "No, no, no! I will not be a party to this! And neither will Lord Hurst!"

"I imagine Lord Hurst, who's also been absent from London, will most happily claim that he had no knowledge of any engagement, and has no idea which rogue might have placed the announcement. If he wishes to disagree, I would be very interested to see how any ranting he does about losing a woman to an untitled Scotsman could possibly benefit him."

"Y—"

Francesca stood. "Beneath any other argument, Victoria, if you stand against me, you will lose. Your indignance only makes you look like a frothing lunatic. Anyone asked to choose between your version of events and mine will choose mine. Especially when the new Mr. and Mrs. MacTaggert return to London in four days, happily wed and with no idea of any confusion they might have left behind here.

"Therefore," she went on, "when they return you may be here to welcome them with smiles and blessings, or you may be elsewhere keeping your thoughts and opinions to yourself. And that is for your benefit. You still have people who will invite you to parties. You still have a chance to meet your grandchildren, God willing. Whether you retain those things is utterly dependent on your own behavior." She took a breath. "I have seen to it that there will be perhaps a few whispers and a bit of speculation about who authored the engagement announcement. Nothing more. No scandal, no ruin attached to the Baxter name, no reason your lifestyle or associations should alter. Think beyond your anger, Victoria."

Her lips trembling, Victoria Baxter glared. It must all be crumbling away, her dreams of being introduced as the mother of a marchioness, of having a title so directly attached to her name, to rising in her social circle to a level she'd probably imagined to be much greater than it truly would have been as the mere mother of good fortune.

"Do as you will," Mrs. Baxter finally spat, standing. "I have a wretched daughter, and I will be happy—happy, I tell you—never to set eyes on the ungrateful thing again. She ruined everything. And you stand there with a smile and help her. The lot of you be damned." With that she flung open the morning room door and stalked out of the house.

Her husband stood. "This is not ideal," he said, his tone much more measured. "I shall have to listen to that for years, now, as I've listened to her ambitions for years. Please inform me when my daughter returns to London. I, at least, would like to be here to welcome her. That child . . . Well, she's no child any longer. She did try very hard to please." He nodded. "Outspoken, though. She didn't get that from me." Charles held out his hand. "Good morning, my lady. We shall do as you suggest. Victoria would not be able to tolerate her life with a scandal in it."

Francesca shook his hand. "Thank you, Mr. Baxter. I shall send word, and I'll see you in a few days."

Once they were gone and Smythe had shut the front door again, latching it for good measure, Francesca walked back up the stairs to Rory on the landing. Then she leaned down and kissed the deer's cheek. Rory, it seemed, wouldn't be going anywhere. And neither would Niall—or at least not permanently.

Seventeen years ago she'd abandoned them, putting all her hope into an agreement that, if Eloise decided not to wed, she could never enforce. One by one, the pieces of her life had begun to fall back into place. Even better, Niall had found happiness in the middle of this mayhem. So while she couldn't—and wouldn't—brag that she'd planned perfectly, she could happily admit to herself that like the mad, half-dressed stag on the landing and despite dubious beginnings, they seemed to be showing quite well. All of the MacTaggerts. Herself included.

Fresh pots of red and white roses lined the shallow turn-in at Oswell House. Two dozen potted flowers at least, alternating in color. It looked . . . hopeful, but Amelia-Rose kept her hands clenched together as she had since they'd first reached the outskirts of London.

"If ye have an apoplexy before we speak a word to anyone, ye'll nae find out what's actually happened," Niall pointed out from beside her, stretching as the coach came to a stop.

"How can you be so relaxed?" she asked him, though the only thing she'd yet seen trouble him was when something stood between him and her. That made it seem simple, that nothing else signified, but she'd been raised to be much more careful.

"I'm nae relaxed," he returned, reaching past her to open the door as Smythe appeared to lower the steps. "I'm in love. And I'm hopeful. Here or elsewhere, it's ye and me, Amy."

She stepped down first, then turned around and kissed him as he joined her on the drive. "It's destiny, yes?" she whispered, smiling against his mouth.

He grinned back at her. "Aye. Now take my arm so the rest of 'em cannae see me tremble."

"Mm-hm." She did as he suggested, leaning close against his side. Only Smythe had emerged from the house, but then he gave some sort of signal and a trio of footmen trotted outside to begin unstrapping the trunk at the back of the coach. Niall had hauled it about on his own, but then he carried sheep about regularly.

His brothers joined them, Aden flexing his back as they reached the doorway. "I'm nae going anywhere for at least a week," he commented. "And if my arse is numb, I can only imagine—"

"There's a lady present, ye heathen," Niall interrupted without heat. "But aye, at least part of me is hoping we've traveled as far as we need to for now."

More than half of her was hoping that. And it wasn't so much that she felt like she'd returned home, but simply that she wanted to wake up and then fall asleep beside her husband in the same bed more than one night in a row. The inns had been the nicest along the road, but she missed soft sheets and mornings without coachmen yelling for their passengers to board or they'd forfeit their fare to London or points elsewhere.

"Ye want me to go in first?" Coll asked.

Niall shook his head. "Nae. But if ye lied to get us back here, dunnae go far because we'll be having a tussle."

Smythe somehow beat them inside the house, and ushered them down the hallway toward the Oswell House library. It was the largest room on the ground floor, full of windows and light and delightful-smelling books, but it seemed more a place for a dressing-down than . . . than whatever else she wanted it to be. They had eloped, after all. Perhaps a happy greeting was too much to expect. She flexed her fingers in Niall's strong hand, and he glanced at her.

"I promised ye happiness," he murmured, smiling that charming, disarming smile of his, the one that made her feel very warm and safe and aroused all at the same time. "A MacTaggert keeps his word."

The butler pulled open the library door and stepped aside. "Congratulations, Mr. and Mrs. MacTaggert," he said with a very uncharacteristic smile, and motioned them into the room.

Before she could take in much more but bottles of

champagne, glasses, what looked like a delicious white cake, and a string quartet in the corner, Eloise squealed and launched herself forward to hug both Amelia-Rose and Niall. "You did it!" she laughed. "And in my dress! Which one did you wear?"

"The teal one," Amelia-Rose returned. "And I'm afraid I'm not giving it back to you."

"No, of course not! Oh, I'm so happy for you!"

"Thank you, Eloise." She couldn't help grinning at her friend's enthusiasm. "I suppose we're sisters now."

"I couldn't have chosen a better one."

"Amelia-Rose."

At the sound of her father's voice behind her, she stiffened. At the same moment Niall moved, putting himself between her and Charles Baxter. "Mr. Baxter. If ye've a complaint, I reckon it's with me."

"Nonsense," Lady Aldriss said, swirling into view. "Of course we knew what you two were about, though I do wish you'd been more patient."

"Yes," her father seconded, though he made no movement to approach her more closely. "You'll never guess, but as a jest someone put an engagement announcement in the newspaper about you and Lord Hurst of all people, daughter. We still haven't figured out who it was. A jealous beau, perhaps, angry that you didn't accept his suit."

She blinked. What in the world had happened over the past week? "I . . . I thought you'd refuse to see me ever again."

"I cannot speak for . . . others," he said slowly, "but time does heal all wounds. And I do not doubt that there were wounds."

Goodness. Slowly she reached out her free hand, and he clasped his around her fingers. "I shouldn't say this is unexpected, but I—I thank you, Father."

"And I hope you have found happiness, Amelia-Rose." He cleared his throat. "I think I shall have some champagne now."

"What did ye do?" Niall asked, facing his mother as soon as they were alone.

She handed him a folded newspaper. "I used my negotiating skills," she said.

Looking over his shoulder, Amelia-Rose stared at the full-page announcement of their marriage, dated on the day they'd actually wed. "And my mother saw this?" she whispered.

"She did. She wasn't happy. Once I explained that our two families knew about and aided the elopement and how romantic we all thought it, and what the likely outcome would be if she chose to tell a different tale, she subsided." Lady Aldriss's brow furrowed, then smoothed again. "I know your brothers did something to Lord Hurst, because he hasn't been seen in over a week. Is there something else I need to prepare for? He could throw a tangle into our yarn."

"He'll be back in London tomorrow," Niall said, tilting his head. "I promised him five thousand pounds to keep his damned mouth shut except to be baffled by why anyone would announce someaught he'd nae knowledge about. I dunnae have that kind of blunt to spare, but if I—"

"Done," the countess said quickly, and leaned up to kiss him on the cheek. "And it dovetails with our current version of things quite well." Shifting, she kissed Amelia-Rose on the cheek, as well. "You've received more than two dozen notes and cards of congratulations. All is well, I believe."

"Thank ye. More than I can tell ye. Amy came with me with nae any expectation of being able to stay in London. I couldnae think how to give it back to her on my own."

"We're not on our own," Amelia-Rose said, hugging Lady Aldriss. "We're MacTaggerts."

"That we are," the countess seconded, smiling deeply.

"Ye gave us a choice when we first arrived here," Niall said, his impossibly light-green gaze on his mother. "Ye said we could call ye Mama or Mother or Lady Aldriss or my lady. But ye nae said which ye prefer. I'd like to know."

With one arm still looped around Lady Aldriss's, Amelia-Rose could feel the older woman's sudden reaction. Oh, she'd married a good man. A kind, strong, man who loved to laugh and who would literally go to war for her if she wished it. Nothing else mattered. Not his title or lack thereof, not where they lived, and most certainly not who else might or might not approve.

"If it's all the same to you," Lady Aldriss said slowly, her voice not quite steady, "I'm becoming fond of *màthair.*"

"Aye. Thank ye, *màthair.*" He bent his head, kissing her on the cheek as she'd done him. Then he straightened again. "I require a word with my wife."

Wordlessly he walked them over by the nearest window, ignoring Coll and Aden arguing over whether biscuits wouldn't be better if they were filled with meat, and took both her hands. "I adore your family," she said, keeping her voice pitched below the sound of the quartet.

"Yer family now, as well," he corrected. "I'm glad they didnae opt for the bagpipes. They're bonny, but nae meant for inside the house, I reckon." He met her gaze. "I grew up with nae a mother. My da's a fair man, but rough. Mac-Taggerts make do, he always says. I shear sheep and mend fences, ride hard, fight hard. Ye're the gentle breeze, the first touch of sunlight in the morning, the patter of summer rain on the window. I dunnae mean ye're soft, because ye're fierce as a dragon. Ye fought for happiness, and I'm glad I could help ye find it. What I mean is, ye're all the important things." He frowned. "That doesnae sound—"

Going up on her toes, she kissed him, sliding her hands over his shoulders. "It sounds perfect," she breathed, barely noticing Coll and Eloise now waltzing in the middle of the room. "You were who I wanted before I knew what I wanted. You're . . ." She thought about it for a moment. Which word or set of words best described him—his protectiveness, his confidence, his faith in his family and in her, his utter lack of care over what anyone else might think.

"*Adae?*" he prompted, an expectant half grin on his face.

"You're my Highlander," she said.

He returned her kiss with a thoroughness that made her blush. "Aye. That I am. Always."

Read the novels in the "thrilling and sexy"
(*Kirkus Reviews*)
No Ordinary Hero series
HERO IN THE HIGHLANDS
MY ONE TRUE HIGHLANDER
A DEVIL IN SCOTLAND

And look for the Scandalous Highlanders novels
THE DEVIL WEARS KILTS
ROGUE WITH A BROGUE
MAD, BAD, AND DANGEROUS IN PLAID
SOME LIKE IT SCOT

. . . and these other wickedly delightful romances by
New York Times bestselling author
SUZANNE ENOCH

A BEGINNER'S GUIDE TO RAKES
TAMING AN IMPOSSIBLE ROGUE
RULES TO CATCH A DEVILISH DUKE
THE HANDBOOK FOR HANDLING HIS LORDSHIP

❀ ❀ ❀

AVAILABLE FROM ST. MARTIN'S PAPERBACKS